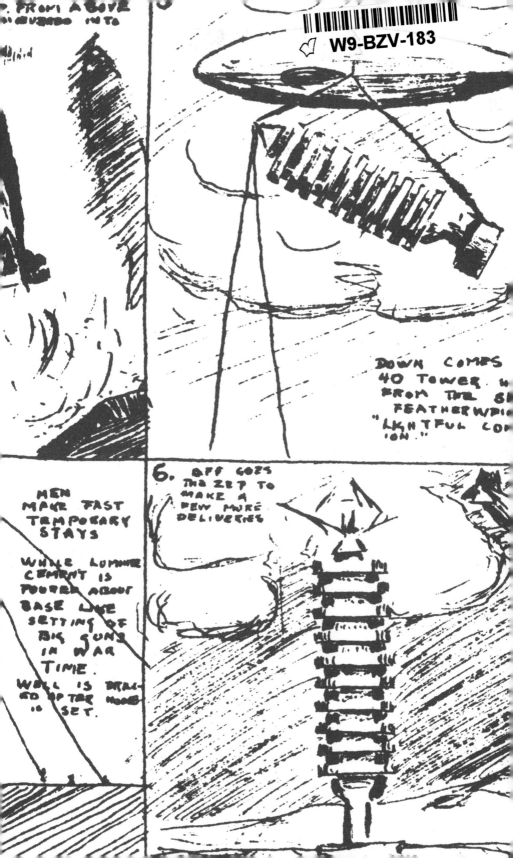

The

EIGHTH WONDER

of the

WORLD

The

EIGHTH WONDER

of the

WORLD

A NOVEL

LESLIE EPSTEIN

HANDSEL BOOKS

an imprint of
Other Press • New York

Production Editor: Robert D. Hack

Text design by Natalya Balnova
This book was set in ACaslon by Alpha Graphics of Pittsfield, New Hampshire.

10 9 8 7 6 5 4 3 2 1

Library of Congress Cataloging-in-Publication Data

Epstein, Leslie.
    The eighth wonder of the world : a novel / by Leslie Epstein.
    p. cm.
    Includes bibliographical references.
    ISBN-13: 978-1-59051-250-0 (alk. paper)
    ISBN-10: 1-59051-250-2 (alk. paper)
    1. Italy–History–1922-1945–Fiction. 2. Mussolini, Benito,
    1883-1945–Fiction. 3. Goebbels, Joseph, 1897-1945–Fiction.
    4. Pius XII, Pope, 1876-1958–Fiction. 5. Italo-Ethiopian War,
    1935-1936–Fiction. I. Title: 8th wonder of the world. II. Title.
    PS3555.P655E54 2006
    813'.54–dc22

                                                    2006000895

Many of the characters in this novel are based on those who lived in the past or are still living now; but they are imagined in a way that so fuses them with others or rips them apart that any resemblance to the people the reader thinks might be their historical models is almost certain to be an illusion.

FOR
SYLVIE, ANNIKA, AND EVE

ACKNOWLEDGMENTS

This book took many years to write and much more erudition than I possess. I cannot begin to thank the dozens of people who—sometimes with detailed expertise, sometimes with a chance remark—helped me. I hope those whose names do not appear here will be forgiving. A few, however, I must not ignore. Len Morse-Fortier drove me here and there with the top down, shared Indian food, and patiently explained to me why a tower that is as much his design as mine or Bucky Fuller's or Frank Lloyd Wright's would not fall down. Donald Altschiller, of the Boston University Library, ran all over town to find me old maps and guide books of Rome; if there are omissions or mistakes, he is the last one to blame. A grant from the Memorial Foundation for Jewish Culture allowed me to wander around Rome long enough to figure out what kind of trees grew on what has become the Via di San Gregorio, and that the meteor I was seeking had better be buried under the Circo Massimo and not the Isola Tiberna. Gwen and Franco Romagnoli stepped into the maelstrom of imminent publication and found and corrected hundreds of *errori* in my tourist's Italian. I owe them a high-class dinner. Harry Thomas, my brilliant and dedicated editor, worked harder to get this book into its final shape than I did. Thanks, Harry: you will shudder to hear me say, Let's do it again. My agent, Lane Zachary, proved once more, by her integrity, taste, and hard work, to be a model for all those in her profession. I also think it is about time to thank my publisher, Judith Gurewich, for believing in this book, and the last one, and in me.

Sapius ventis agitatur ingens
pinus et celsae graviore casu
decidunt turres feriuntque summos
fulgura montis.

As the tallest pine has the farthest to fall
And the highest tower collapses with the greatest roar
So does the lightning aim at the mountain top.

—HORACE

CONTENTS

ETHIOPIA

A Prologue

[1000 BC-1936]

Three thousand years ago the Queen of Sheba, having heard of the wisdom of Solomon, traveled to Jerusalem in a caravan laden with spices and gold and gemstones, in order to test that King with hard questions. He answered them all and dazzled her as well with his wealth, his servants, and his demeanor before the Lord. One day the Queen came across a room in the palace that was floored in glass; thinking that she was about to step into a pool of water, she raised her skirts. The commentators maintain that Solomon tricked Sheba and brought her to his couch, but it would be surprising if this Queen, the setter of riddles, did not know the difference between the surface of a mirror and that of a lake. In any case, once back in her homeland, she gave birth to a son. This was Menelik I, "son of the wise man," who, when he had come of age, set out to visit the father he had never known. The moment the King saw him he recognized, as in a mirror again, not only himself but—such was the boy's lithesomeness and graciousness of form—his own father, David. As the young man prepared for his return journey, Solomon caused the first born sons of the priests and the elders to travel with him; some say that he was also accompanied by the Ark of the Covenant, which he had stolen from the Temple upon his departure. In that manner did the glory of Zion pass from Jerusalem to Axum, and from the children of Israel to what the Ethiopian people to this day consider the embodiment of the kingdom of God: their nation and themselves.

A thousand years later another foreigner arrived at the gates of Jerusalem. This was Titus Flavius, son of Vespasian, who had come to finish his father's task of putting down the revolt of the Jews against the rule of Rome. At his command were four legions, equipped with engines for throwing darts, stones and javelins, together with catapults, siege towers, and battering rams. Over time this force made its way through wall after wall of the outlying quarters, though the desperate Jews made new walls of their corpses to fill each breach. At last the tower of Antonia fell and the battle for the Temple itself began. The defenders were weakened less by the Romans than by treachery, dissent, and a famine so great they were forced to gnaw the leather from their shields. Still the two armies fought not only by day but in a darkness so thick it was impossible to tell one's friend from the enemy at one's hand. Titus, seeing the futility of further attack, and recognizing that his rams, after six days of ceaseless assault against the Temple, could make no impression upon the vastness of its stones, ordered its gates set on fire. The blaze soon spread to the cloisters of the inner court and all their furnishings. Yet the battle, raging more fiercely than the flames, might have gone on without end had not a legionnaire, seized by what the historian Josephus called "a certain divine fury," thrown a burning brand through an open window of the holy house. Thus on the 9th day of the month of Ab, the same fatal day on which the King of the Babylonians had previously destroyed it, did the chief wonder of the world, God's dwelling, burn to the ground.

The slaughter that followed was so terrible and the conflagration within the city so great, that, as we read in the text of Josephus, the flames that consumed the houses were quenched by their inhabitants' blood. In that chronicler's reckoning, eleven hundred thousand perished in the course of the war and ninety-seven thousand were taken captive; but of these last the aged and the ill were slain, those under seventeen sold into slavery, and still others sent off to work the Egyptian mines. The unluckiest, perhaps, became gifts to the provinces, where they were destroyed by wild beasts in the spectacles. The tallest, however, and the handsomest in body, were reserved for the procession of victory, which was to take place when the conqueror returned to Rome.

Had there ever been a triumph like it in the history of the Empire? In all of the city not a person remained at home, lest he miss a moment of the pageant. Vespasian and Titus, father and son, each crowned with laurel, sat on ivory thrones. All the wonders, the varied riches of the vanquished land, uprooted trees and strange species of animals, paraded before them. At the center were the treasures of the razed Temple: the golden table of the showbread and the silver trumpets of the jubilee; the gem-studded crowns and rare purple hangings; the Ark, with the scrolls of the Law; and towering over the heads of those who bore it, the great lamp with its septuple branches that, as Josephus reminds us, "represent the dignity of the number seven among the Jews." Next in the procession, and most acclaimed by the multitude, were the pageant carts. Some of these were as high as three or four stories and each depicted a scene from the recent war: the scaling of walls and their demolishment by machines; the stoning of the populace; the countryside laid waste; the slaughter and the supplication of the enemy; and finally, a miracle of ingenuity and workmanship, the Temple in actual flames, together with the burning houses that fell upon all who dwelled within

3

them. In that fashion those who had remained at home and only wished they had taken part in the battle were made to feel they had actually been present, just as men and women of the modern world are transported to distant conflicts by devices the ancients could never have imagined.

And the conquered Jews? They came last, after the wooden ships, the armies of centuries and centurians, and the waving images of the gods. Among the captives was Simon of Gioras, the leader of the revolt, with the rope that would slay him already around his neck. With every step he was so harassed and tormented that he must have blessed the God of his people when in a sudden hush his suffering was brought to an end. Only then, according to custom, were the crowds free to take up the feasting of that festival day, while the Jews were led off, many of them to complete the work on the famed Colosseum and to begin construction of the great arch that would celebrate the victory of Titus as well as their own ever-to-be-lamented defeat.

Nothing endures, said Heraclitus, but change; and by way of example he remarked that no person can step into the same river twice. Nonetheless, men continue to build their memorials not from sand but from stone; and it is true that on occasion some monument will seem to stand against the flood, like a boulder against the river's rush. Yet that same Arch of Titus, thrust upward like a great pair of shoulders from the throbbing currents of modern Rome, will in time turn to dust. Even the Jews who built it, whose stubbornness in persisting has made them both hated and holy, in the way that some aged rock will become sacred in an aboriginal's eyes—even they must perish, as the Chaldeans perished, and the Canaanites.

Still, what the Greek philosopher neglected to mention was that, since time is infinite and the atoms of water finite, sooner or later the bather must find himself in the precise mixture of elements in which he had previously splashed. Josephus himself seemed to sense this, for when writing of that terrible 9th day of Ab he spoke of an Age of Revolution, as if history were a wheel, endlessly repeating itself, even as it pulverizes those caught beneath it. And not just Josephus. Who among us has not felt that he was once before submerged in the same tide of experience that surrounds him now? When was it? In childhood? In an altogether different life? Or did that clank of metal nozzle on metal fender, the swift swoop and dip and swoop of the telegraph line outside the train's gray window, the bark-bark-bark of an unseen Alsatian, occur not just to you but to others of the race whose senses—the ears, the eyes—you have for an instant been allowed to share?

In the summer of 1936, after two more turns of the millennial wheel, another triumph made its way along the avenues of Rome. The marching prisoners, barefoot and black-skinned, thought themselves children of the land of Israel. Among them, caged, was the last royal descendant of the union of Solomon and Sheba: the Emperor Haile Selassie I, *King of Kings, Lord of Lords, Conquering Lion of the tribe of Judah, Light of the World, Root of David, Elect of God.* For all the honorifics, he stood with his uniform in tatters. At each lurch of his movable cage, his body swayed but, though his hands were tied before him and a rope hung round his neck, never toppled. Indeed, his small, narrow head, with its tufted beard, its tangled hair, remained motionless atop the board of his shoulders.

What struck the milling masses—struck them so forcibly that they either fell silent or murmured, *occhi di Dio, occhi di marmo*—were his eyes, a strip of black iris, a strip of ivory, and the way they stared as fixedly as those in a stone statue of Jupiter to where the great arch rose like a guillotine at the end of the Via Sacra. If those onyx eyes, wide and unblinking, possessed the power of the telescope lens they so much resembled, or could see on the wavelength of X-rays, the deposed King might have taken comfort from the image carved on one of the monument's inner walls; just as the new conqueror of Ethiopia, upright on the reviewing stand, his thumbs hooked in his leather belt and with no cap upon the bony pate of his shaven head, might have felt some unease at what had been carved on the other.

For on the first wall, the artifacts of the vanquished people, carried along in a procession that mirrored the one now passing before him, are all intact: the table of the showbread; the long-stemmed trumpets; and, taller than the Roman soldiers who hold it aloft, the menorah, three new moons recumbent within three old ones, symbolizing the city of Jerusalem, the light of learning, and the seventh day of rest after creation. Opposite, however, on the second wall, the goddess Nike reaches forward to crown the victorious Titus; alas, time has eaten away his head, so that the only laurel we see this day is the shadow of stubble that circles Benito Mussolini's bullet-shaped skull.

———◇———

ALITALIA 607

Taking Off

[2 0 0 5]

1

It has been an odd afternoon, the light tan, or tannish, as if the city and suburbs have been wrapped in burlap. Yes, those sacks of clouds look ready to burst. Which is why, maybe, we've been sitting on the runway. Or else it's the duck I swear I saw wheeling over the macadam, heading for the reeds and rubbish of Jamaica Bay. They're supposed to have men with shotguns to scare off the wildlife. Are they out there now in hip boots? Beating the bushes? I'm half holding my breath in fear of the shots. Leda, on the aisle, and nearsighted, has got the *New Yorker* three inches from her nose. My Antigone. My swan. What's so interesting in the "Talk of the Town"? The cabin smells of kerosene, from the planes in front and behind. The landscape through the window is wavering in the fumes.

It will be dawn and rosy when we land in Rome. There's nothing like the morning light on St. Peter's. As Michelangelo well knew. A shivering, shuddering jellied dessert. *Un gelato. Un montebianco.*

It's silly of me to worry about the wayward mallard. She'll make it back to her ducklings. They don't shoot the birds, these hunters. They aim into the air. Then why this anxiety? This sadness? A stupid tear, I can feel it, is worming its way down my cheek. The right cheek. Out of my right eye. Does that mean that my left-handed tear ducts are frozen? Fool of an old man: Over a duck! I had one for dinner—when was it? At Chanterelle. Exactly a week ago. Those clouds are stretched out like intestines. They're bound to rupture. They're going to cover us with excrement and bile.

But the rains won't come. The engines are humming on a higher note. We advance through the traffic jam, turn, aim ourselves down the avenue of cement. This is the moment to cry out: *Wait! Stop! I have to get out!* That wouldn't do it. *Help! My heart! I'm having a heart attack!* Could any of this Italian crew, over the hysterical whine of the fan jets, hear a word? And what would they do? They're all strapped in, and we are roaring down the runway. Every airliner, while still on the ground, reaches a spot at which it has no choice but to take to the air. I'm afraid that for all my infirmities—*Oh, my heart! My head! My aching back!*—I've already reached my personal point of no return. When? Once I'd stepped into the limousine? Or allowed myself, for the first time in a year, to be shaved? Was it the moment I saw the envelope, with the seal of the Italian Consul in New York? Hell, I knew sixty years ago, when I left Naples on an American troopship, that I'd be back. What I didn't know, couldn't even imagine, was that A.P., returning to America in an army C-54, would make his way back as well.

I can't detect sensation on the left side of my body; nonetheless, there is now a vague sense of pressure. I can almost hear it rather than feel it, as if someone were shouting my name—*Maximilian! Maximilian! Max!*—from a distance. *Annette. Adriana. Orazio. Oscar.* I glance down in confusion. My granddaughter has a grip on my arm.

"Maxie, I'm not really frightened," she says. There's the flash of an unconvincing smile.

"N-n-nothing to be f-frightened about," I answer, though God knows how the words come out.

Then we're off the ground. Leda's squeezing with both hands. She's buried her head on my shoulder. A grown woman, a senior at Yale, yet here she is gasping, giggling into my traveler's tweed.

"I'm embarrassing myself," she says, glancing up, still applying that tourniquet to my arm.

I gird myself for another tongue-twister. "Leda, I confess: I am t-t-trembling too." I don't bother to add that my fears have less to do with taking off from New York than with landing in Rome: the first glimpse of the Forum, the Vatican, the poisonous snake of the Tiber. Indeed I *am* trembling—or half trembling. It's not the tourist's itinerary that produces the shakes, it's all those words, *Trastevere, Circo Massimo, Palazzo Venezia*, the hated *Teatro di Marcello*, that I have expunged from my vocabulary for fifty years. Memories! You think you've strangled them, lopped off the hundred heads; but they lurk, they linger, until you understand they're the ones strangling you. *Philomène. Katya. Shemi. Judit.* Yes, those words too.

My little Yalie is working at her composure. Her magazine has spilled to the carpet. She retrieves it. Now she leans across my strapped-in body to get a glimpse of the outside world. Pea-soup. I catch her eye, small, dark, near-black, nearsighted: my eye, in short. It may be the only thing she has inherited from the Levant. The rest of her has descended not from her grand- but her great-grandfather. Uncanny how she resembles his blond daughter, her great-aunt: the straight, narrow nose, with its delicate, quivering nostrils; the high brow; the golden hair; the long, pale curve of her throat. Even these nervous, twitching fingers.

Now there bubbles into my brain one of those hydra-headed thoughts, one I believed that, like the Christian St. George, I had slain long ago. What if that bright, glistening, olive-of-an-eye had come not from her grandfather, me, her Maxie, but from Amos Prince himself? What if Prince, the great Prince, were for all his fulminations, *because* of those fulminations, also a Prinz—that is to say, P-R-N-Z, the Hebrew consonants for F-R-N-Z, Firenze, Michelangelo's Florence? I make a noise; Leda looks up, but with my good right hand I wave off her concern. It was only a laugh, darling, that grunting sound. If you knew the whole story, you'd be laughing too. What a joke! Amos Prince, notorious for his opinions: an Italian Jew!

The girl gives a chuckle of her own. I glance round at the *New Yorker* cartoon. An alligator is chewing at a man's ankle and his companion, in the caption, asks, "What's eating you?" Now the girl takes a tissue from her handbag and dabs at the side of my mouth. Drooling again, I suppose. Must remember not to laugh.

"Have you finished your speech, Maxie? Did Rosellen have time to type it out?"

"T-t-typed it myself," I answer, and hold up the finger that accomplished the feat.

"Do you have it with you? I mean, is it with the carry-on luggage?"

"No." I shake my head for emphasis. The truth is that the carbon—yes, you are spending your time with the last man on earth to possess and use carbon paper—is in my left breast pocket. Leda, I know, wants to study it. My black-eyed blonde intends to be an actress. She's already been elected chairman—chair, I guess they call it—of the Dramat. She doesn't think I can deliver the talk myself—or, if I start, the drooling, the drone, the derision on my listeners' faces, will bring me to an embarrassed halt. At which point the golden swan, this cowering canary, will take over, the understudy upstaging the star. *All About Eve.* Italian style. The press will be there—and how! And television. Radio? Radio, in the land of its inventor, has gone the way of carbon paper.

"Well," says Leda, "I've got most of it memorized. All but the ending." She starts to reel it off: "*Il Presidente del Consiglio dei Ministri, Signor Berlusconi. Il Ministro della Cultura, Signor Urbani. Ambassador Sembler. Amici della memoria d'Amos Prince. Ladies, gentlemen, my dear friends in Italy. Once again I stand in this room, as I have for thousands of nights in my dreams. Do you see, behind you, that window? There was a bird's nest on the sill during the years I lived in Rome. Those same birds would—*"

"All right. G-good, Leda. You have it m-m-memorized." Why should I feel peevish about it? Doesn't she have every right? I had only married into the family. Here was the great-granddaughter, A.P.'s blood relation. Let her twitter about the swallows, the genius at his drawing board, and conclude with my lame hopes that all wounds were finally healed.

Suddenly the cabin of our 767 is filled with light. *Ahhh*, go any number of my fellow passengers, involuntarily, as we break above the clouds. Through our windows: the setting sun. It looks, as in the myth, like a fiery chariot. Rays shoot out of it, like incendiary arrows that set everything—the wadding of the nimbostrati, the tip of our taut wing, the very flesh of our reddening faces—ablaze. There isn't a sound among us; even an infant, who I now realize has been whimpering, falls still. I think we are worshiping that wheeling disc—as the Greeks worshiped Apollo; as Akhenaton of the Eighteenth Dynasty worshiped Aton; and as in our lifetime Amos Prince built his monument to focus the light of this very sun. The airship banks, slips sideways, and in doing so reveals, jutting from the ledge of vapor, a finger of fire, crimson-colored, as if sheathed in blood.

Apollo, I remember, is also the bringer of plagues; the contagion he scatters was always depicted by a trail of just such flaming clouds.

I first went to Italy in 1936, aboard the *Conte di Savoia*. I was searching for Prince then too. I'd heard of the architect all of my life. The fact is, I grew up across the street from one of his houses, the one that hung so far over Sunset Boulevard that I thought the least thing—the quickening of the breeze, the roll of a child's marble, the footfall of a fly—would tip the whole of the gleaming white structure into the flow of traffic below.

There are twenty-six Prince buildings in greater Los Angeles, and by 1932, when I was about to head east to college, I'd seen and sketched them all—the houses in Topanga Canyon and on Malibu Beach, the church in Hancock Park, the automobile showroom on the Miracle Mile, that crazy mirror-image estate above Sepulveda. Decades later, a lifetime later, after I'd established a practice of my own, I went back to many of them. That church had long since become a synagogue. To me, the black concrete slabs at the entrance looked like the mandibles of a prehistoric beast. I passed between them with a shudder: wouldn't the slightest wrong move—meat mixed with the milk, maybe, or a woman with the men—trip some hidden wire and snap those jaws shut? I also went back to the house cantilevered over Sunset. The owner was perfectly gracious. He gave me a drink. He showed me his paintings, a roomful of Soyers—Raphael, Moses, Isaac. But he could not lure me into the dining room, with its view of what used to be the polo fields and the lights of the city beyond. I was convinced that the weight of the nine-year-old child within me would tip us backward, downward, over the edge of the cliff.

Who was it? Can I remember? Yes! Sir Nikolaus Pevsner. He was the one who compared the experience of entering a Prince building to violating the secret chamber in a pyramid or a Pharaoh's tomb:

you are at one and the same time seduced by the beauty of the painted goddesses and simulated stars, and certain that, because of a dooms- day trick of the ancient architect, every breath is to be your last.

2

My right hand can operate, even if it is as clumsy as the mechanical claw in a penny arcade. I fumble at that inside breast pocket. The fin- gers close, but what they draw out is not the typed speech but the little booklet, spiral bound, filled with handwriting that is as familiar to me as my own. Rosellen brought it in yesterday, along with our papers from the Italian consulate. Who sent it—that's a mystery. *For Leda*, someone had written on the cardboard cover. But I'm not going to let her see it until I've read it myself. Maybe when she falls asleep. Maybe in the bathroom. My God! The diary of Amos Prince.

I take a sneaking look at his great-granddaughter. Why did I allow myself to become vexed with her? This is no Anne Baxter, the betrayer, who takes my hand now in both of hers. There is nothing ignoble about her motives. She's cut her classes, abandoned rehearsals, fundamentally out of comradeship. And loyalty. Family feeling.

Ah, there goes the chariot, into the thunderheads, ready to race round the other side of the world. Here, on the instant, it is night. A sky filled with stars. Pinpricks in cloth, according to the ancients. That threatening finger? Nothing more than the Pariah State Build- ing, as A.P. might call it. Red lights blink atop the old dirigible mast, telling us to keep our distance. That great pointed antenna pulses with invisible radiation, sending its signals to every part of the planet and receiving the dots and dashes, the data, from the metal tubs we have like Jupiter hurled into space.

SPIRAL NOTEBOOK

Gubbio

[1982: 1957]

Cup of tea. Sharpened pencil. I start this journal on an anniversary: twenty-five years to the day that I returned to Italy in 1957. Aboard the *Cristoforo Colombo*. Incognito, I figured. Under an alias. Not with a white hat but a black one. No fuss on the American end. Glad enough to see me go. But in Genoa, a pride of paparazzi. Sometimes I think this headache, this buzz saw that splits my skull in half, started then. The flash lamps. The rays of light. Might as well have been the blades of knives. I tried to see past the glare. I don't like to think about that moment. Makes my heart beat too fast. Makes my head swell, so the old fedora doesn't fit. Used to see Ben inflate like that, his chest bursting his buttons. Blood pressure.

Where was I? At the rail of the *Cristoforo Colombo*. Heart racing then too. Thump-thumping on the gangway coming down. I was trying to see if beyond the bursting flash lamps she was somewhere on the dock. Before the first letter, sent to the loony bin, I did not know if she was dead or alive. Typed. On an Olivetti. In Italian. *Ti aspetterò.* I will wait for you. A voice from the grave.

Doctors did not want to give it to me because it was not signed. Warders, not doctors. Old Weinstein, young Weinstein in point of fact, brought it in. With his sweaty thumb prints on the page.

"My daughter!" I shouted. *Figlia mia!* Two more letters to come. Next one in 1950. *Ancora sto aspettandoti.* Still waiting. The last: end of '57. *Sarò là quando arriverai.* I'll be there when you arrive. But where was she? Not on the dock. Not in the customs shed. Outside, standing next to a taxi, a stooped, black-haired lady. Well, half-black, half silvery strands. Not Aria! Gianna! My servant. My spy. "*A Roma?*" she asked, opening the Mercedes's rear door. No. Never Rome. To see the ruins of my work? I heard every story. The Americans destroyed it. With bombs from their planes. With dynamite at the base. Speer had his eye on it from the start. Did he have time to pull it apart? Section by section? To make his rockets? His tanks? Or did we miscalculate? Did some windstorm, *una tempesta di vento*, blow the damn thing down? Worse: What if it still stood? Rusting in the clouds. Filled with bureaucrats.

"*No. Non a Roma. A Gubbio.*"

Which is where I lived, with my children, before I met up with Ben. I liked the place. Clinging to the side of the mountain. The Palazzo dei Consoli. The Palazzo Ducale. The little ruby-colored cup, *una tazza*, by Andreoli. A train to Florence. A train to Perugia. A hired car. Not a word to Gianna. Not a word to the passengers, who, some of them, did a double take. My first experiment with silence. What was I doing? Where was I going? My son, Franklin—they'd either killed him or thrown him in jail. Aria, if she wasn't dead, might as well be. Nina, my other daughter: she'd married Maximilian, the Jew, the betrayer. Showed up at St. Liz. Wanted the old man's blessings. They had their child, a son, in their arms. Wouldn't see them. Hell, no! The half-breed. Got a letter. When was it? A month ago. In November. With a baby picture. Great-granddaughter. What's her name? Something Greek. Fuzzy-haired. A duckling.

Scared to death on that train. Tongue-tied. Hands always shaking. Didn't know if these Italians would tear me apart. Hang me up by the heels, like they did old Ben. Hid under the brim of my hat. Now I'm going to write about one of the glorious moments of my life. Maybe most glorious. Nothing to do with children. With marriage. Nothing to do with buildings, not even when me and Ben took out our peckers and pissed in the hole where *La Vittoria* was going to rise. The urine of great men: where it falls something must grow. What a laugh I got out of that one. What a shock to the crowd. No, and it wasn't the shout of joy when we pulled up the piece that made us the world's tallest building, tallest thing ever made by man, higher than the Eiffel Tower, higher than the Empire State.

No, no. I mean the end of that train ride. Winter of 1957. December 2. Twenty-five years to this day. Drove up to the old flat, just beneath the Church of San Ubaldo. Night falling. Ravens, or maybe crows, flying over the fields in the valley. Alighting on the stalks, the stubble. Taking off again. Of course the flat was occupied. Two elderly sisters. Foolish idea: to think I could live there again.

I hid in the car while Gianna took two rooms in the hotel. The Villa Montegranelli. Dog-tired. Fell onto the bed. Still trembling. Still in a sweat. Slept I don't know how long. Couple of hours. Washed up. Went downstairs, holding on to banister for dear life. Braved the dining room. Mostly empty. Sat in the corner. Waiter arrives: white napkin on arm, curled up moustache, shining hair. *Minestra*, I mumble. He returns, with the steam rising from the bowl. In a reflex, I remove the black felt hat. Waiter puts dish in front of me. Who knows what he—name of Enrico, aged maybe thirty-five, maybe forty—did in the war? Old enough to have spit on the corpse of old Ben. What he says, on seeing my white, disarranged hair. What he says—oh, my hand shakes: he says, "Enjoy your soup, *Maestro*."

I have lived in this room a quarter of a century. Gianna had a small one on the top floor. Maid's quarters. I like to think I am a gentleman. I don't speak of our relations. Disappeared in 1974. No farewell. No note. Sick of the great man? Of not hearing, from his mouth, a single word? How did I spend my time? Looking in the mirror. Chewing on aspirin. Walking up the mountain, past the cathedral and the palace, to where if you know your geology the ice elbowed its way into the rock, creating the near-vertical gorge.

Can still make the trip, with the help of a cane. Not bad for a centurion—or nearly one. When *was* I born? 1880? 1882? Once counted the steps. Thirteen hundred odd. Then it struck me: I was climbing to the top of our tower. Another hike: around and around the track that surrounds the *campo di calcio*, the football field, where the servants walk their masters' poodles and Pekinese. And another, out of town, now the outskirts of town, to the reservoir at Bottacione. The old dam crumbling, the water bubbling out of the stream bed in the spring, shrinking to a trickle in the fall. White stones in August like the bones of cattle that came there to drink.

Wherever I go, the government is watching me. They may be Italians, but they're in the pay of the CIA. I can see, up in the tree line, the sunlight flashing off their binocular lenses. I don't doubt they've bribed the hotel maids. Did they capture Gianna? To force her to speak? I would not be surprised. Not that she knows my secrets. I know all about J. Edgar Hoover! That FDR. Nixon's no different. Reagan, too. They're all controlled by the Jews.

What about these visitors? The journalists? The book writers? The students of architecture? I get maybe one a month. Maybe two. A girl from Carnegie Tech, curly black hair, red-colored spectacles.

Reminded me of Maximilian: a hero-worshiper. Said he'd seen everything I'd done in Los Angeles. So had she. Glasses, like Max's, slipping down her nose. *Jew-near*, I used to call him. Junior. Like a son.

What did she want? Wants me to talk. We sip tea. She speaks, not I. Does she think I burned up my house? And those inside it? Stole my three children? The charges were dropped. No, no. She's after my secret. She wants to see what I'm building in back of the Montegranelli. In the bicycle shack. Peek through the window at my model. She wants to be the one to announce to the world: Amos Prince is going to launch a planet into the air.

No reason not to write this down. Though the headache is bad. My project? Think of a *Hindenburg* without any gas. No hydrogen to burn. To explode. No helium you got to beg for. Here are the mathematical equations: A sphere, diameter one hundred feet, weighing three tons, encloses seven tons of air. Air to structural weight ratio, about 2:1. Now double the size of the globe, to two hundred feet in diameter. It will weigh seven tons, but the air inside it will weigh fifty-six. Air to structure ratio, 8:1. Double again. A sphere four hundred feet in diameter weighs fifteen tons, but the air now weighs five hundred. Air to metal ratio, 33:1. Let's stretch our minds. A sphere a half mile in diameter. The air inside it will weigh so much that the weight of the structure itself is by comparison negligible. That's old Amos's secret! The surprise in the bicycle shop! What I kept my mouth shut about all these years. A ratio of one thousand to one!

Now imagine the sun shining through the open frame of our aluminum bubble. It is reflected from the concave surface of the far side and begins to heat up the interior atmosphere. When the temperature of that air rises by only one degree Fahrenheit, that's right, *one degree Fahrenheit*, the weight of the air pushed out of the sphere is greater than the weight of the structure itself. What I am saying is, the total weight of the interior air, plus the weight of the metal, is now much less than that of the surrounding atmosphere. The sphere must rise! Goddamn it: it will rise! That's what they want to find out at Carnegie Tech. And the CIA. Fools! Numskulls! Nitwits! All they have to do is look at the clouds. Then they'd realize why the sphere, displaced by the heavy atmosphere around it, must hang in the heavens. Just as mist, heated by the morning sun, loses some of the air inside it and rises from the valley into the sky. All folks have to do is open their eyes.

Don't worry about night. We're going to hang polyethylene curtains that will slow the rate at which the cold air wants to rush back in. We can hang in the sky from dusk to dawn. Thousands of feet in the air. If there are passengers, human passengers, they would weigh next to nothing in the overall scheme. We can anchor. We can fly off from place to place. Or just hang there with lights inside, the way a cloud hangs on a mountain top. Every man on earth will look up and see the work of Amos Prince. All aglow. All silvery light. A man-made moon.

I got the photograph in front of me now. "Born November 9, 1982. Greetings, Great-grandpa. From your—" Yes, that's her name. No duckling. Lover of Jupiter. "Leda."

ARCH OF TITUS

[1936]

1

Maximilian Shabilian arrived at Genoa on the liner *Conte di Savoia*
three days before the defeated Ethiopians were marched through
Rome. He left the next morning for the town of Gubbio, where,
according to the *New York Times*, Amos Prince had been living ever
since he fled Arizona after his twin sons had been killed in the fire
that consumed his famous Tree House.

It took a tramp of only ten minutes through the steep streets
for Max to find Prince's flat, which occupied the third floor of a
building that overlooked the valley below. The door was open, the
windows unshuttered, and the inhabitants—Prince himself; the
three children; and perhaps a female servant, judging by the two
black dresses in the closet and the Singer sewing machine frozen in
mid-stitch over a hem—gone. Prince's clothing, all those white linens, still hung in the closet. The cloth smelled, the whole place
smelled, of the master's tobacco.

Max, a myope, five-foot five, curly black hair, an unfortunate nose hooked to round black glasses—in short, the whole world's notion of a Jew: this twenty-two-year-old Maximilian poked about like a detective at the scene of a crime. The soup pot atop the stove, the wormy cigarettes in the ashtray, the book on the floor, its covers like the roof of a little cottage—all of this seemed to indicate a sudden discovery, a sudden abduction. More alarming, a single broken-heeled burgundy shoe, a woman's shoe: did that mean violence? A struggle? Had the great architect himself been harmed?

A lone Carabiniere, a thin old man under some kind of Napoleonic hat, had been leaning against the ground floor door post when the young American had arrived.

"*Dov'è il Signor Prince? L'architetto. E i suoi figli?*"

"*A Roma,*" the policeman now told him, waving his hand vaguely to the south. "*Chissà—?*" And here he waved westward. "*Forse in America.*"

Maximilian went back to the kitchen, which was covered in pale rose and pale green tile. The mold on the soup, largely evaporated, was a darker green. He took up a tumbler and ran himself a glass of water. Then he took out the page of smudged newsprint and read the headlines yet again:

ARCHITECT AMOS PRINCE FOUND
Fugitive Hiding in Small Italian Town

U.S. Authorities to Seek Extradition
Three Children Safe

Max had first read those headlines that summer, just after his graduation from college. The accompanying text retold the familiar story of how, in 1930, Prince's wife and their infant twins had been killed in the blaze that had raced up the hollow concrete trunk of their house and burst through the sixty-five-foot crown with such force that people twenty miles off in Flagstaff saw the spectacular spray.

In spite of his second-degree burns, Prince had fled with his three older children, two girls and a boy, who had been visiting their father over the weekend. Everyone assumed he had gone to Mexico, and in fact the four of them were soon traced to Navajoa and then Mexico City. How could he not be apprehended? He was, of course, a world-renowned figure, unmistakable in his white linen jackets and with his white shock of hair, his wiry eyebrows, and strong yellow teeth clamped around the holder of a burning cigarette. The eyebrows, it seemed, had disappeared, scorched off in the blaze, and, for all the best efforts of the federal and international police, so had the great man who had worn them.

Now, six years later, Prince had been found. Which is to say, someone had turned him in—almost certainly for the reward that Odaline, his first wife and the mother of the three teenaged children, had offered for his capture. Would Max have been tempted to do the same? Never! He would give everything he had or hoped to have to save the architect and his art, even if the sum of 20,000 lire was roughly equal to the 1500 dollars he hoped would take him through the Architecture School at Yale.

In New Haven, on the Old Campus, he had read and reread the article. The temperature on that summer day had climbed well into the 90s. Even the statue of Nathan Hale was in a sweat of what looked like molten metal. Above his head the leaves of the elms curled and crackled. A wound-up pigeon crossed the stone pathway, head bobbing on its spring. The newsprint, Max saw, had turned his hands as black as a Negro's. Suddenly the boy gave a leap.

He hurled his straw hat into the heavy air. "Hurrah!" he shouted, as young men did in those days. "Italy! Italy! It's off to Amos Prince!"

2

Maximilian spent the night in what might have been the architect's bed and just after dawn started his journey to Rome. Easier, it seemed, to fly to the moon. The trains were overbooked and his route took him backward to Florence and eastward to Pescara. At the end of the day he managed to squeeze into the crowds that burst through the windows and actually lay flat on the roofs of the cars; they chugged into the Stazione Centrale the way that, in newsreels, Indian workers arrived each morning at Calcutta.

There wasn't, it seemed, a single free room in the city. Maximilian trudged in widening circles, stopping at every lodging in his path. "No, no—tutto completo," the porters told him, even before he could bang on the shut, coffered doors. It was well after nightfall before he came to the Pensione Wanda at the end of a little alley behind the Piazza Remuria. Wanda herself led him to a top-floor room, actually an attic, where two mattresses had been spread on the floor. A black man was asleep on one of them, a clean white sheet tucked under the Mephistophelian beard on his chin.

"Tsst, tsst," said Wanda, holding her finger to her lips. "Un Generale!"

Max stared in confusion. He knew the war in Africa was over. Was this an Abyssinian on the run? A saboteur? His plump landlady, her neck dotted with moles, pointed to the uniform that hung crisp, brown, and gold-braided from a hook on the back of the door. She whispered, "Un eroe."

Shabilian pulled off his pants and shirt; he washed as best he could by pouring the water from one ceramic bowl into another.

Then he lay down on the mattress and fell asleep—or into a half-sleep—almost at once. The trouble was that the ground seemed to be shaking. The whole of the Pensione Wanda was atremble. Max could not help but recall one of the earthquakes from his California childhood: the teeter-tottering of his bedside lamp, the rocking of the bed itself, the indelible sight of his pencils, upright in their cup, whirling like a whisk in agitation.

Did the soldier, floating on the ticking of his mattress, feel it? Maxie peered through a squinting eye. Colored light fell on the Ethiope, his taut white sheet, the curving scimitar of his nose. He was as serene as a Christian crusader upon a tombstone, though this black warrior might have fought for the other side. The part of Max's brain that sought to protect his sleep soon transported him again to childhood. Here was the Clyde Beatty circus, filled with lions, with elephants, whose heavy footfalls shook the seats in the Shrine Auditorium, in which he slept drooling against his father's shoulder, the miniature of the grown man—though not grown so very tall—fitfully dreaming now.

In the morning the red sun streamed through the open window. The African was gone, his sheet kicked in a pile. The odd thing was, that linen, which had seemed so white in the aquamarine glow of neon, turned out to be the same khaki color as the uniform that had hung on the back of the door. Max looked again: the sheet, which lay in tangles and peaks, resembled the whipped cream on a cup of coffee once the Italians had sprinkled it with cinnamon. He glanced toward the chair post over which his shirt was draped. It too was covered with cocoa. So was the towel at the washstand; both bowls, the large and the small, each of porcelain, seemed to have rusted overnight. Now he saw the fine suspension of dust drifting through the air. He plucked up his glasses and ran for the window.

Was he sleeping still? There, in the fields below him, were the elephants that had bumped about through the night. And there, on leashes, the lions. He could hear the trumpeting; he could hear the roar. There was no Beatty, with chair and whip, but what Max saw from the open window could have been one of the sets for that actor's movies. Thousands of people, dressed up as soldiers, sailors, airmen, were milling about like extras, while people on ladders, using megaphones, tried to order them in various directions. The whole of the park, the Porto Capena, and the adjoining fields that stretched behind the Baths of Caracalla, had been turned into a staging area. The motorized vehicles—the trucks, the half-tracks, the heavy treads of the tanks—along with the hooves of the innumerable horses and the boots of the uniformed troops, had churned the grassland into a plain of dirt, from which rose the cloud that was already spreading across much of Rome.

Max would have run into the street had Signora Wanda not entered with a tray of soft eggs and coffee. "What is this?" he asked her. "*Che cos'è questo?*"

"*Il Trionfo!*" she said, laughing aloud. "*Il Trionfo! Come Cesare.*"

The noise from the window drowned her out. Max went to it and pulled the panes shut. He wanted to ask her if the famous American architect, the one who had been in the papers, was still in Rome. In his tourist's Italian, in her pidgin English, they managed to establish that she didn't know. "*Che tragedia,*" she moaned. Her body rocked in sympathy. "A big American, no? *Architetto.* Like Michelangelo! *Ma, perché?* Why he want to steal the *bambini?* The little children?"

Max glanced once more through the shut window. What had seemed to be chaos turned out to have a design. Half the milling throng was moving leftward, onto the Via Aventina and from there toward the broad Viale Aventino. The other half meant to exit to the right, onto another tributary—his map called it the Viale Guido Baccelli—which fed into a broad avenue named for the Baths. Both thoroughfares angled north and met on the far side of an open square. Why had he slept so long? He was going to be late for the parade.

Buttoning his shirt as he went, Max trotted down the five flights of stairs. There wasn't a soul to be seen in the Piazza Remuria. The shutters were drawn across all the shops. The side streets were also deserted, save for the cats who looked about in confusion—the way all animals, and primitive peoples too, might stare upward during a solar eclipse. The sun was well up in the sky, just as it should be at that hour; but the thick clouds of dust had transformed its yellow rays into magenta, which made it seem that it was simultaneously rising and setting, and that by some miracle it was both dawn and dusk.

Ahead, on the far side of the Porta Capena, the two lines of march joined together and moved side by side up the Via dei Trionfi. That's where the Romans were, in their tens and hundreds of thousands. They hung like breadfruit from the rows of trees that lined both sides of the boulevard. They leaned over the occasional rooftop and overflowed the ledges of windows. They were singing and chanting and roaring. They waved a million paper flags. Straining, on tiptoe, Maximilian tried to see over the heads of the crowd. All he could make out was a single enormous banner stretched above the thoroughfare. On it a painted lion struggled against the eagle that, clutching the beast in its talons, bore it aloft on outstretched wings. No interpreter needed: the Lion of Judah had been captured by the golden eagle of the new Italian empire.

There was nothing for Max to do but try to elbow his way through the throng. They were packed tight, however, ten deep to the curb, and would not budge. The odd thing was, though those in the back could see no more than he, they all knew when to cheer, or applaud, or sing *Giovinezza*. "*A chi la vittoria?*" cried the multitude, only to shout out the answer to their own question: "*A noi!*" *The victory belongs to us.*

Again and again Maximilian attempted to pierce the wall of spectators. He was always rebuffed. Indeed, as he worked his way northward, the crowd stretched further and further from the avenue, growing thicker, more dense, more solid. Max forced his way ahead, amid the shoulders, the elbows, the hips and buttocks, until at last it became impossible to take another step. Here was a paradox: while he could not move, he was moved; that is, he was spun, buffeted, prodded this way and that by a million other similarly immobilized human beings. Then, as a single molecule in an otherwise motionless fluid or gas will eventually work its way to the very edge of its container, Max suddenly found himself propelled against a series of red and white wooden barricades that were held in place by jagged concrete slabs. On the far side the barrier was an open area, at the end of which rose the curve of the empty Colosseum.

Suddenly, half on instinct, and half thrust forward by the random vibrations of the crowd, Max darted beneath the lowest rung of a barrier into what seemed an ocean of light and air. Three militiamen stood nearby. Max walked toward them; as he drew near the trio turned to light their cigarettes from a common match, and hence did not see the American slip by.

A single soldier stood at the nearest portal; he might have been the twin of the Carabiniere at Gubbio, aged sixty perhaps, with a tuft of beard on his chin. That chin lay on his breastbone. Asleep! Asleep on his feet like a horse! By this miracle of inattention, Max Shabilian—whose ancestors came from Bialystok and Odessa; and before that God knows where, Spain, he thought, Babylonia; and ultimately, inevitably, Jerusalem or Bathsheba or the Galilee—this mini-Max, whose five-foot five included shoes and heels, found himself the only person inside the greatest monument of ancient Rome.

He ran through the arching corridors to the amphitheater. For a moment he stood, struck by the perfection of the ellipse. Story rose on story, each with capitals of a different order. Some of the marble still clung to the brick, and huge stone slabs lay pell-mell among the aisles and seats, as if hurled about by giants in the contest. The floor of the arena had long since collapsed, leaving the network of cells and cages and passageways exposed. Here is where the gladiators waited for combat and where the precursors of Beatty must have stood, bare-handed, with no means of forcing their fanged antagonists to retreat, roll over, or sit yawning on stools.

A roar, but not that of lions, came from without; it seemed louder to Max than when he'd been part of the crowd, as if the circle of stone were some great ear, collecting and amplifying the sound. He didn't wait longer to admire the architecture. Climbing to the topmost level would be like scaling a frozen avalanche, full of ice blocks and chasms and jagged stones. Max made his way up a ruined aisle to the second level, then moved sideways to where he could get handholds on the broken travertine and hauled himself to the third.

But how to get to the small, square windows set high in the sheer face of the attic? He saw the solution at once: a ladder, a series of ladders, that had been abandoned by the craftsmen who must have been at work—yes, he could just make out the iron staples—reinforcing the crumbling limestone. It took him the better part of an hour to reach the spot, but only a minute to climb the rickety rungs. He stepped off the ladder and thrust himself through the brick-lined opening that looked out over the metropolis below.

Far to the south, at the staging area, the dust was still pumping upward; it spread dark and lowering over the city's marble monuments, and over the billowing white banners that moved up the avenue. To Max it seemed as if the brown earth and cloud-filled sky had exchanged places. Was everything topsy-turvy? There, on the ground, were bombers and fighters—the three-engined Capronis and Savoia-Machettis of the Regia Aeronautica—that belonged in the air. Behind them, and no less disconcerting, was a whole forest of palms and pepper trees that moved like a scene from *Macbeth* up the Via dei Trionfi, followed by a field of uprooted ferns and mosses that was waved about by—this time the chorus could have been from *Aïda*—girls in halters and fluted sheaths. Here was a further anomaly: squads of black-skinned Africans, each man with a rifle and sword and wearing, instead of the rags of the defeated, the lion's mane of the victor.

Now another roar began. It swelled, became deafening, ear-splitting, but—was this one more somersault? Had the crowds beneath him been lifted skyward like a heavenly choir?—its origin was not in the streets but in the air. Max looked up. Two aircraft were heading straight for him! They were going to crash into the Colosseum! At the last instant both machines swooped upward, passing so close to where Max lay that he was certain he felt the wind of their wake pass over him. The population below was in a frenzy. They were jumping upward and flinging their arms into the air, as if they wanted to touch the two flashing, silvery craft. Then they bellowed like animals: *L'Etiopia è nostra! L'Etiopia è nostra!* The two planes, meanwhile, had made a full circle and now, wingtip to wingtip, were headed straight for Maximilian again. This time they flew even lower, hurtling down the Via dell'Impero at a height no greater than the wires strung for electrified trolleys. Then, when the daredevils were opposite the Temple of Venus and Rome, they dipped their wings in tribute to the reviewing stand, and pulled back on their sticks to try once more to leap over the obstacle that Titus, in the year 80, had placed before them. Max could see the pilots' straining faces: Bruno, in leather helmet, and Vittorio, his scarf trailing behind him. *I figli di Mussolini*: the Dictator's sons.

Mussolini himself stood off to the left, below. His arm was raised in the old Roman salute toward the departing aircraft. Behind him a Fascist official raised an arm whose hand had been sheared away in the African war. "Duce!" cried il Signor Farinacci, his voice booming from a thousand loudspeakers. "You see the silver angels! They have descended from *Paradiso!* They wish to pay homage to our living god!"

On the dais, the Pope, Pius the Eleventh, shifted unhappily upon a throne-like chair. His living God was on the chain around his neck. He fingered the tortured body. He frowned. Mussolini, however, thrust out his chest and his chin. His arm was still extended toward the two distant airplanes, even as they disappeared into the crimson haze. "Marconi!" said He Who Is Loved By All.

"At your disposal, Duce," replied a small man in a bowler hat. "Can you make contact?"

The creator of radio leaned over the wires and dials of his invention. There was a crackling sound, which amplifiers broadcast through the atmosphere. "*Sì*. I have them."

Mussolini hooked his thumbs into his belt. "THE WHOLE WORLD," he proclaimed, "WILL HEAR THE THOUGHTS OF IL DUCE AS HE SPEAKS TO THESE BIRDS OF THE AIR. YOU, PILOTS! YOU HAVE WON THE GREATEST COLONIAL WAR IN ALL OF HISTORY! THE EAGLE OF THE ROMAN EMPIRE HAS ONCE MORE SPREAD ITS WINGS OVER AFRICA. YOU ARE ITS BLOODY BEAK! YOU ARE THE TALONS THAT HAVE TORN HUMAN FLESH! BECAUSE OF YOU THERE WILL BE NO MORE SUN. BECAUSE OF YOU, NO BLUE IN THE HEAVENS. OUR TEN THOUSAND PLANES WILL TURN THE SKY BLACK. THUS ROME SALUTES YOU!"

There were more crackling sounds. Then a voice, fresh, youthful, masculine, was heard to say, "We fly for the honor of Italy." A second voice: "And in your name, Duce!" Now came an outburst from the crowd. Men and women surged forward. Some had children on their shoulders. They lifted them skyward, as if they meant to dip them into the stream of transmitted words that moved invisibly through the air.

"This is how a Fascist father speaks to his sons!" That was Farinacci. He put his lips to the mesh of the microphone. "And how Fascist sons speak to their father!"

"*No, no!*" cried the multitude. "*Nostro Padre!*"

A quick grin, the flash of white teeth, passed over Mussolini's features. Then, indeed like a father, he stared sternly down. One of the bands marched smartly forward, tootling and drumming, and the tens of thousands of people assembled between the Arch of Constantine and the Arch of Titus broke once more into the familiar anthem:

> *Salve o popolo d'Eroi*
> *Salve o Patria immortale!*
> *Son rinati i figli tuoi*
> *Con la fe' nell'ideale.*

Max, seeing it all from his lofty perch, realized that the two airplanes had timed their appearance to coincide with the arrival of their fellow airmen on the ground below. Each segment of the parade, after moving up the Via dei Trionfi, swung leftward at the first memorial arch; paused briefly in front of the reviewing stand; and then proceeded to, and through, the Arco di Tito, which marked the ceremonial conclusion of the Triumph. Even now, as units of the *Regia Aeronautica* marched under the keystone, carrying the same fasces as the carved Roman soldiers above them, the palm and pepper trees halted before the man who had caused them to be uprooted. He raised his hand in the stiff-armed salute and leaned into the microphone.

"TREMBLE EARTH! TREMBLE IN FEAR, ALL WHO WOULD OPPOSE OUR EMPIRE!"

Not for the first time, Max became aware of a disconcerting lapse—a quarter second, a half second at most—between what he saw and what he heard. Then he realized that the echo was caused by Signor Marconi's invention. Each word from the reviewing stand, the answering roar from the crowd, the endless round of the *Giovinezza*— all of this was pouring from the speakers of every radio in Rome.

"TREES! YOU WISH TO TEAR OUT YOUR ROOTS! TREES! YOU WISH TO MARCH WITH OUR ARMIES. SOON! SOON! SOON THE WORLD WILL SEE A MAGNIFICENT FOREST. A FOREST OF EIGHT MILLION BAYONETS."

Now it was the turn of the black-skinned soldiers. With swords upraised, they stood so near that Max could see that their commander was either the runaway, the rebel, who had slept beside him that night, or his double—the same khaki-colored, gold-braided uniform, the curving nose, the point of the beard on his chin. Then it came to him: these were not the defeated enemies of Rome but its victorious allies, the Eritreans, the Somalis. Mussolini's face, in addressing them, grew dark itself, as the blood rose through the veins of his neck.

"MY BROTHERS! *FRATELLI!* YOU, WHO KNOW HOW TO KILL WITHOUT MERCY! AS A LEOPARD KILLS! A TIGER! WITH ONE BEAUTIFUL STROKE OF THE CLAWS! YOU! *FRATELLI!* WHO HAVE LEARNED TO KEEP A DESERT IN YOUR HEART! WHO HAVE ALWAYS KNOWN IT IS NO CRIME TO BE STRONG! WE, WITH OUR WHITE SKINS,

WITH MILK IN OUR VEINS, WITH PALE HEARTS; WE, WHO HAVE BEEN TAUGHT TO TURN OUR CHEEK AND LOVE OUR NEIGHBOR—IT IS WE WHO HAVE MUCH TO LEARN FROM THE BLACK HEART OF OUR BROTHERS IN AFRICA. THUS ROME SALUTES YOU!"

The crowd roared so fiercely that few heard the pontiff as he leaned toward the man in the military uniform and white moustache who sat beside him. "What is he saying, your Highness? That we are to learn from the heathen? We wished to go into Africa to win new souls for Christ. We wished to create a Catholic continent."

The little King nodded, tapping together the toes of his shiny boots. "You have heard correctly, Your Holiness."

A man, a diplomat from Germany, turned toward an aide. His face, narrow-lipped, hooded-eyed, seemed flushed. "*Ja,*" he said. "And he called these *Negers* his brothers."

The black regiments marched off beneath the Arch of Titus and were replaced, in their turn, by a brigade of sailors hauling a scale model of a sailing ship and an actual submarine. Next came the infantry, the artillery, and, on their prancing horses, the battalions of the cavalry. What a cheer went up. Louder than ever: *forte, molto forte, fortissimo!*

Max thought he could feel the ancient foundations of the Colosseum begin to quake. Was it from the treads of the motorized units that were just now rumbling by the arena? He watched as each tank jerked leftward at the Arch of Constantine, where it was blessed by a tall, thin, bespectacled cardinal of the church. No, more likely this quaver was caused by the concussion of the Blackshirts, Mussolini's own, whose stiff legs and cleated boots fell like jackhammers on the cobblestones.

On the reviewing stand the foreign diplomat, taking note of the goose-stepping warriors, turned toward his Italian counterpart.

"I am delighted, Ciano, to note that Il Duce has adopted our own march as well as the Führer salute."

It wasn't the foreign minister who replied but He Who Never Doubts: *"YOU, RIBBENTROP: IS THIS A JOKE? DO YOU IMAGINE THAT WE, THE DESCENDANTS OF CAESAR, VIRGIL AND AUGUSTUS—THAT WE HAVE BORROWED FROM A PEOPLE WHO DID NOT HAVE THE SKILL TO RECORD THEIR OWN LIVES? THIRTY CENTURIES OF HISTORY ALLOW US TO REGARD WITH SUPREME PITY THOSE FROM BEYOND THE ALPS."*

Ribbentrop, reddening, started to speak but his words were drowned out by new cheers. Now Max saw, moving up the avenue, the same animals he had viewed from the window of the Pensione Wanda. Here were the elephants and the lions, along with one- and two-humped camels, spotted leopards, quivering gazelles, and all manner of exotic creatures—mammals with curved noses and what seemed to be enormous lizards with scales on their flanks but, on their backs, like certain fish, a spiked and fan-like fin.

This menagerie also halted before He Who Never Errs. Max, high above, could hear the crowd laugh with delight at the thought that even dumb beasts could understand the words of their leader. Mussolini struck a new pose, hands on hips, gazing down at these new subjects. His laugh boom-boomed above all the others. The animals, as if aware of the honor bestowed upon them, became calm, still, and dignified. Then, without a word, Mussolini moved to the edge of the stand. In a dumb show he hooked his finger toward one of the keepers. The man pointed with incredulity at himself. The vanquisher nodded. The man stepped forward with his charge, a maned beast that leapt upright, pawing the air with its claws.

"No! Duce!"

That cry came from a pale-faced, dark-haired woman, who also sat on the platform. She had grasped what Mussolini intended to do. He gestured for silence. The woman put her hands over her eyes. Next to her the only other female on the stand, the Queen, covered hers with her gloves. Thus neither of them saw how the new Caesar leaned over the railing toward where the animal, rearing still on its hind legs, had bared its yellow canines. But everyone else saw how the bald bullet head went into the gaping mouth.

A gasp went up from the masses. "Ah, Duce," they moaned, breaking into tears, as if they had already lost him.

The white-faced keeper heaved on the leash. The terrible jaws closed over the Duce's head. Silence fell upon all of Rome. Up in his perch Max counted the seconds: five, six, seven. Then He Who Fears Nothing withdrew the cannonball of his skull and stood erect. His voice, when he spoke, needed no amplification. "BEAST OF THE JUNGLE! IL DUCE HAS HEARD YOU! YOU, WHO POSSESS THE WISDOM OF POWER AND INSTINCT: WHAT YOU HAVE TOLD ME IS TRUE. *BETTER TO LIVE ONE DAY AS A LION*, SÌ! SÌ! SÌ! *THAN ONE HUNDRED YEARS AS A SHEEP!*"

There was applause, laughter, a joyous exclamation of relief. Off went the animals and on came a series of pageant carts, each depicting a crucial battle in pantomime. Here were ambushes and routs. Hundreds of Ethiopians seemed to be drowning in a river that flowed and gurgled and swirled. Another float gleamed with the broken glass that had mutilated the bare feet of the warriors at the battle of Mai Cen. At the base of each cart, in an attitude of dejection, sat a defeated prince—Ras Imru, Ras Sejoun, Ras Kassa; while at the top, arm raised in the salute, was a commander of the Italian army.

"YOU, BADOGLIO! MARSHAL OF THE EMPIRE!" cried Mussolini, when the float that portrayed the capture of the enemy capital stopped before him. "IN THIS, THE 14TH YEAR OF MODERN HISTORY, THE 14TH YEAR OF THE FASCIST REVOLUTION,

OUR VICTORY IN AFRICA JOINS THE BATTLES OF THERMO-
PYLAE AND CANNAE AS A MASTERPIECE OF STRATEGY AND
EXECUTION THAT WILL BECOME PART OF HISTORY. YOU,
WHO HAVE TRANSFORMED THE DUCE'S CONCEPTION INTO
THE MOST BRILLIANT STRATEGY SINCE THE WARS OF CAE-
SAR. ROME SALUTES YOU! THE DUCE NOW PROCLAIMS YOU
DUKE OF ADDIS ABABA AND VICEROY OF ETHIOPIA!"

The last of the pageants moved away. Now it was the turn of
the citizens—representatives of workers and industry, the guilds,
farmers with pitchforks, the university students. On and on they
came, streaming up the boulevard with no end in sight. Had Max,
in the heat, the dust, the constant tumult, dozed off? Or had he,
like the animals under the gaze of Il Duce, fallen into a trance? All
he knew was that the sun, which had once been rising over the eastern wall of the Colosseum, now hung bleeding over his own jagged
wall to the west. The light that came out of it turned the whole sky
the color of an opera curtain. Max watched four large birds, cranes
certainly, beat their way over the city, as if attempting to escape the
darkness that unfurled behind them.

Then the steady ticktock of the march, a marvel of clockwork,
came undone. There were shouts. There was turmoil. Was it—the
same thought occurred simultaneously in a million minds—an as-
sassination? No: there stood Mussolini, his arms crossed on his chest,
his glaring eyes fixed on the Titus Arch, where a crowd, now milling about, had spilled outside the line of procession.

"It's the Jews," said Farinacci.

Pius the Eleventh: "Yes, poor Jews. They do not wish to place
themselves under the arch of their humiliation. It is a sorrow to them."

Mussolini raised his noble head, in form much like that of
Vespasian. "YOU, JEWS OF ROME! CITIZENS OF THE EMPIRE!
WHY DO YOU MAKE THIS DISTURBANCE?"

At that a wail went up. A ripple, then a wave, went through the march as it backed up on itself. Hundreds of women were rushing back to the platform, their left hands raised in the air.

"Duce! Duce!" they screamed. "You see how we love you!"

The diplomat, Von Ribbentrop, turned toward the pontiff at his side. "Why do you tolerate these Jewesses?" he asked.

"They have been with us a long time. They are the descendants of those whom Titus defeated."

"You will pardon me, Excellency," said the German. "Not defeated. I am something of an expert on this matter. A conquered people does not flourish as the Israelites have here. Will you allow me to quote the words of Juvenal? *'The vanquished have made laws for the victors.'*"

The women continued to sway. The last of the day's light fell on their upraised fingers.

"Look, Duce! Look!"

"We are married to you."

"You have our rings!"

"We love you like a husband."

Now it was clear: they were displaying the iron bands that had replaced the gold ones, all of which had been donated to the Ethiopian campaign. They held these dull circles up to their master.

"Duce! You are the father of our sons!"

"We gave them to you!"

"Our rings!"

"Our sons!"

Between the two arches, all was pandemonium. The women were wailing. They were panting. Some of them, in ecstasy, were biting their hair, the cotton of their dresses, their own olive arms.

"*'These Jews!'*" That was Von Ribbentrop, who was once more declaiming the words of the Roman poet:

They'd prefer to dine
On flesh of men than that of swine.

Mussolini moved to the edge of the platform. He spread his arms wide. His words, when he spoke, were no louder than a man holding a conversation.

"Beautiful ladies. You fill my soul with joy. I accept the love you offer me. I know that of all my people you have sacrificed the most. For this, your treasure, your sons, the blood I know you would shed for me, I kiss you. I embrace you. I hold each of you against my beating heart. *Grazie.* Now you must do for the Duce one more thing. It is not big. No, it is small. But it will bring him happiness. Return to the *Trionfo*, eh? Walk under the arch. It is nothing, a matter of ten steps. I will be with you. The Duce accompanies you, his hand is in your hands. Come, let us go."

No animal trainer could have tamed his beasts with more skill. The enchanted women turned about in order to resume their place in the march.

"*Bravo! Bravo, Duce!*" cried the multitude, as they might to a baritone or a basso who had completed his aria. Mussolini, for this performance, took no bows. He struck instead a new pose: his elbow cupped in his open hand, his closed one supporting the weight of his chin with but one finger pointing upward toward the organ of thought. Perhaps this is what, within that iron skull, the new Caesar was thinking: *Who will mourn me, as these Jews mourn the destruction of their temple, after two thousand years?*

The cheers died away. All became still. The women had returned to the threshold of the hated arch. Would they obey their husband, their father, their lover, and walk beneath it? On the reviewing stand Margherita Sarfatti, the green boa over her shoulders matching her green-tinted eyes, rose from her chair. The slick-haired Count Ciano stood beside her. One after the other those on the dais got to their feet. Up went the Fascist Grand Council. Up stood the ambassadors, the dignitaries. All strained to see through the last of the dust-filled light, as thick now as a slab of reddened aspic.

At the memorial, an historic dumb show was taking place. First one Jewish woman and then another stepped ahead, but each fell back, as if a sheet of glass or some other invisible barrier had been stretched across the opening in the facade. Then the men strode forward; they too were repelled. No one, it seemed, was capable of being the first. Finally the Rabbi of Trieste approached the Rabbi of Rome. He took something from the older man's arms. Then he walked back to the monument, until he stood directly under the keystone; there he turned, and held the sacred Ark over his head. His thin, faint, high-pitched voice rose into the air, offering God's blessing, the *Mi-Sheberakh*, upon Benito Mussolini. Then the first Jew in nineteen centuries walked beneath the arch that commemorated his people's defeat.

There was a pause. A girl, she had the wild black hair of a Gypsy, ran after him. Then the community followed, disappearing beneath the stones.

Von Ribbentrop rose from his portable chair. "Duce," he began, "now I see that only a great leader of a great people could have dealt as you have with this detritus of history. You show all of mankind the way." The diplomat's lips were as pale and thin as the edge of the paper he held in his hands. He bent toward the microphone. "In gratitude, and in the name of the Führer, of the Volk, and of the Thousand Year Reich, it gives me pleasure to announce that Germany will be the first nation to recognize your Empire in Africa. All sanctions, and all embargoes, will cease. We look forward—"

"*Basta!*" said Il Duce. He waved the blond-headed man back to his chair. Then he took out a flour-white handkerchief and wiped his head, his neck, his brow. He smiled. He frowned. He smiled again, as each new thought passed through his brain. When he spoke, it was without effort, and without need of the microphone.

"IL DUCE THANKS THE FÜHRER. HE THANKS HERR RIBBENTROP. HE IS PLEASED. WITH EYES THAT PEER INTO THE FUTURE HE SEES A GREAT UNION OF THE GERMAN AND ITALIAN PEOPLES. ABOUT THIS AXIS THE LESSER RACES WILL IN SUBJUGATION LEARN TO REVOLVE."

Another cheer went up, like a mighty thunderclap. High above the scene Max wrapped his arms about his body. The words he had just heard made him realize that it was not the arena that had been trembling; it was he, himself. What had he learned in his old Latin classes? That *arena* meant the word *sand*, the same sand that was strewn to soak up the rivers of blood.

Down below, Mussolini had thrown back his head. He stood with his fists balled at his hips. "NOW THE DUCE ADDRESSES HIS OWN PEOPLE. OFFICERS, NONCOMMISSIONED OFFICERS, PRIVATES, BLACKSHIRTS OF THE ITALIAN REVOLUTION. ITALIAN MEN AND ITALIAN WOMEN—COUNTRYMEN AT HOME AND THROUGHOUT THE WORLD: LIFT YOUR BAN-NERS, YOUR SWORDS, YOUR HEARTS, TO SALUTE THE REAP-PEARANCE AFTER FIFTEEN CENTURIES OF AN EMPIRE, A FASCIST EMPIRE, UPON THE FATEFUL HILLS OF ROME. WILL YOU BE WORTHY OF IT?"

From everywhere, from the earth and air, came the reply. "*Sì! Sì!*"

"WILL YOU RENDER IT FERTILE WITH YOUR LABOR, AS YOU HAVE ALREADY DONE WITH YOUR BLOOD?"

"*Sì, Duce! Sì!*"

"IS THIS A SACRED OATH? DOES IT BIND YOU BEFORE GOD AND MAN?"

"*Sì! Sì! Sì!*"

As if by some remote signal, bugles began to sound from the seven hills of Rome, and bells began to ring from the innumerable churches. Through it all Mussolini beamed down on his people. Then, as the squads of Blackshirts put their caps on their swords and lifted them skyward, a voice rang out above all the others:

"You are our general, Duce! We follow you anywhere!"

Then other voices rose even higher.

"Not our general! Our Emperor!"

There was no stopping the rejoicing. The Romans beat their breasts. They pulled on the strands of their hair.

"*Un genio!*"

"*Garibaldi!*"

"*Nostro padre!*"

The great man allowed the accolades, the exultation, to go unchecked for a full minute. This time the crowd ignored him when he held up his hands. It was only when his flashing, white-toothed smile transformed itself into a tight-lipped frown did they fall silent. They watched as the Conqueror of Addis Ababa struggled to find the words he wished to speak:

"Dear Romans: you exaggerate, you flatter. Il Duce, he is not your Emperor. That honor shall go to his majesty, Vittorio Emanuele the Third, whom I now declare Emperor of Abyssinia. Next to him, I am nothing. Only a man. A poor soldier. An old revolutionary fighter. A schoolteacher, born of plain folk in the Romagna."

Here, the handkerchief appeared once more in his hands. He wiped what was clearly a tear from his eye.

At that gesture of humility, all was chaos. Women rushed

forward, holding their children, even newborn infants, in their arms. Many dropped to their knees or fell in prostration. "Bless us!" they cried. "Divine Duce! Give us your love!"

"*Mussolini divino!*"

"*Mussolini, nostro dio!*"

"*Un Immortale!*"

Now the Duce raised his hand and, as if he were indeed a god, one with the power to create darkness and light, the floodlights that illuminated the Colosseum snapped on. At the same time hundreds of torches lit up the columns of the Temple of Venus and Rome and the two Emperors' arches. The black sky, starless and moonless, was draped over the incandescent city.

Maximilian checked his watch. It was well after nine. He'd been at this perch the whole of this day. He hadn't eaten. His throat and lips were parched with thirst. He knew that, if he did not want to be discovered at dawn, he would soon have to depart; but the dark descent would be perilous, even if he were not feeling light-headed. Now, glancing one last time down the Via dei Trionfi, he could not help but gasp. The spoils of Ethiopia, the gold and silver ingots from the treasury of Addis Ababa, were moving up the thoroughfare. They made a kind of light of their own.

Behind the glittering treasure came a new corps of Africans— hundreds and hundreds, thousands and thousands, a few marching briskly but the greater number dragging a wounded limb or having to be supported by their comrades. At this spectacle the crowd did not cheer; they erupted instead in a low, derisive hooting, a *woo-woo-woo*, pierced by the kind of shrill whistling no bird could hope to replicate. This, then, was the army of the defeated. Row after row they came, some in uniform, some in the folds of their *shamas*, and still others with nothing more than a rag about their loins. Almost all carried the stump of a weapon—spears without points, bows without arrows, or bulletless French rifles. *Clack-clack-clackity* went the drummers, *clack-clack-clackity*, as they beat with their sticks on the sides of their drums.

Further off, the Abyssinians were tugging along a metal cage. Max, squinting behind his spectacles, could make out the figure of the man behind its bars, his body upright and swaying. After the cage came other men, white men and white women; these were not prisoners of war, clearly, but the refuse of the Roman jails, who had been assembled to receive Il Duce's clemency.

And that, Shabilian saw, was the end of *Il Trionfo*, except for the gigantic carved stele that brought up the rear. If the whole parade had been a serpent or an unwinding snake, this plundered obelisk would be its stiff and frozen tail. Thus was the long day of glory punctuated by a horizontal point of exclamation.

The captured troops were not greeted by Cardinal Pacelli at the Constantine Arch. Unblessed, they stood before the genius who had conceived their defeat. Mussolini did not growl or gloat. He looked, if anything, pained by the sight of the misery he had caused. Solemnly he addressed the fallen commanders.

"YOU, DEJIAK NASIBU. YOU HAVE FOUGHT BRAVELY. IL DUCE HAS RESOLVED TO SPARE YOUR LIFE."

The prince, thin as a stick, his bony cheeks and hollow temples protruding from the hood of his robe, inclined ever so slightly the blade of his head.

"YOU, RAS GUGSA. YOU HAVE BEEN A WORTHY FOE OF THE ROMAN LEGIONNAIRES. IL DUCE HAS MADE HIS DECISION: YOUR LIFE WILL BE SPARED."

So the ceremony of benevolence continued through the ranks of the princes, the Shoan chiefs, the Imperial Guard. The last to face Mussolini was the man in the cage. As the mobile prison was brought in front of the reviewing stand, the crowd went into a frenzy. They hurled taunts and curses at the small figure who stood unflinching within. And not just curses: at first there was a chiming sound, a clanging and ringing, as coins of all dimensions bounced off the iron bars; then fruit and eggs splattered against the enclosure, until it was impossible to see in or out. At last Mussolini held up his hand. Instantly the throng desisted. Two Africans moved to the cage and slipped the bolt. Then the Light of the World, Haile Selassie the First, stepped onto the ground. At the sight of the deposed monarch, Max could not suppress a shudder—not so much because his hands were tied before him, not even because he wore a noose around his neck; but because of his uncanny composure, the impassive face, the gaze, like agate or onyx, of his wide, expressionless eyes.

"YOU, TAFARI MAKONNEN! BECAUSE YOU REJECTED THE DOVE OF PEACE, YOU INVITED THE EAGLE OF WAR. FOR YOUR DEFIANCE, YOUR CUNNING, YOUR SECRET COLLUSION WITH THE ENGLISH CRIMINAL, EDEN—FOR THAT YOU MUST PAY THE PRICE. IL DUCE DECLARES YOUR EMPIRE AT AN END. THE LINE OF SUCCESSION FROM SOLOMON AND SHEBA IS OVER. HAILE SELASSIE IS NO MORE."

A cheer went up. The prisoner stood as before, pulp and rind hanging from his uniform like defunct medals of decoration. His black pupils in their white setting did not blink once.

"YOU, TAFARI MAKONNEN, WHO CALLED HIMSELF LORD OF LORDS: LISTEN WELL. ALL WHO HAVE GATHERED HERE HAVE GIVEN THEIR LOYALTY TO THE DUCE AND THE FASCIST REVOLUTION. THE LIONS, THE CAMELS, THE REPTILES HAVE WALKED BENEATH THE ARCH OF ALLEGIANCE. THE MUTE MOSSES AND PALMS HAVE SWORN, ALONG WITH YOUR OWN PRINCES. THE JEWS OF ROME, EVEN THEY HAVE CALLED OUT, *RABBI! RABBI!* THE PEOPLE OF ROME ARE TIRED. THEY ARE HUNGRY. THEY WISH TO

RETURN TO THEIR HOMES. BUT FIRST YOU MUST HELP THE DUCE DECIDE YOUR FATE. YOU, ERSTWHILE EMPEROR, NOW IMPOSTOR. YOU, SO-CALLED LION OF JUDAH: WILL YOU TAKE THE OATH?"

The little coffee-colored man stood without making a sound. His head, on its thin neck, moved neither up for yes nor sideways for no.

"THE DUCE IS MAGNANIMOUS. MORE TENDER THAN THE LIGHTNING-HURLING GODS. WHAT DO YOU SAY TO HIM?"

What the Abyssinian said was nothing at all.

"YOU, TAFARI MAKONNEN: THE DUCE NOW DECIDES." So saying, he raised his arm, as if he intended to give his enemy the Fascist salute. But at the end of his arm his hand was balled into a fist, a fist from which his thumb extended. Then, like the Emperors of old, he turned that thumb down.

There was no reaction from the crowd: the weary multitude let out its breath in a collective sigh. An honor guard of four Blackshirts seized the condemned man and led him off toward the Arch of Titus. From behind that monument a group of *Squadristi* maneuvered a portable platform. The base of that structure rose some four feet from the ground and had what looked like a door frame attached to its floorboards. Instead of a door, however, a hook protruded from the horizontal beam. A muttering went through the onlookers, *patibolo*, *patibolo*, as they slowly realized what that device was.

No ladder, no steps led to the platform. The honor guard seized the Abyssinian and, as if he had been a milk can, heaved him upright on the boards. Then the Blackshirts leaned together, much like the three militiamen Max had seen bending over a match. When they broke apart, none had a cigarette; but one was wearing a black velvet hood. Without assistance he leapt onto the stand. He gathered up the free end of the noose and swung the knot through the hook, where it caught tight, leaving plenty of slack in the line. Then he moved the prisoner directly over the trap and withdrew to the wooden bar that would release it.

"YOU, KING OF KINGS: THE DUCE PERMITS YOU TO ADDRESS TO HIM A PLEA OF MERCY. WHAT ARE YOUR WORDS?"

The captured foe stood mute. With a gasp of sorrow, surprising in one so stalwart, Mussolini turned away, burying his smooth-shaven head in his hands.

The executioner threw the lever; the former Emperor dropped like a shot. What occurred next was so filled with horror it might have caused even Nero to shudder. The thin neck split in two from the impact: Haile Selassie plunged into the pit; his staring head swung free in the air.

"*Ah, maledetto!*" cried the assemblage, like a chorus in Verdi. "*Che orrore!*"

That was but the start of the abomination. The audience could scarcely believe what was occurring before their astonished eyes. The corpse of the King, the whole of his decapitated body, came lurching up from the pit and, its legs thrashing in a reflex motion, dashed crazily from one edge of the scaffold to the other. What was worse, the most appalling of sights, was the blood that shot like a geyser in pulses from the empty collar of his uniform.

"*Aiuto!*" shouted the crowd. Many dropped to their knees. "Save us!"

"Ha! Ha! Ha! Ha!" That was Mussolini. He too was dancing about on his platform. Tears streamed freely from his eyes. He was slapping his knees in glee.

"Ha-ha-ha-ha!" He waved toward the grotesque spectacle. "What a joke!" He hugged his sides as if to hold them together. "*Che scherzo! Che pantomima! Bravo, Arlecchino!*"

All followed his gaze to the scaffold. There the Emperor's dead hands clasped his blood-soaked tunic and in a last reflexive spasm ripped it apart. Inside was another human being! It wasn't a midget, exactly, but a small man, the homunculus of the departed King. There he stood, grinning and bowing to a universal gasp of wonderment, while a few members of the huge audience, those who still happened to possess a short-wave radio or had read a foreign newspaper, recalled that the real Haile Selassie was at that moment in Bath, a town built by the ancient Romans, and thus could not be part of this modern grand guignol.

"*Eh, bravo!*" shouted Mussolini, blotting the tears of merriment with his sleeve. "*LA COMMEDIA E FINITA!*"

3

At that moment a comet flew over the city of Rome. It was no prop in the charade that had just been concluded. The great flaming ball passed directly over the heads of the gaping crowd and briefly turned the nighttime scene into day. Nor was Benito Mussolini acting. His steadfast chin quivered. His deep-set eyes bulged wide with terror. He held up his hands, which in the red glow of the vanishing meteorite looked as if they had been dipped in blood.

"*Si muove,*" he said, in wonder. "It moves."

He was not referring to the falling star but to the gigantic obelisk that sat on its caisson below him. Indeed, in the fading scarlet glow, it did seem to have shifted on its moorings, so that it pointed now like the finger of a colossus toward where the paralyzed Duce stood. Was such a thing possible? Could some embedded ore in the sandstone needle cause it to be deflected by the passage of the iron planetoid overhead?

"*O, Dio!*" Mussolini exclaimed. "I am cursed."

"*No, no, Duce!*" exhorted his subjects. "*Coraggio!*"

But the Duce had lost his bravado. "Margherita!" he called. At once his mistress ran to him, just as that other Jewess, Berenice, had attached herself to Titus after his day of triumph. The two of them clung together.

"Hush," she told him. "*Zitto, Caro. Zitto, zitto.*"

But Mussolini was wailing. "My dream! It comes true! Look! *L'obelisco!* It moves!" He stared in agony at the stele as if it were the pointer and all the panoply of victory a vast Ouija board that was about to reveal his fate. "Ah," he moaned, "I am doomed."

Now the old Pope got to his feet. "Such phenomena, dear Duce, are often not a curse but a blessing. Think of the star that appeared over Bethlehem. Look: there is the monument to the great Emperor Constantine. Did he not see a burning cross in the sky? All of Christ's kingdom, and the might of the Church, are the result of that vision."

"*Imbecille!*" Mussolini cried, pushing the pontiff away. "Ah! Ah! It is torture! Can nobody save me?"

Not a person in the crowd rose to the challenge. Many had fallen to their knees in prayer. Others ran about senselessly in panic. The majority simply waited silently for the end of the world. Then one voice, high and twangy, called out in something like English:

"Wal, I ain't no feelosopher, but I reckon since you axed I can give it the old college try."

The speaker stood among the kneeling crowd of common prisoners. He had a white billy-goat beard on his chin and a white hat on his head. His jailers moved quickly forward to force him to his knees. The pale-faced Mussolini held up his hand.

"Wait. Who are you? Where are you from?"

"Ain't no Your-rump-pee-on, that's for sure. Just a farm boy— like you, Mr. Musty-loin-ee."

The Duce fell into his own version of English. "What's-a the name?"

"Prince."

Max, of course, knew it before the man spoke. In spite of the burnt-off eyebrows, he'd recognized the famous head, the twanging voice. Without a thought to the danger, he abandoned his high perch and hopped like a goat from stone to pillar to slab on the journey downward. He could not hear, therefore, what was said in answer to Mussolini's next question.

"What-a you want, eh? Why you make the speech?"

The prisoner indicated the resting stele. "Wal, it ain't how I go about earning a living, but I know a thing or two about these higher-glee-facts. You want to learn your fate? It's here, in all these scribbles on the side of the oh-bull-ask."

At that point a thin-faced, thin-haired man who had been seated in the ambassadorial section rose to his feet. "Signor Mussolini, you must not continue this farce. That man is nothing more or less than a fugitive from justice. As you know, the American embassy has filed papers for his extradition. I ask—"

"*SILENZIO!* HOW DARE YOU ADDRESS WITHOUT PERMISSION THE DUCE?"

The Conqueror turned back to the man with the bearded chin. "You—what's-a the name? Prince? Signor Prince? I have inna my head many, what-you-call-him? *Sogni.* Dreams. Many bad dreams. Oh, the *cometa!* You tell me, eh? You tell Benito alla what you know."

The prisoner, a chain clanking about his ankles, moved to the stele, which lay horizontally on its high, wheeled carriage. Had the fire in Arizona scorched not only his eyebrows but his eyes? Like a blind man, he stretched upward and began to run his fingers over the owls and cats and little round jugs that had been cut into the sandstone. A full moment went by. Mussolini, his brow in anxious corrugations, stood clutching the hand of Margherita. A hush fell over the crowd. Everyone stared at the American, who continued to move the pads of his fingers over the incised images that were the converse of the raised dots in the system of Braille.

"Wal," he said at last, "I think I know what that comet sig-knee-fries."

"Eh? *Parla! Non mi tormentare!*"

"This here's your horrorscope. It says you are going to live forever."

Margherita burst out, "*Caro!* You see? There is nothing to fear."

"FEAR? THE DUCE FEARS NOTHING. HE KNEW THIS WAS A SIGN FROM HEAVEN."

The ambassador, Breckinridge Long, spoke once more. "With all due respect, Signor Mussolini, this is nonsense. The man is trying to hoodwink you. He stole his children from their mother. That, sir, is a crime in my country as well as yours. And there is some question of arson and perhaps even murder. Don't let him pull the wool over your eyes. He must return to face American justice."

Here a wiry-haired girl, she couldn't have been more than fourteen, cried out. "No! We don't want to go back! Do we, Frankie? Aria, isn't that right? We want to stay here with Papa." The children—the boy must have been two or three years younger than his sister, and the other girl two or three years older—both nodded.

Prince said, with no trace of his farmer's twang, "You leave them out of this. I'll fight my battles on my own, Mr. Ambassador. You hear me? You understand?"

Mussolini looked back and forth, from the three children, to the father, to Long. "What's-a? You gonna *abbandonare* the Duce? Without he say is all right, is okay?"

"Naw, not at all, Mister-loony. With your persimmon, I ain't going to the city of New York. Old Amos, he's got to stay here and enjoy your horse-pit-ality."

"*Sì.* But first you tell the Duce: how he be *Immortale?*"

"Why, it's right here on the higher-giraffe. Your fate is going to be the same as those Egyptian Pharaohs. You're going to have a monument, not some arch like old Tight-ass or old Constant-teen, but something that will rival that of Cheops and Ramses the Great. You will be remembered as long as they."

Mussolini: "*Per l'eternità.*"

"That's the ticket."

"But how it happen, this *miracolo?*"

"Easy as pie. You say this here was the greatest victory in history? Wal, where is its arch? You got to announce a competition. To build a Monument of Mussolini."

The Greatest Italian sucked in the thick, dust-laden air. His chest expanded like the bellows of a furnace. The buttons on his tunic stretched and strained. "YOU, PEOPLE OF ROME, OF ITALY, OF THE HEMISPHERES OF THE EARTH. THE DUCE HAS BEEN TOUCHED BY A STAR. NOW YOU MUST MAKE HIS MEMORIAL. YOU, PEOPLE OF ICELAND, OF CALIFORNIA, OF THE STRAW VILLAGES IN THE SOUTH SEA ISLES—TAKE OUT YOUR IN-STRUMENTS. MAKE YOUR CALCULATIONS. CREATE A THING OF STRENGTH AND BEAUTY, A THING AS POWERFUL AS OUR FASCIST IDEALS. MAKE FOR IL DUCE THE WINGS THAT WILL LIFT HIM TO THE SKY."

That was when Max, his clothing torn and an ankle turned, limped onto the scene. "Mister Prince!" he called. "*You* have to build it. Duce! Duce! Let him stay! That's Amos Prince! The world's greatest architect."

Then, from pain, hunger, or dehydration, the scene before him began to shift. Or perhaps it was the sheer joy of seeing the master in the flesh that made everything spin. Turning before Max now was what had been and what was to be. He knew, if dimly, that history was repeating itself; knew, even, that the Titus Arch, now looming above him, was a portal in time through which streamed the armies of the past and the present and perhaps the champions of battles to come. Had there not been, at that earlier *Trionfo*, another comet? Passing over the head of—Titus, was it? Or Vespasian, his father? Had it not also been interpreted as a sign of glory for the reigning Emperor?

Let us forgive Max Shabilian for not recognizing that it was his own future that was rushing toward him now. For, had he but eyes to see, he would have known that all those who would share and shape his life were standing before him: Prince, of course, Prince above all; and the Duce, mopping with his square handkerchief the expanse of his sweating brow; Marconi, the Nobel Prize winner; Von Ribbentrop too; and the Fascists, Ciano and Farinacci; Vittorio Emanuele, the little Italian King; the squat-bodied old Pope and the thin-faced Cardinal who would soon be the new one; the Rabbi of Trieste, who would also rise, in this instance to become Rabbi of Rome; the American ambassador; Sarfatti, Benito's mistress; the Jewish nymph with the wild ringlets of hair; A.P.'s children, the boy, Franklin; the wire-haired girl; and that third child, Aria, the oldest, blond and sad-eyed. How beautiful she was! And was she not smiling, sweetly smiling, directly at him? As it happened, hers was the last face Max saw before his eyelids closed with the finality of a shopkeeper's shutters, and Maximilian himself dropped to the cobblestones of the old Roman road.

ALITALIA 607

Il Gabinetto

[2005: 1936]

1

We are, the accented captain has told us, at cruising altitude. Already I've forgotten the figure. 35,000 feet? I used to be a whiz at this kind of math. Six miles up, I guess, and change. Mother of God! I can't remember the number of feet in a mile. And of course I'm going to have to pee. Fool that I am, I wanted a window seat. I'll be clambering over Leda all the way across the Atlantic. What did I think I'd see? There is nothing but blackness now, starlessness, and the blink of the bulb at the tip of the wing. Below? Not even a fishing boat's lantern. Not even the glow of an electric eel.

"Let there be light." The words of God? Old Testament version? No, no, only Marconi, when we were all floating angelically a mile high in the air. Though that was no less a miracle when you think about it. Without wires, lines, or cables, he switched on every light bulb in Rome. *Sia fatta la luce.* If I were wearing a hat, I'd take it off to him.

Wait! A mile. 5280 feet. Sixteen hundred and ninety-three meters. Another miracle. One more victory over Uncle Al. Memory restored.

These jets: how smoothly they fly. Alitalia 607. New York to Rome. I still have Prince's notebook in my working hand. He seems to have written it backward, last things first. Will the first ones be last? *Like a son*, he wrote. *Jew-near*. I won't let Leda see it. Not now. Maybe never. I swing my head round to gaze at my granddaughter. She's still lost in her magazine. Her profile, that straight nose, the noble brow: it's like a figurehead on those old-fashioned schooners. Now *that* was a dangerous journey. Braving the storm. Braving the seas. What was that lovely word we used in the old days? For the airport? Before JFK? Speak, muse. Ah: *Idlewild!*

The first person I saw when I woke from my fit was the last one I'd seen as well. What do they say about ducks? That they get imprinted with the first thing they see when they peck their way out of the shell. Whoever it is—whether brooding hen or a tin can on a string—becomes its mother. In the case of Max the Mallard, I was struck dumb by beauty. There was the blond hair, tumbling downward, and the gray eyes—not totally gray, because these seemed to have flecks of green around the circumference of the iris, like the markings on the dial of a clock. How sharp, how focused my vision: the nostrils to either side of the thin curving blade of her nose were reddened, like those of a weeper; they trembled, they flared, with each exhalation. Poor rabbit, I thought, coming to: had she been sobbing for me? I remembered her name. I struggled to say it:

"Aria."

Then another head—a round one, with a round face—leaned down. The pale boy with the cherry lips, the cherry cheeks. He was grinning. "Look," he said. "There's blood."

For all my painlessness, I knew I had split the back of my head on the stones. A crowd had gathered. Women with a hundred little flowers on their dresses. Men with moustaches and hats.

"*Poverino*," they murmured.

"*Dov'è un dottore?*"

"*Sta sanguinando molto.*"

I knew what that meant, roughly. That the blood was flowing out of me. I tried to lift my head. No dice. I could not, I was amazed to discover, raise my hand. *Am I still living?* was the question I had for the girl; to my alarm not a word came out.

Next, Amos Prince, unmistakable in his white whiskers and white linens, moved unshackled to me. He loomed over what suddenly seemed a crowd of five-foot Italians. "What's everybody standing around for like a bunch of wouldn't Indians?"

Then, before my fluttering eyes, he seemed to fall, growing larger, growing closer, until I could see and even smell the streaks of nicotine in the little white beard that hung from his chin. He rolled me into his arms. He stood, clutching the limp doll of my body. With horror I saw the spreading blotch on his linen lapel. I did, finally, manage to speak.

"Sorry, I'm sorry," I said, though I hadn't the strength to point to the stain, more black than red, as if I were leaking bile.

He laughed—oh, how often was I to hear that cackle and wheeze, the *hee* and *haw, haw, haw!* "Don't mention it. Ain't the first time that old Amos has been taken to the cleaners!"

2

Christ, I do have to pee. Now what? At least Burlesque-phony, as Prince might have called him, provided first-class passage. Hell, he probably owns the airline, along with all the TV stations and just about everything else in the country. Mushy-linguine was no billionaire. He had to live off his salary and the royalties from his books. Ghosted by Margherita, including the autobiography. A bestseller. *Safari*, A.P. used to call her. *So-fatty*. Okay. All right. I'm going to do this. Which means hoisting myself up by the seat back in front of me.

"Maxie. What is it? Do you have to, you know, use the facilities?"

I wish I didn't. I wish I were still on the catheter. I wish Rosellen had come along instead of Leda. She knows how to get me into tight spots. And out. My nurse, in theory. Though I've asked her ten times to be my unblushable bride.

"You mean p-p-pee? Isn't that what you m-m-mean?" Oh what a testy old fart.

She makes a joke of it. "*Facilities* is what they taught us to say in New Haven."

Now I've done it. Who is this little Shirley Temple staring at me over the back of her first-class seat? Hello, sweetheart! Did I wake you? Sorry. Sorry. Sorry. Will I scare her with my lopsided smile?

Gruffly, to my own flesh and blood: "Just move your own f-f-feet, will you? I can m-manage."

I hear the snap; she's unbuckling. Now I see but of course don't feel her grip on the deadwood of my arm. God! Is she going to march me all the way into the—what *do* they call it? Restroom, bathroom, lavatory. It's the ultimate port-a-potty. Shithole in the sky.

"Don't be silly, Max. I'm here to help."

So are the stewardesses, every single one of whom, I note, has averted her eyes. Including that one with the olive skin, the boobs, the black hair in a bun. Only the Little Chickadee is watching. Those ringlets! Those curls! I risk the smile. Shirley, solemn, doesn't blink.

Leda pulls me upward, by inches it seems. She bites her lower lip from the effort; two or three beads of perspiration pop out on her brow. Okay, I'm up, on my feet, with one arm over my grand-daughter's shoulder and the spiral notebook left behind on the cushion. Supported thusly, I hobble onto the jade-green carpet of the aisle.

I became a member of Amos Prince's family from the day the architect picked me up in his arms. I slept in the *seminterrato*, the basement, of the tall, narrow apartment that the Duce had arranged for A.P. to rent for the monthly sum of ten American dollars. It was at 8 Via degli Specchi, midway between the Palazzo Farnese, westward, and the Main Synagogue to the east. The building itself, like the street, was dark, anonymous, without distinction. I can't think of the place now without associating it with birds—the doves that the neighbor at number 10 kept on the roof, and the nutty swallows that would build their nests every year on the windowsills of the *piano nobile*. Nutty because they persisted in flying into the house, fluttering and flailing at the walls or circling, like giant moths, the false candles of the dining room chandelier.

Franklin would chase them, waving his hands, waving a broom, without success—at least until the day he shut the casements and three of the birds without a bat's radar flew headlong one after the other into the glass. I knew Frankie well enough by then to suspect he would laugh; he did, one sharp bark. Then his pink cheeks turned pale and he plucked the little corpses from the floorboards. With a finger he smoothed the black and brown feathers. The moment has stuck in my mind not for its unexpected tenderness, but because it was for all that I know the last time in his life the boy shed a tear.

I slept, as I said, in the cellar; but I spent my days at work in the attic. Through that summer of 1936 I sweated beneath the super-heated eaves. Temperature: 42 Celsius on a typical day. "108 degrees

Foreign-hate," said Prince, cackling at the sight of the gadgets—whirligigs with propellers, catapults, a compressed gas rocket—with which I'd surrounded myself on the attic floor. His daughters came up to watch me play with what they called my toys, as did Gianna, our black-dressed servant, whom A.P. always insisted ("Ain't she a member of the Fast-shits Party?") was a spy.

"They're not toys," I told the sisters, though it was hard to make the case when I was on my hands and knees, preparing to launch a missile to the ceiling and watch it wobble down beneath a parachute made from a silk handkerchief—which was precisely the kind of thing I had done as a ten-year-old boy. How to explain that my work was part of the competition that Mousy teeny—how these names stick with you!—had announced to the world? Prince wanted me to build a model, something that at full scale could move five hundred people straight upward at a speed close to a mile a minute—and get them down again just as fast. That's why Nina—that was the name of the younger sister—and Aria had watched me raise a rubber horse twenty feet in the air atop an Archimedean screw. They were present when I completed a Ferris wheel that instead of going around in a circle made a long, narrow ellipse, the weight of the carriages going down in equipoise with those on the rise.

"Go on, blow on it," I said to Aria, who, with a single puff of air sent the gee-gaw spinning. I didn't look at the well-oiled device; I looked at the ends of her hair pooling on the wooden floor and her lips, still pursed, as if preparing for a kiss.

At the end of August I focused my efforts on the kind of contraption—half auto-gyro, half cigar-shaped balloon—on which Jules Verne's passengers spent eighty days going around the world. It didn't have the Frenchman's thirty-seven propellers on thirty-seven masts, but when the family gathered on the rooftop, everyone burst into laughter at the improbability of the launch. Only Prince kept a straight face. "You can aim it at any target you want?"

I nodded.

"And it will come back to where it started, like a bummerang?"

I nodded again, though I had more than a few doubts.

The architect pointed overhead, to where the sun was sending semaphores behind a fistful of clouds. "Let 'er go!"

I tripped the cog that held the coiled springs in check; the thirty-inch ship shot upward, whirling into the sky faster than any of the doves in the nearby dovecote could have carried a secret message. Up, up, up went the little airship, straight for the blazing disc.

Suddenly, from opposite directions, two clouds, like two great purple boxing gloves, slammed together. The sun disappeared. The sky turned black. Rain, a Tyrrhenian Sea of it, engulfed us. We ran for the doorway, for the rickety stairs. We were as wet, already, as swimmers emerging from a pool. We tramped down, flight after flight, while the storm continued to rage. Thunder boom-boomed from one of the seven hills, then from another, as if the city of Rome were under bombardment. We burst, laughing, gasping too, into the dining room, where Gianna was just bringing in a roast on a platter. We took our seats to the accompaniment of a drum roll: that was the hail, beating on the hood and metal top of our parked Fiat automobile. Suddenly lightning flashed. The windows shuddered in their frames and the little wire loops in all the incandescent candles glowed brightly and went out.

"You did this," said Frankie.

"It *was* you, Slapsy Maxie," said Nina. "Like Benjamin Franklin with his kite. When the lightning went down his string."

Aria—have I not mentioned this before? That Aria never spoke? She smiled and nodded.

Then quietly, with no twang in his voice, Prince started to talk. "Back home, when there was a storm like this, all the farmers, all the people in town—they ran like hell for the cellars. *When pigs fly*—? I've seen them go half a mile. I've seen a cow jump way over the moon."

I sat alert, as I always did when Amos dropped his wordplay. On something, maybe his shoe, he struck a match; he brought the flame to the cigarette in its holder. A lightning bolt cracked like a whip over our heads.

"One time when I was eight years old we had a mean twister that dropped down on one house, rose up to skip two, and fell on two more, and so on, like hopscotch, but without the squares; then I swear it turned around and did the same hip and hop back the way it had come. Down in the cellar, the nine of us, from Granny Tropp, well into her nineties, down to my sister Frances, who was only five months: we heard it change its mind again and decide to give us another shellacking."

Back in the cub scouts, at camp, we'd sit like this, around a fire or in the dark, trying to scare each other out of our wits. This, evidently, was no ghost story. "It sounded like a giant, a footstep here, a footstep there, *fee-fi-fo-fum*, haw-haw-haw, *I'll blow you all to kingdom come!* Three passes and he was gone. By the time we opened the cellar the sun was out and a couple of birds that by some miracle hadn't been blown to Antarctica plucked up their nerve and started singing. Raindrops were hanging like opals. Sunshine in the sky. Just like that"—we jumped as Prince snapped his fingers—"it had become a beautiful day."

Our storm, however, was far from done. The wind was howling. The windows looked as if blackout curtains had been drawn across them. Off in the distance the enemy ships continued their cannonade. Prince wasn't done either:

"Then the people came out, after the birds. The trouble with human beings is that they want to find meaning in things. Everyone for two hundred miles looked for a pattern. Why was our farm untouched and Herb Riggs's place turned into matchsticks? But there was no pattern, no rhyme or reason, unless some folk like the ancient Hebrews put blood on their doorposts and so were spared. We didn't have ancient Hebrews. Nor any of your up-to-date Yale University Jews."

I didn't have to see him to know that Frankie, with his thickish lips, his large teeth, was grinning at me. I looked toward his oldest sister, almost invisible in the darkened room. Speechless, of course, her hair obscuring what little I could see of her face. Why did I sense that she was thinking of that other disaster? The fire in Arizona, the death of her stepmother, the death of her half-brothers, too. *That* was the conflagration, I suddenly realized, that had struck the beautiful girl dumb.

But Nina was still thinking about the tornado. "I can't believe it. What you're saying. That there's no meaning. How can there be no meaning at all?"

"You heard me. There was no more sense in all that destruction and misery than a drunken dance by a giant. If you think about it, that's good news. If there is no meaning, no purpose, there's no reason to be afraid. You know where I'll be when Big Ben, Il Doozy, gets us into the next war? When the bombs he dropped on those Abyssinians start falling on us? Not in a cellar. Not in a bunker under the ground. Amos Prince will be out in the open, taking shelter under the iron arch of probability."

"Hurrah!" Frankie cried from the darkness. "Live dangerously! Just like the Duce says!"

There was a pause. The smell of the meat on the table filled the pitch-black room. We could hear, outside, the gurgle of rainwater in the gutters. Then Prince resumed. "Just because there is no reason for things does not mean there is nothing for us to learn. Before that storm we'd had two kinds of trees on the farm. Elms and pines. Now we had only one. Every elm was down. Overturned. Uprooted. But the pines were standing. Wherever I looked—in town, down by the river, on the sides of Sleeping Sam—not a single one had blown over. Oh, they'd been stripped and the branches were cracked, or maybe lopped right off like an arm by a surgeon. I saw plenty that had no crown, no limbs, no leaves—just a trunk stuck in the ground. But the damned things stood. The giant huffed and puffed but could not bring the pines down."

The architect's cigarette had long since gone out. But we did not need that beacon to realize that he had gotten out of his chair. His voice, when he spoke next, came from above us:

"I am going to build the monument with a tap root. Like this. Like a pine."

There was a crack of thunder; a lightning bolt must have struck just outside. On the instant, even through the closed windows, I could smell the fried molecules of air. At the same time I could see, as if a curtain had been whisked from a stage play, Amos Prince, the protagonist, standing with a knife in his hand. He just had time to draw the weapon downward, backward, the way a bowler might extend behind him the ball, and then we were cast once again into what might as well have been the darkness of deepest night.

Someone leaped from her chair and threw her arms around my neck. *Aria!* I heard the thud of the knife blade strike home, but sat unmoving, while the hot breath of the girl fell over my cheek, over my ear; her arms, which I knew were long, thin, and white, clutched me so tightly that I had to struggle to draw a breath of my own. Her legs were over my lap. Her breast was pressed to mine.

"Oh," I moaned. "My sweet girl."

Before I could say another word, the play had concluded and the houselights—that is to say, the myriad bulbs of our chandelier—came on. The first thing I saw was Aria's face, on the far side of the table. I jumped to my feet, spilling Nina, with her scrubbed red cheeks, her kinky hair, to the floor. Upright, aglitter, the bright blade of the carving knife protruded through the wood of the table the way a shark's fin might protrude from water. We stared at the taut, gleaming metal, motionless in the simulated candlelight.

"Careful," said Prince. "It's sharp."

If a waiter tells you a plate is hot, do you not reach out to touch it? I stretched my fingers to the silvery shaft. It did not yield.

"Haw! Haw! Nothing can bring it down. Not a hurry-can't. Not a ty-phooey. Not an earthquack or a sigh-clown. And sure as shootin' not a little old Illinois tornado!"

3

Here we are, at the bathroom's goddamned door. All I have to do is see it and the urge quintuples. Ring! Ring! Time for dinner. Good Pavlovian dog. Leda's propping me up with one hand and reaching for the latch with the other.

"Here we go!"

Unbelievable. She's picked up the cheery singsong of an elder's aide. At least Rosellen growls.

"*We?* What do you mean, *w-w-we?* This is a m-men's room."

"Unisex," she says, her polished teeth lined up in a smile.

"I t-t-t—" I'm surprised to hear how I'm panting. What next? Saliva? Like a German shepherd? Oh, if I could bite! "*Told* you! I can m-manage!"

She's holding the door wide with her foot. She's doing contortions to keep me upright against the jamb. "Don't be silly, grumpy Grampy. I'm a grown up. I mean, I won't look."

But, I note, back in her first-class seat wide-eyed Little Miss Marker most certainly will. Dimples, damn her, and all. At the sight I let my granddaughter lever me inside.

Here's some luck: the pissbowl is toward the tail, which means the aluminum grip is on the right-hand wall. I grab hold. That sends the wordless message: I intend to stay upright. Now the class of 2005 has a new task: lifting the toilet seat. A little clumsy, a slight hesitation: let's give her a B. Straight A, as I might have expected, on pulling the zipper down. Now what? I hold on to the chrome-colored clamp for all I'm worth. Heaven help me, she's kneeling, fumbling in the fly of the thing, digging me out. I close my eyes. This is a part of me that isn't left, isn't right, but right down the middle. Alas, it has no more sensations than my numb nose.

What a time for the airplane to fishtail. A rise, a roll, a fall: nothing more than a bump in the road. She's found, has Leda, what she's looking for. Her hand draws it out. I keep my eyes shut. Her voice, wobbling up to me, is in not much more than a whisper.

"All right, Mister Max, you can start."

Poor kid. This isn't what she bargained for. She was imagining balls of a different kind—music, dancing, the Italian diplomatic corps. She thought she'd hold her hand out for the kiss of the magnate, Bear-lust-horny. Ha! Ha! I wonder if she has the usual rags-to-riches fantasy: if it happened to Grace Kelly, why couldn't it happen to Leda? A smile, a wink to the bald billionaire. She wants to give my speech? Let her. *Il Presidente del Consiglio dei Ministri, Signor Berlusconi. Il Ministro della Cultura, Signor Urbani. Ambassador Sembler.* After all, she is the blood relation. Aria reincarnated, or close to it.

"Maxie, dear. Please. Please go."

"Fool! Are you b-b-blind? I *can't!*"

It's true. My bladder is aching. I feel all kinds of sharp little stabs. But nothing is going to come out. Not while she's got me in her hand.

I open my eyes. I look down at the foreshortened scene below me. I address my words to the gold crown of her head. "I am too ashamed."

She nods, good egg; she withdraws, to wait in the corridor outside. I'll spare you the details of what goes on now, the way the Greek playwrights spared their spectators similar horrors by moving them offstage. I stand, suffice it to say. I wait. *Jirí. Chanina. Tito. Dawid. Consolina. Lazar.* What a time for these names! The sounds, the syllables scroll along before me as—this, at my age, takes time—I do my business. Then out I come.

"Ha! Ha! Ha-ha-ha!"

Who's laughing? Why, it's Miss Curly Top. She can't control herself. The peals of her hilarity fill the cabin. She's in paroxysms, our Little Princess. She's pointing. I don't have to look. I know full well there is a dark stain on the front of my pants.

———◇———

SPIRAL NOTEBOOK

Bughouse

[1982: 1946–1957]

What struck me about the bughouse was how damned ugly it was. A Victorian shitpile. Bricks turd-red. The thought of it makes me ashamed of my profession. Padlock on doors. Bars on windows. Five miles of linoleum. What human beings want is beauty; our job is to allow them to live in it. All the millions who died in Roosevelt's war, plus the Jews killed by gas—maybe they're better off when you think of the ugliness they'd have to endure if they were alive. Up the chimney, they say. How could I know? I didn't know! I got lied to the same as the fellow who sits hours at a time outside this room in Gubbio, chipping and chipping and chipping a single cobblestone for the street.

Whoever put up St. Liz is a genius compared to what got built after the war. Grope-your-ass, Caribou-slay, Mice Vender-rolls, Morsel Brayer: every last one of them climbed up the hill to sit at my feet. What did old Phil Johnson say? "Not at the feet of the Prince. At the feet of the King!" *Off with their heads!* That's what the king was thinking, even when I was handing them tin cans of donuts and tin cans of boiled eggs. We had plenty of kings—and emperors and potentates. Howling for their supper. Drool on their chins. Napoleons in slippers. Any one of them could have designed better buildings. Windows and boxes. Boxes and windows. The great avenues of our cities: it's like walking between slabs in a cemetery. A cemetery made out of glass. I can remember Granny Tropp. Always used a glass vase, because she wanted to show the stems of the flowers in water. That is architecture! If only we could have finished *La Vittoria!* We would have caught every cloud.

My inmate pals didn't howl when they built their buildings out of wooden blocks. Didn't drool either. What they did do was hum. Right out loud. I watched them putting up their castles, their towers, but I listened too. Architecture is frozen music. Best architect who ever lived? Phideas? Michelangelo? Frank Lloyd Wrong? Hell, no! Beethoven! No, no, no: not Beethoven. Mozart. Because he brought the most joy to the most people. The rest of us? Brunelleschi? Palladio? Old Bulfinch? Old Wren? Eye music.

One time Wine-stain asked me did I want to move to a room on the top floor. I'd have a much better view. But the view was fine where I was. Whole joint was built on a hill. I could see the city down below and all of its monuments. Obelisk to G. Washington. What ignoramus decided it should have a pointed pyramid at the top? It needs one that is strong, solid, low. It ain't a pencil! Also saw plain enough the capitol dome, as white and ugly as that set of dentures for Vittorio Emanuele in Rome. Not that Michelangelo did any better: they had to hold St. Peter's together with an iron chain. Nowadays the iron domes are nothing but those chains. But in the eye of my mind I put together the capitol dome and, in the reflecting pool, a dome upside down. That was the origin, or so I suspect, of the secret that is coming to its perfection inside the bicycle shack.

Funny I should end up with a sphere. It's the one basic form
our crazy hummers can't make from their pieces of wood. I couldn't
either as an eight-year-old, playing with my Froebel blocks. Maple.
The feel of them is still in my fingers. That's the trick, combining
the tactile, touch as form, and the inner meaning: the square, integrity; the circle, infinity; the triangle, aspiration. I saw myself at
play in those madmen. "No, thank you, Doctor Weinstein," I answered. "The view is adequate where I am." Didn't tell him the truth.
Didn't want him to think I was a nut case. *No thank you, Doctor
Wane-strain. I fear I will throw myself out.*

Who knows? I might have jumped off that roof. It would have
been a tough decision. To be or not to be, as that other Prince put it.
He was wrong about dreams. The ones in this life are bad enough. I
think he wanted to live. That's why he put on the antic disposition. I
know that game: you go mad voluntarily; gives you just enough elbow
room so you don't have to do it against your will. Here's the catch, as
Granny Tropp used to tell us: *Don't make that face or it's going to freeze
on you.* Once you go round the bend, it ain't so easy coming back. I
look in the mirror, head splitting. I'd like to claw at this mug; I'd rip
it to pieces. Best solution was Aria's: silence. Old A.P. has said too
many words. *Hitler and Mussolini, they're your true leaders.* Yup, and
We need a pogrom at the top. Here's a new question for Hamlet: inside
or out? I mean, does the crackpot spend his time inside St. Liz? It's
hot, it stinks from urine and cabbage, and old Chief Wahoo is carrying on about killing ten thousand white men. Hell, I don't want him
killing ten thousand and one. Not to mention the screaming, the
howling, the sobs. Using tin pans for percussion. But if you're outside, even in sunshine, in the balmy spring, you have to see the shitpile
you've just walked out of. It's a conundrum.

There are, however, trees. The hill was once an arboretum, I
guess. You can still see the Latin names on the metal tags: genus

Ulmus, Ulmus americana, the American fan-topped elm; genus *Quercus, Quercus suber,* the cork oak, bark like an elephant's hide; genus *Prunus, Prunus cerasus,* the sour cherry; genus *Acer* of the Aceraceae, *Acer saccharum,* the sugar maple, of which some craftsman in the last century, oh, in the 1870s say, made my wooden blocks. The beauty of the beech! The beauty of the aspen. Look around: there is no such thing as an imperfect tree. There is no ugliness in nature. It is the body of God. No set of hills, no meadowland, nothing at the shore of the ocean is unbeautiful in any fashion—the only exceptions I know of being certain deep-sea fishes photographed through the windows of Lucius Beebe's bathysphere—and Justice Felix Frankfurter, Justice Cardozo, and Justice Brandeis. Throw in Morgenthau and Bernie Baruch. It's the pressure of thousands of fathoms that has deformed the spiny creatures. What has disfigured the genus *Judaicus?* Thousands of years of inbreeding, maybe, though more likely, in my opinion, it's the unnatural act of circumcision. It must do something to them, after centuries, cutting away at the most sensitive nerves in the body. No wonder they've got these sour pusses.

I had a favorite, all right, genus *Platanus, Platanus occidentalis,* a sycamore. Used to watch the bark peel away, the raw flesh underneath the color of lemon custard. Used to watch its tufts blow like down in the breeze. Over the walls. Sky bound. Seeking other sycamores. I climbed into its branches like a boy. That's where they all came, to the roots, the big-shot architects, the politicians and lawyers, everybody who wanted something. Nina with babe-in-arms, my red-faced, well-scrubbed Nina: "Won't you see Max? Won't you look at the plans for his buildings? Papa, he's making such wonderful houses." Wouldn't let Jew-near. Deepest fish of them all. I saw how he looked at Aria. Did more than look, too, if you can believe what Franklin was always hinting. Had to settle for flat-faced Nina. Stole all his plans, no doubt about it, from me.

69

There they all sat, chittering and chattering on the lawn, gulping the caviar, the wine. With my paint cans full of hard-boiled eggs. My paint cans full of candy. Like philosophers in the days of Greece, with Aristotle up in the buttonwood tree. While in the background, the chorus of true feel-officers, Chief Wahoo and the boys, who couldn't read cat, C-A-T, if you spelled it out for them.

They were trying, my friends, to get me out of St. Liz. Seemed to me they had a case. Old A.P., ain't he presumed innocent until found guilty? But I couldn't be tried because they thought I was insane. But once I was cured of this malady, I couldn't go free because I had to stand trial. And Old Axis Sally, old Tokyo Rose: they got out years ago. Odaline, never the brightest, says *What about President Eisenhower?* Old Ike. *Couldn't we ask him for a pardon?* It didn't take Dick Mosk, my sharp-nosed, sharp-eared lawyer, always in a suit like a penguin, to figure that one out: I was never convicted of any offense, so there was nothing to pardon me for. Round and round we go, like a dog, D-O-G, after its tail, like the tiger in *Little Black Sambo*, and me the nigger boy stuck in his tree. I'm in forever, I figured; they'll never let me out.

And why should I want to leave? I had wine, women, and song—or at least my honeybees humming and humming. Top architects in the world worshiped me like a god. I got, like a bubble in my brain, my new idea. The sphere. Women. I know what Odaline wanted. Supposed to be thankful she dropped her charges. When I could be shot as a traitor! When I could be fried in the electric chair. Let me repeat I did not know about the Jews. Their big mistake was Abraham and Isaac. Substituting a ram for a real knife and a real son. Old Adolf, he wanted to go back to human sacrifice. So does the whole Christian world. People can't do without that bleeding boy. Nails in his hands, spear in his side. If I made a broadcast now I know what I'd say: *Amos Prince speaking. Beware of your leaders when they call for sacrifice.*

Odaline, as I was saying. She followed me from the lawn to my room. Dressed in black. Perpetual mourning for her daughter, her son. Wouldn't listen when I say there's a damned good chance they're alive. Wanted comforting. Sorry. I had all the women I wanted. History repeats. St. Lizzie used to be the hospital for the Union army. Old Hooker, the general, brought the girls in from the capital streets. I don't call them hookers. I call them disciples. Washed between my toes, if I let them. Had to watch out for the three P's: petitions, pardons, pity. Professors and pusskikiatrists, too. Dead set on getting me out. That's why I climbed up into the crotch of my sycamore. Let them lie in the sun and hatch their schemes. There I was, the certified madman, with a peanut tied to a string. The blue jays see me. What a hullabaloo! What a squawking! Ah! Ah, ha! here come my three companions. They don't have a plaque. They don't have a name in Latin. Family Sciuridae, genus *Scurus*, the bushy-tailed squirrel. They ain't afraid of old Amos. They love their nut. Closer. Closer. On my knee. On my lap. Eating out of my hand. Skim-more, Owing, and Marl.

In or out? Out! The Freud-boys, the lawyers, the politicians, they sprung me. Yes, and lovers of the beauty of architecture too. The Pharaohs, they took out their architects' eyes. Or walled them up in the tomb. Because they had the secret to the inner sanctum. The life of an architect is perilous. Bad pun: Perillus. That Athenian made a bull out of copper and zinc, so that the tyrant could burn his enemies alive inside it. The cries of the dying men would sound like the roaring of the bull. But the first person the tyrant locked in was Perillus himself. They lit the fire under the belly of brass. *Let me out! I built my own tomb. They are roasting me alive!*

Did they get old Adolf? Nobody saw the body. I heard he made it to Buenos Aires. He's the one who rescued old Ben. Dropped down out of the sky. Silent gliders. Whisked him right off the mountaintop. The daring of it! The audacity! The bond of friendship. If only Marconi had lived. He could have melted these walls. With his magical ray. The guards. The Carabinieri. They waved good-bye to the boss with tears in their eyes. So long, Doctor Whine-strain. The gliders are coming. Farewell, Wahoo. I'm soaring into the sky. I'll roar, all right: a dandy-lion.

In reality I drove out the front door in an old suit of clothes. Into the city. Under the cemetery slabs. Mozart. Those melodies. I never brought joy to a single person in all my life.

LZ 129

[1936]

1

On the first night of September, still in the year 1936, Amos Prince told everyone at the dinner table to pack a bag and be ready to leave the next morning for an overnight trip. Not a word of where they were going or why. Gianna, in her black dress and black belt, appeared in the doorway, "*Ed io, signore?* I am also to depart?"

"Ain't those your ordures? Can't go no place without you."

Maximilian, down in the cellar, spent an uneasy night. Why such suddenness? Why the secret? Nor was his foreboding lessened when, the next morning, the two cars arrived: a small Fiat and a Citroën six-seater, each with an armed Blackshirt as a driver and an armed Blackshirt as a guard. Shabilian sat on the jumpseat opposite Nina; Gianna was on the cushion next to her, with Franklin on the far side.

"Where do you think we're going, Maxie?" The girl leaned forward, so that their knees touched. Her face, to him, always looked as if it had just been scrubbed with a rough cloth. "To the Lido?"

She meant the Lido di Lallia, where they'd gone on a Sunday to splash in the waves. "I don't think so," Max answered. "Not overnight. Not without swimsuits. These soldiers give me a bad feeling."

Franklin snorted, filling the little cabin with the smell of peppermint. "He's afraid of his shadow."

"Silly Shabby. How can anything bad happen? Papa knows everybody. He's practically best friends with the Duce. He gets a letter from the palace—you know, the Palazzo Venezia—every day. And phone calls too. Gianna, you know it's true. Tell him. How the Duce loves us all."

But the servant only crossed her arms under the swell of her breasts. "*Io?* I know nothing. About the telephone, nothing. About the *lettere*, nothing. You do not ask Gianna such things."

By then both cars had turned onto the Via Cavour; five minutes later they pulled up before the Stazione Centrale.

"The station!" Nina cried. "The trains! We're going to have an adventure!"

At the sight Max only shivered, hugging himself, as if he were indeed about to step into the chilled waters of the sea.

As it happened, their tickets were for the Rome-Milan express. They waited until the train was full and the fat conductor was shouting *Attenzione! Partenza immediate!* before their squadron escorted them across the platform to what Max recognized at once as Mussolini's private car. The steel sides were painted in two broad bands of green and brown. A medallion, the familiar bundle of fasces with the embedded ax, was affixed next to the door. The whistle sounded. They hurried on board.

The interior was laid out in a series of rooms—sleeping compartments, a living room, an office, a den—all lined up along a single corridor. At the far end was a dining area and kitchen, complete with chef and waiter. The largest room, where they settled, was furnished with a leatherette couch and scattered tables and chairs. The paintings on the walls were of battles: broken lances, the big rumps of horses, stricken infantry on the ground. Uccellos, Max thought, or first-rate copies. Apart from the staff, the car seemed empty—or nearly so. A Blackshirt remained stationed at either end of the corridor. One had already lit up a cigarette; the other had spread a day-old copy of *Il Corriere della Sera* over his knees.

Aria had taken a chair by the windows. Nina and Max sat high on the incompressible cushions of the couch. Frankie moved from one seat to another; as soon as they left the northern suburbs, he started to prowl the length of the car. Though it was still early, Gianna laid out a packed luncheon and went off to arrange for glasses and plates. Amos Prince sat with his feet up. "This is mighty white of old Ducky," he declared. Nina laughed. Her sister, however, looked left and right. "Papa!" she said—mouthed, rather. Max, attentive, knew how to read her lips. He thought he was learning how to read the tilt of her head, the nervous twistings and turnings of her fingers and thumbs, like a sign language for the deaf, the dumb. *Papa! Don't talk that way,* was his interpretation now.

But the architect, with his hat over his browless eyes, had already fallen asleep.

Max turned to stare out at the stubbly fields and the occasional stand of oaks. The farmers, behind their horses and plows, were rolling the hay into spindles. At the sight of the bulletproof car, they raised their hats. So did the men and the women in each of the towns and on the platforms of the local stations. Sometimes a sedan or a sporty coupe would try to keep pace alongside. The occupants waved from the windows or trailed their handkerchiefs in the whipping wind.

After an hour two young men appeared at the entrance to their room. One of them, in an airman's uniform, went through the motions of knocking at the entrance. "*Possiamo entrare?*" he asked.

His companion, a year or two older, perhaps twenty, had already stepped inside. With a glance at the dozing man, he said, "I speak English language very, very good, almost with perfection; therefore, it is the desire of my heart, eh, *mio cuore*, to make the conversation with you." He meant, naturally, Aria.

The airman would not be outdone. "*Sì! La Bionda! Bella bionda!*"

Both men stepped over to where Prince's elder daughter was rising from her chair. She smiled and held out her hand.

"We are delighted absolutely," said the older of the two men. "We have heard the talk of Signorina Aria, who has fame all through Rome."

The girl tilted her head up, so that all could see the flush of pleasure that had appeared on her cheeks. She removed her hat from the nearest piece of furniture and gestured for the young men to sit down.

The uniformed Italian leaped to adjust her chair, so that, when she resumed it, it faced the one he claimed for himself. His companion drew up a third. He leaned toward the girl. "My *fratello*, my brother, eh? He and I have much pleasure that you have joined us for this journey."

Nina spoke up, from halfway across the room. "We were wondering about that. We've been racking and racking our brains. Do you know where we are going?"

The younger man, not much more than a boy really, laughed. "But it is only natural that we know this thing. Your father, Signor Prince: he also possesses this knowledge."

Frankie now stood in the doorway. "No. He doesn't. He didn't say anything."

"Yes, this is because his lips are shut. Also mine. This is, how do you say it? A state secret? A secret of state?"

"It's not fair to tease us," Nina said. "Why do you get to know? Besides, it's easy to see that we are going to Milan."

The youth, full-lipped, broad-browed, laughed. "No! It is not true. Absolutely we are not going to Milano."

Nina clapped her hands. "Is it Como, then? The lakes? Do you know what I've always heard? I've heard that they are like paradise. Paradise on earth."

"Ah," exclaimed the airman. "This is the most beautiful place to make a visit. Perhaps today you will see it. Yes, it is possible. The mountains, how they plunge into the blue waters. The wildness of the hills, with here in a spot, or there in a spot, a house that is hidden and you see only the chimney and the chimney smoke. *Bella!* As beautiful as if this were a portrait of da Vinci."

His brother turned toward Nina's sister: "But not so beautiful, American lady, as what I am seeing now with my eyes."

Was it true? Max wondered. Was all of this—the sudden departure, the armed escort, the Duce's private car: could it really be in preparation for nothing more than a excursion to the lakes?

"I know what you are doing," Frankie declared. "You want to flatter Aria. By making up a story."

"But, no," said the airman. "Every word that I speak is definitely true. I swear it. No, you will not see Milano. Yes, you will experience the vistas of Maggiore, of Como: a white sail, a net from a fisherman's boat, the sunlight on the waves. It is *la poesia!*"

"But that's not where we're *going*, is it?" said Nina. "I mean, that's not, you know, our destination."

The youths looked at each other. Simultaneously, they shrugged.

At that moment the train swayed on a curve. That may have been why Prince awoke, blinked, and settled his gaze on the young Italians. "Wal, look who's here. Brew-now and Victrola."

The airman frowned, knitting his brows. But his brother laughingly addressed the group. "*Sì.* This is Bruno. And I—"

"I know who you are! *Vittorio!* You flew in Abyssinia! In the Riccordo Legion! You're a hero!" Frankie turned toward the man in uniform. "I know you too. Bruno! You are the sons of Il Duce." Here the American boy grasped his belt with both hands. He threw out his chest and drew in his chin. It was, for a teenager, a passable imitation of the new Caesar. "*Le aquile dell'aria!* Eagles of the air!"

"I know!" said Nina. "I've guessed it. You are taking us up in an airplane."

"An airplane!" Bruno laughed. "This is nothing. What you will experience is a thing that no one in all of Italy has known. Wait! Yes, perhaps five, ten, twenty fortunate souls. Of our many millions. Even I, even Vittorio—it is for us something completely original."

Vittorio: "*Zitto!* Enough. I propose that we make a *conversazione* about different subjects."

"*D'accordo*," said his brother. "Let us speak once more of *la poesia*. Yes. The poetry of this smooth brow. These gray-colored eyes. The sunbeams of this golden hair. *Le sóle dorato; capelli dorati, più dorati.*"

Aria, to whom these words were clearly addressed, blushed again. She held up the palms of her hands. Heedless, the leader of the Riccordo Legion strode up before her.

"Sometimes I am asham-ed that such a human being as Bruno is my brother. Always he speaks like a person who is crazy from books. Now you will hear the words of a Fascist man. I am in my Corerro 127, yes? My *aeroplano*. Over the river Wa-harui. But this river, it is dry. Dry as a river must be in the desert. But it is not empty. No, it is full. Full with black water. I turn, yes? I look again. Not water. *I negri.* Seven hundred. A thousand. A thousand more. A river that runs with ink. So naturally I make the bombardment. Then, below me, what do I see? The white petals, the orange petals. *Sì! Sì!* My bombs are bursting like flowers. *Come fiori.* This is poetry. Beautiful lady, I offer to you my bouquet."

Amos Prince got to his feet. "You know what people say about my pal, Bent-ego? That he makes these trains run on time. We're getting where we're going all too soon. I'll tell you this much. We ain't any of us going to sleep a whole lot tonight. Let's go now and get our forty winks."

He, with Gianna trailing, left the compartment. Max would have stayed, had Nina not pulled him through the door. Aria remained seated, turning the brim of her hat in her hands, winding the ribbons about the crown. Vittorio and Bruno sat down, laughing and chatting, to flirt with the American girl. The train whistle blew. It was like a signal to Frankie. He grinned, teeth flashing, at the two airmen.

"You bombed them!" he declared. The whistle blew once more. "You blew their black heads off!"

As promised, the small group of travelers did not see Milan; they detrained in a wilderness, that is, in a marsh east of Voghera. The Blackshirts led them through the reeds, out of which startled pheasants took whirring to the air. Three cars waited on an unpaved road. They climbed in and drove some four kilometers to a larger road, which wound its way to the highway north. Also as promised, they saw Como, though by then the sun had begun to fall behind the Pennine Alps, so that the fat, pink underbellies of the clouds lay like fish on the lake's unrippled surface.

They were waved through the Swiss border without coming to a stop. Max, up front, saw through the semicircles of dust on the windshield that they were going through the high Splügen Pass and up the course of the Hinterrhein through mountains that, in the onrushing dusk, were half lit and half curtained. At some point they must have joined the Rhine proper, since, according to the sign-boards, they were skirting first Liechtenstein and then the out-stretched finger of Austria on their right. All three cars put on their headlights, which, at intervals, engaged in brief bouts of swordplay with the beams from the automobiles heading south.

"Ah!" That was Nina, who sat just behind Maximilian on the rear seat. He saw what she did: that instead of growing darker, as any human might expect, the sky was brightening. Then, with a sudden turn, they saw the thousands of lights that sparkled like gem-stones along the shore of the Lake of Constance. "Oh, Maxie," the girl exclaimed. "I never saw anything like this."

The two cars followed the coast past Rheinbeck and Arbon, until they turned into Romanshorn, zigzagging past the glowing windows of the thatch-roofed houses and over the round stones of the roadway that led down to the last of the port's wooden wharves. A steamer rose high above them. Already the sailors on board were hauling in the thick, mossy lines.

Bruno got out of the middle car and waved to his brother, who stood at the back of the car at the rear. Then both Italians began to walk toward the gangplank that stretched from a lower deck to the edge of the pier. "Come," said Vittorio, over his shoulder. "We must make speed."

Amos, with Aria holding his arm, walked spryly over the slip-pery stones. Gianna came after. Nina started to skip ahead, but abruptly halted. "Maxie! Get a taxi! We're going up the gangplank."

Maximilian took a step, then halted. He stared up to where the word *Friedrichshafen* was stenciled on the rusted plates of the prow. His stomach turned, as if he were already suffering from *mal de mer*. Constance was one name for this body of water. The Bodensee was the other. The home port of this ship was in Germany. Every Jew in that country was attempting to flee it and he, sorry Shabilian, was about to step on board a vessel that would take him to the Thousand Year Reich. What a joke! He looked up still higher. Why, even the ship's red and black flag, floodlit and fluttering, seemed with all four of its crooked limbs to be turning a cartwheel at the prospect.

"*Du! Mach schnell! Ja! Du!*"

Above him, at the bulwarks, a man in a blue cap and blue uniform was pointing in his direction. Max, mesmerized, dragged himself on board.

Almost instantly bells started ringing, the moving walkway was winched up behind him and the last lines were cast off. The big steamer began to make its way backward and sideways into the deeper waters. The American found the others at the stern. They all stood by the rail, watching the agitation below them, the froth and the spray, as the ship hove about and aimed itself at some distant point across the lake. The last light faded. The temperature dropped. The water, heated all day by the unclouded sun, sought equilibrium by releasing a mist. The *Friedrichshafen* sliced through it, throbbing in its eagerness to reach the other shore.

Maximilian strained to see that fateful land. But the fog around them was as thick as the smoke that poured from the funnel. There were no lights in any direction, save for those that shone blurrily on board. They might just as well have been sailing across the Atlantic or Pacific oceans—would that they were! thought Max—as upon the waters of the landlocked lake. Then, without a word of command, with neither a warning bell nor a whistle, the diesel engines below decks ceased operation and the ship drifted to a wallowing halt.

"Come, you come," said Vittorio, beckoning to his fellow travelers. "Now is the time."

Bruno, whistling a tune, led them forward along the starboard rail. Everyone in Prince's party must have had a hundred questions;

none said a word. They followed the boy as they might have the Pied Piper leading them to their doom. They stopped where a lifeboat hung waiting, its complement of four crewmen already on board. One by one, Aria, Prince, Franklin, and the others climbed in. Again, Max hesitated. A German oarsman addressed him:

"*Warum zögerst du? Raus, kleiner Mensch. Schnell.*"

Did the sound of that language, its consonants and vowels, stupefy him? He swung his leg over the gunwale and settled onto a wooden seat. At once the supporting ropes went hissing through their davits and the little craft sank toward the waves.

Smartly they struck the surface. The sailors uncinched the lines and in unison lowered their oars. In four strokes they were free of the wash from the steamer; in four more that same large craft had disappeared into the fog. In silence they rowed on, minute after minute. Impossible, in this gloom, for those seated at the stern to make out the faces of those who rowed at the prow. More minutes. No sound but the creak of the oars in the oarlocks and the quiet splash of the blades.

Where were they going? Max knew: to the bottom of the lake. Had the Nazis learned that the sons of Il Duce were attempting to slip into their country? Did they wish to eliminate them for some unfathomable reasons of state? Perhaps the Americans had simply been swept up in the plot. Wait. Wasn't Mussolini the first of Germany's allies? The only man in the world the Führer actually admired? Hadn't they agreed to form an Axis around which all of Europe would be made to revolve? How could the Reichskanzler risk wounding his only partner? Unless—horrible thought—Mussolini had determined to do away with his own sons. Monstrous! It was monstrous! But wasn't the history of Italy filled with such episodes? Look at the Borgias. Look at the Emperors of Rome. Fratricide, patricide, matricide, rivers of blood. What was the loss of two sons?

Max stared at the young men. Even the veil of fog could not turn them pale. They seemed eager, excited, yet eerily calm. Too eager. Too calm. *They* were the ones who had ordered the plot! Yes, yes, Max saw it all: these dashing airmen were executioners, not victims. Amos was the target, Amos and his entourage. The architect had proved himself an embarrassment. He was jeopardizing the relations of the Fascist state with both Germany and America. But Mussolini couldn't simply hand him over to the latter nation without losing face. After all, he had offered him his personal protection. Nor would Germany take him—certainly not with his Jewish assistant—lest it risk further antagonizing an already hostile Roosevelt administration. *Ecco!* The solution: a word whispered in a son's ear.

"*Halt!*" Bruno gave the command. In response the oarsmen lifted their dripping oars. This was, Max knew, the fatal moment. Amos Prince and his little family were about to disappear.

Their momentum carried them forward another ten yards. Max in his fever was growing light-headed. It seemed to him that just ahead the sky was brightening, as if some midnight sun were burning away the mist. Then he heard Gianna gasp. He saw her make the sign of the cross. Frankie, forgetting himself, started to rise, as if he were on dry land and not on a craft as tipsy, almost, as a canoe. Even Vittorio's mouth fell wide, as if he wanted to say something but was unable to form the words.

Nina spoke instead: "Oh," she said, "It's like a god."

There, rising before them, towering ten, twenty, thirty stories high, was an incomprehensible form. Was it some sea animal? A dragon? A fish with silvery scales? The shape, certainly, was that of a whale, round and bulbous, and as white as the fabled Moby Dick. But this strange beast was many times larger than any creature that had walked or swum the earth. Higher and higher it loomed, like a pale moon that had fallen from its orbit to the surface of the planet below.

"Look," cried Franklin. "Lights! It must be a ship."

Max saw them too. A line of luminescence glowed through the swirling vapors. Yes, it must be a ship. But the only craft this size was the Queen Mary; it would indeed have been easier to bring the moon to earth than to sail that great liner across the continent of Europe.

Bruno gave another command. The Germans, who had twisted about on their seats to stare, now dipped their oars. Max kept his gaze fixed on the apparition. There wasn't just a single row of lights, he noted, but a second, below the first, shimmering, glimmering. Of course: that was the original illumination reflected on the lake's surface. Then he looked again. What he saw made him remove his glasses, scrub them on his shirt front, and put them on again. There was a *third* row of lights, also a reflection; but it was beyond the first mirror-image and could only be the duplication of a set of lights on the *other side of the ship*. That meant that the great vessel was not on the waters of the Lake of Constance but was floating above them. Nothing like this had ever appeared on earth. Was it, then, from another planet? Some place, in another galaxy, where the laws of gravitation did not hold? For an instant Max thought that the world he had known had been taken over by alien beings. But only for an instant: before the cold sweat of fear could break out on his body he heard the faint tinkling notes from a piano playing, of all things, "Stars Fell on Alabama."

"Look," said Nina. "Look at those rings."

One of the Germans glanced over his shoulder. "*Ja, das Olympisches Symbol.*"

Maximilian recognized the interlocked circles, symbol of the 1936 games. His eyes slid forward, until they were able to make out a word painted in black Gothic script:

HINDENBURG

Just then, Amos laughed aloud. "Here we are, folks. Floating beneath the world's biggest dodge-a-bull."

2

It was the *Hindenburg* indeed. The light from its cabins fell directly onto their lifeboat, which drew up into the shadow beneath the leviathan's belly. Now everyone could hear the sounds—laughter and music and the clank of cutlery—of a cocktail party in the air. As they floated below the bulging, silver-sided cloud, a panel on the belly fell open and a gangway with built-in stairs descended. The sailors maneuvered their craft beneath it; then the airship, which must have been tethered by lines fore and aft, was winched downward until even Nina, the smallest and youngest of the travelers, could grasp the rails and climb on board.

They gathered in the depths of the Zeppelin, while the panel closed tight behind them. After their voyage through the mists, even the low-watt bulbs that hung overhead made them squint. It seemed to them that they were in a vast hangar, or a factory whose superstructure had remained exposed. Below, a steel girder stretched backward as far as the eye could see, as if after all they had boarded an ocean liner and this were the keel; in addition— and now Max thought of a four-master or a brigantine—all the space above them was filled with enormous canvas bags that rose into the murk like so many sails, taut with hydrogen instead of the force of the wind.

"Ladies and gentlemen. Will you be so kind as to come, please, this way. You are now on B deck. Here there is storage. Here sleeps the crew. Also the *Toiletten* and shower bath. Follow, please. This stairway takes us to deck A. There all is in readiness for your comfort and pleasure."

The speaker, a man in his sixties, wore a starched uniform with double brass buttons on the front of his coat and three gold bands on his cuffs. A steward, Max presumed, though he was surprised to see binoculars hanging from a strap round his neck.

"*Il Dottor Eckener,*" said Vittorio, sotto voce. "*Il Capitano.*"

They followed the officer up another flight, past a bust of Hindenburg himself, and forward along an interior corridor, off which other corridors led to the various sleeping compartments. Max, glancing back, was startled to see a contingent of Blackshirts, who seemed to be guarding a stateroom at the rear of the passageway. Before he could react, their party turned right, into the starboard section. There, outside the cabins, was a brightly lit room filled with chrome-edged tables and tubular chairs. A large portrait of the master of the Reich hung on one wall, and on the other was an outsized Mercator projection of the world.

Some two dozen men and women sat on the furniture or stood in bunches, all of them nodding in conversation and raising pale or dark drinks to their mouths. Children, some mere babes, played in the promenade that ran along a series of Plexiglas windows; these slanted outward at an angle of forty-five degrees and had surely been the source of what had seemed such a bright and mysterious line of light.

Someone, an American apparently, was playing another hit tune at an aluminum piano. A woman, her short, wavy hair parted in the middle, sat beside him. Her red lips were wet and shining. In a high, accented voice, she began to sing the words:

> *The Continental, it's so ex-citing*
> *It's so divine, I must de-clare*

Where had Max seen her before? Instantly he knew, and blushed at the recollection. This was Paola Borboni, the actress, whose posters hung one above the other on the Via Nazionale. Why blush? Why look down at his shoes? Because she was famous for once having exposed her breasts and saying, in response to the ensuing scandal, "I am playing a mermaid. A mermaid does not wear a brassiere."

These thoughts were interrupted by the captain, who removed his braided cap and addressed Amos Prince and the others: "I invite you to relax in our lounge. I must now return to the controls. We await one last guest. Then we shall depart and you may retire for the night." He bowed, inclining his close-cropped head. He repeated his name to each of them: "Eckener, Hugo. Charmed. Eckener, Hugo, a pleasure." Even Gianna shook his outstretched hand.

A female steward in a red skirt and with a red cap over her corkscrew curls, came up to Max with a tray of glasses. "Martini cocktail? Manhattan cocktail? Scotch whiskey?" He chose a glass with an olive and stepped over the low railing that separated the lounge from the outer promenade. The only thing visible from the angled windows was the reflection of their lights on the black water. Two children, tow-headed girls, were actually lying with their elbows on the treated glass; they stared, as children will, at nothing. Another child, a much older boy, came up to the American.

"I am Harald," he announced.

"And I am Maximilian."

"How did you come aboard LZ 129?"

"By boat. The lifeboat from the steamer. The *Friedrichshafen.*"

"I am aware from a boat. But who gave you—what is the word in this language? *Autoritiät.* Yes, the authorization?"

"I don't know. I left Rome this morning. With Amos Prince. Do you know him? There he is—" Max nodded to where A.P. stood with his empty cigarette holder in his mouth. "He's a famous architect."

"Do you think I am ignorant of this? That would be insolence. My father, he is even more known in the world than this man who protects you."

The boy, blond, sturdy, and solemn, glanced toward a figure who might have been his genetic opposite: short, thin-boned, dark-haired. The man stood with his head inclined, staring down at the celebrated cleavage of the singer. At the sight of him, Maximilian felt as if someone had injected his heart with ice.

"Isn't that Herr Goebbels?"

"You do not ask questions," the boy shot back. "I ask you."

"But I told you what you wanted to know."

"You have told me nothing. This man, the architect: Does he expect to defeat Herr Speer in the competition?"

"I am certain he is going to try."

"This is an absurdity! The result of vanity. And why does he employ you? What is it you do for him?"

"Well, he calls me his pen-soul. Or maybe it's pen-soil. I draft various designs."

"And what do you design for him? What is this great new monument?"

Max stood tongue-tied. How explain that he had spent the entire summer on a series of model toys?

Harald smiled. "Speechless. Naturally. It is an absurdity to think that a Max, a Herr Max Goldberg, a Herr Max Goldstein, a Herr Max Goldbloom would dare to design a new arch of triumph, a new Colosseum, a new Pyramid of Giza. No: you are the one who will be lifting the stones."

There was a burst of applause. For an awful moment Maximilian assumed that all the passengers were hailing *der Jüngling's* speech.

What next? Would they beat him? Behead him? Throw him over-board? But they were only cheering Signorina Borboni, who had fin-ished "The Continental" and was standing with one hand splayed on the piano's pigskin cover. Then she bowed, revealing, in her low-cut gown, what the world had already seen of the *sirena*.

Now it was Harald's turn to blush—not because of the two ex-posed breasts but because Aria was approaching the two young men. Max took pity.

"Harald, this is Fräulein Prince. Aria, this is Harald Goebbels."

The boy snapped his heels together, even as he wrung his hands in perturbation. "Harald Quandt," he intoned. "The Minister of Pro-paganda and Public Enlightenment is my beloved stepfather."

The girl barely glanced at him. She took Max by the arm, her lips forming her favorite word: *Papa*.

She led him back to the center of the lounge, where her father stood a full head above the crowd. Max had seen most of them months before, on the reviewing stand: Farinacci, the former Party Secretary, with his missing hand; Ciano, the new Foreign Minis-ter; and his German counterpart, Von Ribbentrop. Prince directed Max toward a man with a starched white collar and black cravat. Max recognized him too: the world-famous Marconi.

"Here he is," said Prince. "My Maximum. My Shabby-lion. *Senatore*, he is the one who is going to solve our last problem."

The Italian took Max's hand in both of his own. He stared at him with surprisingly blue eyes. "We are grateful for what you have done," he said, in hardly accented English. "And for what you will do."

What could those words mean? What had he done? He barely had time to stammer that he was honored to meet the inventor of radio when a German woman stepped between them. "Herr Marconi, the Führer has said we must look to the future. Is it true that your wireless rays may be used in all sorts of new weapons? I have heard that you can send a signal that could drive a man mad. What a contribution to science. And to our Axis."

Goebbels, hearing this, spun toward the woman. "Magda. You have had too much to drink. Such talk is nonsense."

Marconi himself only smiled. "Oh, I am sure it is only a joke. I wish to help mankind, not to harm any person."

Farinacci stepped forward. "Yes, *Marchese*, what you have done for mankind brings you into the orbit of Italians of myth: Augustus, Caesar, Virgil, and Dante. For you have brought the voice of Il Duce to the ears of every member of the Fascist state, even to those in the forests, in the fields, on their fishing boats, and within the most humble home. Over the invisible ether you have spread that voice to the ears of the world."

At this a honey blonde spoke up. "Yes, and for this he wins such fame. But what of the voice that speaks over his instrument? The voice that will bring to all men a new *Pax Romana?* I do not understand it. Explain it to me. Why is it that Marconi wins the Nobel Prize and the Greatest Man on Earth does not?"

In a flash Max realized that this was Mussolini's daughter. Ciano, her husband, took her arm. "Edda. *Stai tranquilla, per favore.*"

But the young woman only stamped her foot. "It is a plot. The Americans. The Swedes. They are all against him."

Her brothers came up to the group. Bruno said, "*Sì, Sì,* it is a scandal."

Vittorio: "Worse. It is a crime."

Prince gave a laugh. "What does it matter, who wins or doesn't win that No-bull Praise?"

A tall man, slick-haired, fine-featured, laughed too. He held his hand out to the architect. "Herr Prince, I am Speer. I think tonight we are to be in competition. I want you to know I very much admire your work. I have made a study of your system of cantile-vers. Long ago, in school, I made a talk on your residences. At this moment, at our meeting, I feel both enthusiasm and humility."

Prince shook his hand. "So you're saying I was your in-speer-ation. Peas-to-meat-ya. Let's see who wins: Germany or America."

Farinacci: "It is not to be thought that a monument to Il Duce could be raised without the contribution of an Italian. Against the American entry we oppose a German-Italian axis, which reflects our new alliance in the political world. Butocci! *Lui, dov'è?* Ah! Stand up! Let us see you!"

The minister called out to a man at one of the tubular tables. The strings of his hair fell almost to his shoulders; in the cup of his hand he rested a pointed, poorly shaved chin. He couldn't stand, how-ever, because the film star, Borboni, was sitting on his lap. "This is my friend," she declared. "The new Donatello. The new Bernini. He is going to win the contest. But he won't do the two-step with me."

"Ah!" cried Vittorio. "It's a good idea. We should have music. We should have dancing."

The actress pulled at Butocci's necktie. "Come. Come, Georgio. Let's do the boogie-woogie."

"But Paola. You see, there is no dance floor."

Goebbels, of all people, limped over to their table, seized it, and—as if it were made from nothing more than tin foil—placed its legs up on the top of another nearby. "Now there is," he declared.

Vittorio laughed. He turned toward the pianist. "Play for us something. From America! From the Negroes!"

The man, though clearly American, hesitated.

Speer spoke up: "Putzi, why not do it?"

The pianist responded with "St. Louis Blues." Decadent mu-sic, Max thought, to the master race—which is why he was surprised to see the German Minister of Enlightenment and Propaganda bow to the Italian actress and take her hand. Von Ribbentrop did the same to Magda, Goebbel's wife, and led her into the tiny open square. There was hardly room for the others, but they pressed in nonetheless, wriggling their shoulders to what at another time they would have called a jungle rhythm.

Nina came up to Max and seized his hand. He looked for Aria, but she was already whirling about in Vittorio's arms.

"Have you seen Frankie?" Nina asked, while stepping on Max's toes.

Shabilian, stumbling, looked about. The boy was nowhere in sight. Putzi, the pianist, switched to "My Blue Heaven." More and more people pushed into what seemed less and less space. Max saw Bruno grasp his brother by the shoulder and cut in to dance with Aria. He enclosed her waist with both hands. Edda and Ciano hung their chins on each other's shoulders. Farinacci, with his good hand, spun the cocktail stewardess about in a circle. The slick-haired Goebbels pressed his cheek to the mermaid's world-famous breasts.

Suddenly the music stopped. So did the dancing. A woman had entered the lounge. Everyone drew back, as they might before an infectious patient. Max had seen her before. He strained to remember her name. Her lipstick was smeared over her teeth. Her round, pale face was surrounded by a cloud of dark hair, like an octopus by its ink. Her dress, gathered at the waist, was hiked askew on one side. Her feathered boa dragged at her feet and a blouse button was missing. Max had it! Sarfatti. The mistress of Mussolini. It wasn't her dishevelment that made the crowd part. It wasn't the crazed look in her eyes. No, they cringed in something like terror because of the burning cigarette in her hand.

"*Nein! Fräulein! Nein!*" That was Frau Goebbels, who had spoken with relish of death rays and new kinds of weapons. Now she shrank back, her cheeks twitching, at the tiny red glow of the ash.

"Margherita! *Fermati! Non ti muovere!*" That was Ciano, who had lost his diplomatic savoir-faire. "Stop! Don't move!"

Dreamily, tipsily, the woman continued toward them.

Von Ribbentrop: "*Diese Jüdische Schwein will uns alle umbringen!*" The Jewish sow will kill us all.

Now Speer addressed her. "Fräulein. I will explain to you. The buoyancy of our ship is created by hydrogen. This is a flammable gas. The least spark—"

Sarfatti nodded. She gave a wave with the hand that held the cigarette. "I understand," she said. "You don't want to let me dance. You won't let me smoke. You are going to take away every pleasure."

The next instant three stewards rushed forward. They were like athletes, like soldiers. They surrounded her. One took her wrist, twisting it. Another seized her from behind. The third slapped the cigarette away and crushed it with the rubberized sole of his shoe.

"No! No!" Margherita twisted about in their grasp.

Then, at first far away, but drawing rapidly closer, there came a buzz-buzzing. Everyone heard it: like a bee, that's what it sounded like, or a horsefly. The idea of an insect, free, following its instincts, in an environment meant to be purified, sealed from the natural world, caused almost as much consternation as the now-extinguished cigarette. All the passengers looked about, here and there, high and low. Even the portrait of the Reichskanzler seemed, with the eye not covered by a black triangle of hair, to be peering out at the miscreant. The drone continued, growing louder. Then from the promenade, one of the children cried, "It's not here! It's outside!"

Vittorio exclaimed, "The airplane!"

Bruno: "*Attenzione!* Il Duce arrives!"

There was a spontaneous burst of applause. Everyone listened to the sound of the engines. They grew louder still, and lower, until it seemed that they must be coming from just outside the silver skin of their tethered craft. There was a rush for the windows. People knelt. They craned their necks upward. Over the roar of the descending machine, somebody screamed. It was Margherita Sarfatti:

"No! No, Duce! The fog! The darkness! The mist!"

It was almost as if the pilot had heard her. The howling engines changed their pitch, they growled in what sounded like anger, and then rose upward into the starless heavens.

In the lounge of the *Hindenburg* there was a sigh. A little man wearing a neat white beard, black boots, and ribbons said, "*La signora ha ragione.* He must return to the airport."

"Yes," said the piano player. "It is too dangerous to land on the water."

Bruno leaned furiously into that American's face. "*Pericoloso?* Dangerous? We are speaking of Il Duce!"

Had the distant aeronaut heard those words as well? For no sooner had they been spoken than the craft he controlled circled about and began to speed downward again.

"But he must be mad!" exclaimed Speer.

"Or a daredevil!"

"Does he want to commit suicide?"

Once more the motors roared. They came closer and closer. This time, when they seemed directly overheard, they ceased, with as much suddenness as if someone had crushed the buzzing insect with a rolled-up newspaper.

"Oh, no! *O, Dio!*" cried Edda, the Duce's daughter, as she dropped into her husband's arms.

Everyone in that lounge, including the stewardesses and stewards, held his breath. But there was no crash. Instead, both engines sputtered back to life and then, just as they had before, faded into the night.

The little Goebbels children burst into tears. Many of the women were dabbing at their eyes. Even Vittorio stood pale-faced, with a sheen of sweat on his cheeks. After another moment of silence, Herr Ribbentrop declared: "He has come to his senses. He will wait until *die Nacht, der Nebel,* has lifted."

No sooner had those words escaped the diplomat's lips than they all heard the distant drone of the seaplane's engines as it began to spiral downward on its third approach.

"What a man! All honor to the Duce! *E imperturbabile!*" That was Bruno, whose shining eyes, like the black balls for billiards, were bulging from their sockets.

"*Un leone!*" said Farinacci, whose only official position was Friend of the Duce. "With a lion's heart!"

Down came the aircraft, its engines coughing, choking, like a man who has swallowed a bone.

Then, just when it seemed the tension could not be tolerated a moment longer, the Jewess, Sarfatti, rushed across the lounge toward a thin, bespectacled man who had not once moved from his table in the corner. This, Max realized, was the cardinal who had stood at the Constantine Arch, blessing the parade of the tanks. The wild-haired woman dropped to her knees before him. "Please. Excellency. I beg you. Ask God to save him. This is the Duce. The hope of all the world. Ask for a miracle."

The papal secretary closed the book he was reading, keeping a finger between the pages. "It is not for me to ask of our merciful God a special favor for any one man. What will be will be, according to His will."

"Oh!" cried Sarfatti, though whether at this act of defiance or at the sudden roar of the airplane engines it was not possible to tell. How loud they were! Louder than ever before! Even the glasses on the tabletops began to shudder and, across the ship, on the port side, the plates and cutlery in the dining room began to chatter in response.

"*O, Dio! O buon Dio!*" sobbed Sarfatti. "*Benito mio!* Save him! Show him the way!"

Her prayer was answered. There was, of a sudden, a bright flash of light, which lit up all the windows. A second flash followed, as dazzling as the first. "Oooh," cried the tow-headed children and, truth be told, many of the adults.

Now the sound of the engines rose to a screech that even inside the hermetic tube of the *Hindenburg* reached a hundred decibels. Then nothing, a silence so complete that everyone on board could hear the splash of a perfect landing.

"*Un miracolo!*"

"*Ein Mirakel!*"

The passengers were shouting with delight and pounding each other about the shoulders.

Only one other person, besides Max, realized that the miracle had been performed by Eckener, the captain, who had sent up rockets to illuminate the surface of the lake. It was Amos Prince who, above the excitement, the tumult, declared:

"I don't know about the Daze-he. I don't know about mirror-kills. What I do know is that he sure as hell did it with flare."

Five minutes later the Duce, still in his flying helmet, entered the lounge. He was accompanied by a youthful female with curly black hair and bright white teeth set into gums that glistened wet and pink when she smiled. Not even her heavy camel-hair coat could conceal what in those days was called an hourglass figure, with more sand in the upper chamber than in the one that collected minutes and hours beneath.

At first, seeing this couple, everyone stood motionless. Someone in the crowd murmured, *O, Dio, è* Claretta Petacci."

Then the little gentleman, the one with boots and ribbons, came forward and inclined his torso, even as he thrust out his right arm.

"Duce!" he declared. "I offer you a Roman salute."

"Majesty," came the reply. "You must not bow. We greet each other as equals."

Maximilian looked twice, and then a third time. Was this the King, Vittorio Emanuele? The same one he had seen on the reviewing stand? But there was no time to marvel at the sight of the Emperor of Abyssinia; already Marconi was moving toward the end of the lounge. He actually knelt before the man who stood before him, chin out, hands on hips.

"Duce," he quite simply said.

"*Senatore*," said Mussolini. "It is I who should kneel before you."

At such graciousness a sigh of appreciation rose from the Italians, and perhaps from the Germans too. Now one after the other Mussolini's countrymen came forward to bow before He Whom The Whole World Fears:

"Duce," said Ciano. "We marvel at your airmanship. Through the mist. Through the darkness of night."

"*Niente, non era niente*, Ciano. A few wisps of fog."

"Duce," said Edda, the great man's daughter.

"Duce," said Bruno, her brother.

"Duce," said the famous actress, making a curtsy, a deep one, before him.

"Charming," said Mussolini, gazing downward, his eyes as wide, almost, as the goggles that were plastered to his forehead. "Il

Duce approves. Who can say? Perhaps tonight he will take the blood from your lips."

Before she could respond, the Friend of Friends took his turn at the head of the line. "Duce," he declared. "On behalf of the Grand Council and all your ministers—"

The daring airman crossed his arms over his chest. "Ah, here is Farinacci! He wants everyone to think he lost his hand because of a grenade."

"But it was a grenade, Duce. You know that."

"Ha! Ha! *Sì*. But not one of the Abyssinians'. One of ours! Il Capitano Farinacci, he was fishing!"

Who had the audience next? Butocci, the architect. "Duce," he said, like all of the others.

Then, surprisingly, a child got up from under the aluminum piano and ran the length of the lounge. He wasn't one of the Goebbels's blond-headed brood. He was dark-haired, dark-skinned, and couldn't have been more than nine years old. "Duce," he piped, bringing his hand to his brow. "Your son salutes you."

"Get up, Romano," said his father. "Some day you will fly through the sky like your brothers. Before you know it that day will arrive. *Vai, vai.*"

The boy scampered away, to be replaced by the oldest of those siblings. "Duce," said Vittorio, bowing like all the others.

"Vittorio, I am happy to see you. I want you to fly the Marchetti back to Rome. I want you to be there when I arrive."

"No, Papa! I won't go. Everyone else is flying with you. I will too."

"Papa? I am not your Papa."

"Duce, forgive me."

"I am not Duce, either. I speak as Commander of the Fascist Air Forces. Your officer has given you an order."

Like his little brother, Vittorio saluted. "*Sì*, Comandante." He turned on his heel and marched down the passageway, looking neither left nor right.

The next person to come forward was not an Italian. There was a murmur of surprise as Amos Prince, in his loping stride, moved to where Mussolini stood waiting. He didn't kneel. He didn't bow. But he did touch the brim of his Panama hat.

"Douche," he declared.

There was a gasp from those standing nearby.

Putzi, the pianist, stuck a chord, then stood at the keyboard. "All Americans greet the Duce. When you come to New York you will see it. Even the Statue of Liberty offers the Duce the Fascist salute."

He struck another chord, which was lost in a burst of merry laughter. Mussolini unfolded his arms and embraced the architect. "He's my dear *Americano*. I love this Amos-a."

Farinacci stepped forward. "It is a breach of protocol for a foreigner to greet you when not all of your countrymen have done so." He was staring pointedly at the table in the corner where the cardinal, in his flashing spectacle frames, was sitting. "He refused to pray for you. He would not ask God for a safe landing. It is practically treason."

Mussolini's grin faded from his face. He peeled off his leather helmet, which had been stretched like a second skin over his scalp. "WHAT? DOES IL DUCE NEED A HEAVENLY HAND? HAS HE FORGOTTEN HIS SKILLS? PERHAPS YOU THINK HE HAS GROWN OLD?"

"No, no" cried the assemblage. "Never!"

Ciano said, "Our faith is in you, Duce. You landed your airplane on the waters. Tonight you will carry us safely over the Alps."

Mussolini looked skyward, as if with eagle eyes he could see those jagged peaks. "OH, ALPS! YOU RISE LIKE A DAGGER TO

PIERCE THE FLESH OF OUR BALLOON. WE ACCEPT THE RISK WITHOUT GUARANTEES FROM GOD. IT IS HYDROGEN, NOT PRAYERS, THAT MAKES US LIGHTER THAN AIR."

At this the cardinal rose from his chair and spread his long, thin fingers on the table top. "Do not forget, Duce, who made this hydrogen—yes, and helium, and nitrogen, and the very oxygen that now fills your lungs."

"YOU, PACELLI: DID THIS GREAT BEING ALSO MAKE THE POISON GASES? INCLUDING THE MOST POISONOUS GAS OF ALL? DO YOU KNOW OF WHICH ONE I SPEAK?"

The churchman stood rigid; not a word came from his mouth, which was clamped so tightly it looked as if it had just devoured his lips.

"*INCENSO!* HA! HA! HA! *FUMO D'INCENSO!*"

Another wave of laughter filled the lounge; it was like a wind that blew the Pope's secretary of state back into his modernistic chair.

Now, unsteadily, Margherita Sarfatti made her way through the crowd and, like those before her, knelt before the chief of state. "Duce," she said.

But it was the Duce's companion, Petacci, who gave the reply. "What? Is *she* on board? Who allowed this? Look: she is *ubriaca*. Drunk. She will make a scandal."

"*Io? Io?* I make the scandal? It is you who bring disgrace to the Duce. It is you who wish to steal him from me." With that, the older woman sprang upward and clamped her hands around the throat that rose above the camel collar.

Claretta fought back, thrusting her own hands into Sarfatti's dark locks and pulling so violently that the features of her face became as distorted as the famous gargoyle on the Via Giulia in Rome. But instead of water, a stream of curses poured from her mouth.

"*Cagna! Porca! Prostituta!* I am going to kill her! The bitch! I am strangling her!"

Claretta only pulled harder. "It is I who will kill you!" she shouted. "Duce, how can you love such a hag? And a Jewess! She's as old as Sarah in the Bible."

"Haw! Haw!" bellowed Amos Prince at the sight of the two struggling women. "It's like a night at the Italian up-roar!"

The Dictator was not looking at either of the female antagonists. He directed his black, flashing eyes to where Prince's elder daughter was standing with Bruno. Max turned too. He saw how she tipped her head back to drain the last of her martini. The flesh of her throat rippled as the alchohol descended down it. For an instant Max felt himself crazed with envy: if only *he* could have been that green olive, or the red pimento inside it.

Mussolini: "Who can tell me the name of that woman?"

After a brief pause, a voice rang out: "I can!"

Everyone, including the rival mistresses, turned toward the speaker. Max gave a gasp. So did Nina. For there, under the arch of the lounge, stood Frankie. He wore a Blackshirt's peaked cap—clearly borrowed from one of the guards in the passageway—that was a full size too large for his head. He raised his right hand toward the Dictator. "Duce, I have the honor to present to you my sister. Her name is Aria."

Mussolini turned toward the boy. "You. You bring here the *sorella*. The Duce, he's gotta look at this woman. She has such a boootiful name. Yes, and many boootiful hairs. Go. Bring her. I'mma taste already, like roast pigeon, that neck onna my tongue."

Franklin clicked his heels together, as if he were wearing a German instead of an Italian hat. But before he could move, someone at one of the tables started to giggle.

"What is the matter with me? I drank only one glass of wine. Already I am tipsy."

Maximilian glanced down to where Magda Goebbels was sitting. She stared at her wine, which, like the colored liquid in the trick glass of a magician, was tilted, rising at the front of the crystal, falling at the rear.

Then Putzi, holding his goblet aloft, said, "Then I am a drunkard too."

Everyone looked at his own drink. The water or wine or whiskey seemed to be spilling backward in every glass. "An angle," said Albert Speer, while assessing his own snifter of grappa, "of eight degrees."

Just then a spoon slid across a table, as if its surface had been greased. The boy, little Romano, took an India rubber ball from his pocket and set it on the floor of the lounge. At first nothing happened. Then, as if tugged by an invisible string, it moved an inch, and then another inch, and soon was rolling aft. Everyone stared as it disappeared down the passageway. The passengers were pale. Not one of them spoke. Were they thinking the same terrible thought as Max? That the gas must be escaping from the rear of their craft? That they were about to crash into the Bodensee?

"Hurrah! Hurrah!" That cry came from the blond-headed children at the slanted windows. "We're moving. *Wir sind abgehoben!* We're off!"

There was a rush to the promenade. People were pushing each other for a better view. Maximilian squeezed among them. He was able to see lights playing on the water and, in the center of that illumination, a toy airplane with a toy aviator standing on a play pontoon. Not a toy! It was the seaplane. Already it was contracting, shriveling, shrinking away. That was Vittorio, waving a scarf. He too seemed to be falling, dropping like a stone into a bottomless well.

But he wasn't sinking. They were rising, nose up, without the slightest sensation of movement or the least sound.

What had happened to the mist? The huge mass of the *Hindenburg* had displaced it, as a ship displaces its volume in water. Up and up they rose. There were the lights of a ship; it might have been the *Friedrichshafen*, on a final midnight crossing. There were more lights, a thousand of them; that might have been the town of Friedrichshafen itself. Then everything grew dark. Had the mists been sucked back around them? No: their lights were playing on the coils, like lemon taffy, of a cloud.

Max realized that not only were they rising but they were moving forward as well. He heard—but when had the sound begun?—the hum of the outboard engines. They were pushing the great ship ahead, at a velocity that would be impossible to distinguish from a standstill were it not for the streaming wisps and rag-ends of the clouds. After another moment—or perhaps it was another hour—time, in the absence of any feeling of motion, seemed to have stopped: soon, then, those clouds disappeared and all the men and women inside the airship, the notables and nonentities, a cocktail waitress and a King, found themselves hung at the center of an upside-down bowl that was painted with uncountable stars.

3

Maximilian, ready for bed, walked through the maze of passages to his assigned cabin. It turned out he was to share it with Signor Butocci, the architect, who had already filled the tiny space with the odor of his stockinged feet. There were no windows; on the wall was a button for water and a button for wine. The furniture consisted of a folding washstand and writing table, along with two bunk beds, each with its own eiderdown. The Italian had climbed into the upper berth, from which one of his legs now dangled. With each of his snoring inhalations he sucked up what little remained of the breathable air. After an hour of this, Max rolled off his bed and opened the cabin door, gasping at the fresh mountain currents that the dirigible's ventilation system had funneled into the hall.

Then he gasped again, but for a different reason. Twenty yards off, was that not Aria? With a man! He Of Unrivaled Powers? No, that was Bruno's arm snug about her waist; the two of them turned down a corridor of cabins. Max blinked; they were gone. Not only that, but the lights in the passageway had grown dim, either because of the thick curtain of blood that had dropped over his eyes, or because the steward had turned off the illumination for the night.

He put himself into motion, heading toward the same hall-way down which the lovers—horrible thought!—had disappeared. He squinted through the thick, round lenses that perched on his nose: no sign of anyone. He tried to read the names on the slips next to each door; there wasn't enough light. Through one of the portals he thought he heard a high feminine laugh, followed by a masculine guffaw. Next came a thump. Giggles. A squeal of a bedspring. Aria! The most painful of memories overwhelmed him: he lying wounded and she bent over him. Her hair like a halo. Her throat as white as the cotton on a swab.

"Psst! Psst!" hissed Maximilian. "Aria! My dear one! My darling!" He rapped on the cabin door. At once it jerked open. On the threshold stood Putzi, the pianist. He was stark naked and on the bed behind him, wearing long stockings, was Edda Ciano, née Mussolini.

"Beat it!" hissed the musician, in their shared idiom, and slammed shut the door.

Now, from the corner of his eye, Max saw the shadow of a woman fleeing down the main passageway pursued by the silhouette of a man. Could it be they? He dashed back to the corner, only to be nearly bowled over by the cocktail stewardess. She stopped, panting, looking over her shoulder. Her hat, on its little red strap, hung over one ear. Her blouse was unbuttoned and one breast swung freely, propelled by the physics of arrested momentum. She was so close to Maximilian that, by an association of senses, he caught the scent of pears. "*Was für ein Mann!*" she exclaimed. What a man!

She meant Joseph Goebbels. He came lurching along the hallway, his suspenders flapping at his knees. The stewardess gave a laugh and darted into a cabin two doors away. The Minister of Propaganda and Enlightenment, in accelerating, ran out of his specially made shoe. Listing leftward, he sped by the silent Shabilian and pounded on the shut cabin door; it sprang open long enough for him to disappear inside.

All, for a moment, was still. Nothing could be heard but the drone of the powerful engines. High in the nighttime sky the airship slipped over the jagged prominences below. Then, from halfway down the corridor, Max made out the sound of sobbing. Someone was huddled there, a woman, with her knees drawn to her chin. Was this Prince's daughter? Had Bruno abandoned her? Broken her heart? The American made his way along the shadowy hall. When he drew closer the woman cried, "Oh, he doesn't love me. He never loved me. Sweet talk! Sweet talk and lies!" To Max's amazement she threw herself toward him and clasped him about the knees. It wasn't Aria, of course. It was Claretta Petacci. "Help me. *Aiutami*," she sighed. Shabilian stood frozen. What could he do?

Opposite, a door opened—first a crack, then wide. A short man in a robe stood illuminated by the light bulb behind him. *Il Re!* Emperor of the Abyssinians! "*Vieni.* Come. You will weep on my shoulder." At the royal command the young woman got to her feet, took the first of five steps that brought her to the threshold of the state-room, and stepped across it.

The silence resumed. Like a sailor on a ship, someone, some-where, started playing an accordion. A mechanic or steward on B deck, no doubt. Now, from that same deck came the sound of laughter and voices. Were the crewmen having a party? Shabilian moved toward the iron stairway. The sounds grew louder: a bellow, the slap of footsteps, a gasp, a grunt. The shriek that came next was not from a sailor. Who was this on the staircase? With a wild head of hair dripping water from every strand? Paola Borboni! The mer-maid! Up she came, her steps ringing, clutching the tiniest of tow-els to her streaming body. At the top of the stairs she sprang onto A deck and shook her head, which, like an atomizer, covered Max with a spray. She paused long enough to give a quick laugh, and then ran off, even as the staircase began to clang from the approach of the man behind her.

It was, of all people on earth, Guglielmo Marconi, covered in soapsuds. He vaulted like an Olympian up the last three steps. "*Ferma!*" he cried to his fleeing prey, even as she disappeared around the near-est corner. For a moment the great inventor stood, clutching his chest. "*Che donna!*" he gasped. "She will give me a heart attack." Then—with each footfall leaving a damp impression, the way a god in a legend will leave a clue to his passage, or a film star will cast his feet or his palm print in cement—the lathered laureate thudded after his paramour.

To Maximilian the congress within these busy corridors had become more suffocating than his crowded cabin. He wanted noth-ing more than to return to his bed. He started back down the main passageway. By now he was not surprised to come across Claretta, on her knees and weeping, much as he had seen her before. Nor was he startled when a cabin door opened and another robed man stood on the threshold. As he half-expected, that figure said, "Don't cry, my daughter. *Perchè piangi?* Come. I will dry your tears." But nothing could have prepared Max Shabilian for the shock he experienced when he realized that the comforter was the pious and puritanical Pacelli, Vatican Secretary of State.

Madness! he thought. Romans and Sabines! Like a play by Schnitzler! In a daze he staggered toward the refuge of his cabin. When he arrived there he found that the door was blocked by Prince's daughter—not Aria, alas, but Nina, who was nothing more to him than a playmate. Her face, always ruddy, now seemed inflamed. Heavens! She was reaching for him. Max drew back. Was there something in the molecules of hydrogen, a few of which must have slipped into the atmosphere of their ship? Or had something been placed in the drinks they had been served, a potion so powerful that it could transform the features of even this innocent child? Child? There was no mistaking the leer on her lips. Why, she was licking them with her tongue. She reached for him again; again he retreated.

Then both of them stopped the twisted game of tag. They stood in their tracks. Here was Franklin, still wearing the borrowed cap of a *Squadristra*. He was leading a female figure down the corridor, toward the rear of the airship.

Max saw at once that the woman in his grasp was Margherita Sarfatti. Her tresses, where Claretta had pulled them, stood out on her scalp, more like antlers than human hair. Her lips quivered. Tears like dewdrops clung to the lashes of her eyes. She never stopped murmuring, perhaps to her escort, perhaps to herself, perhaps to the love of her life: "*È vero?* He wants me? *Benito mio? Sì! Sì* I knew it. He always returns to me. He never stops loving me. *Mai!* Never! Ah, *Caro! Mio Caro!* I can't live without you."

The two of them continued down the hall, which was so dark that nothing could be seen at the end of it save for the gleaming crossed boots of the Blackshirts, who stood guard before the last of the staterooms.

Nina stood dumbstruck. Max seized the chance. He slipped inside his cabin and stood, heart racing, against the closed door. There was no plea. There was no knock. Slowly he felt his way through the rank air to his bunk. He lay on his back, atop the eiderdown. A moment passed. Then came the familiar sounds of men and women chasing each other like beasts: the far-off slam of a door; a pause; the slam of another. A shout, a sob, somebody panting, the laugh of somebody else. The faint strains of the accordion. Footfalls. Now a scream of—was it pain? Was it pleasure?

Max, flat on his coverlet, now heard a thing that made his heart stop: the click of his very own door. He watched it slowly creak open. A man stepped inside. Max gasped at the sight of Farinacci. The ex-party chief paused. Then he stepped closer. The stump of his arm emerged, standing upright before him. Max could not have exhaled had he wished to. He could not have uttered a cry. Farinacci's erect limb stretched upward, outward, over the American's head; it butted against the leg of Butocci, which hung over the edge of the upper bunk.

"Wake up! *Stupido!* Wake up!"

But Max was the one who obeyed. He opened his eyes. There indeed was Farinacci. There was the architect's foot, inside its stinking stocking.

"*Wake up!* It is four in the morning. Time for the battle."

Could it be? Had he been asleep all these hours? Aria. Bruno. Putzi. Edda. Goebbels and the stewardess. The mermaid and the inventor. Even Clara and the cardinal. That poor Margherita. Had the whole of that carnival been nothing more than a moment's dream?

4

Shabilian swung his feet off his bunk and followed Butocci and the one-handed man from the cabin. The corridors were silent. You could hear the passengers snoring at peace. At the end of the hallway they turned not to the right, toward the lounge, but leftward, into a dining room that must have measured a full fifty feet. The tubular tables had been pushed together, as if for a formal banquet; but instead of a tablecloth, with silver and linens, the entire surface was covered by a large green cloth. There was no Mercator projection on the interior wall, only a series of paintings of what a passenger might have glimpsed from the windows of the *Graf Zeppelin* on its South American passage: the Canary Islands, a full-rigged ship, seagulls and sharks, palm trees on a coastline, and finally Sugarloaf rising above the harbor at Rio. From the slanting windows of the *Hindenburg*, however, nothing could be seen save the black of night.

A steward appeared with a pot of milk and a pot of coffee. A stewardess—yes, the one from his dream, with her corkscrew curls—held a tray of cups. Max, with a sweet tooth, took his with cubes of sugar. Now the two opposing teams began to gather in the room. To one side stood Shabilian and Amos Prince, chewing on his cigarette holder in lieu of a cigarette. At the other was the Axis entry: Speer, standing with Goebbels, Von Ribbentrop and, inexplicably, Cardinal Pacelli; and, a few feet off, Butocci, with Farinacci hovering about him like a boxer's second.

And where, thought Max, was the great referee? Everyone had finished his coffee. The small talk had ceased. Nothing could be heard save the drone of the powerful diesels. Then the nine-year-old Romano came bounding into the room. His father, wearing a tunic and riding breeches, with a riding whip in his hand and a tufted black cap atop the plate of his cranium, strode through the portal.

Claretta Petacci, apparently the winner of a different competition, had her arm crooked through his. "YOU, ARCHITECTS OF ITALY," Mussolini began, chin high, balled fists on his hips. "OF GERMANY. OF AMERICA. THE DUCE OFFERS HIS CONGRATULATIONS. ONLY YOU REMAIN FROM THIS CONTEST OF THOUSANDS. OF MILLIONS."

Von Ribbentrop dared to break in. "Were there truly a million entries, Duce?"

By way of reply, Mussolini dug into his leather tunic and removed a folded piece of paper, which he spread wide. "I HOLD AN ENTRY FROM CALABRIA. ITS AUTHOR IS PIERO CIPRIANI. EIGHT YEARS OLD. WE LISTEN TO HIS WORDS: '*Duce, here is my idea. Build a statue of Hercules like at the harbor of Rhodes. But Hercules will have the face of Il Duce. You will live forever—per l'eternità—on Olympus. We worship you like a god.*'"

Mussolini paused, refolding the paper. "HA! HA! *ERCULE!* A GOD! THIS PIERO, HE IS A SIMPLE SCHOOLBOY. ONE OF THOSE MILLIONS WHO DREAMS OF THE MONUMENT TO IL DUCE."

There was, from the small gathering, a patter of applause. Amos caught his apprentice's eye, and then his ear: "'Course every schoolboy dreams about his *Dolce*. A *tira-Mu-ssolini*."

"MILLIONS? TENS OF MILLIONS! IN TRUTH, ALL FASCISTS ARE BUILDERS. IN THEIR BOSOMS THERE HAS AWAKENED THE INSTINCT MANIFESTED IN NATURE BY THE BEE, EVER INDUSTRIOUS, AND THE ANT, SEEMINGLY LOWLY BUT ABLE TO CRUSH ANY FOE IN HIS JAWS OR LIFT IN HIS ARMS TEN TIMES AND TWENTY TIMES HIS OWN WEIGHT. O, ANT! O, BEE! THE TERMITE! THE SEA CREATURE THAT SLOWLY SECRETES IN HIS GENIUS THE SHAPE OF HIS SHELL. THESE SIMPLE ANIMALS POSSESS THE ARCHITECTURAL

IMPULSE THAT MODERN MAN, DRUGGED BY DEMOCRACY, HAS FORGOTTEN."

Again, from the audience, applause. And from Prince: "This Bean-eat-o, he's amazin'. Why, he knows how even a insect bee-hives."

"*COMPETITORI!* ARE YOU PREPARED TO SHOW ME SOMETHING TRUE TO THE SPIRIT OF THE AGE OF MUSSOLINI, SOMETHING NEW, DARING, MODERN, NEVER SEEN BY ANY MAN BEFORE; AND AT THE SAME TIME, *SIMULTANEAMENTE,* A THING THAT WILL HONOR THE GLORY OF ROME'S PAST, ITS GRANDEUR, ITS NOBILITY, ITS UNENDING TRADITION?"

Farinacci stepped forward. "We are, Duce."

"YOU, BUTOCCI. YOU, SPEER. YOU MAY ATTEMPT TO ASTONISH IL DUCE."

At once the two men walked to either side of the table and rolled back the oilcloth. There was an exclamation at what was revealed underneath: a scale model of Rome, from the Villa Borghese in the north to the Terme di Caracalla in the South; with, to the east, the great cemetery of Campo Verano and, at the western boundary, every building of the Vatican, down to the flower beds, flower-filled, in the gardens.

"Ah! *Bene! Meraviglioso!*" Petacci exclaimed.

Goebbels leaned over the model, like a tour guide pointing out the sights. "*Hier ist die Pantheon. Und hier der Römische Forum. Ja! Man sieht das Villa d'Este und das Colosseum.*"

Signora Ciano said, "This is miraculous. I can see every ancient monument. But where, I wonder, is the one that is new? The one that marks the triumph over Abyssinia?"

Farinacci, wiping his brow in excitement, gave a sign to the Axis partners. Speer and Butocci dropped to their knees on either side of the table. Romano, the boy, couldn't help giggling at the way the two men had disappeared. When they stood up again, he clapped his hands together in wonder. For each held what looked like half of a silver crescent moon. They leaned forward, suspending the shining metal shards above the tiny buildings, the maze of the streets, and the serpentine curves of the Tiber. Then they leaned forward, clicked the two pieces together and set them into the model. When they at last stepped back a gleaming steel band rose from the Terme di Caracalla, soared high over the Colosseum, and plunged back to earth at the Giardino del Quirinale, which in real life was at least a mile and a half away. There was, from every throat, a gasp.

Von Ribbentrop: "*Hier ist das Tor der Mussolini.*"

Farinacci: "*Il monumento per Il Duce.*"

All turned toward the Conqueror of Ethiopia, who seemed to have been struck dumb at this realization of his command: a thing never before seen by the eye of man. The other great arches, of Titus, of Constantine, would seem no larger than garden hoops to those Romans who would some day watch this great span of metal disappearing into the heavens.

Speer, cocreator of the wonder, turned to the man whose exploits it honored. "Duce, your monument stretches over and protects all of ancient Rome, and will be visible from its furthest suburbs. It will shine in the heavens like a permanent rainbow; it will mark your blessings on the Italian people, just as legend has it such a sign sealed the covenant of God with the Jews."

Quickly Herr Goebbels added, "But this bow is curved like a weapon, Duce, ready to launch for all eternity the arrow of your will."

No one had taken his eyes from the Dictator. His finger was crooked in his collar, as if it were choking his throat. Suddenly a button burst from the cloth and landed at his feet on the carpet. With an audible pop a second button flew from his tunic. Mussolini was expanding like a pneumatic tire. Yes, the very hasp of his belt buckle was bending, like a crane that buckles under too much weight. Yet even as his lips sucked in the atmosphere of the dirigible, they uttered not a word.

Farinacci stepped before him. "Permit me, Duce, to declare that, as you demanded, this design is fully in accord with our heritage. The arch, invented by Romans, remains a symbol of the endurance and strength of our civilization. Upon that foundation stand our aqueducts, our ancient buildings, the Colosseum, the triumphant memorials to our Emperors. If Caesar, if Titus, if Augustus possessed steel instead of stone, they too would have contemplated such a monument."

Off flew another button. The skin of his face was darkening, reddening, as if all the blood in his body were being forced upward under pressure. Yet there was no hiding the smile that cut like a knife blade across the crimson flesh.

Now it was Speer's turn to stand before him: "We have labored to meet all your requirements, Duce. This structure not only honors the ancient empire but reflects the new Fascist age. The construction of the catenary curve is of not one but two layers of steel. Between the two, there is a network of equilateral triangles, each piece welded with a plate on the interior surface. You commanded: something modern for the Century of Mussolini. We obeyed: here is an arch with the precise structure of an airplane's wing. It will last far longer than the Colosseum's concrete and stone."

The great chin slowly dropped, like the movement of a lock on an ocean canal. The mouth, with its white teeth, red tongue, and interior of blackness opened wide. But the words they all heard belonged to Joseph Goebbels:

"*As long as the Colosseum stands, Rome stands.* This famous maxim will now apply to *das Mussolini Tor. When the Arch falls, Rome falls.*

When Rome falls, so falls the world. Do you see, Duce? Your monument will hold up all of the sky."

At last the Conqueror held up his hand. His voice, when he spoke, was at first choked with emotion—*"Bene. Grazie, amici. Come è bello"*—but soon it grew in volume: "YOU, ARCHITECTS OF THE AXIS. YOU HAVE WON THE PRIZE. YOU SHALL WEAR ON YOUR BROWS THE WREATH OF IMPERISHABLE LAUREL. SOON, THE *ARCO DI MUSSOLINI* SHALL FILL LIKE A STREAM OF STARS THE SKY OF THE ETERNAL CITY."

"Bravo!" cried Farinacci.

"Bravissimo!" Butocci echoed.

The Germans, all together, cried *"Wunderbar!"*

But Amos Prince said, "Hold yer hearses. The competition ain't over. Now it's the turn of the old U.S.A."

Von Ribbentrop stared at him in genuine bewilderment. "But you have heard the words of Il Duce. The decision has been made."

"The trouble with you boys, you ain't seen the light."

"What light?" asked Claretta.

The cardinal was standing at the port side promenade. "Is that it?" he asked, even as his spectacles began to gleam.

Everyone turned toward the specially treated glass, through which they saw a single pillar of illumination that shot upward and hung tremblingly in the sky.

Goebbels laughed. "Is that your monument? *That?* It is what you Americans call, *alter Hut,* old hat. Herr Speer has already done this at Nuremberg. It was his Cathedral of Light."

Farinacci: "Il Duce does not wish stage effects. He will be commemorated in steel, not searchlights."

"Listen, fellas. I don't mean to gum up the works, but this ain't no ex-Speer-mint. And it sure ain't no Catheter of Light. What it does is tell us we've arrived at our destination."

"And where," said the sneering Von Ribbentrop, "is that?"

The answer to the German's question came from the portal, under which Marconi and Captain Eckener now stood. The latter, with his binoculars still around his neck, was the one who spoke: "Longitude 12 degrees, fourteen minutes east. Latitude 41 degrees, forty-eight minutes north."

But no one was paying attention. It was now apparent to all that the great airship was heading straight for the glowing beacon that stood so silent and unmoving that, with its bouquet of clouds at the top, it might have been a gigantic Corinthian column. Closer and closer they came; the beams from the searchlight were brighter than the fluorescence in their dining room. Suddenly Eckener plucked up a speaking tube from the wall and spoke a few quick words of German into it. Instantly the engines began to roar. The effect, palpable to everyone, was as if someone had applied a set of brakes. The dirigible slowed, and slowed further. Then, almost as if it were coming to rest at an actual mooring mast, it glided to the crown of the column, nothing now but a crazed fountain of photons, and came to a halt. It hung to its tether of light.

Eckener: "Speed: zero. Altitude: 1609 meters."

"Yup," said Prince, "that's what you call one A-merry-can mile. It's the height to which the Deuce of Spicks will arrive each morning."

Ciano: "I don't understand. Arrive each morning? I thought you were going to build a monument."

"I am. A skyscraper one mile high."

Some of the passengers gasped, others burst into laughter. Farinacci said, "Duce, this is an insult to you and the Party. You called for a memorial to a great warrior and his victory. And what has he given you, this *Americano*? An office building!"

Prince tugged at the brim of his hat, which sufficed to alter his voice considerably. "An office building that will hold the entire

apparatus of the Fascist state, a hundred and fifty thousand government officials: your generals and admirals; your ministers; a city
of public servants, all consolidated and working literally under the
Duce, whose own quarters are above—"

"It is just as I said," Farinacci interrupted. "The vision of a
bureaucrat."

"Above the clouds," Prince went on, "above the high-flying
birds, a place where he will be able to view every part of his city and
where every Roman can see him, the burning light in his window,
working for their welfare late into the night. And by day? The gold
leaf of the pinnacle will be visible from three different continents."

The Romans, and the foreigners too, turned toward the Duce.
His arms were crossed over his chest. His brow was furrowed with
thought. "This building: how's-a she going to stand up and not fall-
a down?"

"The way a tree stands, Duce, a pine tree, with a taproot deep
in the bedrock."

Max just had time to think of the dinner table, the blade that
Prince had thrust into it, before Farinacci broke into laughter:

"Ha! Ha!" The Fascist, in a paroxysm, was waving the stump
of his arm. He addressed the architect in English. "Yooo are stoopid.
A foool. Do yoo think yooo are in New Yooork? There is, in
Rooome, no bedroock." He spoke in Italian to the others: "Why
do you think we Romans have not long ago built our own Eiffel
Tower? Our Chrysler Building? Our edifice of the Empire State?
We, who discovered the arch? Who spanned mountain peaks with
our aqueducts? Who connected all of Europe with our roads? It is
because without the granite of Manhattan such feats cannot be
done."

Butocci: "True. True. Under our city there is only ash from
ancient volcanoes and pumice that is half made from air. This build-

ing will not rise far before the excavation collapses from the full force of the Tiber. The solid earth will turn once more into lava—a lava of mud."

Prince, unrattled, replied: "There is bedrock. We shall find it. Enough of it to raise a building five miles, if we wished to. Or ten miles. Or until there is no more oxygen left in the sky."

Pacelli, the cardinal: "You wish to challenge God. What you say is blasphemy."

"Excellency, give no heed to the challenge to God." The speaker was Albert Speer. "The challenge to man is quite enough. Let us say, for argument's sake, that the building is constructed. That would not take, in my opinion, a miracle. We are speaking of five hundred stories. How will a population of a hundred thousand reach the upper floors? How will they reach even the middle?"

"That problem has been solved by two *Americani*," Prince answered. "Alexander Graham Bell and Elisha Graves Otis. Without the telephone, there wouldn't be a hundred and fifty thousand arriving every day; there would be four or five million. And without the elevator—"

"Pardon me," said Speer, "but the lift creates more problems than it solves. Even with express stops and transfers and lounges, the shafts would take up all the space of the lobby and lower floors. Do you think that we, in the Third Reich, have not studied this? At most, and even this is awkward, a system of lifts might serve a structure of seventy or eighty stories. Your building is magnificent in conception, Herr Prince; it fails on the most mundane and practical grounds."

"We have made studies, too. At least my assistant, Mister Shabilian, has. Isn't that right, Maximilian?"

Max started, not only because he hadn't the least idea of what the architect was talking about, but because this was the first time he'd heard either of his names without a punning play on the words.

"Go on," Prince said. "What else have you been spending your time on but this very problem? All right, what's the solution?"

Then, without any thought on his part, the whole of the summer, with its gadgets and geegaws, fell like kaleidoscopic pieces into place. Max actually shouted the words he heard himself saying. "The elevators go on the *outside* of the building!"

Prince: "Correct. It will be a vertical highway filled with self-propelled cars. Each car will be three stories tall. Speed: a mile a minute. Only they won't go a mile. The top fifth of the building belongs to the Duce. He won't take a lift to the top. Instead—"

Here the architect removed one of Shabilian's toys from his pocket and wound the propeller on its rubber band. Squatting, he released it. With a whir it rose to the dining room ceiling, fluttering there like a bat at the roof of its cave.

"He's going to fly. The landing platform will be five thousand feet in the air. Duce, you can cruise there in an autogyro from any part of your empire, or arrive in twenty-five seconds from a dead stop on the ground."

The helicopter tumbled back to the carpet, where Romano pounced on it. His father grinned.

"It's a *meraviglia!* The Duce will live inna the air. In *un nido di àquila.* The nest of the eagle!"

Von Ribbentrop: "That, too, is stolen from the Reich. Only the Führer lives in *das Adlersnest.*"

Goebbels: "Speer, tell us. Is such a thing possible? A lift on the exterior? An autogyro?"

"Yes, Herr Minister. These things can be done."

"But why should they?" demanded Count Ciano. "Why should the Duce consider such a building? It does not commemorate the victory over the Abyssinians. It does not connect him to any past Emperor. It is not a memorial at all."

Prince paused, his hands in the pockets of his rumpled white linens. "What does a memorial do? What is it for? It reminds those in the future of the glories of the past. It is a timepiece that counts years and centuries and millennia, instead of minutes; even as it stands itself, imperishable, like a boulder in the river of time or like a pyramid above the blowing sands."

"Don't listen, Duce," said Farinacci. "These are only words, pretty words. We must not allow language to seduce us."

"Words?" echoed Prince. "But don't you see? Our monument is *literally* just such a clock, a gigantic sundial, with the tower as the gnomon and all of Rome as the face. The shadow of the Duce's memorial will move across his city for eternity, and all the other monuments will be nothing more than figures on the dial."

At this Mussolini gave a low groan, as if he were experiencing an act of pleasure. "*La mia ombra*," he murmured. My shadow.

Prince threw back his head, so that with his cigarette holder and unlit cigarette he looked like the jaunty photographs of the American president. "It's not just a sundial, keeping time, or a calendar, marking seasons; it is also a gigantic radio mast from which your voice—traveling on a new kind of Roman road—will echo across every ocean and into every continent; and it will do so not only during your lifetime, Duce, but long after your death."

The flesh of Mussolini's face went as white as the strong bones underneath it. "Death? *Morte? Morte?* Why you wanna say a thing like that? The Duce: he drink the milk! He performs the *esercizi inglesi.* He's got-a woman every eight hour. Alla the night. Alla the day. Like a *stallone!* You make mistake, eh? You no mean death of Il Duce?"

"But I do. This monument will not only be a place of work for the living but a resting place for the dead. It is your office and your home; but it is also your tomb. Here you shall be buried—not in the earth, but a full mile above it."

"*Traditore!*" With that the Dictator pulled out a pistol. He waved it in the air. "You make plot? You kill-a Mussolini? Mussolini, he kill-a you!"

"No, Duce!" That was Edda, the Duce's daughter. She stepped between the gunman and his target. "Don't shoot! You will puncture the balloon."

Prince was as calm as ever. "Duce, my monument does not remember you as one of the Caesars but as one of the Pharaohs. This is your pyramid, where you shall be secure forever."

"This is more nonsense," said Von Ribbentrop. "The whole world knows that the graves of the Pharaohs were looted, even though their tombs were blocked by enormous slabs of granite."

"That is true. But when the looters arrived at the sepulchers of Ramses, of the great Cheops, what did they find? Emptiness. Where had the great kings gone?"

No one answered. He Who Is Irreplaceable stood pie-eyed, his great jaw hanging as if from a broken hinge.

"Into the heavens, to take their place among the constellations. Duce, no man will reach you from below. But above there will be a single small channel. There, at the winter solstice, a solitary ray of light will enter. Thus shall the sun god Ra arrive to claim his child."

"I'mma all mix-up," said Mussolini. "I'mma filled up with *confusione.* I'mma not dead, inna this tomb? I'mma live?"

"Imagine, Duce. The ray of the sun will penetrate your crypt. It will activate a solenoid. And then, as if this solid tower were a rocket ship carrying you into space, your voice will hurl at the speed of light on radio waves that, like a decreasing decimal, can never be extinguished. Your spirit will travel through the galaxies, Duce, for as long as the sun shall shine—no, longer, for the stars that we see have long since burned out; but their light, and your words, shall travel forever."

Once again Mussolini clawed at his collar. He had begun to swell anew, as if, like the hovering *Hindenburg*, he had been inflated with gas.

Goebbels said, "Do not be fooled, Duce. I have become an expert on the power of radio. It can send words from one spot to another. And that is all. In reality it is nothing more than an invisible megaphone."

Prince smiled, as if he had been expecting such an objection. "Duce, with your permission, we would like to demonstrate the power of this invention."

The Dictator, still with his finger crooked in his collar, looked from one man to the other. "*We? Che cos'è, questo noi?*"

"Myself, with the assistance of Captain Eckener and his airmen." That was Marconi, wearing a stiff collar of his own. "You see, I have here a key. Beneath our airship are the wires of our antenna. I can, if you wish, shut off the column of light."

Mussolini said nothing. Prince said, "Yes. Turn it off now."

The inventor depressed the key, of the sort that telegraph operators use to send alphabetical letters in code. On the instant the towering beam disappeared. So did the lights inside the *Hindenburg*. The whole dirigible went dark. The sensation—Max felt it in the pit of his stomach—was like that of falling, as if the pillar of light had actually been a material column that had supported their weight.

"Ooooh," said everyone inside the dining room, as though they had been watching exploding fireworks instead of all-encompassing darkness.

"This is nothing," said Von Ribbentrop. "It is all too easily explained. All you have done is send a signal to a person on the ground, an ordinary man who turned off an ordinary searchlight."

"And is that man," said Prince, "also turning off every light in the city of Rome?"

"Rome? Who said anything about Rome? When we get there you will see its lights."

"But we *are* at Rome, Herr Ambassador." That was Captain Eckener. "I told you: longitude, 12.14 degrees. Latitude, 41.45. That puts us directly over the city. To be precise, directly over the Circus Maximus."

Everyone reflexively glanced out the darkened glass.

"But where are the lights?"

"Where is the city?"

"There must be a mistake."

Maximilian was as confused as the others. There was definitely nothing to see. They might have been over the empty Atlantic or still skimming the uninhabited Alps.

Von Ribbentrop said, "There has been an electrical failure."

Farinacci replied, "Italian electricity does not fail, I assure you."

"Then it is a trick," said Goebbels. "A bit of your commedia dell' arte."

"Or sabotage." Those dark words came from the cardinal.

"Our demonstration is not complete," said Prince, who turned once more to Marconi. "Senatore, will you please continue? Press the key once more."

With a slight bow, Marconi complied. "*Sia fatta la luce*," he said and instantly the lights of Rome, the streetlamps, the illumination of the monuments and fountains and buildings, even the lights in the apartment houses and private homes—all came on. If the impression before had been one of falling, now it was of buoyancy, as if the plummeting airship had been caught in the blanket of illumination. Throughout the room people were exclaiming in wonder. Prince's voice rose above the others':

"What you have seen, Duce, both the suppression of light and its rekindling, has been accomplished through the genius of your great countryman's invention. All matter is indestructible; it is conserved by transforming itself into energy. What the Marchese has shown us is how such energy, a stream of electrons, might be turned into words—or into a force that can create or extinguish light. Duce, you too will be transformed into spirit, into energy, into wavelengths, into thought. Will you not then be immortal? Shining among the stars like all the Pharaohs, like a living god?"

With three rapid pops, like the sound of a cork leaving a child's toy gun, the buttons flew from Mussolini's tunic. The Conqueror threw wide his engorged arms:

"EVEN CAESAR IN HIS TRIUMPH KEPT A SLAVE IN HIS CHARIOT. THIS WAS TO REMIND HIM THAT HE WAS HUMAN, NOT DIVINE. THE DUCE HAS DONE AWAY WITH THAT SLAVE. YOU, PRINCE: YOUR VISION IS FASCIST. YOU WILL BE THE ARCHITECT OF IL DUCE. YOU WILL BUILD THE NEW ROME."

"May I congratulate you?" Marconi stepped forward with his own arms outstretched.

Those gathered in the dining room gasped. To them it seemed that the inventor had just performed another miracle. The pillar of light did not come back on. The lights of the city of Rome did not go out. But from out of the Adriatic and from over the Apennines the great god Ra was sending his crimson rays into the sky. In the language of modern life, here was the dawn.

Max glanced downward through the tinted glass. Already the sunbeams had illuminated the details of the city. It was much like looking at the Axis model; except that, at five thousand feet, it was clear that the model was looking back: what traffic there was stopped and so did the agitated dots that represented Italian women and men.

The whole city stared upward at what must have seemed to them a silver-scaled fish swimming through the sea of the sky. Imagine their delight had they known that their leader, the Duce, was hovering above them.

The new Caesar spoke. "YOU, CITIZENS OF GERMANY, CITIZENS OF ITALY. YOU MUST APPLAUD NOW THIS ARCHI-TECT. HE WILL SEND THE DUCE'S THOUGHTS INTO THE HEAVENS, LIKE THE RUMINATIONS OF A DEITY. IT IS ON HIS BROW THAT I SET THE LAUREL."

There was, in fact, a burst of applause. Eckener, the captain of the *Hindenburg*, moved to where Prince was standing. "I too congratulate you, and I salute you." As he spoke these words, he slipped the strap of his binoculars up and over his own head and lowered it, as if in lieu of those laurels, over that of the architect.

Amos Prince: "I thank you. We have more work to do together. We shall need your great dirigible to build our monument. I do not mean the *Hindenburg* itself, but the *principle* of the lighter-than-air ship. We shall use them—in their dozens, perhaps in their hundreds."

There was another round of applause. Everyone felt the airship give a slight lurch upward, as if it too wished, with this dance step, to join the celebration or demonstrate how eager it was to get to this work.

Speer leaned close to the man who had bested him in the competition. "Take care," he said. "All those who labored on the tomb of the Pharaoh were immured within its walls. And the architect, the possessor of the Pharaoh's secret, was blinded."

As if those words were not frightening enough, a cry rang out from the opposite side of the airship. "*Nein! Oh, nein!*" What had happened? What was wrong? All rushed for the exit. They moved quickly across the dirigible's A deck to the lounge on the starboard side. No one was left to hear the laughter of Amos Prince: "Haw!

Haw! A tomb. A sarcophagus. A Mauso-lini. His thoughts are going to fly through the uni-wurst. The thoughts of a god! Haw! Haw! Haw! Thanks to Marconi. And his ray-dio!"

5

In the lounge, breakfast had been prepared. Those passengers who had just rushed in could smell the hot coffee and the toasted rolls. But no one was eating. Everyone was gathered at the raked windows of the promenade. The stewards and stewardesses were there. So were all the other passengers, the late risers who had not witnessed the competition. Max ran forward. Even before he saw the opened glass, he could feel the cold blast of air in the room. Those gathered at the bank of windows were holding each other. The women were weeping; the men looked ashen. Maximilian pushed his way through the crowd. He saw, caught on the window's aluminum edge, a length of green feather boa, half fur, half feathers. Margherita Sarfatti! Was that why the airship had just given that upward lurch? Because it was jettisoning its human ballast? He remembered how, the night before, he had seen her making her way back toward the Duce's stateroom. Was it possible, he wondered. Had the whole of that carnival *not* been a dream?

Before he could put all these facts together—the missing woman, the weeping passengers, the open window—Frankie came running toward him. He wasn't in uniform now. He didn't swagger. He threw himself on Shabilian, sagging against him and clutching him in his arms. "Oh, Max," he exclaimed, with a shudder. "He wouldn't have her. He made her leave. He chose someone else."

Something was shining at the row of windows. One of the stewardesses cried, "Oh, look!" Maximilian disentangled himself from the grip of the boy and moved toward the glass. Outside, an aircraft was glittering in the sunlight. It was the double-hulled sea-plane. He saw Vittorio in the open cockpit. His goggles were atop his helmet. His scarf flew out behind him. Waving, flashing a smile of bravado, he gaily commenced looping the loop.

ALITALIA 607

Rough Weather

[2005: 1937]

1

Ding, ding, ding—and from the cluttered attic that is now my ruined hemisphere I drag up, *Goes the trolley.* Ding! Ding! Ding! again, right on cue. Now what's the rest of it? Dig through the junkyard: *Goes the bell!* But it's not the trolley that's sounding the warning; it's the pilot of our 767: rough weather ahead. Though now, high above the clouds, I don't feel a thing. We could be sitting on the tarmac. This could be my armchair at home. With my working ear, I hear the laggards snapping their seat belts shut. I've been dozing, I guess. That is how we older gentlemen spend our time. I sneak a glance at Leda. She's studying her script for the Dramat, a paperback of *Julius Caesar.* How pat! Apropos. The overthrow of the demigod. The murder of the tyrant.

Clang, clang, clang, that's how the song goes. How did this minnow get caught in the fishnet of my brain? Hell, it's got enough holes in it to drive ten trolleys through. Wait! I've got it! Judy

Garland. *Meet Me in St. Louis.* I saw it in Milan, in May, only a week, maybe two weeks, after old Mushroomy got hung up by the heels. Diamante, that was the name of the theater. The U.S. Army had requisitioned it. No wops allowed. Not even Partisan fighters. Not even the Brits. I snuck in, the way I used to do as a kid—into the Rosemary, the Hitching Post, the Dome. Somehow or other they'd found popcorn. Jesus Christ! Popcorn! My dead nose couldn't detect a skunk if one has been smuggled aboard this plane; but I swear I can smell that butter. The roasted kernels. The boots of the soldiers. The mustiness of the plush red seats. I stuffed the treat with both hands into my mouth. Technicolor! It made my head spin. I felt as if I'd been released from an Italian prison, a jailhouse in black-and-white. *Zing, zing, zing went my heartstrings.* America! Why did I leave you?

I am as ravenous now as I was then. I wonder if dog drool is dripping from my chin. A stewardess, in Alitalia green, a bit of a double chin, hair pulled back in a bun: here she comes, pushing a tray of snacks. Ah, the World's Fair! Ah, the Palace of Electricity! All around me, the soldiers were weeping. Swiping the back of their wrists, the cloth of their shirt cuffs, over their eyes. I, too, was overcome. I gulped in the depths of my sorrow. I hiccuped. The old Hollywood corn? No, no. There sat the loneliest man in the world.

A groan: am I, foolish old fellow, weeping now? The sigh comes again—not from me but from Leda, wrestling with her part.

"W-why are you c-c-carrying on? It's Shakespeare, darling. Not Stan-Stan-Stan: not Stanislavsky."

My granddaughter puts her thumb between the pages of the old Signet edition. She blinks, as if coming from a trance.

"Was I disturbing you? Oh, Max! It's such a hard part. I thought it would be easy. Sixty lines. Portia, the Constant Wife. But she's a nutcake. You should *see* the things she says—" Here she thrusts the dog-eared text before me. I note the stars of exclamation that, in red ink, she's strewn in the margins. "And what she *does!* It's weird. Stabs herself in the thigh, which, of course, is meant to be sexual, attacking her vagina. Then she kills herself by swallowing fire. *Swallowing fire!* Burning out her insides, destroying her womanhood. It's *inconceivable.* Don't look at me that way, Maxie. I know what you're thinking. How can poor little Leda—Ethical Culture, Fieldston, Yale—enter such a twisted mind? It ain't easy, pal! Even if half the girls in my class are self-mutilators. Either that or they are throwing up their guts after every meal. There's a problem, all right, but it's not because I can't relate to unhappy women."

"Too bad the Dramat can't do Noel C-C-Coward. How about Cole Porter? Wasn't he a Y-Yale man?"

"Don't you dare joke! Don't laugh at me. Burning the womb! I've got to understand that. Unimaginable. Never to have children."

"I'm n-not laughing, dear h-h-heart. It is a serious business. Why, if you wanted to p-p-p: *perform* this play in Italy, in the d-days when I was there, the Duce would have th-thrown you in jail."

"Oh, I don't want to hear his name. I know all about him. About my great aunt. About Amos. That Mussolini: scary!"

The sound I make, like dishwater disappearing, will have to do for a laugh. "He wasn't so b-bad. Once he banned *C-C-Caesar and Cleopatra.* You know? By Sh-Shaw? It wasn't because Caesar was a tyrant. Oh, no. It was because he was b-b-bald!"

Leda giggled. "Really? Is that true?"

"*E vero.* And then he turns around and shaves his h-head, so he would look *more* like the D-D-Dicator for Life."

"Ha-ha-ha! But why did he shave? *Wasn't* he bald? In all the pictures—"

"*Sì,* I AM BALD. IT IS BECAUSE I HAVE SUCH BIG BRAINS, THEY PUSH OUT ALL THE HAIRS."

I say this, stutterless, in the big voice of Mussolini. People look around. Breathless, exhausted, I slump back in my seat. The gong goes off again. This time I believe I can sense the frame of the aircraft give the slightest of shudders.

Leda leans toward me. "Maxie? Did you feel that?"

Instead of replying, I concentrate on firing up the pistons in my left-side lobe, which by some hidden spring allows my right hand to rise. I fumble at my breast pocket. "Here," I say. "F-forget about Shakespeare. You can finish m-m-memorizing this." I draw out, I hand over, the pages of my address. *Il Presidente del Consiglio dei Ministri* and all the rest.

Leda holds it between two fingers. "What is this? Your speech?"

"*Your* speech. You are the one who is g-going to give it."

"Me? Oh, no. Only if you have trouble. I am just going to turn the pages. You know, like for a pianist."

"Listen to me. I *am* having trouble. I can't even ask that stew-stewardess for p-p-p. For p-p-p. Wait. Let me. *Peanuts!* What a travesty."

"No, no, Maxie dear. It's an honor. A great honor. But not in that crowd. Not with those people. I can't."

"*Can't?* What do you m-mean, *can't?*" I give way to the spasm of irritation. "You-you-you are an actress. So act! You are honoring your own ancestor. A great man. You don't even h-h-have to pretend."

"I know what you think. You think I'm a dumb blonde. An actress. But I know history. I certainly know *this* history. *She'll* be there, won't she? What's her name? Mussolini's granddaughter. Alessandra. And who am I? The great-granddaughter. Of who? Okay, *whom?* A traitor. And Mussolini. He's a hero all over again. He Who Made Us Great. That's why they've elected her to Parliament. They elected this Berlusconi—"

"Burly-crony."

"It's not funny! He's a Fascist. He doesn't need thugs. He doesn't need castor oil. He owns every television station in the country. He's got more power than Mussolini ever had."

"You've got things m-mixed up. First of all, A.P. He was no traitor. N-not in Italy. He's a hero."

"Yes, and besides, she's famous. This Alessandra. A senator in parliament."

"D-don't worry. I used to know her father. Romano. The jazz pianist." Dig in the junk pile: ah, here is the little boy with his rubber ball, the toy helicopter, crouching under the aluminum piano. "Do you know who—s-s-sorry, *whom*—he married?"

"My God, Maxie. Romano! Is *he* going to be there? Mussolini's son! Aria, aunt Aria: Wasn't she supposed to marry his brother? Wasn't it all decided? Then wouldn't I be part of that family? It's like something *Greek*. Like a curse."

"L-let me finish, okay? R-romano married Sophia Loren's sister. She might be there. Speaking of actresses."

Leda stares back at me, entirely blank. I have to remind myself of all the things she does not know. The World Wars. The Vietnamese War. Jack Kennedy. Hepburn. Olivier. Picasso might as well be Titian. Frank Lloyd Wright. Brando, even. Hell, LBJ. We might, the two of us, inhabit different planets. But I see that she is glancing down at the speech. The airplane, back in the tail, gives another quiver. She looks up.

"It's not easy, Maxie, being who I am. Did that ever occur to you? Even if he were just a great man, an architect, it would be hard enough. But Amos Prince! Tell me something, will you? Tell me the truth? I know he died in 1982. I know it was at the end of the year. Did he know I even existed?"

It is, as it happens, a question I can answer. Nina and I sent the photo. Of the fuzzy-haired infant. The duckling. Prince got it, all right, first class to Gubbio. "Yes, darling. You have my w-w-word. He knew he had a g-great-granddaughter. He knew that you had been born."

For six straight days in January the temperature never rose above zero degrees centigrade. No one could remember such a phenomenon. Had the British, the enforcer of worldwide sanctions, punished sunny Italy by plugging the Straits of Gibraltar? Or had the Ethiopians, praying to Ra, persuaded the sun god to withhold his favors? The Tiber had a crust of ice so thick that thousands of Romans were able to careen across it in their moustaches and homemade skates.

Thousands more streamed to the Circus Maximus. Where were they going? To see how this American was going to build a monument five thousand feet into the sky when it was impossible to dig a single meter into the frozen ground. Even if the excavation could be completed, to what would the building be anchored? Hadn't the whole world learned from the example of Pisa what was bound to occur unless one built on the one thing that Rome could not offer—a foundation of solid rock? In other words, those who were gathering now in this ancient oblong were filled with the same mood of exuberant malice as those who had once thronged to the Colosseum. They wanted a beheading, not a horse race.

The head they were after—goateed, un-eyebrowed, the white thatch of his hair hidden by an unseasonable Panama hat—belonged to Amos Prince. He stood well off, near a team of six steaming horses that made the spectators think they had come to a chariot race after all. It occurred to me, bundled into three sweaters, that there were now more people at this site than at any time since it had fallen into ruins in the fourth century A.D. They sat on both sides of the U-shaped track. Mussolini and his entourage had taken over the Palentine embankment, while behind them were assembled the whole cast of familiar characters: Pius XI and his bespectacled papal secretary; the little King in his riding boots and ribbons; Ciano, Ribbentrop, Farinacci; Bruno, the young airman, sat next to Aria, who, to my sorrow, was pulling on the five plump fingers he dangled over her shoulder. From each of the thousands of mouths rose little clouds of warm mist, like taunting white handkerchiefs at a sporting event.

There were no speeches. There was no ceremony. Prince, at the open, river end of the U, nodded his head, so that the cigarette at the tip of the holder he clenched in his teeth wig-wagged in the air. In response, the teams of horses, all hitched together, strained forward, their iron-clad hooves slipping over the surface of the frozen ground.

They were pulling, or attempting to pull, the Ethiopian obelisk. It lay on a series of rubber-wheeled caissons, blunt end forward. For a full moment the half-dozen horses pawed and snorted and lunged, to no effect. The mass of stone did not budge. The crowd hooted, like Spaniards taunting a recalcitrant bull. The stallions hurled themselves forward again, until the windblown spittle covered their flanks, black as the shirts of the Fascists. Still the great needle remained unmoving, as if the pattern of animals and eyes that covered its surface had cast a spell of immobility. Then Prince settled a shoulder beneath the carved stone; with that small increase of force, the series of wheels, each with a red hub at the center of its whitewalls, began to turn. The charioteer turned toward the seat of the Dictator.

"It's just basic physiques," he declared. "The power of I-urge-ya."

The caravan crept up the near, or Aventine, side of the Circus. When the lead horses finally reached the closed end, they swung leftward along the circumference of the arc and lumbered along in front of the dignitaries and their guests. It took them a full twenty minutes to reach the western exit, where they turned and began coming back, inside the track they'd already made. On and on went the laboring steeds, up one side of the arena and down the other, slowly, methodically, like plowhorses preparing the furrows for next year's crop.

"*Basta!*" some brave soul shouted out. "It's freezing! We'll be here all night."

Night indeed fell. The row of streetlamps along the Via dei Cerchi came on, lighting up the hoarfrost spread like lace over the untrampled ground. Suddenly Prince strode forward, into the path of the oncoming caissons. The stele shuddered to a halt. "Did you see? Did you?" the architect called. Then, in words that echoed those of Italy's ancient astronomer, he cried, "*Si muove!* It moves!"

There wasn't, from anywhere in the dark stadium, a sound. In the obscurity the tip of the American's cigarette pulsed and glowed. The Duce, pale-faced beneath his black, tasseled kepi, leaned forward. He stared through the gloom to where the stele lay trembling. Trembling? A monument of a hundred and sixty tons? I could hardly believe my own eyes. I removed my spectacles, wiped them, and placed them back on my nose. A gasp went up from the assemblage. I gasped too. We all saw how the tip of the obelisk ducked a palpable inch toward the ground.

"We build here." Prince calmly uttered the words. "We go all the way down where it's meatier."

My mind was spinning. Was this some kind of trick? An hallucination? Hypnosis? The same thing, I recalled, had happened during the triumphal parade. That was when, as in Vespasian's time, a comet had passed overhead. Was this obelisk nothing but a gigantic dowsing rod, a blown-up version of the twig customarily used to find water but now responding to the iron pyrites in a long-buried meteor?

Before my eyes I saw the monument twitch again.

Il Duce, gaping, half rose. "*Un miracolo,*" he murmured.

Those nearby echoed, "*Un miracolo, un miracolo.*" The words spread from row to row throughout the stadium.

Immediately the teams of horses plunged forward against their traces, pulling the monolith off toward the river end of the Circus. Through that same opening there came a rumble and roar. A moment later a huge diesel tractor came lurching forward. Smoke belched from its vertical exhaust. Its headlights, drunkenly crisscrossed, stabbed now upward, at the vault of the sky, now down at the rutted ground. Around it danced the shadows of men, black men, the same vanquished Abyssinians who had been paraded up the Via dei Trionfi some months before. Stick-thin and clothed in blankets, they ran forward with two-headed picks in their hands.

With a whoop these scarecrows hurled themselves at the magical spot on the ground, attacking it with their tools. The crowd shouted encouragement.

"*Coraggio!*"

"*Più forza!*"

"*Ancora di più!*"

Alas, to no avail. The picks rebounded from the frozen soil; the shafts of the shovels and spades broke in two; the blades went skittering. Then the tractor turned, swiveling so that the machinery at its rear was centered over the target. Now the engine grunted and growled and the smoke poured upward like the black clouds from a steamship's funnel. With a high-pitched screech the drill bit spun on top of the crust of earth. A cheer went up from the multitude. No one wanted to abandon his seat now. They were determined to see what was going to happen.

The wait was not long. Only the top ten centimeters of the ground were frozen. In a few minutes the shrieking noise was replaced by a low, effortless buzz. Now the Africans scurried about among suspended sections of pipe, attaching each new length to the one that had just burrowed through the pumice and ash that held, as rock holds fossils, the broken ruins of the old civilization. At one point water shot skyward, so that the workers slid on an instant layer of ice. Still the drill swiftly sank, segment after segment, until at last it stuck fast in bedrock. The tractor coughed, as if something had lodged in its throat; then it reversed its gears, bringing the long snake of pipe to the surface, where it fell in hollow pieces. At last the bit rose from the hole, glowing like Prince's cigarette. Prince himself did little more than glance at the chunk of red-hot metal.

"*Signori*," he declared. "A star is borne."

A shout went up from both sides of the arena. Those who had been standing fell to their knees. Others raised their hands in prayer.

"*Una Stella!*"

"*Un miracolo del cielo!*"

"*Lui è un dio!*"

At this blasphemy Pius, in white, rose from his chair. So did Pacelli, in his cardinal's purple and red. The short, stocky Pope was waving his arms in anger. The tall secretary of state bowed his head in resignation.

But it was left to a much younger man to take action. He leaped from the stands and ran onto the stadium grounds.

"Frankie!" That cry came from Nina, his sister.

It was indeed Prince's son, hatless, round-headed, with his breath coming in puffs from his mouth.

"Come back!" Nina shouted. "Max! You, Maxie! Stop him!"

I heard her voice, but what was it she wanted me to do? I trotted toward where Franklin stood, near the spent diesel engine. But before I arrived he began to shout. "You! Romans! Good people! Do not be fooled. Look! Do you see what I have in my hand?"

I recognized the object at once. Long before, on a hot summer day, Prince and I had walked the length of the Circus Maximus, up one side and down the other, until the compass I held started to spin. I had no doubt that the magnetic needle was moving in the same crazed circles now.

"You see?" Franklin cried. "It is a trick. There is no miracle. He knew it was there all the time!"

I glanced up at the rows of seats. Bruno was shaking his fist at the boy. Aria had buried her face in her hands. Nina stared back at me, as if she thought I should do something to stop the scandal. I moved to Franklin. I took his arm. But he twisted aside, shouting still:

"A miracle worker? A god? He is a fraud!"

Now Amos Prince came loping toward us. Frankie, in response, stepped away. His eyes were wide and his mouth twisted downward in a grimace of fear. As it happened, he had no cause for apprehension. The architect was not heading toward where his son now cowered behind the ticking tractor. He veered to the mounds of earth that surrounded the excavation. All eyes were on him, though I do not think anyone in that great assemblage had the least idea of what I suddenly realized he was about to do. It had always been the stuff of legend. But the moment he spread his legs and reached for the vent of his trousers I knew that what I had so often heard was no myth.

The arc of his urine fell steaming into the mouth of the sixty-foot chasm. Il Duce was not to be outdone. He clambered over the barrier in front of the grandstand and walked on his bow legs to the spot. He raised the cliff-edge of his jaw as he fumbled with the buttons of his britches. What emerged was as thick as a forearm, with a helmet on the end like a German soldier's. His stream splashed noisily on the high rim before dropping like a rope into the depths. Thus did patron and artist, Missile-peenie and Prince, consecrate with this downpour the great tower to come.

2

What a time to think of peeing! The seat belt sign is on. No one is allowed to stand. Even if it weren't, I'm damned if I will allow Leda to prop me up in the aisle. I'll hold it all the way to Rome if I have to. I glance at my granddaughter. She looks more like Aria than ever, her face as pale as the cover of the paperback she holds in her hands. Her nostrils, like a rabbit's, like her great-aunt's, are reddened and quivering. She turns toward me. Her eyes, my eyes, incongruously black, are wide with fear.

"Did you feel that?" she asks. "That shaking?"

"D-don't worry," I tell her. "These planes are engineered for stress. El-El-El: hell! *Elephants* could walk on our wings."

Instantly, to rebuke me, the wind takes us upward on an elevator ride, then throws us willfully down. There is a moaning sound, perhaps from the stressed metal of the plane itself. I see, through the window, the wingtip light jerk in mindless semaphores. Then we straighten out, as if nothing has happened.

My right sleeve is yanked up my arm, which means that Leda is pulling on the left one. She's saying something inaudible beside me. The sight of her lips moving, her tongue moving, gives me a chill: Aria reborn! I remember the play she is reading. Didn't Caesar go to his death because the words of warning were whispered into *his* deaf ear? Then I hear her:

"Oh! Oh! Maxie! I knew this flight was cursed. I *knew* it. Are we going to die?"

Without a stutter—a sign that I am lying?—I say, "No it's just a hole in the air. You know, sweetheart, like a hurricane's eye."

Leda: "Then why are you crying?"

"Wh-wh-what are you talking about?"

But I know. I don't have to feel the tears on my cheeks. It *was* me, old Maxie, who had groaned before. I'm on a crowded airplane; I could as easily be with the G.I.s in that theater, the Diamante. Weeping from loneliness. Not just loneliness. Truth to tell, from shame. I raise my right hand, to push up my glasses, to get at my eyes.

"See? You won't tell me. Something is wrong. We're going to crash."

I don't answer. I don't tell her how I fear going back to the scene of the crime. How I'm little better than a war criminal myself. Instead, a new series of names come floating up, squeezing into the space between my spectacles and my eyes: *Malachi. Ilse. Anja. Bernät.* And more: *Leon. Leopold. Vida. Ota. Jules.*

At that moment the head of Little Miss Marker pops up over the seat back in front of us. Her milk teeth are gleaming. The coils of her curls bounce. "Mister, are you sad? Don't be! I thought of a joke."

I peer through the thick glass of my spectacles to bring her into focus. "T-tell it."

"What's the difference between a girl and a boy?"

"I d-d-don't know," I answer. "What?"

"They're both kids!"

Leda bursts into a peal of laughter. "Oh, my God! Oh, that's *wonderful!*"

The Little Princess pouts. "I didn't tell *you*. I told *him*. So he won't be sad."

"And it w-worked. Look, Bright Eyes. No more t-t-tears!"

"That's because I'm a cheerer-upper. Nothing bad happens to people if I'm around."

"I'm g-g-g—" I want to say I'm glad to hear it, but before the words can get around the obstruction, she's gone.

Leda says, "What's the difference between a snowman and a snowwoman? Do you remember that? From when I was her age?"

Oddly, I do, though as Rosellen is always happy to point out, there are times I can't find the newspaper when I am holding the damned thing in my hand.. "Sn-sn-sn—"

"Right! *Snowballs!* How brave of me! I thought I was being risqué!"

"Ha! Look. You're b-blushing now."

True. Two small dots, doll's dots, have come out on her cheeks, just as they did when she first dared tell me the joke.

Total recall: a yellow dress with blue bows on her shoulders. A summer dress for a summer day. Light bounding through the open windows; air blowing in too. The thirteenth-floor view of the Hudson: boats and barges, the treetops on this side, the far-off Palisades. The winter before, Malcolm, our son, had died in his automobile. Run off the road. Into a Merritt Parkway tree. His widow, a busy woman, often dropped Leda off to stay with her grandparents. I worry about the little girl's perch at the bank of windows. Before I can say anything, Rosellen wheels out Nina, half-hairless, fumbling first with the green wrapper, then the silver foil.

Here, sweetie. For you. Doublemint gum!

Leda hops from her crow's nest above Riverside Drive, Riverside Park, and takes the sugary stick from her grandmother's fingers. She folds it, puts it into her mouth, dutifully chews.

What do you say to Nana-Nina? asks Rosellen.

That's when her cheeks turn bright red. Meaning she has made up her mind: out in a rush comes the query about the unseasonable snowmen. It occurs to me now, as it has not before, that she too wanted to be a cheerer-upper, though the spectacle of Nina, with her head drooping, a spider's thread of spittle stretching from chin to shoulder, made her task almost superhuman.

"Am I? Blushing? Really?"

My mistake: I thought that in the time it took the memory capsule to burst in my brain, our 767 might have crossed half the Atlantic; in fact, we've flown—what? In these two seconds? Not even a mile. Well, further than that: maybe we've covered only a moment or two of the great circle's arc; but we've also leaped back five thousand days, to the little girl, the daring girl—*Snowballs!*—on the thirteenth floor. *Fourteenth*, I should say, since the co-op board, of which I used to be a member, also believed in curses.

It took the better part of a month to complete the excavation. Eventually an enormous ditch, some eighty feet deep and stretching thirty-five by twenty-five meters, cut across the surface of the ancient arena. The crowd never left the site—that is, they returned in growing numbers to gape from the top of the earthworks that lined both sides of the Circus. A row of Carabinieri had to be installed when the shaft neared the buried planet. Everyone was afraid a mob would rush the field the way spectators did at soccer matches or, for all any one knew, as the Romans had when the winning chariot crossed the finish line.

At last the gangs of Ethiopians reached the cold, colorless surface of the bedrock. They stopped their work, staring in fascination, as if they had in their imaginations taken the long journey back to the Mesozoic era, the age of clams, or to the bird-filled Paleocene, out of whose skies the great rock had tumbled. Standing at the site, staring with them, I could not help but wonder if this was why, at the dedication of the Titus Arch, Josephus and other historians reported the flash of so many comets. Was it possible that the lump of ore had attracted the other planetoids, as it had drawn the flaming star over our heads when we witnessed the mock execution of the Lion of Judah?

With no warning something clapped me on the shoulder. I reeled to the very lip of the chasm. A voice boomed over me: "Haw! Haw! I told 'em. And there it is! Our very own ass-turd-void!"

The arena soon came to look like any construction site: cement mixers lined the edge of the pit, and the wet slurry slid down the chutes to harden around the steel rods that had been trucked down from the foundry high up on Montespaccato. That was where the real show was taking place. The smokestacks, working overtime, soon created a permanent haze that hung over the city and that, in darkness, reflected the glow of the open forges. The Mussolini Works, that's what everyone called the plant—either that or *Il Vulcano*, after the biblical model of the cloud by day and the fire by night.

What no one could guess—after all, its grounds were enclosed by electrified wire and the roads that circled the plateau were patrolled by armed guards—was what the foundry produced. Steel rods? Without doubt, though these could have been secured from any number of sources, in spite of the international embargo. At the end of February, however, two enormous wooden crates, each like a pair of wings, or the V-shaped pasta the Romans called *maltagliati*, were loaded one on top of the other onto a shallow barge at the Ponte di Ferro. They smashed through what was left of the ice and floated all the way to the ruins of the twin temples that sat on the riverbank, just fifty meters from the open end of the Circus.

On site the crates were sawed open, releasing mounds of sawdust and excelsior that protected the huge chunks of metal that had nested within. Then each of the curved planes was lowered into the pit, facing one another, so as to complete a gigantic ellipse that was quickly joined at the vertical seams. A second barge brought two other sections, each in its *maltagliato*, and these in turn were set atop the anchored plates, welded, and secured against the walls of the pit by a fresh paste of cement. More loads followed, so that in the course of a few weeks a great steel funnel rose first to ground level and then, amazingly, began to step even higher, into the unresisting air.

Now there was a new fire by night—the fountain of sparks that flew from where the goggled metalworkers joined the ascending planes. This shaft would eventually be the core of the monument— a monument that, because each new section was designed to be imperceptibly narrower than the one below it, would continuously taper as it rose toward the clouds. Already the laborers who gathered below had to crane mightily to see the top. To them the black ellipse looked less like a ship's funnel than the ship itself, a black, gleaming prow that created the illusion of steaming forward and backward, east to the Baths of Caracalla and west to the Tiber, at one and the same time.

One morning, a spring-like morning, with the last icicles falling in chime notes from the nearby eaves, Aria opened my cellar door and leaned so far over my sleeping body that I could feel her warm breath against my cheek.

"Get up, Maximilian," she whispered. "This is the day."

I didn't want to get up. I wanted to go on sleeping. What might happen next in this dream, this fable of beauty and beast? Anything! Everything!

Then I opened my eyes. Nina was the one leaning over me. "Maxie! Get a taxi!" she exclaimed. "We're leaving in five minutes."

Spindle-legged, in boxer shorts, I rolled from my pallet and threw water over my face. I got into pants. I pulled one sweater over the other. Upstairs, outdoors, Amos was pacing the intersection. His daughters were already inside our old Fiat Berline. The architect was pale. Even his nicotined beard seemed leached of color. I got into the back; he slid onto the seat in front, next to the fat-necked party member who had long since become our driver. Off we went, making left turns, right turns, *a sinistra*, *a destra*, toward the construction site.

We didn't get far. Renato, the driver, swerved and halted. A crowd filled the Via del Portico. The Berline retreated, shifted its gears, and roared the wrong way down the Via Progresso. But the crowds, pouring from shop fronts, from the courtyards of the shuttered apartments, blocked that route too. The red-faced driver struck the horn with the meat of his palm. He gunned the motor and tried to force his way through. But the masses of people grew more dense, more compact. Between two stuccoed buildings I caught a glimpse of the river. Prince did too.

"Get out," he commanded. "We'll walk the embankment."

We abandoned the Fiat and wound our way to the Tiber, coming out at last near the Ponte Fabrizio. The bridge was lined with people. It looked as if, down on the Isola, all the patients from the Ospedale Fatebenefratelli had been let out of the wards. Everybody was looking up, open-mouthed. They were pointing skyward too. Reflexively we threw our heads back. There was nothing to see. The blue morning sky was smeared by mist and what had become the habitual smoky haze. Sea gulls slipped sideways, keeping an eye out. Swallows too.

"What are they looking at, Papa?" Nina asked. "What do they see?"

Prince, his eyes shaded by his hat brim, peered upward. His lips were curled back in a grimace, showing his tobacco-tinted teeth. "Wait. A moment more."

But before that moment was up, the crowds on the far side of the river began a low-throated murmur, oddly like the rumble of a tram car. *Olo-olo-olo*, I heard, and saw a thousand fingers pointing directly at me—no, directly over my head. Then the cry was picked up by those who packed the island: *olo-olo-olo*. Still nothing appeared in the smudge of empty sky.

Now a gasp, a sigh, began on our own embankment, and the rolling O's, like some Alpine cry, broke out on every side. Suddenly, above the dome of the Main Synagogue, the rim of a huge black disk hove into view. *Olo-olo: Colosseo!* Yes, it was as if the Colosseum had risen from its foundations a little more than a mile to the east and was now floating above us. The rest of the vast circle soared over the dome top. The great ring filled the heavens—not a ring, precisely, but an oval, an ellipse, with gleaming wires that stretched from the circumference to a hub at the center. The dimensions, firm in my head, were indeed much like those of the Colosseum, 190 by 160 meters, but the effect was of an unimaginably outsized bicycle wheel, one that had been squashed in some accident but was still held together by a hundred shining spokes. *Colosseo, Colosseo*, the crowd contined to chant, staring upward, though not a soul among them thought that this was any more likely to be the ancient monument than a flying saucer from Mars.

For a moment, none of us moved. We watched spellbound as the huge disc passed overhead. Then the odd, ululating cry died out, though we could hear it picked up and passed along, like a roundelay, as the enormous form followed the course of the river. In the new silence I could hear another sound, a distant drone. I looked higher. *Was* this an invasion from space? *Had* the universe lost its bearings? High in the sky, above the layer of soot and smoke, hung a dozen orbiting moons. Moons? Blimps! Balloons! Six-ten-twelve, fourteen in all. They floated high and pale in the sky, though everyone could hear the pulse and groan of their engines and see, stretched from the bottom of each, the taut cable that held up what I knew to be the first three stories of *La Vittoria*, the Monument of Mussolini.

At the Circus Maximus all was chaos. The grounds of the old racetrack were littered with equipment. The crowds, trotting along beneath the apparition, flowed over the earthworks and mingled with the workers. Our little party elbowed its way past Santa Maria in Cosmedin and into the stadium, above which the great horizontal wheel was already hanging, some two hundred feet in the air.

Minute after minute went by. The huge oval did not seem to move so much as an inch. How, I wondered, would those in the far-off blimps, whose movements would have to be precisely coordinated, know when to begin? I looked to where Amos Prince was standing a few yards from the core; I wanted to see if he intended to give a signal, then realized that from the perspective of those in the soft-skinned airships, the architect was nothing more than one light-colored dot among a thousand dark ones. Prince, in any case, was not peering skyward; his gaze was directed across the arena to a small wooded shed at the closed, eastern end of the Circus. I noticed two things at once—the antenna on the shingled roof and the black-coated man at the window. Marconi! Just then another man, heavy-set and sweating, ran to the shed and stepped inside. Renato! Our driver. It was to the two of them, the famed inventor and his assistant, that Prince now nodded.

Instantly, and from a great distance, there came a subtle hissing: the venting of hydrogen gas. The sound grew louder, and then—I could not help but think of a pneumatic tire deflating—the ring began to descend. A cry, more like a whimper, came up from the crowd, many of whom began to cross themselves, as if what they saw were a vision from the Old Testament, or from Revelation. Slowly, yet perceptibly, at what I guessed to be a foot every few seconds, the wheel dropped down. Ten minutes ticked by: the rim halved the distance to the ground; soon it halved that. The people became uneasy. The hissing noise, accompanied now by a piercing shriek as the gas rushed over the opened metal valves, was deafening. Suddenly, the entire crowd was in motion. There was a pell-mell rush, a stampede, as the shadow of the spokes and the shadow of the rim fell over the frightened people, like the bars of a gigantic cage.

The axis of the core ran east and west; the axis of the descending structure was aligned north and south. That meant that the hub of the wheel was turned at right angles to the circumference, like a drawing of an atom or the pupil in a cat's eye. The hissing stopped. There was a hollow clang, a clank, as the hub dropped over the vertical spike. The last of the crowd had escaped from the penumbra of the falling planet. Only Prince stood rooted. Ringing now like a gold piece, the whole of the satellite moved down the shaft, lower, lower still, until, just as it had been engineered to do, it halted twenty-eight feet above the floor of the stadium and twenty-one feet nine inches above the Panama hat of the man who had conceived it.

For an instant it rested there, with a perceptible wobble, or shudder, moving from end to end. Then, simultaneously, the fourteen airships released the steel cables from their underbellies and leaped upward; it was as if fourteen boys had opened their hands, causing their freed balloons to jerk dizzyingly into the sky.

I hardly knew where to look: at Prince, standing with folded arms beneath the first three stories of what would eventually be a five-hundred-story building; at the twelve meters of those joined floors, as they continued to tremble with what might have been the final oscillations of a dropped coin; or at the blimps, which had finally reached equilibrium in the atmosphere. As I watched the last, one of the airships detached itself from the others and with a roar of its engines made a wide, descending circle. It looped well out over the Palatine, crossed the river and then, still dropping, recrossed it, heading toward us at what was ultimately little more than a flagpole's height above the arena's earthen sides. When it was directly over-head a window opened at the side of the gondola, and a man in a leather helmet leaned outside.

Now Aria took out her handkerchief and waved it over her head. I saw her lips form, repeatedly, the word *Bruno*. And I could read them when they said, *Tesoro mio!* My treasure.

Il figlio di Mussolini waved back, releasing his white flying scarf with such dexterity that it snaked through the air and fell coiled at his mistress's feet. Then the engine roared, louder than ever, and the blimp swept back up to the sky, where the rest of the fleet was docilely waiting, like a herd of cows that were lighter than air.

3

This is no cow we're in; it's certainly not lighter than air. Still, jet planes are designed to fly above the weather. No cumulonimbus stretches as high as our thirty-seven thousand feet. I used to know meteorology. I taught myself to be an expert on winds. What's the point of modesty? I'm the one who persuaded A.P. to bunch the stories in threes and leave a gap between each set all the way to the top; yes, and to place the axis of the core at right angles to that of the building itself, so that the prevailing sea breezes from the west would slip over the former's aerodynamic ellipse, and the real storms, which thundered down out of the north, would never strike the mass of the structure broadside. Or so went the theory. I had, nonethe-less, my doubts. So did Prince. We spent endless hours trying to figure out how to lubricate the hubs; we wanted to set them into grooves in the core, so that the stories would all turn in such a manner that the point of the prow would perpetually face into the teeth of any wind. The monument would be a weather vane. It turned out that the ball bearings would use up more grease each month than the Italian army had expended through the entire Ethiopian campaign. *La Vittoria*, fixed in place, would have to take its chances.

And Alitalia 607? What are the odds on us? Not so hot. Oh, everything seems normal enough. No more roller coaster rides. Our flight path is steady. The crew is starting to cook our dinner. *Pastina in brodo, risotto con funghi,* and—what is the main course on the menu? Let's see: *Tonno.* And some kind of scaloppine. Ah, the aromas must be delectable, delicious—or they would be, if I had any sense of smell.

The trouble is, the sign is still on, the one that forbids us to unbuckle. Worse, what are these wiggles and wobbles on the outside pane of the window glass? Above the weather? We're under it, in every sense of the phrase. Aha! A lightning flash, off in the coils of the clouds. Maybe only a cripple can sense this: we're yawing, off angle, like a man who has ducked his head into the blast of wind. Diagnosis, doctor? Ice on the wings.

"Maxie, I want you to tell me the truth. That was lightning. I saw it. And—can't you feel it? I can. We're going down. Always going down."

In turning toward me, Leda's hair ripples and falls over her forehead in the peek-a-boo style of—uh, oh: here comes Uncle Al. What the hell was her name? I used to see her in Rome. At the Cinema Quirinetta. They showed American films. Everybody spitting sunflower seeds. The boys and girls kissing. Ah! Aha! Veronica Lake.

"Would they be c-c-cooking our dinner if we were in trouble? It's just that you've never—"

Damn: Leda's not listening. She is digging in her handbag, taking out a tissue. Has she started crying?

"Silly Maxie," she says. "Don't worry, my baby. Don't. Please don't. Remember? The elephants? We're safe. I know we are. Here. Isn't this a pretty handkerchief? I'll do it. Let me."

Baby! Pretty handkerchief! What next for grandpa? A rubber duck? Oh, here's Curly Top. Watching over her seat back. Can't say I blame her. What a cascade. Niagara Falls. It's got nothing to do with our 767. The Boeing people know what they're doing. Was it the movie theater? Not the Quirinetta. The Diamante. That might have been the last time I let myself give way to tears.

Oh, Christ. My shirt is soaked. And I don't feel a thing, any more than the faucet feels the gush once someone has turned the tap. Apparently it won't stop. The pretty handkerchief is drenched. So are my pants. So is the cover of A.P.'s notebook. Lord, here comes the stewardess. The one with the bun. The breasts. She looks like she wants to pick up her *povero bambino.* Instead she tucks, under my chin, a linen napkin; she lifts my thick lenses from my beak of a nose and folds them into my pocket.

True enough, that day in Milano: I did not know a soul in the world. The Douche, gone. A.P., taken away. Aria, missing. And the Jews? Where were my Jews? *Have yourself a merry little Christmas.* Margaret O'Brien. But it wasn't Christmas; it was springtime. This fit won't stop. The liquid is pouring out, like the contents of a cracked aquarium. My eyeballs, like a couple of carp, are going to be swept out of their sockets. *Sasha. Renata. Yamin. Éliane.*

Am I saying these names out loud? If not, why are the other passengers starting to turn around? The next thing I know the pilot will call out on the intercom, *Prego, signori: c'è un medico a bordo?* And if there is, what will he do? Sing a lullaby to this grown-up infant? Or just give me a shot?

"Mister. Hello, mister," says, in English, a voice from out of the blue. It's Heidi herself. "What is the best time to see the dentist?" Then, rushing, not waiting for an answer: "Tooth-hurty!"

No one laughs. The chin of the Little Princess starts to quaver, as if she might start to shed tears herself.

"Mister, why are you crying? Why, Mister?"

Geörgy. Sofrontja. Szymon. Lilianan.

Oh, Dimples. If only you knew!

SPIRAL NOTEBOOK

On Trial

[1982: 1946]

I came back to America on a plane. First time I flew in my life. Also last. I suppose one night on the *Hindenburg*, above the Swiss Alps, does not count. American army picked me up in a jeep. Drove me all the way from Pisa to Rome. I kept my eyes shut in case *La Vittoria* was still there—and in case it wasn't. Saw it anyhow; my eyelids might have been penny postcards, each with a color photo, *Souvenir of Italy*. How real! Every detail. A stereoscopic effect. Wasn't on the Zeppelin when it crashed. Might as well have been. I was the biggest victim. Would have finished the tower, if it hadn't burned. Be a mile high in the sky.

Didn't open them, my eyelids, until we were well out over the Atlantic. First thing I saw was the headline of the—*Herald Tribune*, was it? *Stars and Stripes?* This damned headache! Like an ax blade. Splits me in two. One of those papers, folded on the lap of GI Joe. *Truman Sends Envoy to Paris to Meet de Gaulle.* Funny, I remember every word. I turned to the soldier in the seat beside me: "Who is this Truman? Is his name Warren Gamaliel?"

What a look. Like a man staring at an animal. "Where you been, bub, all last year? In a hole? That's the president. Harry Truman." Ah, the light that came over me. The warmth of the light of day. To hide my emotion I turned to the window. What did I say? Banalities: *Look at that. Isn't that amazing? Takes my breath away.* Silly soldier boy: he thought I was marveling at the sight of the clouds, the sunlight glittering, the blue of the sea. Oh, no! No, no, no! It wasn't the splendor of nature. The old man was dead. The old man was in the ground. No wonder they put me on an airplane. No wonder they were sending me home. They wanted me to build a monument to FDR!

Yes, I was in a hole. A bear, an old grizzly, dumb enough to hibernate all spring and summer and fall. Not that I was sleeping, not with the floodlights. Then, when they dragged me from my den in winter, they threw me in a hole again. The District of Columbia jail. It dawned on old Amos that they had not brought me across the ocean to build a monument to the hero of World War Two. No. It was to face the music. The judge, Bernard A. Katz, like in some allegorical farce, was a hawk-nosed Jew. No bail. Couldn't be my own lawyer either. Charges too serious for that.

And what might these be? That yours truly,

a citizen of the U.S.A., and owing allegiance to that country, did knowingly, intentionally, willfully, unlawfully, feloniously, traitorously and treasonably *blah, blah, blah,* adhere to the enemies of the United States, to wit, the Kingdom of Italy and its military allies, *and babble, burble, booble,* for the purpose of giving aid and comfort to said enemies, *bibble, bumble, bobble,* and did in the presence of one R. Giovagnoli and X to be disclosed, *blip, bloop, blop,* on or about December 11, 1941, and on or about July 19, July 22, 23, and 24, 1943, and on or about October 15th of that same

year 1943, *qua, quo, qui, quack quack quack,* speak into a microphone in Rome, Italy, and *fibble, furble, flabble,* cause racial preju-
dice and distrust of the government of the U.S.A., stating that
Mussolini and Hitler are your true leaders and *popsie, poopsie, piffle*
thus acted contrary to his duty of allegiance to the U.S.A. and
toodle, twaddle, twiddle against the peace and dignity of the *Yooooo
Nutty Hates.*

In plain English, treason.

Who the hell was Signor Giovagnoli? Never heard of the fellow. How come he heard of me? I looked around the courtroom.
No one in the family section except for Odaline, weeping, with
wattles, you never would guess she'd been a world-class dancer,
hopped around for Diaghilev, was a swan, a Cinderella, for the
Ballets Russes. Nina beside her, also in tears, hair sticking out as
usual, like the cartoon character with a finger in a socket. Who
else? Seedy government prosecutors, three of them, and a gaggle
of reporters from the American press. Mothers never told them
not to chew gum.

Aha! The back of the room. There sat a familiar figure. Fat
jowls. Hair in a horseshoe around a dented scalp. Turning and turning the brim of his hat. Renato! Took us all over town in our Fiat
Berline. Meat of his hand on the horn. He was also Marconi's assistant. Monitored the radio waves inside the tar-paper shack. Why,
what an ass is Amos! I figured Gianna for the spy. She sure couldn't
cook! Renato, all along. Maybe a double spy too. What did they pay
him? A sawbuck? A grand?

"That's him," I said to my lawyer. "Giovagnoli. Their witness."

Mosk, balding, in black: "We don't need to worry about him.
It takes two witnesses in a trial for treason. It's in the Constitu-

tion. Two eye-witnesses. That *X* means they haven't got their second man. I'm going to move for dismissal. In ten minutes you'll be free."

Clever Penguin! The only other possible witness was Nina. Even if she were willing to say she'd seen me at the microphone, she wouldn't be allowed. Not a wife against a husband. Not a daughter against dear old dad.

Mosk rose to his feet. Before he could speak, someone else stood up too. He was so short he'd been invisible behind the padded shoulders of the prosecuting attorneys, and their thick necks and bowling-ball heads. Seeing him upright, you could only make out the top two buttons of his shirt and, a new touch, his bow tie, his poorly shaved face, the mop of his hair. Maximilian. I had not seen him since Milan, when they hauled the Doozy up by the heels. He looked, at the Piazzale Loreto, right by me, through me, as if I hadn't been standing there at all. He was staring now. His black eyes magnified in the black spectacle frames. A half inch of glass. Not saying a word. Poor old Mussolini. Dripping like a dolphin, but not from seawater. Not from blood, which had all drained away. From the spit of his fellow Italians. From the urine of the women who, skirts up, had squatted over his body.

The prosecutors, all three of them, got out of their chairs. They asked to approach the bench. Five-foot Max went with them.

"Here," I said, in not much more than a whisper, "is Mister X."

I knew why. It wasn't because of the broadcast in 1941, or in July of '43. He only cared about what I said later, in October. With the moon rising. The middle of the night. There he was, tip-toed in front of the bench. Talking to his coreligionist. The eyes of the magistrate were rimmed in black. Like charcoal. Problems with his liver. Too much cured meat.

"You! Junior! Maximilian! I know why you're doing this. I should have guessed. You Jews stick together."

The judge brought down his gavel. Max turned, his glasses, as usual, slipping down his nose. "No," he said. I could barely hear the three words he uttered next. "Because of Aria."

It's starting to rain. No surprise. Been cloudy for days. Gloomy Gubbio. What will happen in such weather to the floating sphere? Going to make a pretty rough landing. Must be some way to capture the sun's rays, the way a rain barrel captures the rain. The way stones soak up the heat of day. Wind another problem. Junior's idea: the double ellipse. Air blows free between the stories, grouped in three. Not just rain. Cold. Feet cold. Legs cold too. And, on the back of my head, Paul Bunyan swinging his ax. All the strong men: Atlas. Hercules. Vulcan. They're splitting me in two. Look at that: tea in the cup half frozen.

Old Weinstein, he had a chunk of Mussolini's brain. Must have flown it over packed in ice. The Douche, he figured he was going to join the Pharaohs. Up in the stars. The thoughts of a genius flying on radio waves. *Perfectly normal*, said the kikiatrist. Plain old human tissue. Will they put mine under a microscope too? Try to find the source of the pain? Here is a decision, the last of the year. Do I ring for Enrico? Do I ask for a fresh cup of tea?

Mosk stepped forward. But he did not ask for dismissal. What he said was that the defendant was not in full possession of his mental powers and was therefore unfit to stand trial. The judge? Old Katz? He said they'd observe the defendant and hold a hearing. Bang went the gavel. Imagine that. The absurdity of it. Bonkers! Me!

On came the pussykikiatrists. Young ones, Mr. Squirmy, Mr. Sleazy, and Mr. Slime. All led by Wine-stain. A hairy Jew, hair on the back of his hands. Claimed to be a lover of architecture. Of all my early work. His diagnosis: delusional, paranoid, egocentric, grandiose. Hell, that might have been a clinical description of FDR. "The treason is in the White House," I told him, "not in my brain."

Mosk and Dr. W., they practically went crazy themselves. Didn't I know about the Nuremberg trials? Old Adolf, Himmler, Goebbels. They had all killed themselves. The others were about to be hanged. And A.P.? He was in the very prison, the very cell, from which six German spies had been taken and put in the electric chair. Was there, I wondered, a mark on the wall? A swastika? A cross? A calendar of crossed-out lines? Then I heard that Lord Haw-Haw, who used to speak on Radio Berlin, had been executed. That was when I told old Wainscoat, Washboard, Wastebasket— that was when I told Wineskin that I had a queer kind of feeling in my head, as if the upper third of the brain was missing and was topped off instead by some kind of fluid. Besides, it was impossible to get flat enough in my bed at night. Seemed to me the mainspring was busted. Too tired to talk. Held my tongue. Laid out on the floor. Haw! Haw!

Watch out! Remember what Granny Tropp said. That face is going to freeze. This beating on the head. The bone-weariness. The silence. I heard at an electrocution the fire leaps from your head. Black smoke comes up from your toes. Brave boys! Brave Germans! Crossing the ocean on a submarine. I never dreamed I'd eat hard-boiled eggs. Or tin cans of donuts. I figured, if I was lucky I'd get hung by the neck. I remember. I remember what I read in the paper five years ago: Old Gerry Ford, President Ford, gave a pardon to Tokyo Rose. *Poor American soldiers. Poor American sailors. How can you get home? Home is so far away. And you have lost all your ships.*

No need to worry. I got my marbles. Benjamin Abramson, William T. Berry, Thomas H. Broadus, Ethel M. Christie, and so forth and so on, in alphabetical order. The members of the jury. The prosecutors pulled a fast one. Called on Squirmy and Sleazy and

Slime. What they said, the Fraudians, was that old Amos was eccentric but capable of standing trial.

Doctor W. stood up for our side. Said his young colleagues were mistaken. Said defendant was paranoid. Once a great architect but now subject to delusions. Out of touch with reality. Said he'd give an example. It was *La Vittoria*. For ten years the defendant had devoted all of his energies to the idea he could build a monument one mile high.

Giggles in the courtroom. Tit-titterings. Jurors nudged each other with elbows. Put their hands in front of their laughing mouths. The doctor: *"Even Don Quixote did not dare tilt against such a windmill."*

Well, they laughed at Fulton. At Edison. Ditto Columbus. Take a look at that breed of hyenas: A Katz, a Mosk, a Weinstein, and Abramson—no middle initial, just good old Ben. Definition of a lunatic: an animal surrounded by Jews. Amos Prince speaking: "It's no delusion. I ain't Quixote. You only need a tap root. A pine and not an elm. Like after a tornado. We got bedrock. A meteor. An anchor from outer space."

Hawk Nose was banging his gavel. Bang. Bang. Bang. Because the representatives of the people, guaranteed by the Constitution to be the peers of old A.P., were laughing more than ever. Out they went for deliberations. I knew my fate. What I felt was joy. Let the smoke come out of my nostrils! I'd roast my executioners like a dragon! With a tongue of fire! But when the jurors came back three minutes later what they said was, "Unsound mind."

Enrico! Enrico! Get up here! The tea is cold! Better bring a blanket too. Can't feel a thing in the frozen logs of my legs. Bang! Bang! Bang! Ah, now I understand. Not a gavel. Not an ax. Not inside my head at all. Nope: and it's not that shutter going back and forth in the wind. It's the old man, the old mason. Down in the street. Chipping, chipping, chipping at his cobblestone. He does not mind the weather. He's got his chisel. He's got his hammer. Tap, tap, tap. He hammers away. He has got to earn a living.

CURSE OF THE PHARAOHS

[1937-1941]

1

The bitter winter of 1936–37 came to an end. The sun at last shone over Rome. Soon the ice in the Tiber, the crusts on the fountains, cracked and melted away. Then the barges, each one loaded with a pair of pasta halves, the giant *maltagliati*, sailed one after the other from the dock at the Ponte di Ferro to the two temples downriver. The crews that welded the pieces of the core together continued to work day and night. The great hollow ellipse, one point to the west, the other east, rose higher and higher. Every seven days precisely— Mussolini was able to make more than the trains run on time—a new three-story unit of hub, spokes, and rim would rise from some secret spot on the heights of Montespeccato and sail improbably over a city whose residents had seen so much—the Emperors and Vandals, the revolutionaries and all the great Popes—that they no longer bothered to look up.

Max did not miss a single flight. He watched as the hissing blimps lowered each hub over the core, the way he'd seen the Capehart machines of those days drop a stack of 78 rpm records onto a spindle. As soon as one of discs—or *frittelle*, hotcakes, as the Romans called them—settled, a number of iron rods would spring outward from various spots along the circumference. These were designed to be the temporary cranes, or pulleys, that would haul building materials from ground level—everything from steel plates and the men who would weld them together, to the rivets for the new riveting guns, the furniture for the offices, and finally the very glass for the windows, through whose gaping frames all the other supplies had already passed. In the end, the rods would fold down and be secured to the face of the building. Thus had the young American envisioned the monorails up which the self-propelled elevator cars would carry a hundred thousand public servants from the earth to their desks in the sky.

At that rate of construction—a leap upward each week of fifty new feet when converted into American units of measure—Max calculated that the tower should reach its planned height of a mile in two years' time, even allowing for another winter freeze or a tightening of the embargo on steel by the League of Nations. With luck, he thought, they might dedicate the monument in *Anno XVII, Anno Diciassette*; he might be able to return home by, converting again, the winter of 1939.

Home? And where might that be? Los Angeles, where he had grown up and where what remained of his family still resided? What would he build there? Houses on stilts? More houses cantilevered over the canyons? Storefronts for the Miracle Mile? He knew that he would inevitably end up imitating what A.P. had already done. This, the five-thousand feet of crisscrossing ellipses, would be the only miraculous mile in his life. New Haven, then? The School of Architecture? How could he attend classes when he had already studied with a master and helped him to build the tallest building in the world?

Standing in the Circo Massimo, turning over these thoughts, Max knew he was fooling himself. Home was wherever Amos Prince decided to continue his practice. In all probability, that meant Rome, widening the boulevards and resurrecting the Tomb of Augustus. It certainly would not be America. The charges over the architect's children, the issues of custody, of kidnapping, still stood. His *children*. He gave a start: it had suddenly occurred to him that it was not Prince he would stay for; it was his daughter. Through the wind-blown dust, the scraps of excelsior that constantly tumbled about the site, he looked for her. Not Nina, who stood chatting with Renato through the open window of their ten-year-old car. She, sensing his eyes on her, turned to wave. He had already looked away, toward where Aria, like a figure in a Greek sculpture, had bent over to adjust the strap of her sandal. Now his heart began to swing violently inside his chest, as if an invisible boxer were using that bag for practice. He could not breathe. He could not swallow. He simply stared at her, knowing at last what it was he was going to do.

In three more weeks, on the Seventh of May, *Anno Quindicesimo* of the Fascist Revolution, he worked up the courage to do it. It was already a day of celebration. That morning, when the blimps completed their weekly flight from *Il Vulcano* to the Circus Maximus, the tower of Mussolini would stand at 435 feet, a full thirty-one feet higher than the dome of St. Peter's. Of course there would be a celebration: *La Vittoria* was about to become the tallest building in Rome.

The usual dignitaries—the Papal Secretary of State, Farinacci, Count Ciano and his wife, members of the diplomatic corps, the King and Queen: all gathered atop the steps at the rear of the monument dedicated to that same King's father, the first ruler of a united Italy. The Duce was there, wearing a red-and-green sash across his chest and an especially tall fez with a spread-winged eagle on the front. His wife, the rarely seen Rachele, sat in a special armchair, with Anna Maria, their youngest daughter, on her lap. All three of his sons were present too. Bruno, the middle youth, was not wearing his aviator's uniform or the leather helmet he donned when guiding the flotilla of lighter-than-air ships. A spectator to this morning's passage, he wore a black suit with the red rosette of the *Regia Aeronautica* in one lapel and a small white flower in the other.

Prince had pressed his linen suit and, it seemed to Maximilian, cut at least the tips of his hair. For the moment, he stood behind one of the fluted columns, sucking the smoke from a Tigrina cigarette through its tobacco-colored holder. Franklin wore his customary black shirt, though for this occasion he had added the black scarf, complete with gaping white skull, of a Young Fascist Musketeer. Nina wore a new dress, light green in tone, whose straps kept slipping from her bony shoulders. Her sister was in white, with a white shawl against the morning chill. Max took all this in through a haze, as if someone had left thumbprints on the lenses of his glasses. *Now!* he told himself. But he did not move.

At ground level a military band had started to play, drawing a crowd. Their uniforms gleamed as bright and white in the sunshine as the mountain of marble that rose above them. They went through a medley of marches; then, at precisely half-past the hour of eight, they fell silent. A group of men, all in dark suits, came shoulder to shoulder from the front of the Palazzo Venezia. Like pallbearers they moved in stride across the broad avenue, where policemen held up square signs to halt all the traffic. Slowly the Grand Council members climbed the steps of the monument, until at last they were able to drop into the row of chairs that had been set out for them. The band struck up again, this time overtures from operas, while the ministers caught their breath and wiped what could have been the morning dew from their brows.

Toward nine o'clock people began to glance up at the sky. The Emperor of Abyssinia thrust out both of his little arms and looked at his watch. To no one in particular he said, "What has happened? Shouldn't they be here by now?"

It was a fair question. On any other morning the blimps would already have unloaded their burden and been on the way to the military aerodrome at Lago Albano. On this trip, of course, there was a detour, away from the river and over the *Monumento a Vittorio Emanuele II*. Could the airships, taking that dogleg, have gotten lost? In any case, thought Max, this delay was the very opportunity he had sought. *Now*, he told himself, yet again; and again he remained rooted to the spot.

Aria, as if sensing his dilemma, solved it for him. He could not move to her; she, smiling, her eyes a brilliant, freshly rinsed blue, moved to him.

At her approach Max also broke into a smile. He removed his right fist from his pocket and, fully extending his arm, opened it.

"Oooh," said the Queen of Italy, Empress of Abyssinia. The sound was echoed by Rachele and Edda, the Duce's wife and daughter; by Gianna and seven-year-old Anna Maria; and for that matter by most of the women and even a few men in the crowd.

The ring that lay in Maximilian's palm sparkled like a little sun. At the sight, Aria halted.

Could the others read her lips? Her suitor could. *Oh, Maxie!*

He was as tongue-tied as she: "We—I mean, you—Could you—? What if—?"

Aria shook her head from side to side, which in Europe and America signified *No*. Then she began walking again, toward where Bruno stood waiting, wearing a smile as wide and brilliant as her own. She took his hand. The couple turned toward the Duce, who stood scowling, his arms folded over his chest.

Bruno: "I wish, Duce, before all of Rome and its representatives, to address you as a son does to his father. May I speak?"

He Who Fathered A Nation neither approved nor disapproved, though his scowl cut deeper into his face, like the line of an advancing army.

"I have found the woman I love. The one I wish to join my life. We desire to marry. Will you, Duce, *e caro Padre*, permit this engagement?"

A gasp went up from the gathering. Some of the ladies took out their handkerchiefs. One of them exclaimed, in English, "It's wonderful! I'm so happy!" It was Nina.

Max stood frozen, as if the glittering stone in his hand had the power to turn whomever it touched to ice. He could not take his eyes from the happy couple. They stood, he in black, she in white, atop these layers of marble like—yes, he gave way to the malicious thought—the marzipan figures on a wedding cake.

Meanwhile the brass ensemble below, perhaps at a signal from the would-be groom, began to play the famous melody from *Lohengrin*. Bruno now had one arm around Aria's waist. He leaned toward the man who was not only his father but that of his nation as well. "Speak, Duce, I beg you. Will you approve? *O, Dio!* This is like *tortura!*"

"Say yes!" cried one of the ministers from the Grand Council.

"*Sì*, Duce," came other voices. "Don't leave them in suspense."

The great man propped his chin on one fist, in the manner of Rodin's thinker. With his other hand he made a palm, thrusting it outward for silence. Thus he ruminated. Then, ponderously, as a great boulder might be hauled upward from the depths of a quarry, he raised his head.

"*Forse sì. Forse no.*" Such were his mysterious words. But was that not a light, like the first star to appear in the darkened heavens,

that shone in the depths of his eyes? "It depends—" Yes! The corners of his mouth: were they not, like either end of a Viking canoe,
turning upward? "Will the bride give or not give her *papà* a kiss?"
Sposa! Papà! That meant he agreed! A cheer went up. "Hoorah!"
Mussolini took a stride toward the girl. His throat, Max saw,
had begun to swell over his collar.

"Hurrah!" cried the assemblage a second time.

But not everyone was cheering. Aria's cheeks, in bloom from
happiness, from the freshets of a May morning, had gone as pale as
the cold marble columns behind her. Reflexively, she drew backward.

Max had to force himself not to intervene. He looked to
Franklin. He looked to Prince. How could they allow this to happen? To their own flesh and blood? Didn't they know about Muscle-
weenie? His powers were mythical. No one could resist him. *Every
Eight Hours.* That was practically a slogan on the city's walls. If those
hours went by, he was in anguish, in unbearable pain.

"Ha, ha, ha!" laughed the Living Legend. "PEOPLE OF ROME.
DO YOU SEE? SHE STEPS AWAY FROM THE DUCE. SHE IS
TIMIDA. HA! HA! SHE IS COY."

The Dictator took another step toward his would-be daugh-
ter-in-law, who involuntarily shrank back again.

No! That word caught in Maximilian's throat. All he could do
was gaze upward, while silently uttering the following prayer: "Stop
him! Don't let him!"

Oddly, a number of other people were looking up too. Max
shielded his eyes. Nothing to see but the blue of the sky. But he
thought he heard something, a hum, a distant drone. The military
musicians must have heard it too. They lowered their instruments;
then they brought them back to their lips—the trumpets, the flutes,
the horns and trombones—and began to play the triumphant march
from *Aïda.*

The streets did not fill with conquered Ethiopians, as they had the year before. There were no palm trees, no dancing girls to entertain the victorious Pharaoh. But there were elephants—not on the ground but in the air. A pack of lumbering dirigibles, fat-bellied and gray, appeared on the western horizon. They nudged each other over the Tiber and continued eastward, more or less following the route of the Corso Vittorio Emanuele. Max's prayer had been answered. Everyone's eyes, including the dark, deep-set ones of the Duce, were fixed on the armada and on the great spoked form that hung beneath it, its steel rim glittering in the morning sun.

Up went the cheers again, louder than ever. The ministers rose from their chairs and applauded. Here was the new landmark that would surpass in the Fascist Era the achievement of Michelangelo in the Renaissance. On came the high-flying pachyderms, making their way between the *Teatro di Pompeo* and the Parthenon, relics of an empire that had now been eclipsed.

Suddenly, from that same Palazzo Venezia, a horseman came on the gallop. There was a feather stuck in his cap and his steed, a stallion, had a plume in his halter as well. At this sight the band ceased its music. Once more the policemen raised their little square signs—though there was no need to do so: the drivers had stepped out of their automobiles, just as the passengers on the trams strained through their windows, to see.

The horseman—he had a silver stripe that ran the length of his breeches—raced straight across the broad avenue to the base of the gigantic staircase. His agitated mount, seemingly unstoppable, actually clattered up the first half-dozen steps before coming to a halt. The rider slipped from the saddle and continued upward, fly-ing over stairs by twos and threes, as if he were one of the marble statues scattered over the monument, the messenger Mercury, with wings on his brow instead of his feet. He halted, panting, before the Duce. He gave the Roman salute with his right arm; with his left he handed his master a communiqué.

Mussolini, not wishing to employ his reading glasses, squinted down at the stiff piece of parchment. Instantly the tanned tint of his face, like bathwater, seemed to drain down the pipe of his throat. He staggered, which drew an exclamation from the crowd. For a moment he bowed his head and closed his eyes. Then he spoke. "OH, EVIL DAY! DAY OF INFAMY!"

From all sides came murmurs of consternation. Those on the monument, those in the multitude below it, braced themselves for his words. "ROMANS! *CORAGGIO!* THE DUCE MUST INFORM YOU THAT THE NOBLE AIRSHIP OF OUR AXIS PARTNER, THE GREAT *HINDENBURG*, HAS EXPLODED IN THE AIR."

"Ah!" came the cry from a thousand throats.

"Una cosa terribile!"

Maximilian was no less stunned. Instantly he pictured the stewards and stewardesses, the girl with the curls and the little red cap. What of the crewman on B deck, the man with the accordion, the cooks in the galleys? Had they all perished? The poor passengers, what of them? What of the captain, Eckener, himself?

"It's awful, awful," murmured a voice close beside him. Nina took his arm. She laid her head on his shoulder.

"THINK OF YOUR DUCE! WAS HE NOT ON THIS AIRSHIP ONLY A FEW MONTHS AGO? WHAT IF HE HAD BEEN ON THIS TRIP TO AMERICA? WHAT IF THIS WERE A PLOT TO KILL HIM?"

"Do not say it!"

"Do not think it!"

"God has saved you!"

As if this were a hot day instead of a cool one, sweat began to pour from beneath the edges of the Duce's fez. He seemed, next, to be mumbling to himself. "I knew this would happen. I felt it. This is a curse! Prince, Amos Prince! He brought on this *calamità!* He dared to challenge the kings of Egypt. To disturb the sleep of the Pharaohs. What pride: to build higher than their pyramids. Now they take their revenge. *Maledizione!* A curse! *Malocchio!* Why did I listen to this man? Why did I tempt the gods?"

Prince was by then on his third or fourth Tigrina. As if he feared he might ignite the gas in the balloons that had now moved directly overhead, he removed it from its holder and stamped it, still glowing, under his heel. "The *gods!* Jew-peter! Jew-hover! The evil eye! I would not believe it if I did not see it. The Dunce is afraid."

"The Duce is never afraid!" That was Farinacci, waving his truncated arm in indignation. "He enters a cage with a tiger. He puts his head into the mouth of a lion."

The lion-tamer's next words came out in little more than a whisper. "It is true, my dear Farinacci. But I must respect my fate. The Pharaohs have made a curse."

Now the Cardinal Secretary of State rose to his feet. His high, reed-like voice cut through the throbbing engines of the machines above him. "There was a time when the grandest building in every town was the church, and the greatest building in every city the cathedral. These were the houses of God, dedicated to His glory. What do we see in our modern age? The great buildings are offices, dedicated to Mammon. Or else they are dedicated to Caesar. Now this abomination has come to the holy city of Rome. St. Peter's is to be supplanted by *Il monumento a Mussolini.* It is not Pharaoh who is angry. This is no curse of a pagan spirit. It is God who thunders in His majesty. He will not lose His home."

Prince, in his agitation, plucked at the little yellow tuft of his beard. "I don't think I ever heard such rub-itch. The *Hindenburg* exploded because it was filled with inflammable gas. Anything else is bull-loony."

But Mussolini had already made, quickly, surreptitiously, over the expanse of his tunic, the sign of the cross. "It is true, what this Pacelli tells us. The wrath of God threatens the Duce. This delivery is a blasphemy. It must not occur."

But how, everyone wondered, could it be prevented? The fleet of airships was a thousand feet above them, the pulse of their propellers making a steady drone. Nonetheless, the Conqueror of Abyssinia threw back his head, cupping his hands to his mouth:

"YOU! *PILOTI! DIRIGIBILISTI!* YOU MUST STOP! PILOTS OF THE AIR! THE DUCE COMMANDS YOU! GO BACK! GO BACK AT ONCE!"

Naturally, whichever of those words that had not been whipped away by the wind, or diminished by distance, had been drowned out by the buzz of the diesel engines. The people on the monument glanced at each other. Had their leader taken leave of his senses? Appalled, they watched as he once more put his hands to his mouth:

"*EIA, EIA, EIAAAAA! ALALÀ!*"

It was the cry of the Arditi, by which those brave fighters called to each other from peak to peak of the Alps.

"*EIA, EIA, EIAAAAA! ALAAAAAALÀ!*"

To the amazement of all, the blimp at the front—as if heeding the trumpet call from below—began to turn northward, toward the Palazzo Colonna, the Quirinale, and away from the Circus Maximus in the south.

"*A-LAAAA! A-LAAAA! ALÀ!*"

Now the other ships, as if following the lead elephant, made the turn too. Then the whole humming herd made its way back the way it had come.

What a victory for the Pope! And for his Papal Secretary of State! St. Peter's would reign as the tallest structure in the eternal city. Some of those who stood that morning on the lesser monument would later swear they saw the thin, ascetic lips of Pacelli spread ever so slightly in a smile.

And what a triumph for the Duce! His voice, the sheer power of his will, had extended outward into space and forced the faraway pilots to obey his command. What could a man of such powers not accomplish?

It was, however, a defeat for Amos Prince. He took off his Panama hat and held it beseechingly in his hands. "Duce, let me explain. It is a mistake to use hydrogen. Stupid! Ignorant! To think of it puts me in high dudgeon. But there is to this problem a solution. A gas that can't burn. That can't be hex-ploded. We'll fly with *helium.*"

Mussolini turned toward the American. "Signor Prince. The Duce, he no hear what you say. Is no *possibilità.* I'mma give the order. The *palloni*, alla the fleet: she grounded-ed."

"But Duce, it *is* possible. Helium has 92 percent of the lifting capacity of hydrogen. That was a fleet of fourteen airships. Add two. That's more than enough to make up the difference."

"No, no. Italy, she need these weapons. What about we gonna have war? Eh? The Duce, he notta saying. Is just thinking. But what about? We keep these *palloni* for the *ricognizione.* For the *bombardamenti.* For kill-a the people."

"Then use balloons! Hot-air balloons. Weather balloons. *One* dirigible can pull all the rest. It's lift you need. Not whores-power."

The Duce turned toward his middle son. "Bruno? *Dimmi. È vero?*"

"*Sì*, Duce. The one could pull the many."

"Did you hear?" Prince exclaimed. "Duce, it is not too late. Call back the airships. This is your moment. In only an hour your monument will be the greatest in Rome. Tomorrow—or in one week, two weeks, it will be taller than the sin-agog in Turin. The tallest building in all of Italy. Next: the Awful Tower in France. Your monument will be the greatest structure in the history of Europe. Then there is only a single step left: the Impure State Building! Then the monument to Il Duce will become the highest in the world. You are the new Caesar; the old Caesars are buried in the past. So is Michelangelo and the Rainy-sauce. So too the age of the Popes. A curse? The wrath of God? It's just jealousy and superstition. Duce, remember that your words will live forever. Your thoughts will reach the stars. I ask you: make this decision. Let us complete together the work of your monument."

What, everyone wondered, would the Duce do? For the moment, nothing. He stood, his head raised and blankly staring, like a statue on Easter Island. A minute went by. Another one followed. No one, no thing, dared move. Even the few wispy clouds in the sky seemed to stop in their windblown tracks. Only the tassel on the Duce's fez swung slowly to and fro, like a pendulum that recorded the passing seconds, or a marker that reflected the ongoing conflict—first that notion was on top, then this one—beneath the woolen headgear itself.

Then one voice broke through the deep silence. "I know what it would take to make up the Duce's mind. And so do you."

The speaker was, of all people, the Young Fascist Musketeer. The person he addressed was his older sister.

Everyone, Max included, looked to where Aria stood. Her face, so pale before, was now flushed. She dropped the hand of her fiancé. She stepped forward, toward the master of the Italian nation.

"Duce": that was the word she formed with her expressive lips.

Though she had not made a sound, he heard her. On the instant the mouth, shut tight in contemplation, opened wide, revealing the powerful teeth in their rows.

"*Sì?*" answered He Who Never Sleeps.

Again those lips, so clearly atremble, pushed forward. They did not form a word, however. They were pursed for what everyone recognized was a kiss.

Instantly the Dictator shot out his arm, as quick as the tongue of an amphibian, and seized his prey by the wrist. "NOW THE DUCE EMPLOYS HIS MAGNETISMO."

No! Once again the word rose in Maximilian's throat; once again it stuck there, strangling him, choking him. He turned toward the architect, imploring him with his eyes to step forward, to intervene, to save his daughter's honor. Amos Prince did not move.

In any case, it was too late. Mussolini had the girl in his arms. His throat was once again spilling over the confines of his collar. His chest expanded so forcefully that the sash that had crossed it on the diagonal broke in two. Now he placed a single leg, stout as a pillar, between her two slim ones. He bent her backward—yes, with his invincible magnetism, the way a mentalist might bend a spoon.

The silence resumed. All those on the monument, all those below, simply waited. Was Maximilian the only one to see how the girl's hands, at the ends of her dangling arms, clutched and opened, and once again clutched, as if she were trying to capture something, or else set something free?

At last her father brought himself to speak. "Well, Duce: have you come to a decision?"

A shudder passed through the body that was clothed in gray and green and black. The great man raised his head and, like a deep sea diver who has lingered under water in his search for an oyster, a pearl, took a breath.

This time Bruno, the beseeching groom, asked the identical question. "Duce, tell us: have you reached a decision?"

The Dictator nodded. He said, "*Sì*."

At that moment Nina dashed to her sister and clasped her in her arms. She led her—*weeping?* Max wondered, yes, *weeping*—aside.

"And what is it?" asked Amos Prince.

"Signor Prince. The Duce, he gives the forgiveness. We will make another flight. Maybe, we make two. Maybe three. With helium gas. Not hydrogen. *Sì*, we gonna be more tall than the *Duomo*. More tall than the what-you-call-him: the *tempio a Torino*."

"No, Duce," said his middle son. "It is our *fidanzamento* I ask you to decide. And our marriage."

"*Bene*, Bruno. I will do so." So saying, He Who Tames Lions stood fully erect. "YOU, PEOPLE OF ROME. YOU, COUNSELORS OF STATE. REPRESENTATIVES OF FOREIGN NATIONS. HEAR THE DUCE'S DECISION."

Naturally, everyone leaned forward in his or her seat. These are the words with which the Duce addressed them:

"HE DOES NOT APPROVE THIS ENGAGEMENT. THIS WOMAN, BRUNO, IS NOT FOR YOU. NOT YET. YOU ARE TOO YOUNG. YOU MUST WAIT A YEAR. YOU MUST WAIT TWO YEARS. UNTIL YOU ARE TWENTY-ONE. UNTIL THEN, YOUR FATHER, THE DUCE: HE DENIES HIS BLESSING."

In spite of himself, Maximilian felt at this proclamation a surge of joy. "*Grazie*, Duce," he exclaimed, even as he returned his own ring to his pocket.

Nobody heard his words. Down below the band once again started to play—not *Lohengrin* this time, not Mendelssohn either. It was a jaunty tune, a chorus from Mascagni, perhaps, or a sextet from Bellini. The crowd took this as a signal to depart. Chatting and laughing, they made their way down the steep staircase to the street. There the traffic was circulating as usual. The cars were sounding their horns, the trams their claxons, the bicyclists their little bells. In no time the monument was deserted. The sky, once filled with more than a dozen motorized balloons, was empty, save for the ponytails of a few cirrus clouds. Alone on the steps of the memorial to Vittorio Emanuele II, Maximilian paused. It had occurred to him that of all the dignitaries present that morning, the one notably absent had been Guglielmo Marconi. Was that how Mussolini exercised his magical powers? Did the inventor, in the radio shed, or on his famous yacht, or from any other location, send a prearranged signal to the pilot in the airship: *Go back. Turn around. Return to Montespaccato?*

It was not until some hours later, while reading the afternoon paper, that Shabilian realized that the *Hindenburg* had exploded in Lakehurst, New Jersey, at about 7 p.m. the previous day. That meant that those in the Palazzo Venezia, connected to all the capitals of the world, must have learned of the disaster at midnight, or at the latest 1 a.m. Max put down his copy of *Il Messaggero*. He put down his coffee cup too. All the magic, the *magnetismo*, the projection of the Great Man's thoughts into the air: Had it all been nothing more than a stage trick, an organized charade, much like the execution, with all its fake blood and mock horror, of the Ethiopian King?

2

The Mole Antonelliana was begun by the Jews of Turin. Over the years it grew higher, gallery on gallery, colonnade upon colonnade, until at more than five hundred feet it became the tallest brick structure in Europe. Eventually the community, in some dismay, decided to give their temple to the municipality. "We want to pray to God," the chief rabbi declared, "not join him for supper." All that *La Vittoria* required in order to surpass the Mole in height was six more stories—that is, two more flights of three stories each. But when would these deliveries be made? The whole month of May went by. No *palloni* appeared in the sky. The first week in June went by as well, then the second: still no balloons, motorized or not, crossed the Tiber to the Circo Massimo.

Amos Prince raged. He made call after call to the Palazzo Venezia; none was returned. He had Renato drive him the few blocks from the Via degli Specchi to the Via Astalli, from which street he stormed into the palace itself. There, Count Ciano told him that his father-in-law was at home, at the Villa Torlonia, still brooding over the catastrophe of May 7th, a day of evil influence that had been ripped from every government calendar.

Finally, in mid-June, a first flight was announced; on the 19th it actually occurred. After all the fuss, the armada was composed of the same blimps as before, with two more added to make up the difference in lifting power between the element H and the element He. How to explain that yet another full month passed before the second, record-breaking, flight was announced? No one understood the caprices of the Protector of Rome. Certainly he did not—on the day his monument was to become the highest structure in the new Roman Empire—desire a celebration.

On that morning in July there was no band. There were no dignitaries or government officials, much less the Duce himself. Nina had arranged a table and tablecloth, whose corners the breezes threatened to send upward, upsetting the glasses of champagne that awaited the workers, the riveters, and those who operated the pulleys and cranes. When Renato sent the signal from the radio shed, and the hub of one ellipse had settled over the core of the other, Prince was the first to raise a glass. He did not toast the tallest building that had ever been raised on Italian soil; he saluted the fact that they were now exactly one-tenth of the way to their final goal.

As it happened, the Duce decided to send a delegation after all. Four sailors in blue and white uniforms arrived on the site that evening. They marched up to A.P., who was standing at the base of the monument, where the stray sparks of the welders were exhausting themselves on their way to the ground. They invited him to accompany them to their Lancia Lambda, which was waiting behind the poplars on the Via dei Cerchi. Only Franklin went with him. If this historic day were to be marked by a celebration, it was going to be held in private.

By midnight neither Prince nor his son had returned home. His daughters, and Maximilian too, alternately paced the floor or stared out the second-floor window. Something, clearly, had gone wrong. Nina turned on the radio. Nothing came out of the speakers but dirges and funeral music. Finally the announcer informed them that Pharaoh had cursed them once again. The man who had demonstrated that Herzian waves would follow the curvature of the earth, and so made possible the music that once more poured from this Philips *Superinduttanza Sei*, had fallen ill and—one moment after saying to his physician, *If my heart has stopped beating, why am I still alive?*—suddenly expired.

The funeral took place the next day. Dressed in his Royal Italian Academy uniform, the Marchese was brought first to the Farnesina and then, in a great parade, to Santa Maria degli Angeli. The flags of the city were at half-mast. Every doorway, according to custom, was left half open. The wreathes in the cortège filled twenty-five carriages and nine army trucks. The one from the Reichskanzler trailed a red pennant, with swastika attached.

The two girls, Nina and Aria, stood on the Via Cernaia as the horses drew up in front of the basilica. Max, on the first step of the church, kept looking for Amos Prince. He had long since been made an honorary Academician, but among this group of bearded and beribboned Immortals, the tobacco-tinged whiskers of the architect were nowhere to be found. The person that Maximilian did see, was Frankie. Black-shirted, with a gun and holster and crossed bandoleers of bullets as well, he was in the middle of the *Squadristi* who stood at attention immediately behind the flower-draped hearse.

Now He Who Mourned Most, in green with black leather flaps on his breeches, stepped out from amidst his brothers-in-arms. In a voice that made a flock of pigeons wheel skyward, as if at a gunshot, he cried:

"*CAMERATA* GUGLIELMO MARCONI!"

"*Presente!*" a thousand voices replied.

Then the honor guard, with Bruno and Vittorio and even little Romano among them, carried the bier over the cobblestones and up the shallow steps and into the church. Now the crowd pushed forward as well. It took some time for Max, Nina, and Aria to force their way through the throng and make their way inside. The service seemed to have already started. An organ was playing. A choir sang. Max saw that the coffin, propped up on a catafalque, was resting halfway down the nave. Candles as tall as grown men burned around it. At each of the four corners palm leaves stretched upward, forming a canopy. The family, widow and daughter, were on their knees. Beyond the chancel rail, their backs turned, bishops were praying. A choir, white-bibbed, oddly like pilgrims, sang back and forth to each other. Spangles of colored light moved in elongated ovals across the floor.

Where was Amos Prince? Max stood on tip-toe to see. How could he miss him, a giant towering over the squat Italians, in habitual white against the dark mass of suits and shawls? He wasn't with those standing in the aisles. He wasn't seated in the pews. He was no-where to be found.

Then, as Maximilian began to turn from the crowd, he saw, amid all the white, unfamiliar faces, one that he thought he knew: a woman, dark-haired beneath her shawl, green-eyed, with, aston-ishingly, the cylinder of an unlit cigarette in her hand. Just as he started forward to discover who it could be, Cardinal Pacelli, his spectacle frames and spectacle lenses gleaming, swept by. The en-tourage behind him was so large that Max was forced to retreat to a small, candle-lit chapel at the rear of the nave. The rest of Prince's family was already there.

Nina had been searching for the architect too. As Max drew closer he heard her confront her brother. "What are you doing dressed up like that? Where is Papa? Is he here, inside the church?"

The boy, rosy-cheeked as ever, only grinned.

Max joined the interrogation. "You must know. You were taken away together. Why isn't he with you? Has he been arrested?"

At that word, *arrested*, Nina began to pull at Franklin's black silk shirt. "He's hurt, isn't he? He's in danger. Tell us!"

Again Frankie grinned, this time opening his mouth wide enough to display the white circle of mint on his tongue.

Max: "Why are you standing there? Why are you grinning? If you know where he is, why don't you tell us?"

"Tell you? The only person who can hear this is Aria."

At the mention of her name, the girl moved forward, as if in answer to a summons.

Franklin pointed to a large, brown confessional—it looked, in fact, like an enormous version of their six-tube radio receiver—and said, "The priest in there knows everything."

Aria walked toward the wooden box. Frankie leapt forward and held the door open for her. The moment she slipped inside he closed the door and took up a position in front of it with his arms crossed over his chest, as if he were on duty as a sentinel.

Max stood frozen in perplexity. A priest? Why a priest? What had this to do with Amos Prince? Reflexively, he turned again to look for the architect among the crowd of mourners. Again he was missing. Where, for that matter, was the winner of the Nobel Prize? Not his body, which was in his wooden coffin, but his spirit. Was it, like those electromagnetic waves he had charted, doomed to follow, like some poor wandering ghost, the curvature of the earth? Or would it reassemble itself as a series of dots and dashes, freed from gravity, in the heavens?

The music, the chanting, the heat of so many bodies on this hot summer day—all these things, together with an anxious, sleepless night, filled Max with confusion. Wherever he looked he saw a cross: on the altar, in all the paintings, on the breasts of the cardinals and priests. That was where Jesus had suffered and died. But it was the wrong symbol for Guglielmo Marconi. Max could not see them but he knew that on every coastline there were masts, wireless masts, and that there were others on thousands of ships. These, the countless antennae on every continent, were the crosses that formed the inventor's true monument.

There was a bang, like a shot, and the confessional door slammed open. Max whirled about in time to see Benito Mussolini step out. Before he could react, Nina strode toward the Dictator. "What have you done to him?" she demanded. "Have you killed him? Have you thrown him into the river?"

Mussolini seemed more amused than insulted. "Who? Amos-a? We *Fascisti*, we no have to kill-a such peoples. Poor baby, eh? Poor *bambino*. Open the mouth. Open for Papa. You gotta take *la medicina*. The *olio di ricino*. Here's the little spoon. *Sì*. And also the *manganello*. The stick! The stick! The stick!"

Max was no longer listening. He peered into the open box of the confessional, in the dim corner of which Aria was sitting. She was slumped and trembling, her arms crossed, like her brother's bandoleers, over her chest. Her mouth, smeared now with lipstick, was attempting but failing to form human words.

Maximilian turned back to the Duce, whose face shone from perspiration like one of the saints in the religious paintings. "This *architetto*. He make the *malocchio*, the evil eye. Maybe he worship the *Satana*, *il Diavolo*. How he make that *Hindenburg* fall down outta the sky? How he put the poison inna the *brodo* of Marconi. *Arsenico*. *Cianuro*. He make the curse on the Duce. He gotta so many *peccati*. Terrible sins. He gotta make the *confessione*."

So saying, the Prince of the Adriatic turned and indicated, on the other side of the chapel, a second confessional. Max gasped at the sight. For there, on the floor beside it, and in plain view, was a Panama hat. It rested upside down, like the receptacle of a man asking for alms. The beggar, however, was nowhere to be seen.

"His hat!" cried Nina. "A.P.'s hat! What have you done to him?"

But Max was already striding across the stone slabs to the coffin-like booth. He yanked open the door. Amos Prince, his hands tied behind him, tumbled out. Both girls screamed and ran to where he lay, his knees doubled against his chest. They had not killed him. His linen trousers were soiled, however, from the forced doses of emetic; there was blood on his chin, on his jacket, on his shirt front, from the blows of the cudgel. They sat him upright. Nina removed the gag from his mouth. Instantly, in full voice, he started to speak:

"Dutchy, listen! Listen to me. We got to finish the tower. It wasn't me who did those things. Why would I? You're making a mistake."

"What? What you say? THE DUCE IS NEVER WRONG!"

"But it wasn't me who brought down the *Hindenburg*. That was a plot by the Chews. That's right. A plot by the kikes and hyper-kikes against the Not-sees. You got to follow the voice of the great Roman. Old Cicero. *Cui bono? Cui bono fuerit?* I'll ferret it out. The Chews, they wanted to put a dent in Mr. Hot-leer's prestige. So they blew up the Zeppelin with aplomb."

Nina: "Papa. Be calm. Don't speak. Don't say any more."

"*Ma, no.* Is *molto interessante.* I gotta the same idea. *Naturalmente*, I got it first. The Jews. The Jews. That make the Duce think." Here, in an instinctive movement, he raised his fist to his chin.

Aria had moved from her booth to her father. Now she knelt beside him, cradling him. To the others she formed the word *Hospital.*

Mussolini ignored her. "Amos-a, you tell the Duce. Why you make the *maledizione* number two? If you no put the poison inna the soup of Senatore Marconi, who did?"

"It was the international bonkers, that's who. The fine-ass-ears: Barnyard Barracks, Organ-thaw, Victor Spittoon—they're the ones who put in the sigh-a-night, maybe, or arse-lick. Strict-nine. You can bet he didn't die of a heart attack or a stroke."

"*Sì, sì,* again the Jews. The Duce, he gotta take the actions against these peoples. But, *cui bono?* Eh? Ha! Ha! The Duce, he speak like Cicero. In Latin. These Jews, why they wanna do such a thing?"

Prince dropped his voice. The words that came from his split lips bore no hint of a Yankee accent. "Duce, you know that the great Marconi was no longer working with radio. No, he was studying microwaves. He was building you a secret weapon. A death ray. To kill at any range. To burn out a brain. To make the blood bubble. Do you think Franklin Roosevelt would stand for that? That he would let such a weapon fall into the hands of the Axis? No. He put his Jews to work."

Strangely, Mussolini's voice changed too. Gone was the stage Italian. "It is true. *Un raggio,* a ray, *della morte.* And more: *Un raggio dell' immobilizzazione.* It stops an engine faster than a driver turns the key of ignition. Tanks run off the road. Airplanes drop from the sky. Why did I want a mile-high tower? For a monument? A tomb? So I could live forever? Do you think I care if my thoughts travel to the stars? Like the Pharaohs? Do you think I really am such a *buffone?* I perform like Pagliaccio for these stupid peoples, these *contadini.* Imagine: from such a height, a mile in the sky, this beam could bring the whole earth to a stop. The Duce would rule the world."

Suddenly, as if in celebration of that idea, the bells of Santa Maria degli Angeli began to ring. It was high noon. The service was over. The mourners, on their way out, began streaming by the entrance to their little chapel. At once the Duce raised his chin. Then he struck his chest with his fist, causing tears, real tears, to fly from his eyes.

"AH, GUGLIELMO! GUGLIELMO! *CARO AMICO!* WHY DID YOU LEAVE THE DUCE ALONE? NOW HE HAS NO FRIENDS. IT IS HIS FATE ALWAYS TO BE ALONE. *TUTTO SOLO!* HE MUST WORK BY HIMSELF DAY AND NIGHT FOR THE GOOD OF HIS PEOPLE."

Those same people, at this sad sight, shook their heads in commiseration, then continued out of the church and into the light of day. Maximilian fell in behind them, squinting into the overhead sun.

Everywhere mourners had gathered in groups, chatting and eating *gelati* in little cups. The bunting on the waiting hearse, the pennant of the Reichskanzler, snapped and curled in the stiffening breeze. The noontime bells were still ringing. Max could feel the sound waves through the soles of his shoes. Then, as the tintinnabulation far and near died away, a strange thing happened. The crowds crisscrossing the Piazza della Repubblica drew to a halt. The cars and trucks, and even the bicycles, moving rightward on the Via Cernaia slowed and stopped. Every vehicle that moved left on the Via Venti Settembre ceased its motion too. All was silent. The very birds in the trees stopped their twittering. It was as if one of Marconi's rays had immobilized the entire city. The only audible sound was a high note, far off, throbbing, as if someone were playing an enormous harp.

Then Max remembered: twelve noon in Rome. That was when, in tribute to the creator of radio, every station, every broadcasting facility on earth, would for a full two minutes fall silent. One of those minutes went by. But before the second had passed, the high, humming note increased in volume, as if an invisible chorus were hidden in the clouds that were racing across the sky.

Maximilian started to run. Through the Piazza dell' Esedra, down the Via Nazionale, and then, southward, through the winding streets of the Via del Viminale. And always, from every direction, he was surrounded by the hum and twang of these unceasing reverberations. The worldwide tribute had long since ended by the time Max came panting out of the Via degli Annabaldi directly in front of the Colosseum, which, like the enormous horn of a Victrola, seemed to be spreading the sound.

Onward Max plunged, down the Via dei Trionfi. From there he could see the top of *La Vittoria*, with its crossed lozenges, stunted at thirty-nine stories. He halted. Sweat dripped from his cheeks, his chin, and poured from the tips of his fingers. To a passing Roman he might have looked like a fountain by Bernini, a curly-haired elf, a bespectacled satyr that spouted perspiration instead of water. Catching his breath, he staggered forward again.

At last, reaching his destination, Maximilian pushed through the rows of dusty poplars that stood along the northern embankment and half-tumbled down to the floor of the Circus Maximus. The great oval was deserted. The machinery, motionless, unattended, lay scattered about. Then he saw, sitting on one of the empty cartons, a *maltagliato*, a lone woman. Not just a woman: the same one he thought he had recognized in the basilica. This time he knew her at once—yet that knowledge forced him to think that he must once again be in a dream. Margherita Sarfatti! *So-fatty!* Mussolini's mistress. He trudged toward her, through the dust of the arena. No, no doubt now. The wind whipped the tendrils of her hair about her cheeks. He worked up the courage to speak:

"Signora Sarfatti? I was on the *Hindenburg*. Didn't you jump from the window? Weren't you killed?"

"I wanted *him* to think so. Not that it made any difference. Soon I will be—and so, my American friend, will you."

"What do you mean? You—"

She cut him off with a wave of her cigarette. "I should say, I might as well be dead. I am leaving for South America. And while there is time, so should you."

"But why? My work, my—"

"You do not know what he has in store for us. For me. For you. Madness. Madnesses. Worse than the Germans. I know his plans. I give you this warning. Terrible things are going to happen. I mean, Signor Shabilian, terrible things for the Jews."

It was as if, at those words, a shudder went through nature. As abruptly as if a switch had been thrown, the light in the skies went out. It was of course only a cloud. But its passage caused the temperature to drop. It made the wind blow harder, sending tornadoes of dust across the site. Simultaneously the high, haunting note increased in volume. Max looked up. The invisible breeze was playing over the taut wires of the great steel wheels; it made them sing over the city of Rome, like the strings of an instrument that had just been plucked.

3

There was to be a *maledizione* number three—and this the one that would strike closest, most painfully, to the Duce. Perhaps it was he who had, all unknowingly, set it in motion when, on the steps of the *Monumento a Vittorio Emanuele II*, he had refused permission for his son to marry until he had turned twenty-one. That would not occur for two more years. Those years slowly passed while the lovers waited. At last, in November 1939, the couple announced their plans for a June wedding. As it happened, that was the very month that the Man Of The Century declared war on Great Britain and France. Naturally, all leaves for military personnel were canceled. Instead of taking his bride on a honeymoon to Capri, Bruno found himself stationed in Pisa with the *Bombardamento a Grande Raggio*. The wedding was postponed for yet another year, until August of 1941.

Not only was Bruno unable to marry Prince's daughter, he was no longer available to fly the lead blimp in the armada. Indeed, once war was declared, all flights by lighter-than-air ships came to a sudden end. Over the course of the previous three years, those flights had dwindled from a high of one each week to one every three months. Still, those dozen shipments had enabled *La Vittoria* to surpass the Eiffel Tower's 984 feet in the spring of 1939 and go over the symbolic barrier of one thousand feet in the course of that summer. There had been no celebration on either occasion. In fact, the Duce left Rome for what he called a working vacation on both dates, as if he feared his presence in the same city would cause some new calamity to befall him.

But how could the nation not mark the day that the monument to Il Duce became the tallest building in the world? That wondrous event was certain to happen at any time after the end of April 1940, when the final flight brought the tower from one thousand to one thousand two hundred and thirty-eight feet, just four yards below the Empire State Building on the isle of what Prince called Mad-hatter.

That day did not dawn. Instead, Mussolini stood on the balcony of the Palazzo Venezia and announced that THE HOUR, SIGNED BY DESTINY had arrived. While no one dared suggest that his motive was anything other than to share in the spoils of an already defeated France and a prostrate Europe, it remains true that he also managed to postpone his son's wedding to Aria—and Aria's to his son—while simultaneously removing the risk of the wrath of the vengeful Pharaohs and the jealous gods.

More months rolled by. Still the tower remained within a few tantalizing meters of being the greatest structure ever raised by human hands. Why the prolonged delay? The Ethiopian workers, once so vital to the project, had been shipped back to their homeland to help defend the Empire that had enslaved them. Some said there was a shortage of steel. But how could that be, when everybody in Rome could see the smoke from the stacks of the Mussolini Works by day and the glow of its furnaces at night? A more likely explanation was the scarcity of helium. The United States controlled virtually all of the world's supply and, almost as if its motive were to maintain its supremacy in man-made buildings, it shut down all exports except to Allied countries. The real problem, Max suspected, was less with the element He than with the human HE, He Who Loves His Country Most. If he held a supply in reserve, it was not going to be expended on La Vittoria.

Thus for more than a year at the Circus Maximus the pulleys labored to draw up crates of window glass and marble tiles for the flooring; specialized crews began to snake tubes for the pneumatic system and plumbing through the four utility cables that stretched out to each of the hanging rims; but the monument itself did not rise another inch.

Then, in the first week of August 1941, the Duce drove up to the site. Max, dressed in coat and tie, watched while the Protector of Rome climbed out from behind the wheel of his little red Alfa Romeo that sat, still throbbing, at the head of a line of black limousines.

"Hail, Do Say!"

Mussolini ignored the architect; instead, he struck a pose, fists on hips, leaning backward to gaze not at the flag affixed to the topmost story but far higher, as if he could actually envision the gold glistening atop his mile-high tomb. Everyone fell silent, out of respect for this moment of—*communion?* Max wondered. *Reverie? Prayer?* Yes, the Duce's lips were moving, owing either to a new tic, a tremor, that no one dared mention, or to the words he was exchanging with a higher power.

As the moments passed, Max felt his breath grow short. He knew it was he, Signor Shabilian, or rather the fruits of his years of labor, that had drawn Caesar to the scene. The young man pushed his heavy spectacles up the slippery crescent of his nose, and craned his head backward too. He followed the course of the monorails, three sets of them, all the way to the terminus at the ninety-third floor. Now the Duce himself would choose which of the final prototypes would carry a hundred and fifty thousand people up those tracks to the top of the vertical city.

"Duce, will you allow me the liberty—?"

That was Farinacci, the Faithful Friend; he trotted to where Max and his mentor were standing; he shouldered his way past them, and came to a stop next to the architect's three children, who were standing beneath the overhang of the steel parabola.

"Excoooz, Signorina Aria," he said, demonstrating his command of English. "I have the privooolege to carry informations. The Duce, he wishes to make his sooon-to-be-daughtoor the invitation. You will have the honooor definitely to accompany him as with legendary skill he pilooots to the heavens the *ascensore.*"

Everyone followed the stump of Farinacci's arm as he gestured toward the three closed cars made from brushed, burnished metal.

Aria, of course, said nothing. Her brother, however, clicked his heels, more in the German than the Italian manner, and said, "Please tell the Duce that our family is grateful for his courtesy. My sister, the signorina, is happy to accept."

At these words, Mussolini broke both from his trance and into a grin. "*Bene.*"

But the Duce spoke too soon. Aria was shaking her head back and forth, saying silently, repeatedly, the single syllable: *No. No. No.*

Nina spoke for her sister. "Aria wants to say she is happy. Happy for your invitation. But she has to tell you, her future father, *no, grazie,* she cannot accept." She paused, watching as Aria nodded her head in agreement. "She has a feeling—isn't that right, Aria? A feeling about being up in the air. Yes, it's true. She is afraid of heights."

There was, from Mussolini, a gasp. He lifted the cone of his hat and wiped, with his snow-white handkerchief, the sweat that was beading on his brow.

"What? She no wanna fly with Il Duce? Such a *àngelo,* she gotta maybe her own wings? A-ha! Ha-ha-ha!"

Farinacci: "Signorina. You foooget yoooself. You misspeak the wooods. She not frighted. She cannooot be frighted. Il Duce, he is the mooost skilled aviatooonist in alla Italy and alla wooold."

Aria, her hand clutched in her sister's, looked down at the solid ground. This time her father spoke in her stead:

"My daughter ain't no Friday Katz. She'll go up in the machine."

Now Mussolini strode purposefully forward; the medals on his chest made a faint ringing sound, like a gunslinger's spurs. As he drew near the row of gleaming capsules, each of the doors magically withdrew inside its metal shell. Without pausing, the Duce marched to the middle cabin, performed a military about-face, and stood in the doorway, arms akimbo, the flesh of his throat puffing out, like that of certain lizards, above his collar.

"Signorina Aria. *Figlia mia.* You gonna come with your *Papà?*"

The girl stood frozen. Max saw how her hands were again clenching and unclenching, as if she remembered all too well the last time she had found herself enclosed with Mussolini.

Franklin stepped forward, took his sister's arm in his own and half-pulled, half-led her toward where the Dictator was clawing open the buttons at his expanding throat. "Duce!" he said. "Do us the honor to take with you this member of our family who will soon be a member of yours."

"No!" That was Max, who was amazed to find himself actually saying the word out loud. "Duce," he continued, "You must take this one, this one here—" He pointed to the *ascensore* on the right, which was propelled by compressed gas. "It is smoother. It is faster. I will operate the one in the middle. It is too slow for you."

Instantly Farinacci came running forward. "What is yooo speak? Too slow? You tradooor? Yooo looonatic? The Duce, he ride a hooorse: is mooost fast hooorse inna woold. He drive oooto-car: is mooost fast oooto-car inna woold. *Una bicicletta?* Is winner of Tooor of France. *Fascismo*: it is speed! Speed! Speed!"

"Maybe," said Mussolini, in a small voice. "Is better take this one over here."

No one heard because Farinacci, waving his stump, had reached his peroration. "Ergooo, if this *ascensore* is manipooolated by Il Duce, is not dispoootable: she gonna winna the Race to the Clooods."

In the moment's confusion, Aria slipped her arm from her brother's and darted off to the side. Mussolini leaned toward his minister and muttered, sotto voce: "*Una donna. Una donna per Il Duce!* Eight hours! Eight! Eight!"

Farinacci whirled, snapping the fingers of the one hand that he possessed. Immediately a door on one of the black limousines on the Via dei Cerchi sprang open; a woman in black, with a black veil over her features, stepped out. She moved down the embankment to the floor of the site and then skipped quickly to the oblong egg of the central capsule. She was soon joined by He Who Is Always Right, his chest bulging, eyes popping, his whole body swelling at such a rate it seemed he would fill the entire cabin himself. A sudden gust of wind lifted the woman's veil. Max recognized the plump cheeks, the cupid-bow of the mouth. Claretta Petacci! Then man and mistress stepped inside, and the photoelectric current slid the door shut behind them.

Franklin glared at Max. Then he pointed to the right-hand lift. "You take that," he ordered, as if his black shirt had given him the authority of an officer. "Maybe it's not as fast as you think, eh?" Then, turning over his peppermint with a quick flick of his tongue, he disappeared into the cabin on the left.

Max, undecided, did not move. But when Nina ran toward him crying, "Will you take me up with you, Slapsy Maxie?" he hopped into the nickel-plated cockpit and heard the hiss of the door behind him make what might have been a sigh of relief.

No sooner had Shabilian stationed himself at the control lever than he heard what must have been a shot. Startled, he moved to the row of glass bricks that ringed the cabin at a height of sixty-eight inches—in other words, high enough to make it impossible for this operator to see through unless he strained upward on the tips of his toes.

What he saw was Farinacci with a smoking pistol at the end of his unshorn arm. For one mad moment Max assumed that the minister was aiming at him—because he had questioned the skill of the Duce, perhaps; or simply out of the exuberance of *fascismo*, the joy that the sole of the boot experiences as it expresses the juice from the bug. In ducking, however, the bespectacled beetle saw, flashing by the line of windows, the bulk of the two other ascending capsules. That was the starter's gun! The race was on!

Max swung back to his station and threw the lever forward. There was a hiss of escaping gas; the lift, with hardly a tremor, rose smoothly upward, accelerating almost as quickly in its journey to the sky as had the stone that Galileo dropped from the tower of Pisa on its way to the ground.

There was no question that his cabin was the fastest. But it was only a model. The actual *ascensori* would be built in three levels, so that every passenger—eighty to each story, not the handful who could squeeze into these capsules—could exit directly onto the floor of his workplace. No one knew for certain whether a jet of gas could propel the full-sized, fully loaded module; or whether they would have to fall back on a car powered by the familiar weights and pulleys, like the one piloted by Franklin on the left; or choose the one with a self-contained engine now being manipulated by Mussolini.

Up and up Max rose. The specifications for this model allowed for a top speed of forty-four miles an hour, which meant that an express to the top of the finished monument would take less than two minutes. Max felt his own chest swell—but from different motives than that of the *Capo del Governo*. His design had worked!

Above him, the sets of stories were flashing by. Below, at his feet, he could sense the chill of the carbon dioxide as it condensed on the metal plates. There, up high, that shadow—it was the middle car, chugging along in a pale plume of exhaust. Mussolini! He was going to catch him! In mere seconds he did so, and then passed him by. Now, farther up, a second shadow: that was Frankie's car, rising swiftly as the block of tricolored weights descended. Max was going to catch him too. Indeed, as he drew alongside he strained to see through the glass. There was Frankie, peering back. His mouth, on his round, adolescent face, formed a black scowl. He pointed down; then, with that same finger, he made a slashing motion across his throat.

Max understood. How could they think of beating the Duce? It would be like overturning the laws of nature, much less those of the state. He dove for the lever. He throttled back to half speed, and then cut his velocity in half again; he was soon rising no faster than a man could ascend the monument by climbing its core's interior staircase. Still, the Duce's car did not reappear. Max brought his own to a dead stop. Frankie halted his too. For a time Max remained unmoving, six hundred feet above the ground. A seagull, one of thousands in Rome, flew by and then circled back, as if it sensed, at the sight of this outsized clamshell, the raw, pink meat inside.

Next came a click and a whir. Franklin had resumed his climb. Max did likewise, slowly ascending to the station on the ninety-third floor. He slid back his door. The landing was open to the elements. The rush of the wind, its force, its near-hysterical whistle, surprised him. Frankie, holding onto his military cap, had stepped out as well. The two of them leaned out, staring down the parallel rails. There was the middle car, stuck halfway down. Was it an illusion? The effect of the sunlight beating on the heated metal? Or was the capsule actually vibrating as it clung with its steel talons to its perch?

What to do? The young man and the boy could only return to their cabins and move at a steady pace, braking heavily, back to earth.

Here was their sole hope: that if Caesar had not beaten them to the top, he might still rally and be the first, the victorious first, to reach the ground.

No one paid attention as the two lifts returned and their operators stepped from the cabs. All eyes remained fixed on the Duce's aerie so high above. The bells from San Anastasia struck the hour, and so did those from Santa Maria in Cosmedin and San Vincenzo di Paoli. Still that *ascensore* remained unmoving. Max, shading his eyes, began to feel uneasy. Had something gone wrong? Could the electrical line be cut? Had the automatic locks become frozen? Was the great man stranded in midair? There was no signal, no sign of distress. Not even a handkerchief dropped from the service box at the bottom of the lift.

Then, from the recesses of his mind there rose a terrible thought—or, rather, a terrible vision: the two passengers, the Duce and his doxie, lying in a heap on the floor of the lift. Unconscious, comatose, unbreathing, dead! Could it be? Had something gone terribly wrong with the system of ventilation? Was it possible that through some horrible error the fumes from the diesel engine had been sucked into the cabin instead of fresh air? What if it weren't an error? What if it were sabotage? Yes, it was all too conceivable: the Duce assassinated! And the first person to be blamed would be Maximilian Shabilian.

The American was just starting to think of how to mount a rescue mission—should they use the adjacent monorail or should they send up a car from directly below?—when two things occurred: high overhead a faint cobalt cloud joined the white puffballs rolling about the bowl of the sky; then, precisely one third of a second later, the sound of the igniting engine traversed the three hundred feet to the ground. A cheer went up as, like a chariot of the gods, the lift descended. Down it dropped, precipitously, plummeting lower, with as much daring as an eagle about to swoop on its prey.

Then, at just thirty feet, the vehicle slowed and with a flourish and a shudder touched ground. Out stepped the charioteer.

"*Viva! Viva Il Duce!*"

"*Bravo! Bravissimo!*"

"*Salutate l'eroe!*"

"He has won!" they were shouting.

"He has broken all records!"

"*E un' aquila.* This eagle rules the sky!"

The Duce did not look like a winner. His face was pale, his cheeks sunken and covered with the stubble of a beard, though these whiskers were gray-colored, as if the capsule he had just emerged from had speeded him not only through space but through time. He raised, in response to the adulation, both arms. Max was shocked to see how his thin wrists stretched from the loose folds of his sleeves. Were those fingers a-tremble? Did they shake?

"*Basta,*" said the Dictator, in a low, cracking voice.

But the crowd would not be silenced.

"Which *ascensore* do you choose?"

"Which one is the winner?"

The minified Mussolini stood there, his shoulders slumped, his neck so withered it was unable to support the weight of the mighty head.

Farinacci intervened: "Foolish people! You know already the answer to your question. The car that Il Duce pilots is the one that wins the race!"

The Blackshirts surged forward. They dug into their tunics and took out handfuls of petals—rose petals, pink ones, and the white buds of geraniums. With these they pelted the chrome-colored surface of the middle car.

Max shook his head in dismay. Not only was diesel fuel strictly rationed, any engine capable of propelling the triple levels upward at even twenty miles an hour would have to be as big as the lift itself.

It was Mussolini, not Max, who disrupted the demonstration. He waved a limp arm at the three machines. "*Basta*," he repeated. "These machines, they do not matter. They hold no interest for Il Duce. They are the past. In them you see the technology of the nineteenth century. They are good enough to transport the ants to the top of the anthill, eh? Ha! Ha! Ha! Yes, the laborers, the bureaucrats behind their desks, all the little people! The fighters with pencils and pens! Like beetles, let them crawl up the sides of the building! With ropes! With the stink of oil in their noses! With the gas-jets pushing them, like *peti*, eh? Ha! Ha! Ha! Let them fart themselves into the sky!"

The Fascists laughed too, *ha! ha! ha!*, echoing their master. What a man he was! Before their eyes they saw the depleted Duce revive: he stood straighter; he filled his loose clothing; the skin on his head, like a metallic reflector, starting to shine. Max marveled. It was as if he had had a transfusion of—what? Blood? Electricity? The expanding bubbles of CO_2?

"YOU, ROMANS! HEAR THE DUCE! HE WILL NEVER STEP INSIDE SUCH A VEHICLE! DOES HE RIDE A CART DRAWN BY MULES? IN AN AMERICAN MODEL T FORD? NO, NEVER!"

"*No! No, mai!*" the chorus responded.

"HOW DOES A HERO OF THE FASCIST CENTURY ARRIVE AT THE TOP OF HIS MONUMENT? HE FLIES! HE SOARS! BEFORE THE WORKER BEES HAVE EVEN REACHED THE TENTH FLOOR, THE DUCE ARRIVES AT THE SUMMIT. HOW? IN HIS AUTOGYRO! THE MACHINE OF THE MODERN FASCIST MAN. HEAR THE DUCE! TOMORROW! TOMORROW AT DAWN! THIS *MACCHINA* WILL BE TESTED. THE DUCE COMMANDS IT TO

LEAP IN A SINGLE BOUND OVER THE TOWER OF PISA! IN SUCH A WINGED VESSEL WILL HE FLY TO HIS HOME IN THE CLOUDS!"

You can imagine the response of the Blackshirts. They were cheering. They were saluting. They danced what looked like a tarantella, clicking their heels a foot off the ground.

Max was filled with wonder. What had caused, in the great Caesar, such a transformation? Why had he first, and so suddenly, grown old? Did it have to do with being spurned by Aria? Or by *not* being spurned by his paramour, Petacci, who remained still within the confines of her capsule? And how had the Duce recovered? He was once again bursting from his clothing, so that the boots on his feet and the trousers that covered his iron buttocks and the collar about his neck all seemed to have been manufactured for a much smaller man.

"Dunce," said Amos Prince. "Does this mean that the balloons will once again fly? That we shall add the next segment to *La Vittoria?* That you wish your monument to become the tallest building in the world?"

"*Certo,*" said He Who Drained The Marshes. "Within a day, two days, a week at most."

Suddenly, above Maximilian's head, like that of a cartoon character, a light bulb seemed to fill with light. He wanted to shout, as Archimedes is rumored to have done, *Eureka!* For the fact was he had the answer not only to why the Duce shrank and expanded, but also to why he had gone only part way up *La Vittoria*; and not only that, but to why the monument itself still existed when so many other projects of the new Roman Empire had been abandoned. Lastly, he knew why the great tower had not been completed but had been allowed to linger in this state of imperfection, forever unrealized, forever unfulfilled.

Max looked again at He Who Cannot Fail, a Jupiter now, with eyes black as coal chunks and fists made from steel. Of course the monument could not be abandoned: it was to be the tomb of this living god. But its completion, the final floor, that golden dome, would be like the passing of a death sentence upon him. Thus the ambivalence of Caesar, his tortured indecision, his inability to go more than halfway. If the tomb were destroyed, he could never have perpetual life. As long as it remained unfinished, he would never die.

4

That night, the night of the elevator trials, August 6, 1941—and for reasons that will soon become clear, August 7, like that same day in May, would never again appear on the calendars of the Fascist regime—Max Shabilian returned to his room on the Via degli Specchi. Because of the heat in his subterranean chamber, he dropped onto his mattress with neither pajamas on his body nor so much as a sheet on the bed. At once he fell into a deep and dreamless sleep.

A dreamless sleep? Does such a thing exist? Or do we forget the phantasmagoria that parade before our shuttered eyes? Max, who always slept flat on his back, never failed to recognize Aria when she appeared, even if she disguised herself as another woman, or a schoolchild—or, like a figure in a Greek myth, a horse, or a tree, or the moon. You couldn't fool Shabilian: he knew the telltale signs of the girl—the pale flowing mane of this Pegasus, the trembling white limbs of that beech, the glow on the face of the heavenly orb.

Now, once again, she came to him—like Iris in the shape of a bird. He recognized her at once by the blondish tips of the wings and the eyes, gray-colored, flecked not only by the green marks of radium but also filled with so many tears that they spilled onto his own closed lids. From such a dream he did not wish to wake. He slumbered on as the weight of the bird pressed against him and the shower of tears continued to fall. His eyes fluttered open to the first faint streaks of the dawn.

Aria, in a nightgown, was on top of him; her hair pooled on the bedspread on either side of his face. "It's horrible," she said, through her tears. "It's terrible! Oh, Max!"

Yes, he knew it. He had been sleeping. And was sleeping still. How else to explain that this figment of his dream, unlike the girl in real life, was speaking? Yet he palpably felt the full length of her human body pressed against his. She groaned, wrapping her thin arms around him.

"What is?" he whispered. "What's horrible? Do you mean the Duce? But you didn't go into his cage."

"Oh!" cried the phantom. "If only I had! Then this wouldn't have happened. They did it to punish me."

"Did what? What's happened? Are you in pain?"

"Yes! Yes! I'm in pain! It hurts! It hurts so much. It will never stop hurting!" She lowered her face, from which the tears were still streaming, against his. Now her legs wrapped themselves around him too. Her hot breath rushed by his ear:

"Don't believe them! Don't listen to them! Oh, my darling little Max. I want you to know this. They are going to say it was an accident. They'll say that something failed. That somebody made a mistake. It won't be true! *He* ordered it! The murderer! The monster! Jealous of his own son! Oh, I know. I know what will happen. He'll make a big funeral. He'll cry his crocodile tears. Don't believe them. Promise me, Max. Whatever happens, you won't believe them."

What had happened? *Had* anything happened? Was *she* the one having a dream? He did not know. He did not care. He clung to her. "Aria. My beautiful girl. Do you know? Have you guessed? It's true. From the beginning. When I fainted. When I was lying on the street. When I opened my eyes. From that moment. I've loved you."

She had not, through her sobs, heard a word. "Why didn't they kill me? It should be me! Why him? We were going to be married. In just three days! We were going to Capri. To be together on the beaches! In the streets! Holding hands! Isn't it silly? Silly to think of such things? Eating ices!"

"I don't understand. What has happened? What have they done?"

The tears fell now in a torrent. She raised her head. "Oh, my lovely Maxie," she said, her lips trembling, her nose trembling, her eyelids trembling too. "Make it go away. Make it go away. Hold me. My sweet, sweet Maximilian. Maximilian, my dear."

In response to those words the center of his body sprang upward. At that very moment he heard, echoing on the staircase, the steps he knew must belong to the messenger of doom. The door to the cellar flew open. Franklin, in an unbuttoned tunic, his hair loose in his eyes, stood on the threshold. He peered into the darkened room.

"Have you heard? Shabilian, have you heard the news?"

Max clung to Aria. He didn't dare take a breath. Even before her brother resumed speaking he knew, from the note of triumph in his voice, that the third curse on the monument was about to be pronounced.

"Bruno has been killed! The son of Il Duce! He was testing the autogyro. At Pisa. The rotor came off. He crashed to the ground."

In Max's arms, Aria shuddered. Excitedly, the boy continued, as if he too sensed that he was declaring the Pharaohs' revenge.

"What will happen to your tower now? What's the matter? Don't you hear me? Your monument will never be built!"

He took a step forward, blinking in the gloom. Then, with a grin already forming on his features, he pulled the beaded cord that shed a hundred watts of illumination on the scene of defilement and shame.

ALITALIA 607

Forced Landing

[2005: 1941]

1

It looks like they are going to keep up the charade. Everything normal. Nothing to worry about. Let's all smile. *Dolce far niente.* Or, in
the Fascist version, *Me ne frego.* I don't give a fuck. Here comes the
stewardess, olive-skinned, rouge-on-cheeks, hair-in-bun. Eyes me a
little warily, wondering, I guess, whether the crying fit is over. What
would I prefer with my dinner? White wine or red? "G-g-ginger,"
I growl. "Ale." I point to my toe. She doesn't get it. "G-g-gout."
It comes out like a gargle. "*La gotta.*" I get for my troubles a toothy
smile. All's right. All's well.

They can't, with this show, fool Slapsy Maxie. Even with half
a brain I pick up the signs of danger. Why, for instance, are these
cabin lights growing dimmer? I'd say it was my own senses, falter-
ing, except for the fact that Leda squintingly holds the menu card a
half inch from her nose. And why, if the idea is to climb above the
weather, have we been steadily descending? Oh, I don't trust my

own inner ear. I've got a private altimeter: the angle of the plumb line of the curtain that separates us from business class, from steerage, is—now we are in the area of my expertise—170, 160, not a level flight's 180 degrees.

Suddenly I hear, from outside, a crack, and then, from behind us, a dull thud. Is it my imagination? Or does the fuselage shiver? The stewardess hears it too. She gives a little jump. Even the paint on her cheeks seems to go pale. There it is again: a crack, a thud. It's not a lightning bolt, not thunder. The ice, I realize, is breaking off the wings and banging against our aluminum skin. We are, ladies and gentlemen, not out of the woods.

Three weeks after Bruno's death, with the nation still in mourning, Gianna woke me from a fitful sleep. An officer was waiting for me on the street outside. This was how, just two days after the tragedy, Prince had been arrested—in the middle of the night. My clothes were laid out, as if I'd been expecting my turn. I only wondered what had taken them so long. The work on *La Vittoria* had come to a complete halt. The perimeter of the Circo Massimo was fenced and guarded. With the work on the elevator systems completed, I was no longer needed. Still, as I slipped my arms through my jacket sleeves, and pulled on and laced up my shoes, my pulse held steady. It's not that I had no fear of the dungeons of Regina Coeli; I did. Then why, at such a moment, did I catch myself whistling? That was easy: for the first time one of us was going to see Amos Prince again.

When I opened the front door I discovered a motorcyclist, all in black, standing next to his motorcycle. He was, save for the white holster on his hip and the slash of a cigarette at his mouth, almost invisible. He motioned for me to get into the sidecar. I started forward. Nina, nightgowned, rushed down the stairs.

"Don't go! Max! Maxie! We'll never see you again!"

Gianna came just behind her, carrying a jumble of sweets wrapped in a handkerchief. "For the Maestro," she said.

I stepped into the little metal pod. The driver buttoned the strap of his chin guard and pulled his goggles over his eyes. Off we roared, through the lamplit streets, and then through a section in which all the bulbs had been darkened, as if the authorities were already rehearsing a blackout. We were not, I noted, heading toward the Regina Coeli, on the far side of the river, but in the opposite direction, toward the center of the city.

We pulled up on a small street at the side of the Palazzo Colonna. Two Blackshirts stood at the heavy wooden door. They swung it open. My escort directed me across a courtyard to what seemed a marble staircase in the northern wing. We climbed to a suite of government offices on the second floor. To my surprise, people were sitting all along the corridor. Most were men, still in their nightclothes or shabbily dressed; others wore the business suits in which they had passed the day. There were women, too, and whole families, crouched in a row against the wall. When I glanced back, the officer in black leather had gone. When I looked again at the figures in the crowded hallway I gave a start of recognition. I knew them all. Rather, it had dawned on me that each of them— whether petitioner or prisoner—was a Jew. Only then did I note the black lettering on the frosted glass of the nearby door: *Ministero della Demografia e della Razza*.

I did not take a seat on the floor. With my hands clasped behind me, as if I were already in handcuffs, I paced the corridor. Periodically a clerk would open the office door and call out a name. What filled me with unease was that whoever responded—a family, a couple, a lone individual—would walk in but never come out again. Where were they going? Alas, I feared I knew.

Signora Sarfatti, of course, had been right: in 1938 Mussolini had taken action against the *Ebrei*. His regulations were as severe as the decrees the Germans had issued at Nuremberg. Since then, things had only gotten worse. Everyone knew that now all foreign Jews— defined as any person not a citizen of Italy in *Anno Primo*, 1922—were being interned in camps or, far worse, deported to their country of origin: not the United States, symbolized by the worn, green-covered passport I'd thought to put in my own back pocket, but to France, Holland, Czechoslovakia, Austria—or any of the other countries occupied by German forces, even, unthinkably, to Germany itself.

I waited a half hour, than a full hour more. At that rate I would not be summoned until the following afternoon. There was no guard in the hall. Couldn't I simply walk back the way I'd come? I could take an all-night taxi to the Via degli Specchi. Even better, what if I took the short walk to the Ambasciata Americana on the Via Veneto? I'd show them my passport. I'd demand asylum.

No sooner had I worked myself up to the point of action, than the door to the ministry opened and the clerk called out, "Signor Shabilian."

Insanely, I could not help but feel a stab of pride. *Kershenovich! Bezmozquis! Henocks! Franks!* this same man had called, to summon the others. But I, the *signore*, was being treated as a person worthy of respect. The clerk, deferential as a doorman, held the door open. With renewed confidence, I stepped through the portal.

The office inside was furnished with a desk and three chairs— one behind the aged mahogany fixture and one in front; the third, in a corner, was immediately occupied by the clerk, who sat, pad and pencil poised, to take notes. Behind the desk sat a plump man in a rumpled suit and what was obviously a dark, slick, imperfectly fitted toupee. One of his eyes was narrower than the other, though possibly it was only squinting against the smoke that curled from his Fiume-brand cigarette. This man rose an inch from his seat, as if any further movement might dislodge his hairpiece altogether, and gestured toward the empty chair. I sat in it.

"Signor Shabilian? Am I not correct?" asked the official in Italian.

"*Sì*," I answered.

"I am Delle Donne, Michele, of the Office of Demography and Race."

Without a conscious decision, I found myself taking a hard line: "It is a quarter of two in the morning. May I ask why I was brought here at such an hour?"

"Oh, we have so much to do. Think of it: I, a vice minister, am also obliged to be here instead of asleep in my bed. But perhaps we may begin? I must ask, do you own a radio?"

The question left me stammering. "Yes. No. I mean it's in our flat."

"Does this instrument contain six or more vacuum tubes?"

"Yes, I think so, but—"

Delle Donne raised his palm, as if to indicate he would direct the traffic of the conversation. "We have information that you have visited the public beaches at Lido di Lallia. Is this true? And is it also true that you have done so numerous times in the last three years?"

"I don't know how many times. Not often. We have been working so hard on the monument for the Duce that—"

At the mention of that word, signifying the Prince of the Adriatic, Protector of Rome, the clerk reflexively started to his feet and even the vice minister rose, this time three inches, before he disguised his reaction by reaching toward his ashtray and grinding out his cigarette. "So? You dare mention that name?" He looked significantly toward the clerk, who even in sinking back toward his seat had begun to scribble on his note pad.

"I only wanted to say that I have been too busy for excursions to the beach."

"Might I ask you to tell me what I am displaying before you?" So saying, Delle Donne removed a heavy book from a right-hand drawer and dropped it onto the desktop.

"A telephone directory. For Roma."

"And for what year—?"

"1941."

"*Anno Diciannovesimo.*"

I noticed the piece of paper that stuck out toward the end of the volume. I knew, even before the official began riffling through the pages, what it marked. "Yes, my name is listed."

Delle Donne continued his search. "Can this be? Should I not make certain? It is of course a serious infraction."

"An infraction of what?" I asked, though I knew the answer all too well.

"Signor Shabilian, in each of these actions you have violated the decisions of the Grand Council of Fascism and the Royal Legal Decrees that have made them the laws of the state. I do not mention your attendance at public events, the theater, the cinema, the—"

While the official went through this list, I looked around the room. Aside from the mandatory bust of He Who Is Greater Than Napoleon, made of plaster but painted in gold, the only hint of decoration was a full-length drape that hung from floor to ceiling against the left-hand wall. This curtain did not quite obscure the hinges of a doorway that opened onto—what? The next office? A hidden passageway? A staircase? Wherever it led, there was no question that *Kershenovich, Bezmozquis, Henocks, Franks,* had gone through it—

perhaps, as Nina had warned, never to be seen again. Was that my destination as well?

"Please," I said, my voice slightly cracking. "I do not mean to be disrespectful, but what are these offenses? Really, they seem no more than technicalities, five tubes, six tubes, a day at the beach: what have they to do with me?"

At this, even the half-shut eye of the vice minister opened wide and his brow, wrinkling in perplexity, caused a sudden movement in the position of his toupee. "Are you making a joke, signore? You do not mean to deny, I hope, that you are a Jew?"

"I do not practice."

"I did not ask if you were a rabbi. Petraconne, would you accommodate us—?"

The clerk, a small man with a shaved head, in the style of the master, consulted a card he withdrew from his vest pocket. "Mother, Dina; the grandmother, Sarah, born Bialystok; father, Julius; grandfather, Joseph, or Joe, birthplace unknown."

"Article 8—"

This time the clerk had the information inside his hairless head. "Article 8 of the Royal Legal Decree, 17-11-1938—XVI n. 1728, converted to law 1-5-1939—XVII n. 274 subsection 3: *Children of mixed marriages who have more than 50 percent Jewish blood are to be considered in every case of the Jewish race.*"

"All right," I said. "I do not deny that I am Jewish. I am also an American, as you already know."

Delle Donne nodded to his assistant, who rattled off what turned out to be subsection 5 of the same decree: "*Also, children of parents of foreign nationality must be judged for the purposes of racial ascertainment according to the Italian racial laws.*"

There was, in that spare, dun-colored room, a brief pause. I pushed my spectacles back in front of my eyes. "I think, Minister Delle

Donne, that we should speak frankly with each other. Over the last four years certain sums have been paid to members of the Racial Court to ensure that they would overlook such small matters—attendance at the Cinema Quirinetta, for example, or the spa at—"

"Stop," Delle Donne commanded. "I too will speak with frankness. You are making a charge of bribery. You are calling the Racial Court corrupt. You charge that in return for cash payments, its members have ignored the violation of the decrees."

"I would say it was less the money than the recognition of the services I have performed, and will continue to perform, for the monument of the Duce."

Again the two servants of the state half-rose from their seats and cast a quick glance at the plaster bust that stared back at them from its pedestal.

"I told you, Shabilian: your people are forbidden to mention the august title of our leader."

"Excuse me. I ask you only to consider the work I have done. Weigh that against how petty these offenses are, mere details that—"

With a thud the vice minister brought his fist down onto the desktop. He leaned forward, staring at me with one eye open, the other completely shut, as if taking aim with a gun. "*Particolari!* You call these *particolari?* A petty offense! No! No! No! What we accuse you of is no technicality. It is no less than the defilement of the Aryan race, a race that once gave the ancient Roman people their warlike spirit and has been reborn in our Fascist legionnaires."

For one mad moment I thought that it was the bust of He Who Conquers that had opened its mouth and begun to speak. What terrible words! *Defilement of the Aryan race.* In response I could only stammer, as if my own mouth and tongue had been set in plaster: "But what have I done? I don't understand. What is my crime?"

Once more Delle Donne nodded to his colleague. Petraconne took another card from the pack in his pocket. "*That at some hour between the night of 6 August and dawn of 7 August, Anno Diciannovesimo, the accused welcomed to his bed and, in violation of Article 12 of Royal Legal Decree 121-19-1940, XVIII, 3121—engaged in sexual intercourse with a female of the Aryan race.*"

Delle Donne leaned forward. "Does the Jew Shabilian admit the truth of this accusation?"

I felt a spasm of pain, as if some toxic liquid had been injected into my heart. *She came to me!* I wanted to shout. *She was grieving! She was in despair!* But what I said was, "Yes, it is true. Sort of. More or less."

Delle Donne sprang to his feet. "And on the Day of Mourning! The day of the death of the son! It is sacrilege! The vice minister's face had turned violet, as if, like the bust of his master, it had been dipped in paint. "You pained the Duce! You made him weep!"

It occurred to me then that they were going to kill me; I half-expected them to pluck up the statue of Mussolini and stone me to death with his image. The only thing that happened, however, was that Petraconne, the clerk, said almost matter of factly, "Would you kindly hand to me your passport?"

Like an automaton, I obeyed.

Delle Donne, too, had grown calm. The only sign of his outburst was his toupee, which had slipped over his forehead, in the German manner. "It will be returned to you when you depart from Italian soil."

I felt myself fill with two contrary emotions. The first was a surge of joy: after all, one moment earlier I had been convinced that I was under a sentence of death; now I knew I would suffer no more than deportation. But my second emotion was despair. "You mean," I asked, "that I must leave Rome? Before the monument has been completed?"

"*Sì*," Delle Donne replied. "And you will do so before the end of this year, *Anno Diciannovesimo*."

"But I don't want to!" I wailed, all too aware that I was sounding like a child.

The vice minister wrinkled his brow. He wrung his hands, as if he were the one feeling dismay. "Signore, I ask you: be reasonable. Be charitable, eh? What is Italy? A nation at war. Our young men are everywhere fighting for their lives and the life of their country and the Fascist idea. They are in Africa, in France, in Greece and Croatia. Soon they will face the ice and wind of a Russian winter. *Sì*, a Russian winter! A nation at war, signore, has enemies both outside and within its borders. You agree? You also agree it must take prudent measures? Let us consider, my friend, the nation of England. It is a democracy, no? With its famed Magna Carta? Do you know what it has done with its Israelites? All those who fled there from Germany, from Austria, from Belgium, from France? They were deported. Or put under surveillance. Or placed inside of camps. Is it fair to criticize Italy for taking similar precautions? Especially when she is allied with the persecutor of those same refugees?"

It made, I realized, a terrible kind of sense. I bobbed my head in agreement, as if this were nothing more than a pleasant conversation among equals. But what my interlocutor said next chilled me through.

"Ah, but I remember! Your ship will not take you to *Inghilterra* but to America. Land of Negroes and jazz. Miss Ruby Keeler! *Footlight Parade!* You see, I, a poor public servant, also attend the Quirinetta. Yes, America: even at peace it turns back the ships with the Jews. What do you think will happen when it is at war? Eh?"

I didn't know what to say. I only braced myself for what he said next.

"I will tell you, Signor Shabilian, exactly what I think. Soon, very soon, America will have no choice but to enter the war. I tremble, then, for its refugees, especially for its Japanese, even though they are citizens. How fortunate they will be if, following our humane example, they are only deported. If they are only put into camps."

Had I heard him correctly? Japanese? *Giapponese?* Perhaps the error was in my own Italian. But before I could ask him to repeat the word, Petraconne, the bald clerk, interrupted:

"I have for you a ticket. On the *Rex.* Sailing from Naples on December 11th. Please, be so good as to accept it."

"What? The *Rex?* But I told you, I don't want to go."

Delle Donne leaned back in his chair, so that his eyelids, like a doll's, dropped over his eyes. In that dozing posture he said, "You do not realize how difficult this was to arrange. Go by the embassy of your country. Look at the lines in the street. These are not only Jews. They are Italians with relatives in America. Yes, and real Americans too. Once war breaks out between our countries, every American in Italy is going to be interned for the duration. *Internato.* That is a nice word for it. Those people are desperate to buy at any price what we have handed you as a gift."

With those words the vice minister rose, stepped from behind his desk, and took the packet from his clerk. He held it toward me. I hesitated. I looked toward the purple curtain and what I knew lay behind it. I seized the steamship ticket. Then I actually took a step toward that hidden door.

"No, no, signore," said Delle Donne. "Please be so kind as to exit here. You see? The way you came in."

Petraconne had skipped to the doorway; now, as if he were again the servant and I the employer, he held it open wide.

Once more I felt myself puffing with inexplicable pride. I stepped into the corridor. If anything, it was more crowded than it had been before. There wasn't room for people to sit against the walls. They were on their feet, circulating, as mammals do in their cages. As soon as they saw me, a hush fell over the hall. Everyone drew back to allow me to pass. Head high, I moved toward the stairs. Suddenly a woman, dragging a bundle behind her, blocked my way. "Tell me," she said, in makeshift, accented Italian. "How you? Who you? How is possible you alive?"

In an instant the others gathered around. They plucked at my clothes. They clung to the hem of my jacket. One boy wrapped himself around my legs. "Wait, wait," I told them. "*Aspettate!*" I reached for the little package that Gianna had thrust on me and began to hand out sweets—first to the boy at my feet, then to the crowd.

They all pushed forward. There was a crush. People were struggling to get near me. It could not be hunger. Many of them, I saw, had food of their own: fruit, cheeses, bread with meat rolled inside. They simply wanted to take something from my hand.

Then, from the other end of the hallway a familiar voice rang out: *Luisada!* At once the corridor fell silent. No one moved. Everyone watched as a bald, middle-aged man in a black suit walked to where the clerk stood waiting at the door. On his right he held the hand of a little girl, on his left the hand of a little boy. The door shut behind them.

Then the crowd surged around me, more tightly than before. "*L'uomo dei miracoli!*" someone cried. Miracle worker. "Tell us!" "What is the secret?"

"What is your power?"

I tried to force my way ahead. I used my elbows. But they would not give way.

"*L'uomo dei miracoli!*"

"He will save us!"

"*L'uomo dei miracoli!*"

2

"Hey, Mister: I thought of a new one. All by myself." It's the Littlest Rebel. She's not propped up on her seat back. She's in the aisle. She's got a round lollipop—*an all-day sucker*, we used to call them—in her hand, and when she leans across Leda's knees to pose her puzzle I can tell from the rush of her breath that it's peppermint. "What's black and white and red all over?"

A Jew's-paper, a nose-wiper, a noise-piper: but before I can summon the answer, the debacle begins.

First, the aircraft seems to rear upward, standing somehow on its tail. *Oooo* say the passengers, as if they, gathered from at least a half-dozen different countries, spoke a common tongue. Wee Willie Winkle topples backward out of view. Now we go over the hump and start steeply down. From well behind us, deep in the coach section, there is a rumble, which grows both louder and nearer. The lollipop reappears, followed by its owner, who clings to the armrest for balance. She opens her mouth, but whether it is to complete her riddle, or cry out in alarm, or simply to lick the sugary circle I can't determine; for at this instant the avalanche from the rear of the plane comes roaring through the curtain.

"No!" cries Leda. She leans outward to protect the mop-haired girl, which causes the blunt metal prow of the food cart to strike her instead. Exit Curly Top, presumably into her parents' arms. My granddaughter hangs unconscious, her head in the aisle. A thin stream of blood drops from under her hairline onto the carpet. I poke at the catch of the seat belt; I yank at the strap. I succeed only in cinching myself more tightly to the cushion.

"H-H-H-H—" *Help! Help me!* that of course is what I want to cry; but even if I had forced out the words, no one would have heard my old man's voice in the hail of exclamations that now fill the cabin.

Prayers, are they? Animal shrieks? Shouts of command? I can't distinguish one word from another. Over everything there is a loud clicking sound, as if the teeth of all of us were clattering in terror. Down and down we plunge. Dimmer grow the lights in the cabin. What time is left us starts to run out. I know the calculation by heart: 32 feet per second per second. The velocity of a falling stone. Involuntarily I start to do the math, vectoring our forward speed and free fall: if we were at, say, thirty thousand feet, then in ten seconds we'd now be at twenty-eight, but in another ten seconds all the way down to twenty-three, though the achieved speed of eight hundred miles an hour would rip the wings from the fuselage as easily as the Cyclops of myth, sitting down to dinner, ripped from their sockets the arms of the Argive band.

Talk about an all-day sucker! I must be a madman, a crazed mathematician, to sit here coolly assessing numbers—forty seconds equals forty-four hundred feet and a thousand miles per hour—until the sequence is interrupted by a slight, near-bald, very tan man who is clambering as best he can over the obstacle of the aluminum wagon, which has wedged itself in catercorner fashion across the aisle.

"*Scusi,*" he says. "*Sono il dottor Mamiglioni.*"

He has, I see, a hinged bag of cracked black leather; I watch him open it as if it contained, among its instruments and vials, the hope of our salvation. All he takes out, however, is an ordinary handkerchief, or what looks like a handkerchief, with a design of stems and cherries sewn along the border. He lifts Leda's head and presses the cloth under the fall of her hair. "*Per arrestare il sangue,*" he says. Stop the bleeding.

"Thank you," I say, childishly pleased that what are quite likely to be my last words on earth have been uttered without a hitch.

The doctor sits so that Leda's head is propped on his raised knees. I see that his trousers are blotted with his patient's blood,

which causes me an ache of concern no less quixotic than his efforts to save her. I look away. The cabin lights flicker, as faint as a
single candle. There: snuffed out. All the cries have ceased. The
clacking, the clatter has stopped as well. The only sound is the low
whistle of the wind, at the pitch that a boy will produce while blowing over the lip of an empty bottle. I don't count the seconds. I don't
add up the figures. I glance through the window. Blankness. Blackness. And then, rushing up to meet us, the hard white-capped edges
of the waves. I close my eyes. The engines, those old lions, give a
last roar, lifting us hopelessly, and then allowing us to descend, and
keep descending, until the deployed landing gear touches down on
the macadamized runway of the airport at—oh, A.P., what fun for
you in these names!—Gander, in the province of Newfoundland.

SPIRAL NOTEBOOK

Pisa

[1982: 1945]

Double-crossed. In Milan. By that four-eyed bastard. Treated him like a son. Taught him all I knew. Even worse: pointed the finger at me during the trial. Then he had the nerve to come to the bughouse, with his baby in his arms. Hell, no, I wouldn't see him. Or Nina. So I got a great-granddaughter now. What's her name? Forgot it already. Must be getting old. That's a joke. Oh, to be ninety again! Another joke. Leda! Last of the line. Franklin gone. Aria probably too.

Drove me first, the American army, from Milan to Genoa. In a canvas-covered truck. To CICHG. Counter-intelligence: aptly named. They got no blood from this stone. What could I tell them? I had no secret weapon. Nobody was going to put a death ray on top of my tower. Christ! And all that time they were sitting pretty on their atom bomb. I asked the questions: What did you do to my son? What did you do to my daughter? Did you put TNT under the monument?

Another ride, this time in a jeep. Handcuffed to a rapist. Ramirez, I believe. Maybe Puerto Rican. Seemed like a nice enough fella. Above Pisa, the detention center for all the other rapists, the thieves, the murderers in the armed forces. Asshole of Italy, they called it. Of Europe, of all of God's earth, I'd say. Of course I didn't see Buchenwald. I didn't see Belsen. Nobody told me about poison gas. Nobody told me about Jews in ditches. All right. It's true. I didn't ask.

Arrived in the middle of the night. They took Ramirez off. But the hospitality suite wasn't quite ready for old A.P. Sat on my bum watching the blue light of the torches. Acetylene. Figured out in the morning they were putting together my cage. Special accommodations. Welded the mesh of a landing strip to the metal bars. A gorilla couldn't escape. What lifted my spirits was the thought: they weren't worried about King Kong breaking *out*; oh, no, they're shitting their pants that their number one prisoner—that would be yours truly—was going to be sprung by the *Squadristi* and the *Bersaglieri* and all those loyal to the memory of Benzine and Clarineta breaking *in*. Six foot by six-foot-one-half inch. Tar paper on the roof against the sun and rain. Cement floor to sleep on. Coffee can to take a crap. Never once in six months on the other side of the bars. Two steps one way, two steps back. No belt, no suspenders. First ape in the world who had to use both hands to hold up his pants.

Sun and rain? That wasn't the worst of it. That would be the wind and the dust. We were off the Aurelian Way. Trucks on the side road kept kicking up dirt. Covered everything. Coated the buttercups. The clover. My tongue. Inflamed my eyes so that half the time everything in a blur. Like my cataracts now. But I didn't—

Well, it's close to a half-hour later. Snapped my pencil point. Force of emotion, I guess. Rang for Enrico. No answer. Then did something stupid. Shouted, *Gianna! Dove sei?* As if she were still up in the attic. As if she were still alive. No answer from anyone.

Like I was one of the prisoners in solitary. They had it worse than I. That's what I was about to write. I didn't suffer the way they did. Stuck in a cement box for some crime: trying to escape maybe, pouring lye on their feet to get out of drilling, a wisecrack about FDR. Like a beehive, that box, with only a hole in the top. God! The sight of their hands sticking out. I got resources: I gnaw on the pencil. Make a new point with my teeth. Miracle of nature I got any left.

No one allowed to talk to the gorilla. Shove in the tin plate of food. Take out the coffee can. Not a word. Except for the niggers. They're the ones who smuggled in my treasures: methenamine, so I could piss; blankets, not to cover me, but to lay on the cement floor. A stick. Pieces of paper. *Doen you tell nobody I get you this*: a Swan fountain pen. Funny, those guards. Black as Africa. Every last one of them named for a president: Jackson, Jefferson, Harrison, Tyler. Washington, of course. Probably named their children for Rosenfelt. Biggest gift, though this one must have been official: a little pup tent, a cell inside a cell.

Forgot to say, my cage, the one with the metal mesh, was the last in a line of ten. Death row: the nine others held those who one by one were taken out to be hanged. At Averso. Replaced soon enough by others. Figured my turn would come any time. Rather be dead, for that matter, than rot away, the sun burning down by day, a beam from a reflector turned on all night. Used the Swan pen to write last words of the boys on their way to the gallows. Letters from Uncle Amos, they called them, shouting the lines from cage to cage.

> *Don't believe what you hear about me.*
> *I'll always love you, Candy.*
> *Remember me*—like the ghost in Hamlet; and the opposite:
> *Just pretend I never was born.*

What time is it? Seems like I've been writing for hours. Rain has just about stopped. The stone mason kept on right through it, *tap-tap-tap*, cutting the edges of his octagon. I'm guessing middle of the afternoon. At Pisa, if the wind was right, out of the south, I could hear the bells of the leaning tower. When the mists lifted I could see it, poking up behind the laundry lines. Looks like they never hit bedrock. No meteor to serve as an anchor. If I had better eyes, insect eyes, I could tell time by the rate of tilt. Three or four microns every night, like a second hand ticking five meters off the vertical over nine centuries.

Hell, a blade of grass grows faster. Might as well watch it, and the ant on the blade, which to him must be a shoot in a bamboo jungle. There: he puts out a forefoot, afraid of a fall. And the cricket singing taps. The white-chested martin. The half-notes of blackbirds on the barbed wire. The camp dog. The camp cat. Another clock: the white ox that went over a hill every morning to plow an invisible field. Just behind, a farm girl in a red dress with white marks like commas. Came back every night when I couldn't see them, not with the reflector in my eyes. Somehow overnight they both had a bath. To wash off the dust. One time she waved. Waiting for a second wave might have kept me alive. Knobs for ankles. Black hair. Black eyes.

Stick helped too. Sawed-off broomstick, I suppose. Used it as a pool cue, a rapier, a baseball bat. Mostly I played tennis. In the summer, when I didn't bother to wear my pants. Set after set of doubles. Making up for the game I couldn't play at Salò. Me and Frankie against the Axis. Macaroni and the Fearer. Beat them every time. Brought them to the net. Lobbed it over their heads. Watched while they started to bicker. Laughed out loud. Franklin: once an apple-cheeked boy.

One hot night I heard a Negro playing a harmonica. Like a full symphony orchestra. "Lady Be Good." What else? Dwarf morning glories. A grape swelling beneath a wild grape leaf. The smell, under my tent flap, of mint. Boom-boom of the drum, while the men marched, pulling the shit-full honey wagon. How did that dress, morning after morning, stay so red? The tail of the ox, swishing away flies.

A journal. Is that what I'm writing? More likely a last will and testament. Nothing to leave. No one to leave it to. Junior. Old Slapsy Max. Got to give him credit. His idea to put the lifts on the outside of the tower. I remember telling Speer, can't put up a skyscraper without the elevator, without the telephone. Just as important as steel. Hell, you also had to have the invention of the revolving door. Equalizes the pressure inside the building and out. Same principle as my artificial planet. Too old, I know it, to go back to the bicycle shack. But the globe is ready. Just put it out in the sun. Those are my instructions: to Enrico; to the Shabby Lion, if he should ever come back to old Italy. Put it in the sunlight. Watch. Soon enough the atmosphere inside, and the aluminum too, will weigh less than the atmosphere around it. Look, Leda. Look, sweetheart. Do you see it rise?

Uncle Amos, big-shot architect. All I could do was put up my pup tent a hundred different ways. Like a Japanese man folding paper. Mostly settled on a pyramid. Old Pharaohs had it right: a perfect form, stresses on one side canceled by stresses on the other. Old Ikhnaton, first man to put all the gods together and worship the sun. Jews got the idea from him. Another way to tell time: lie on my back, note the shadow of the tent pole moving across the tent peg.

None of us can match the forms in nature. Used to watch the mountains, used to watch the architecture of the clouds. That brown-bellied spider spinning her web. Or, at the end of May, the wasps getting to work on their nest. On a tree limb. Out of mud. Four chambers, I remember, like a human heart. To a termite, his mound was a much bigger monument than a mile was to Moo-so-loudly. Those fifty feet by comparison are in the exosphere.

A son of a bitch named Jack the Ripper tore the buttons off the prisoners' blouses. Just to delay their clemency by a couple of months. Inside the cage the wire mesh, the naked ends of it, the jagged coils: an invitation to slit my wrists. Why not? Or make a break for it and get mowed down like the others who tried to escape. Shot over and over by the Browning automatic rifles. Why not? Why not? Why not? I can't answer my own question. The mint, maybe? The struggling ant on his springboard? Or the June day that the shining green wasp, only a youngster, new born, poked his head out of the bottom of his nest and took a long look around.

HERCULES

[1941]

1

Deported! That was all Maximilian could think of in the weeks following his visit to the *Ministero della Demografia e della Razza*. He was as outraged as any Italian. Were they going to throw him out of his own country? With the monument only one-fifth of the way to its ultimate goal? And, most important, with its architect, the great Amos Prince, rotting in jail? Every day, all day, he spent on the tortuous process of appeal. For untold hours he sat at the Superior Council of the Office of Demography and Race. When it was clear he was not to be admitted, he petitioned three different judges of the Racial Court. Then he wrote to the office of Salvi, Minister of Justice, and after that to Buffarini, Minister of Internal Affairs. He even applied for a hearing at the Grand Council itself and took to loitering in the vicinity of the Palace, on the off chance of presenting himself to a staff member of the King. Finally he trudged up the Via Veneto to the American Embassy. As Delle Donne had warned, it was so besieged by frantic petitioners—the line stretched

223

from the garden grounds to well down the Via Boncompagni—that he could get nowhere near the gates.

Every few days he would break off this futile pursuit to cross the Ponte Mazzini, where one or another of Prince's family—Aria, Nina, even Frankie or Gianna—would be standing outside the Regina Coeli prison. This vigil was as hopeless as his own quest. They were never allowed inside. No one accepted their parcels of food or books. Not once, though they never stopped looking, did the prisoner appear, however fleetingly, at the small, dark, barred windows.

The heat of summer passed. The cool days of autumn began. On one October morning Maximilian, after being shooed away from the Quirinale by one of Vittorio Emanuele's personal guards, found himself wandering aimlessly near what was then called the Palace of the Caesars. Glancing up, he saw the top of *La Vittoria* amongst the freshly laundered clouds. If his mind had not been preoccupied by the approaching deadline in December, he might have noticed the first signs of trouble: the bray of distant sirens and the shiny black sedans, windows curtained, barreling through intersections against the lights. As it was, he only noticed the rushing crowds when he was among them, funneling southward down the Via San Teodoro toward the Circus Maximus.

Breathless, Max came to a halt at the eastern end of the excavation. The crowd was already five deep on every side. In places they had trampled down the construction fence, so that the beleaguered Carabinieri had to link arms to hold them back. Everyone was peering upward, to where the tumbling clouds, moving smartly west to east, created the illusion that all ninety-three stories of the tower were about to fall. On the grass embankment along the Via dei Cerchi several squads of Blackshirts were shaking their fists in the air. "*Salta! Salta!*" they shouted, basso profundo. Jump! Jump! Many had picked up small boys and planted them on their shoulders. They shouted the same thing in their falsettos: "*Salta!* Ha! Ha! Ha! *Salta!*"

Max craned backward, his eyes leaping from one three-story segment to another. There! A man was perched on—what? The thirty-third floor. His legs dangled over the pointed edge of the outer wheel. *Amos,* thought Max, for one crazy moment, even though he knew the American was locked up in a dungeon. Besides, A.P. was tall, thin, a beanpole, and this man, though seated, was clearly stocky, even squat; and finally, conclusively, Amos Prince wore nothing but suits of white linen, while this unhappy soul was dressed entirely in black, as if in anticipation of his own funeral.

Why, then, were Maximilian's knees literally knocking together? Why had a sob, like a knot in a handkerchief, caught in his throat? Was it because he was about to witness a spectacle, a human sacrifice, that might have been devised by Nero? No. It was because he instinctively understood that this victim was a Jew.

There was not, clearly, a moment to lose. He pushed forward, all the way to the gate through which the workers and their equipment normally entered the site. "Let me in!" he called to the guards. He rattled the padlocked stanchions. "I work here! I'm Shabilian! Max Shabilian! Prince's assistant!" The uniformed men looked at each other. Then one of them shrugged and pulled the barrier against its chain, so that it opened just wide enough for the young man to slip through.

Now what was he to do? Run up the core's interior staircase? Man the controls of one of the lifts? Wouldn't his ringing footsteps, the approach of the metal cage, cause the poor man to jump?

Ahhhh, went the crowd, shaking Max from his deliberations. He looked up. The wretch had gotten to his feet. He teetered, arms flailing. But he wasn't preparing to jump. Instead, he was trying to catch his hat, which a wind gust had blown from his head. The

Jew—if in fact he was one—scampered across the roof of the ellipse, snatching at the headgear that just managed to elude him. At
this sight, so familiar, so commonplace, even the Blackshirts fell
silent. They watched with everyone else as the hat's owner made one
last lunge, just at the tip of the precipice, only to have the homburg
tumble over the edge. It dropped like a stone at first, but then, caught
in an updraft, soared skyward and spun out of sight toward the Baths
of Caracalla. The man stared after it. Even at this distance, Max
could see that his head, shining in the sunlight, was completely bald.

There was a disturbance at the gate. A few people murmured,
"*Il Rabbino. Il Rabbino Capo.*" Max recognized the plump, white-
bearded man trudging into the oval. This was the Rabbi of Trieste,
Zolli, who years before had led the Jews under the hated arch. Was
he now the Chief Rabbi of Rome? In his hand he held a cardboard
megaphone. At the base of the tower he tilted his head back and
started to speak.

"Brother! My brother! My fellow Jew! You, like me, are a citizen of Rome! All here are citizens of our beloved fatherland!" The
voice, already high, came shrieking out of the large end of the cone.
"Yes! First you are a Roman! I call on you to think of the Roman
virtues. We are courageous in the face of adversity. We are stoic.
We stare without blinking at the most powerful foe. Come down!
Your children need you! Think of them. Little Lorenzo! And your
Antonia! Already they are motherless. Will you deprive them of their
father too? Stop this madness! Be a man! Be a father! Be a Roman!"

Before these last words had left the rabbi's mouth he had his
answer.

"Ha! Ha! Ha! Ha!" The sound rang out like a car horn, chill-
ing all that heard it. "*Figlio mio! Figlia mia!*" cried the would-be
jumper. Then he forced out once more the klaxon of his terrible
laugh.

Zolli seemed to be petrified by the sound. He might have been made of stone. Suddenly Roberto Farinacci strode forward and snatched the megaphone from the rabbi's frozen fingers. He directed it not upward, to the thirty-third floor, but parallel to the flat earth at the base of the tower, where a squad of armed soldiers stood waiting. "*Avanti!*" he commanded. "*Voglio quell'ebreo vivo o morto.*" The half-dozen troopers trotted forward, to take their man dead or alive.

At this show of strength the Blackshirts found their voices. "*Bravo! Bravo il potere del Duce!*" They continued their cry until the last of the soldiers had disappeared through the ground-floor entrance to the core. Then they turned their attention to the man they were seeking. "*Salta, Ebreo! Salta!*"

Max tried to calculate how quickly the stalkers could reach their quarry. They would have to climb the spiraling interior stairway. Then they must make their way through one of the four service cables designed to carry utilities—water, electricity, gas—from the core to the compass points at the rim. Would the widower, the father of two, want to play cat and mouse? If he moved quickly he could drop into the roof hatch, make his way through one of those same cables to the core, and then hide in any one of the upper stories. It would take half the Italian army to find him.

Hurry! Hurry! Max said to himself. His legs reflexively lifted and fell, as if he could by example demonstrate to the poor fellow how he might yet escape. But the bald man stood rooted to the spot. Didn't he know they were coming after him? That with each passing moment he had fewer places to hide?

"Run! Run! Run!" This time Max shouted the words aloud, as he had once done as a child when a doe on a movie screen had been similarly endangered by a hunter with a gun. The deer had escaped. But the Jew remained, his coattails whipping about him, awaiting his fate. It arrived soon enough. The squad had split into two parts. Three men emerged at the north tip of the ellipse, three more at the south. They held their pistols at the end of outstretched arms. Still their target did not move. On came the advancing forces, until they were only a few yards from either side of their prey. That is when the man jumped.

A gasp went up from the crowd. Everyone's eyes were fixed on the falling body. It plummeted past the first three sections, nine stories in all. Then the west wind seized it and thrust it against the facade. It seemed for an instant to stick to the spot, like an insect that had been crushed against a moving car's windshield; then it resumed its downward journey until another gust squashed it against a lower story. That was how the building had been designed: so that the prevailing winds could not gain any purchase against the segmented side of the tower but would instead blow right through it, splitting to either side of the streamlined core. Now all this skill in aerodynamics, which had been exercised to prevent a catastrophe, was bringing one about.

Maximilian could not keep his eyes from the man, who, almost as if he had been aimed in his direction, plunged toward him. Before he could utter a prayer, or move, or think, he landed practically at his feet. Instantly Max recognized him. The black suit; the round, bald head; the line of black moustache: this was Luisada, whom he had last seen going into the office of the Vice Minister for *Demografia e della Razza*. The dying man knew him as well. His mouth just managed to say the words *Il Creatore dei Miracoli* before it filled with blood. Something, Max saw, was clutched in his hand. Hurriedly, before the others ran up, he removed the piece of paper.

Lorenzo, Antonia, it read. *You no longer have a Jewish father. Now you are Italians.*

"Ha! Ha!" That was Farinacci. "This is how a Jew dies," he declared, in a voice loud enough to reach all those on both sides of the ancient circus. "To save the price of a bullet!"

In that multitude, however, not a soul raised his voice in an answering laugh.

2

When, one hour later, the Chief Rabbi left the sunken oval, Max left too. Zolli walked past the twin temples of Vesta and Fortuna Virile, past the Teatro di Marcello and the Great Synagogue. So did Max. Whenever the clergyman stopped, whether at a newsstand or a traffic light, Max halted as well, keeping his eyes on the spot where the rabbi's thick neck bulged over his collar. Why was he following him? He did not know. What did he want to say to him? He did not know that either. His one great fear was that at each pause—for instance now, at the Ponte Garibaldi—he would not be able to start forward again, because the blood on the soles of his shoes would stick fast to the pavement.

The light changed. They continued northward, along the embankment. At the Ponte Mazzini they crossed the river, turned right on the Via della Lungara, and followed it all the way to the Borgo Santo Spirito. By then Max realized that the Chief Rabbi was leading him to the Vatican. Indeed, after another five minutes they joined the stream of seminarians and tourists on their way to St. Peter's Square. To Max's surprise, Zolli did not hesitate; if anything, he moved even more quickly across the Piazza, heading toward the group of tall buildings to the right of the basilica. Stepping between the pillars in the great colonnade, he came to a halt at last before a doorway that was flanked by two Swiss Guards.

"Wait! Stop!" Max was amazed to hear himself shout those words. And more were to come: "*Signore, il Rabbino!* Rabbi! Rabbi! Don't go in. Wait! I have something! Something I have to ask you."

The clergyman turned, staring at the young man from over the top of his spectacle frames. "*Che cosa desiderate da me?* What do you want of me?"

Max came panting to within an arm's length of the *Rabbino Capo*. "Nothing. No. Something. I was at the tower. The poor man! Signor Luisada. I know why he did it. It's terrible! He died in front of me! In my arms! I heard his last words. I—"

Zolli held up his hand. "Why do you tell me what I saw with my own eyes? What is it you want to ask me?"

Max stood, tongue-tied. He saw how the rabbi surveyed him, from his unhatted head to his battered shoes, which he once again imagined to be covered in blood, along with his pant cuffs, his pants. He was soaked in it! By force of will he addressed the older man:

"What is going to happen to the Jews? The ones who are being deported? The ones being held in the camps?"

"Why this concern for the Jews? These are not your countrymen."

"I heard you! You called him a fellow Jew. I am one too."

Once again Zolli's gaze seemed to pass over him from head to toe. "Yes, that I can see."

"Our people are suffering. Work, schools, pleasures, dignity— it's all been taken away."

"The Christians are deprived as well."

"But rabbi! The Jews are your people. If they can't work they will starve."

"The Italians suffer in their own way. My heart is sore when I see them. They line up at the cinema. They stand in crowds at the saloons. And meanwhile the little church remains silent and empty down the road. Is this not suffering? Is it not starvation? The emptiness of these souls!"

Max answered in a voice that was not much more than a whisper. "Rabbi Zolli, you do not answer me. What will happen to the Jews?"

With both hands, Zolli removed his glasses and then put them on again. "They are going to be killed. Sooner, for those already deported. Later, for those who wait in the camps."

"No! We can't let this happen!"

The rabbi turned again toward the doorway. Max clutched his arm.

"I can save them!"

To the young man it seemed there were two Maxes: the one who had blurted out those words and the one, totally astonished, who had heard them.

"What are you saying? You are a fool. Nothing can be done. Haven't I tried? Haven't our friends in the church? Mighty America cannot save them. England—England, France, they cannot save themselves. Even—" And here Zolli barely whispered: "Even the Duce, with all his magnificent legions, is powerless here."

"I told you: I can save them."

"And how can you do this when the greatest powers on earth can do no more than weep?"

Once again, Max felt he was no more than an audience to whatever speaker had stolen his voice:

"I have a plan."

"May I ask: what plan is that?"

"I can't tell you."

"Who can you tell? If the *Rabbino Capo di Roma* cannot hear your secret, who can?"

Max's lips came together; then, spasmodically, they flew open in a series of popping P's: "Papa! Pius! Pacelli! Pontiff! Pope!"

For a heartbeat, a second heartbeat, Zolli merely stared. Then he turned, signaling to the Switzers, who took a step to the side. The rabbi beckoned Maximilian to follow; the two of them entered the papal apartments together.

The older Jew moved quickly, down a hallway and up a flight of marble stairs. Max skipped to keep up. Were those Raphaels on the walls? The madonnas and crucifixions passed in a blur, along with the allegorial figures of—what? Heavenly paradise? The tortures of Hell? All these masterpieces of the Renaissance registered on him with no more force than would walls of blank stucco. Room after room went by, hallway after hall. They passed a group of cardinals standing with teacups; they climbed a second, grander Scala Nobile. Still Max paid no mind. All his faculties were focused on Zolli's question: *What plan is that?*

The truth was, he hadn't the least idea. The words had tumbled from his mouth like so many dice from a cup—and just as randomly, without order or meaning. What had possessed him? His thoughts raced: what *could* save the Jews? Conversion? No, no—the racial laws did not recognize anyone who had become a Christian since *Anno Primo*, 1922. Flight? But where could they go? All of Europe was, or soon would be, a part of the German Reich. Ransom? A bribe? Hopeless! Even if there were someone who could pay it—a Rothschild, a Morgenthau, a Bernard Baruch—the Leader of the Master Race would not take a million dollars for a single Jew, since he was already spending a hundred times that much, a thousand times, billions of marks, to destroy them all. What remained? Mercy? Begging? A change of heart? Must they resort to prayer?

There was nothing to do but stop, retreat, confess that he had no plan at all—and he might have done just that, had they not at that moment stepped into an enormous room, a full two stories high, with marble wainscoting taller than any of the Swiss Guards who stood at every exit. A prickly, multibulbed chandelier cast a green light over everything within. "*Sala Clementina,*" said the rabbi, pausing to catch the breath that either their quick march or the sheer splendor of the room had taken away.

Max stared up at the enormous fresco that covered the whole of the far wall. What caught his eye was not the seascape or the boat under full sail, but the poor man with an anchor around his neck who was about to be thrown into the waves. "Saint Clement," said Zolli, with a note of reverence. *Saint Shabilian*, thought Max, whose own neck was bowed under a weight greater than any anchor. What was he to say? What was he to do? He was going to drown!

Zolli clamped his hand on his elbow and led him to a door on the right. This time the guards recognized him and wordlessly cleared the way. They moved through a dim, book-filled room—was this the papal library?—and past an open archway through which Max glimpsed six or eight men bent over a table, sewing away at a worn tapestry.

"Take care, the step," warned the rabbi as, still holding his arm, he guided him up a sagging wooden staircase and through three more rooms, each dimmer than the one before, as if they had been designed by an optometrist gradually to enlarge the pupils of a patient's eyes. The last was so dark that Max did not immediately see the fat, black-clothed man seated in the corner, wearily leaning his chin in the palm of his hand. Zolli approached him; the two men murmured a few words to each other. Then the official took out a pocket watch and wrote what must have been the time in a green and black ledger that lay open in his lap. Zolli crooked a finger at Max to join him at the door. One after the other, they went into the blinding light.

It was only sunlight, and late afternoon sunlight at that; but the combined effect of the ever-deeper gloom through which they had just passed and the naked rays pouring through the three outsized windows dazzled him to such an extent that, just as he had not noticed the man in black in the darkened anteroom, he did not see now the man in white who for all intents and purposes was camouflaged by the play of the mote-filled beams. Zolli had no such difficulty. He crossed the room and knelt like a pilgrim at the knee of the Pope. Then he kissed the hand, or the ring on the hand, that was extended toward him.

Max was still blinking: the sunlight beat back from the glass of the Pontiff's spectacles and danced the length of their golden frames. His robes fell about him like splashed milk. His skullcap seemed, at first glance, and amidst the darting illumination, to float above his head, as if kept aloft by the force of thought emanating from the narrow scholar's brow beneath it.

"Come," said Zolli, revealing, in his smile, two rows of a smoker's stained teeth. "The Holy Father will hear you. What you have to say interests him. Come, greet His Holiness. Do not be shy."

Maximilian started toward where Pius XII sat behind a book-covered desk. Even as his feet sank into the sand-colored carpet, as if he were indeed crossing a stretch of beach, he was confronted by a new dilemma. How was he to greet the Pope? He could not, like Zolli, get to his knees. Wasn't there something in the Constitution about that? Forbidding Americans to kneel before a foreign power? But he couldn't, in the manner of his countrymen, simply thrust out his hand. In the end he settled on the sort of awkward half-curtsy that the winners of Wimbledon, Helen Wills Moody or Alice Marble, employed to pay deference to the British crown.

To Max's surprise, the Chief Rabbi of Rome knew his name. "Your Holiness, may I present Mister Maximilian Shabilian."

"I am pleased to meet you," Max said in English.

The former Papal Secretary of State replied in the same language, and with something of an English accent. "I know you. Were you not on the *Hindenburg?* Yes, you were. I welcome you now, as I welcome all whom the Chief Rabbi brings to me."

"Thank you. I am honored."

"You are," continued the Pope, whose nasal tones reminded Max of a clarinet, "an American?"

"Yes, yes, Excellency. I am American, though I have lived in Italy for the last five years."

"You know, five years ago, in *Ottobre*, the month of October, I arrived in your country aboard the *Conte di Savoia*. I traveled throughout the land. I saw your Grand Canyon. I saw your deserts and forests and all the wonders that manifest the hand of God."

Max thought he saw an opening. "Excellency, did you not also visit the wonders made by the hand of man? The width of the great Boulder Dam? The height of the Empire State Building?"

Zolli: "The Holy Father saw everything. He took airplanes to every corner of your country. The newspapers there called him *The Flying Cardinal*."

Pacelli said only, "Yes, I stood atop both of those structures."

Maximilian: "I know you are aware that the hand of man is also at work in the city of Rome. Soon our monument to the Duce will surpass the building you stood on in New York. It will rise five times higher than that."

The light from the lenses of the Pontiff's glasses seemed to concentrate on the young American, like the lamps used for an interrogation. "I am all too aware," declared the Pope.

"Forgive me," said Max, "but those monuments of man— might they not be inspired, like the ancient seven wonders, by the example of the original creator? We are constructing such a wonder.

When you climb to its top, will you not be above the clouds? Close to the ear of God?"

"I can assure you that God did not speak to me from that mountain of stone in Manhattan. Nor will he speak from this monument to Caesar. In America, he chose to show Himself in His own work, at the Falls of Niagara."

"Oh," said Max, with a little laugh. "That's where people go on their honey—"

Zolli cut him off in mid-word. "Hush. Respect His Holiness."

The Pope was now sitting in silence, his pale hands on his knees. He stared straight-ahead. Impossible to make out, beneath the drapery of his robes, the rise and fall of a chest. Then, quietly, he said, "I saw in the rising mists, the flying drops of water, the *arcobalena*, the rainbow. I was for the moment convinced that this was the Holy Mother. Yes! With arms extended, she was calling for me in a voice that was obscured by the roar of the falling water and yet possessed by all the force of the turbines for electricity: *Eugenio, Eugenio.*

"I cannot express to you in words the tenderness of that smile. Perhaps, I cannot be certain, I allowed myself to be blinded by pride. Was it that sin that allowed me to think that from this crowd of holidaymakers the Immaculate Heart had made a manifestation before me? Foolish man! Even now I wonder if it was only a trick of the mist. The vapor of my own wishes. I blessed the great falls and all the young people who come there to begin their wedded lives."

There was a pause. The lenses of his glasses were, in the nearly horizontal sunbeams, two blazing discs of light. "I know I am a mere man. A man of decaying flesh. But I have perfect faith that I shall yet live to see Her."

Maximilian stood, half petrified. He thought these last minutes must be a fantasy of his own. Had Pius XII, famed for his reticence, his asceticism, actually spoken the words he had just heard? And what was he now seeing, on the Pope's chalky cheek? He tracked, with as much astonishment as if he were seeing blood on a statue, the descent of a human tear. Then he heard himself say:

"I have a plan."

"A plan," Zolli interjected, "to save the lives of our suffering Jews."

Pius looked away. The tear, when he turned back, had evaporated. "There was, I remember, in America, a priest. He spoke against the Jews. On the radio. I demanded that he hold his tongue. Since then you have not heard from him a single word."

"Father Coughlin," said Zolli.

"Sì. We ache for the pain of your people. We pray continually for their well-being. Some imp of a devil has entered the soul of a certain individual. The ruler of the land to the north. I do not bring myself to say his name. I pray, too, that this possession be ended. Thus far we have not been successful.

"But it is not because of him, or our beloved Germany, that a darkness has descended. No, what we see about us now was foretold by Our Lady of Fatima. I fear that only She can undo the cataclysm that our sinfulness and lack of faith have brought upon us. Bolshevism! Bolsheviks! She saw that they would conquer. She predicted their triumph over all of the world. Let us pray that your country, my son, does not enter this conflict on the side of stubborn England and Soviet Russia. Godlessness would then spread through all of Europe. Our Lady saw this: every church in flames! Think of it! The horror of it!"

Once again, tremblingly, Zolli interrupted: "The Jews, your Holiness. Their suffering—"

"I cannot believe that the Holy Mother, Mary, will allow such a fate to befall us. Until She mercifully intercedes on our behalf, we mortals must do what we can. So, my young American, we are pre-pared to listen with a hopeful heart to your words. What is your plan?"

The trouble, of course, was that Maximilian had no more idea of what he meant to say now than when he had first blurted out the words. He swallowed. He wrung his hands, as if he could somehow knead between them some crumb of inspiration. The two older men leaned forward, the rabbi on the soles of his shiny black shoes, the Pope from his straight-backed chair.

Suddenly, from a corner of his eye, Max saw, hovering in mid-air, a flash, a blur of color. Blue. The color of Mary. Were they about to be visited by the Virgin? The other two men did not stir. Was he the only one to notice the whirl of azure, the streak of cerulean, as it darted across the ceiling and then plummeted in a fit of agitation to the corner of the desk? A pigeon! A parakeet! Papageno! *Il Papa's* pet!

"The Jews! The Jews must work on the monument! Don't you see? They must be forced into labor! They will complete the monu-ment of Il Duce just as they did that of Titus and of the great Pha-raoh before him. The Jews built them all. That is why they have lasted and why they will always stand. The Jews have to build this monument too. The Duce must speak to the man with the devil inside him. He must tell him, *We can't make deportations. We can't put the Jews in camps. We need them. All of them. Not just our Jews. Your Jews! The ones in France. The ones in Holland. In Greece and Croatia!*"

Maximilian, in imitating the voice of He Who Knows All, also assumed his stance, chest out, hands on hips. His words, no less than Mussolini's, were like those of a man possessed: "*YOU, REICHSKANZLER, HEAR ME: ALL THE JEWS OF EUROPE WILL GATHER HERE TO COMPLETE MY MONUMENT AND MY TOMB. ROME WILL BE THE NEW JERUSALEM!*"

Then, returning to his own voice, he was no less manic: "Yes! And if the Jews are saved, if the Duce creates this refuge for all those who are threatened in Europe, then perhaps America need not enter the war against him. Yes, yes, yes! They might even release to the Duce the helium for his balloons! Don't you see? It all fits together. It solves every problem. It's the perfect plan. Max! Oh you Max! *L'uomo dei Miracoli!* Ha! Ha! Ha! The wonder worker!"

That last burst of laughter broke from Maximilian's breast with such force that it seemed to blow the parakeet from the desktop back to its perch above the window frames. For a moment there was nothing but silence. The two Jews leaned toward the master of the little bird, which was now strutting along the cornice, bobbing its head, as if jabbing at a line of grain. The Pope, all smiling, watched his darling. He followed, with a nod of his own head, its peck-peck-pecking.

"Ah, Pipi," said Pius, with such fellow feeling that it was difficult not to note how thin, frail, and bird-like this Pontiff was himself. Indeed, the twin glass discs, between which the point of his noise protruded, created the impression of two perpetually open eyes. Was he, thought Max, a necromancer? Searching for an answer not so much in the entrails of the bird as in the pattern of its movements, the code-like taps of its beak against the painted wood?

"Holiness," said Zolli. "I beg you. The Jews. The danger. The plan."

The parakeet, hearing these words, gave three light taps, like the rap of knuckles on a wooden table. At once Pius XII came out of his daze. He gathered his slippered feet beneath his chair and placed his hands on the surface of his desk.

"This is our idea," said the Pontiff. "That the Duce be informed that these unfortunate people would be willing to work on his monument, just as the Jews of pagan times, in antiquity, worked on the

monument to the Emperor Titus. What do you think, Zolli? Will
this appeal to him? He has much pride. He is stuffed with it *come
una melanzana*, an eggplant, is stuffed with mozzarella. What is your
opinion?"

"Holiness! You have had a divine inspiration." The rabbi, while
saying this, fell to his knees. "Is it the Son of God who has sent this
thought to you? Is it the Immaculate Heart who has whispered the
secret of our salvation? Or the spirit of the Lady of Fatima? *Bravo!
Bravo!* With this solution you will make a mark in history. Only
you could have given us such a brilliant idea."

What was this? The *Pope* would make history? The *Pope* had
had the brilliant idea? Max opened his mouth to object; then he shut
it again. Maybe the whole plan did belong to Pacelli. Certainly Max
had not thought it out himself. He was no more responsible for the
words that had come out of his mouth than a radio was for the
sounds that poured through its speaker. Perhaps he had merely inter-
cepted the notion that was already in Pius's head, the way the antenna on that same radio could pluck transmissions out of the ether.
For all he knew, the blue bird, with its blurred wings, had borne
with it the wavelengths of thought, or had tapped them out with
its beak, the way a telegraph operator will signal speech by the repeated pressing of a key.

"*Bravo!*" Yes, it was he, Maximilian Shabilian, who was shouting that word. And, yes, it was this same Shabilian who was falling
to his knees. Together, the two Jews cried out in praise: "*Bravo!
Bravo, Il Papa!*"

3

Anno XIX, the year 1941, drew toward its close. Nothing except the
temperature changed. The steel works went on making steel, but

whether the ingots became part of tanks and bayonets and artillery shells, or were instead cast into yet more sections of *La Vittoria*, no one knew. The tower itself remained moribund. The *frittelle* continued to hang in the sky at one and the same time higher than the Eiffel Tower but frustratingly, tantalizingly, lower than the building named for the Empire State. One more flight by the fleet of balloons, one more section dropped like a child's wooden ring over a child's wooden rod, and the monument to Mussolini would be the tallest structure in the world. That flight, however, did not occur.

Nor was there any change in the situation of the Jews. If anything, their lives grew worse. In the past those who had been interned in camps remained visible, subject to visits by friends, family, and even the representatives of the International Red Cross. As winter began, however, those Jews seemed simply to evaporate. Were they being deported on camouflaged trains? Were they being imprisoned somewhere out of sight? Or was what was occurring to them even worse?

Max was thrown into despair. How high his hopes had been! Higher than the Duce's tower. But while that monument still stood, his own dreams had been dashed. Had he really thought that his plan might have rescued his people? Scarcely a foreign-born Jew remained in the city; indeed, even those who had been born there, the descendants of a community that had lived in Rome longer than any of the Romans, were beginning to vanish.

And Max, their would-be savior, was about to disappear as well. He had no choice but to board the *Rex* on December 11th. After that date he was going to be ushered like all the others through the purple door. If that did not mean death, it surely meant imprisonment—and for how long? At least through the endless years of the coming World War. It would be foolish to delay. He had to secure his passport and confirm his booking. If he did not, his berth might

well be given to one or another of those he had seen in the clamor-
ing crowd.

Then, on what happened to be the last day of November, A.P.'s
children received a telephone call: they were to appear at the Regina
Coeli prison that same afternoon. Was it their turn to be arrested?
Or had their countless petitions to see their father at last been
granted? The loyal Renato came by in the Fiat. Max and Gianna
squeezed in too. They arrived at the jail before the first signs of dusk.
To Max's surprise, all five of them were ushered inside.

They did not, as he had feared, descend into moss-covered
dungeons. Nor did they climb to where, from the small, square
windows, solitary monks had once gazed out over the whole of
Travestere. Instead, they walked up a single flight of steps and continued on toward the rear of the building. They might have been in
a hotel, with doors lining either side of a long corridor; or a suite of
company offices, filled with busy typists and filers. Why, there was
even music, a tenor, who was singing "*Notte a Venezia*" and "*Lolita*."

"Listen," said Nina. "I know those tunes."

"*Sì*," said Gianna. "I too."

But the lighthearted melodies chilled Max through. He feared
that these high notes, these castanets, were played at such ear-
splitting volume in order to mask the cries of those being tortured
within.

At the end of the hallway they came to a pair of glass doors
with white curtains unfurled against the interior panes. A guard in
a soft green cap rose from his chair as the little party approached.
Saluting with one hand, he pushed open the doors with the other.
Aria stepped through first, then halted, her palm to her mouth. Max
saw why: it was clearly a hospital ward, and one meant for patients
so ill or disabled there was no need for bars on the bank of large,
arched windows that looked out onto the courtyard below. Max

picked up, mingled with the odor of medicaments, the smell of oranges; at a glance he saw the little orchard, which might have been planted by the celibates three hundred years earlier. Those trees, still green-leaved, were hung with improbable globes of the fruit.

"Is he sick? Is he dying?" cried Nina, pushing up behind. "Where is he? Where?"

Nowhere. Only three of the thirty-odd beds were occupied, two of them by men with their legs raised in a sling. The third patient was wrapped in bandages, with only his dark, pock-marked face showing—a burn victim, perhaps, though in Maximilian's imagination this mummy had been lowered into either a pit filled with dogs or a vat of acid. His groans, soft and pitiable, and the sharp tick of the wall clock's second hand—three fifty-two, Max noted— were the only sounds in the room.

"Signorina," said the guard, taking Aria's arm. He pointed to a screened-off corner of the room, where another guard in a green cap sat with what looked like a comic book on his lap. "*Guardate vostro padre.*"

But Aria had already broken from his grip and was running toward the enclosure. The second guard—little more than a boy, with a boy's sparse moustache—threw down his illustrated booklet and rose, just in time to restrain her. The girl opened her mouth, but no words came out. If Max had hoped her voice had been permanently restored, he'd been disappointed. No sooner had Bruno been placed into the family vault than she had once more fallen mute, as if her voice had been buried with her fiancé. But as she twisted about in the arms of the guard, it was easy enough to see what she meant to say: *Let me go! Let me see him!*

The others came forward in time to hear the guard—or was he, unarmed, a nurse, an orderly?—respond: "Please. Calm yourself. Your father, he is sleeping."

With that he rolled aside one of the screens to reveal Amos Prince unconscious on his back. At the sight, the three women gave a collective gasp. Max was no less stunned. The architect's little yellow beard lay like a stain on the bed sheet; the narrow head above it was long, brittle, breakable, as if made from pumice stone. Enough light seeped through the gathered screens to make out the single foot, with toenails as long as a Chinaman's, that protruded from the lower hem. Instinctively Max moved forward, intending to cover it. Before he could grasp the swath of cotton, Prince's eyes popped open. So did his mouth. Impossible to know if the words that came out were an expression of paternal affection or—those glaring pupils, that wrinkled brow—a cry of alarm:

"Jew-near!"

The next instant Frankie clamped both hands on Maximilian's shoulders and spun him around. "What do you think you are doing? You don't belong here. You aren't part of our family."

Nina: "Hush, Frankie."

Gianna: "*E io, signore?* Is Gianna also to depart?"

Max: "I do belong. Didn't he say my name?"

Then they all fell silent as the architect spoke:

"How long I been in this Vagina Cooler?"

Nina said, "Oh, Papa, ever since Bruno died. It's the end of November now. Almost four months!"

"I guess I lost track of the time. Here's what I want you to tell me: How high is our tower now? Wait: let me tell you. Four months. Ought to be, lessee, one flight a week: that's six hundred more feet. Eighteen hundred altogether. Hell, we're one-third of the way!"

"No, no," Max blurted out. "We haven't raised a single floor."

Prince began to cough. Red-faced, he choked out his next words: "What? What did he say? What the hell did that Chew say?"

Aria rushed to Max and put a finger across his mouth.

Nina dropped to her knees beside her father's bed. "That's right, Papa. It's just the way you said. Every week there is a new flight of balloons. Haven't you seen them from your window? Haven't you heard their engines? Oh, your beautiful tower! How high it is now! How high it is going to go!"

At these words, Prince struggled upward, first onto his elbows, then to a full-seated position, as if he were attached by cords to these merely verbal balloons. He looked around, dazed. "I don't know. I didn't see them. I didn't hear them. I guess I don't remember. My head has been hurting."

Nina: "What have they done to you, Papa? Oh, just look at you!" She turned on the orderly. "Did you beat him? Did you starve him? He's skin and bones! You are torturers!"

"No, no, Signorina. We do not beat him. Orders of the Duce. It is his head. *Pazzesco, è pazzesco.*" Here the young man twisted the fingers of one hand next to his own temple, in the international sign of craziness.

The architect did not miss the gesture. "Nothing wrong with me. I saw those balloons, all right. Out of this window. What a sight! Why are you looking at each other? You think I'm bonkers? It's not true! I'll prove it to you. What did you say the monument was at? One third of a mile? That's 1760 feet, which is 536 meters, five-hundred thirty six point, lemme see, five-eight-five. How's them apples? Is that a brain that's gone bonkers? Am I not Amaze-us Prince? Boy, I sure could use a cigarette. Sons of bitches won't let me light up. I guess those balloons are full of helium, eh? Hydrogen too risky. Fire! I guess old FDR gave us the gas after all. Did you know that a one-liter balloon filled with helium weighs one gram less than if it were filled with air? Yup. Everything follows from that. You could lift the Queen Mary. 'Course you'd need one hell of a balloon. Lessee, what's the radius? Seventy-five feet times seventy-five is, is—What's wrong? My head is not working. It's aching! Aching!"

Everyone remained silent, aghast. Aria's eyes, Gianna's eyes, then Nina's, filled with tears. A.P. saw them. He stopped his calculations.

"Please. Don't worry, children. I am in my right mind. I understand. You did not dare tell me. But can we not get one more flight? One! Is that ass-licking too much? Another story will make us the highest building in the world."

Nina, still on her knees, put her hand against her father's cheek. "No, no, Papa. You remember. You saw the balloons. How tall we are now! And we will be even taller. A mile in the sky."

Now Franklin stepped forward, leaning over his sister. "Enough of this farce. You are not talking to a child. In the Fascist Era, no one is permitted to turn from the truth." He paused to run his hand over his hair, which was slicked to his scalp, as if every strand had been set in plaster. "*La Vittoria* is not going up. Not by an inch. It's coming down! I don't mean the R.A.F and its bombs. No! The Duce will do their work for them. Oh, how he loves his monument! Yes, every ounce of steel that is in it. Now we are marching into Russia, to destroy the Bolsheviks. We are returning to Africa, to master all of that continent. The tower is going to be melted into bullets and guns!"

"My God!" cried Nina. "You've killed him!"

For an instant, it seemed she must be right. Prince fell backward, his eyes still open, his mouth open too, as if he had received the death blow.

The color drained from Franklin's cherry cheeks. He was just as pale as his father. "But I only told him the truth."

Nina sprang upward to face him. "The truth! Are you mad? You might as well stab him with a knife."

Gianna: "The Maestro, he must believe the tower grows. That it becomes the most tall in all the world."

Franklin hooked his thumbs into his military belt, as if they were bullets. "And what if *that* were the truth? What if another flight *could* be made?"

Maximilian: "What are you saying? That the Duce will start work on the tower? He won't do it. Not any more. Even if he were not at war. Even if he had enough gas. It's finished."

Franklin scowled in disgust. "Have you all made an agreement? To play dumb? There is only one way to persuade the Duce. You know what it is as well as I."

"But I don't," Nina insisted. "The Duce is frightened. He thinks *La Vittoria* is cursed. How can we make him change his mind?"

Frankie: "By giving him what he wants."

Max: "What he wants? What is that?"

Instead of replying, the boy turned to his right and stared wordlessly at his older sister. Aria blushed. She got redder and redder. Then she began shaking her head, left and right. *No! No! No!* Anyone, a speaker of any language, could decipher those words.

"I can't believe you said that," cried Nina. "You talk about Max not being part of the family. But you are her *brother!*"

Franklin drew himself up like a soldier, a *Squadrista*, in order to bear with stoicism what he knew he would hear next.

Nina: "Tell me you're joking! It's a bad joke. No one's laughing. Do you hear me? No one's laughing!"

Gianna made a fist and shook it in the young man's face. "*No! Voi siete uno sporco protettore! Ti disprezzo.* Pimp! You are a pimp!"

As for Aria, she had backed up against the far wall; her arms were stretched out before her, as if to ward off whatever—a truck, a trolley, a maddened bull—was charging toward her.

Frankie turned aside, to where Amos lay unmoving on his bed. "Don't say *brother* to me. Don't talk about *family*. This is A.P. Our father. You know if work on the tower doesn't start, he'll die. Do you want to save him or not? If you do, this is the only way."

Now the full import of what Franklin was suggesting dawned on Max Shabilian. At once every bone in his body turned to water. His voice, when he forced it from his voice box, sounded wobbly and distant, as if it were under water too. "Wait. There is another way. I have a secret. It's a secret plan. *That's* what we have to bring to the Duce. That's what will change his mind."

"What is it?" cried Nina. "Oh, Maxie, tell us!"

"You aren't going to listen to *him*, are you? To this clown?"

"The Jews have to build the monument. All the Jews in Rome. In Italy. All those left alive in Europe."

Franklin laughed, almost gaily. "What a plan! In another few months there won't be a single one of them left."

"Wait!" Nina exclaimed. "Listen!" She was pointing to what was not yet a death bed. There Prince, propped on a pillow, had started to speak:

"Pharos of Alexandria, a lighthouse, tallest structure in the world. Hanging Gardens of Babylon. Temple of Artemis. Statue of Zeus, made from ivory and gold. Mausoleum at Halicarnassus, tomb of King Mausolos. Colossus of Rhodes, big as the Statue of Liberty."

Nina bent toward him. "What's that, A.P.? What are you saying?"

Maximilian: "I know. The Seven Wonders. The ones from the ancient world."

Prince smiled. "Jew-near! Shabby-lion! Smart boy! That's six of 'em. All gone. All destroyed. Earthquake. Fire. Flood. Marauders. But not the seventh. No sir! I'm talking about the Pyramid at

Geezer. And why is it still standing? Because it was built by the Chews. They built the Titus Arch. It's standing too. We'll explain all that to Massive-peenie. He'll stop believing in curses. His Jewish slaves will build our tower."

"Max! Oh, Max!" That was Nina. She rushed to him. She hugged him and kissed his cheek. "You were right! This is the other way!"

Franklin: "It's rubbish. You are making a mistake. The Duce is no fool. He only plays one. He does not believe in superstitions. Don't talk to him about the Pharaohs. You heard him: he wanted the tower to control the world. With Marconi's ray. Aria, here is A.P. You can see him with your own eyes. You hear him with your own ears. He's weakening. He's dying. We don't have time for this mumbo-jumbo. I ask you: Are you going to the Duce? Or are you not?"

"No! She's not!" declared Maximilian.

But everyone else stared at the girl. She stood, clutching her arms. Then she walked to the bed and leaned close to her father. *Papa?* That's the sound her lips made. They could almost hear the unspoken question: *Papa?*

To the astonishment of all, Prince broke into tears. They jumped under pressure out of his eyes. In an instant they had soaked his beard. "Poor old Cheops," he moaned. "Old Pork Cheops. How he wanted to finish his tomb! But he had no money. Not a drachma. Not a dime. Poor old man. What could he do? He presto-touted his own daughter. Right there inside the pure-a-maid. Oh, that young girl! That innocunt girl! Charged the price of one finished block of limestone. It's a traga-ditty! It's terror-bull. She must have suffered. But think of this. There are more stones in that tomb than all the cathedrals of France put together. The magnificence! Oh, yes. That poor girl. Darling girl. Sweet daughter. But remember this:

the Seventh Wonder of the World is still standing; her name is lost in the sands."

Nina gasped. Max strode toward Aria. But she put her palms up, one ahead of the other, in the ancient Egyptian manner. Without a sound she walked from the ward. A moment later—such a terrible moment that, as in the Fascist custom, Max would tear November 30th from the calendar of his mind—she left the prison and went into the streets.

4

Five passengers had squeezed into the Fiat Berline on the way to the prison, and five passengers took the old sedan back to the Via degli Specchi. Aria, however, had been replaced by her father. The two young guards brought out his linen suit and dressed him. They helped to carry him to the waiting car. Franklin and Maximilian managed to lift him up the stairs of Number 8 and settle him into an armchair. To Max's despair, he weighed no more than the lamp that stood beside it, and was almost as thin. Franklin was the first to notice the four green and red stubs that, in place of a handkerchief, rose from his breast pocket. "What's that?" he asked.

Max knew: the design of the Linea Italia tickets matched his own. "They're for a steamship," he said.

And so, on examination, they turned out to be: for the *Rex*, ten days hence, the same sailing, and from the same port of Naples, as his own.

Prince raised his head from the pillow that Gianna had thrust behind it. In a croak of a voice he said, "Start to pack. Pack everything. All the clothes. The books. My instruments. We are sailing back on that steamer."

"You're mad," Franklin stated. "You're out of your mind. Where did you get those tickets?"

Prince: "Gift of the Italian Government."

"You're running away. You're a coward. You're afraid of being caught here if America enters the war."

Nina: "But that's the best reason to leave. We have to get out of this country. It's horrible! Look what they have done to Papa. If they want to get rid of us, we should go."

Prince: "You don't understand. I am going to talk to FDR. Old Stinky Rosenfeld. If I can make him listen to me there won't *be* a war."

"I am going too," said Maximilian. "On the same boat. We can't stay. We're Americans. If war comes, we'll be enemy aliens. They'll put us in jail."

Franklin: "Oh, you should go. Yes, get on the boat. Run, Shabilian. Hide. Dig yourself a hole. But you are making a mistake if you think you'll be any safer in America. They will get you there. They will get you anywhere. The Axis has conquered all of Europe. Can you have the least doubt it will soon conquer the world?"

A.P.'s next words were spoken so softly that only he might have heard them. "Once I talk to FDR he'll see reason. He'll give us all the helium we want. Then we'll sail back. The tower will rise."

Nina struck her forehead with her palm. "What are we thinking? It's impossible. We can't leave Rome."

Prince: "What? Can't leave? What are you saying?"

"Oh, Papa!" his daughter cried, rushing to him. "How can we? It's Aria. Who knows when she'll come back?"

Not that night, as it happened, and not the next one, or the one after that. The bags were packed, the steamer trunks ready, and still the vigil continued. Everyone, even Franklin, moved through the emptied rooms of the flat, and up and down the stairs, without saying a word. Prince sat glowering in his overstuffed chair. Shame, Max thought, that's what made them slink about—and he the most disgraced of all. He could have stopped her, by force if necessary; but he had done nothing. He could not sleep or eat. Nor could he free himself of the stink of orange blossoms, which clung to him like a vile perfume. A fourth night passed. Still the occupants of 8 Via degli Specchi moved about on tiptoe, not so much from shame, perhaps, but so that they would not miss a footstep, a knock, or the distinctive rasp of the front door's bell.

It sounded at last on *il 5 di Dicembre*, at a little past noon.

"Aria!" everyone shouted.

Nina threw open the window and leaned out. "It must be her. There is a taxi in the street."

Max was already bounding down the stairs. He yanked open the door. It was, of all people, the Chief Rabbi of Rome. Before the dumbstruck American could say a word, the older man said, "I know what you wish to ask me: *Why do the Jews of our city continue to suffer?* This I cannot tell you."

"Aria!" That was Nina, leaning over the banister of the landing.

"*Signorina*," cried Gianna, standing just behind her. "*Salite. Benvenuta nella famiglia.*"

"It's not her," Max shouted. "It's someone for me."

Zolli: "Have I come at a difficult time?"

"Yes. No. I mean, what is going to happen to them? The Jews? It's not just foreigners. Citizens are disappearing too."

Upstairs a door slammed. Then a second door, from farther away.

The rabbi did not seem to notice. "I try to warn them. They do not listen. Even the most ignorant Polish Jew understands the danger that confronts him. But not our pleasure-loving Italians. I would save them if I could. Alas! I have the power to see, but not to act; others, who have the power to act, do not see."

"But what about Pope Pius? He can act. *And* he sees. Didn't he agree to the plan? I thought he was going to speak to the Duce."

Zolli's hand emerged from the black cloth of his sleeve. It plucked at Maximilian, drawing him across the threshold, into the sun-splashed street.

"Yes, Pius the 12th. He is our hope. Do you know when I was young, a youth like you, I could not help but compare my own religion with that of the Holy Father. The Church: how grand, orderly, splendid on the outside; but on the inside, nothing. And Judaism: how shabby on the exterior, how threadbare; but in the interior, what riches, everything! That is what I used to tell myself, Signor Shabilian. I do so no longer. The Jews of Rome do not appreciate, and are not capable of appreciating, the scholarship of their rabbi."

"What are you saying? Are you saying that you are going to abandon them? When they are in such danger?"

"I will tell you one more thing about my youth. In childhood, at a cruel moment, I focused the rays of the sun on the wings of a moth until the poor creature burst into flames. I am haunted still by the tiny soul that I believed I could see in the sudden puff of ash. What power I held in my hand! Like a god's!"

"I don't understand. Why are you telling me this? We have to think of a way to help the Jews."

Zolli did not respond. For a moment there was no other sound on the street than, from just a few feet away, the low throb of the taxicab's engine. Then the rabbi held up his hand. "Here it is. Do you see it? I was mistaken. It is only flesh. The magnifying glass merely a toy. The power is in the sun. Do you see that as well?"

Here the clergyman threw back his head to gaze at the disc that was blazing at them from the highest part of the sky. Max had to put his hands over his spectacles, to shield his eyes; but Zolli, as if immune from the rays, continued staring. "Only that fire can melt my flesh and release my eternal soul. It is trapped. Trapped in this body. The Holy Father has seen the spirit in those flames. He has known the Lady of Fatima in the burning sun. He sees the robes of Mary in the mist. I see nothing. No voice that cries, *"Zolli, Zolli, Zolli!"*

Max drew back. Was the man mad? *Rabid Zulu*, as Prince might call him. Why was he talking of Mary, of Fatima, of a holy spirit? Was the Rabbi of Rome a Jew at all? "Please, why have you come here? Rabbi, what do you want from me?"

"I want what you do: to relieve the sufferings of the Jews. You must believe that Pope Pius will free us. I know that he has mentioned the secret plan to the Duce."

"Then why has nothing happened? I thought the Jews were going to work on the tower. That no one could touch them. Didn't we all agree?"

"These things take time. Can we be certain that the decision is entirely Il Duce's to make? There are other powers. Remember? The *imp of a devil*? I believe the person possessed by that devil is now or will soon be in Rome. That is when our fate will be decided."

"What do you mean? Do you mean *him*? The papers say he is at the eastern front. Fighting the Russians. How can he be in Rome?"

Instead of answering, Zolli turned on his heel. He walked to the back door of the taxi and pulled it open. He leaned into the interior. When he emerged he was holding two large leather-bound books, each one twice the size of the telephone directory that vice minister Delle Donne had placed on his desk.

"What is that?" asked Max.

"The lists of the Jewish community. Names. Addresses. All family members. One for our Roman citizens. One for those not naturalized by 1922."

"Why are you showing them to me? Take them away."

"I am not showing them to you. I am giving them to you. For safekeeping." The rabbi stepped forward, his face reddening with the effort of holding out the tomes.

Max jumped back, as if these books were an explosive with a lighted fuse. "No. I don't want them. What have they to do with me?"

"Nothing. Which is why no one will suspect you have them."

"But it's not possible. It's too much responsibility. I can't do it."

"Please be calm. The Jews may yet be protected. Sometimes I question my own fears. *The sound of a driven leaf shall chase them. They shall fall when none pursue.* That is Leviticus. The words mock my alarm. It may be that the danger will pass. Still, what if *he* is in Rome? What if his soldiers came to the synagogue and seized these lists? What would your responsibility be then?"

"Don't ask me to do this. It's impossible. I'm sailing to America."

"Perfect. When the danger has passed you can return the volumes to us."

"I won't be coming back," Max said. "Our countries are going to war."

Zolli smiled, revealing his stained teeth, though he never seemed to possess a cigarette. "Yes, I have heard of this war." Then, after placing the books in Max's arms, he ducked into the black and yellow vehicle, which then drove him away.

Maximilian, for all the cool of this December day, broke into a sweat. He was certain that, from every window of every building on either side of the narrow street, people were staring down at the sight of an

American holding such strange, oversized books. He could not be seen taking them into Number 8. Instead, he began running—southward to the Via Arenula, where he turned right toward the Tiber, as if the two registers were indeed bombs whose burning fuses could be extinguished only by throwing them into the water of the river.

As he neared the embankment, however, he began to hear hammering that did not come from his beating heart. He stopped. He looked up. Three workmen, unhatted, the blouses of their uniforms half-unbuttoned, were struggling to unfurl a banner from the top of the Ministry of Justice to the cornice of the building across the street. At the sight of the dread letter *H*, and then the dread letter *I*, the two volumes began to slip from Max's arms, as it is written the tablets of the Law dropped from those of Moses. Along the riverfront, he saw more crews setting out boxes of tear-stained pansies and dwarfed evergreens. It was true, then. *He* was in Rome. This was to be the route of his parade.

Clutching the lists close to his breast, Max raced back the way he had come. On his own street, he again came to a stop, listening now not in horror but in joy. Coming through the same window that Nina had thrown open, he heard—music to his ears!—a number of voices, chief among them Amos Prince's. The words were unintelligible but the clear notes of triumph were not. He dashed through the gaping front door. He took the steps of the staircase by twos. There was A.P.'s voice again. And A.P.'s laugh. This could only mean one of two things: that Aria had returned or that work on the monument would be resumed. Or both! Why not both?

Breathless, he ran into the front room. Franklin, Gianna, and Nina were standing together, leaning over and obscuring a fourth person, who was jabbering away in Italian. Prince was not in his wing chair. He was up and pacing the floor. "Shabby-lion! Where have you been? Hot-leer is here! Can you guess why? He's going to help dedicate the monument to old Misaligned-knee. It's true! I swear it! He wants, does old A-doff Hatter, to see what I've done. We're going on, Jew-near! We're going to be the tallest in the world!"

Max's head was spinning. What was he hearing? He already knew that the ruler of the Thousand-Year Reich was now in Rome. But what had that to do with *La Vittoria*? He turned toward the others. Huddled together, their heads almost touching, they seemed almost as excited as Prince himself.

Nina, flush-faced, caught his eye. She grinned. "It's true!" she declared. "Just listen."

Then she and the others pulled back to reveal the dark brown face of the stranger. It was the *Superinduttanza Sei*, whose chatter continued to pour excitedly through the cloth mesh over its mouth. Max caught the gist of the announcer's diatribe: All of Rome, *tutta Roma*, welcomes our ally, the Chancellor and his Director of Armaments. All of Rome, *scoppia d'orgoglio*, bursts with pride at this manifestation of architectural progress, *una cosa mai prima creata da mano umana*, a thing never before created by the hand of man.

Frankie's eyes were shining. "I told you. You didn't believe me. We did it! It was the only way!"

Gianna: "*Meraviglioso! Il grand'uomo. Il Cancelliere!*"

Nina: "Isn't it wonderful! Slapsy Maxie! There is going to be another flight! The Duce and the Chancellor are going to the ceremony!"

The young man felt none of their joy. "And Aria?" he asked. "Where is she?"

He might as well have asked the whereabouts of a complete stranger. They stared at him, their grins fading. He might have felt guilty, as if he had committed a social gaffe, had he not been overwhelmed with a sudden foreboding: Had they already forgotten her? Would they ever see her again?

Then, with a familiar grinding sound, somewhat like the starter of an automobile, the doorbell sounded. For an instant they all stood frozen, while the man inside the forbidden Philips babbled on:

Questo monumento è una Meraviglia del Mondo, un monumento a Mussolini, un monumento all'epoca del Fascimo, che rappresenta la forza, la visione del' Duce e—

Frankie switched off the radio. "There!" he exclaimed. "I knew she'd be back. Why not? She's finished what she had to do."

Nina began to run toward the landing. Her brother caught her arm. "Stop," he said, as if in command. "You take care of A.P. This was my idea. I'll bring her up."

Maximilian moved to the still open window. He leaned out. What he saw below—a shiny black sedan with two motorcycle escorts—made him think that this time Aria had indeed arrived. He watched as the three vehicles sat trembling in the blue cloud of their own exhaust. Then a man in a striped suit came from their front door, took four quick steps, and ducked into the rear of the Lancia. That meant that the girl must be in their building. These men had delivered her, as one might deliver jewelry, glassware, or something that might easily break. The motorcyclists gunned their engines; the caravan drove away.

"She's here," Max announced, addressing the others. "She's coming up now."

But the only person who came up the stairs was Franklin. He was grinning, wet-lipped and open-mouthed, with the leer of a man who has just conquered a woman.

"Where is Aria?" Nina cried? "Who was at the door?"

The boy stopped. He came to attention. He raised his chin and started to speak. "It is my honor to relay to you the wish of Il Duce. Each of you will now listen to what he commands you."

Max saw that he held a cream-colored envelope in one hand and a cream-colored card, embossed with the profile of He Who Has Been Sent By God, in the other. It was from this note that, taking a deep breath, the boy intended to read. But before he could do so, A.P. stepped forward and snatched away the invitation. It was he who declaimed the Duce's words out loud:

His Excellency, Il Duce, Head of State, Master of Albania, Protector of Rome, and his distinguished guest, the Chancellor of the German Reich, request the presence of the Honorary Academician, Signor Amos Prince, and family at 5 p.m. on the Seventh day of December, the Palazzo Venezia, for the ceremonies that will dedicate for all mankind and for all time—

Here Prince stopped. He wiped his eyes, either because the rise of his emotions made it difficult for him to see or because he was not quite able to believe the last words that he pronounced to them all:

The Eighth Wonder of the World.

5

Two nights later a black limousine pulled up on the Via degli Specchi. Max thought it was the same Lancia Augusta that had brought the invitation the day before. Everyone gathered in the foyer: Max in a rented tuxedo; Nina in a more formal version of the green dress she had worn on that fateful spring morning of 1937; Franklin in his uniform and a black leather jacket that closed round his waist. Amos Prince was the last one down the stairs. He wore a cream-colored formal jacket and cream pants with a satin stripe. "My mockery suit," he called it. He kept his squashed Panama tilted back on his head and a cold Tigrina, in its holder, rakishly upright in his mouth. Nonetheless, he was pale, and his hands shook so much that Nina had to make the knot in his butterfly tie.

Together, they climbed into the sleek saloon. Max, in front with the thin, moustachioed, hatchet-faced driver, allowed himself the following fantasy: since there was no jump seat, on the return trip Aria would have no place to sit except in his lap.

All the streets leading into the Piazza Venezia were barricaded. Soldiers lined the steps of the *Monumento a Vittorio Emanuele II.* Their car was stopped at two checkpoints—the second one manned by German Stormtroopers—before they were able to drive into the square and pull up beneath the balcony of the palace. They entered the guarded doors and climbed the staircase past the library on the mezzanine. Then they walked down a corridor lined with empty suits of armor, like the carapaces of fantastical insects, and were directed into the enormous Sala del Mappamondo. The old renaissance torches had been electrified; by their light they saw the banquet table that had been set up in the middle of the room.

The Duce sat at one end and, beside him, in the place of honor, was neither the Reichskanzler, nor the wife of Mussolini, nor Claretta, his mistress.

"Aria!" cried Nina, rushing toward where her sister sat, dressed in a tight maroon sheath, her hair falling freely in back.

Instantly Aria jerked back in her chair, twisting to rise. Her consort reached for her hand, pinning it to the table. She sank back, staring down at her plate of uneaten food. Franklin took Nina's arm and drew her aside.

Max, meanwhile, was astonished to see, at the opposite end of the table, wearing a red cap instead of a white one, Pius the Twelfth. A Swiss Guard stood behind him, as weaponless as a footman. Speer sat across the table from Von Ribbentrop, the German Foreign Minister. And there, with his wife, was Goebbels, grinning like a slick-haired jockey who had just won the sweepstakes.

The fact was, Max recognized all the guests: Farinacci, sawing away at his meat with his good hand; Butocci, the Italian architect, with, around his neck, a velvet cravat that billowed up under a chin still covered with irrepressible stubble; Vittorio, in his airman's uniform, and the adolescent Romano, side by side; Edda, Il Duce's daughter, and Ciano, his son-in-law, chattering like newlyweds; and *Il Re*, the little King, erstwhile Emperor of Ethiopia, sipping, with one finger extended, a glass of wine. The American was seized by an overwhelming sense of déjà vu. Yes! Of course! It was as though the great airship, the LZ 129, had not exploded in sheets of flame but were taking all its previous passengers on a return trip, perhaps to the Lake of Constance, or even a little farther, to the home of the guest of honor, who was surprisingly nowhere to be seen.

Prince, too, had noted that absence, for he now blurted for all to hear, "Where the hell is A-daft Hater?"

All chatter stopped. Forks fell with a tinkling onto the china plates. Ciano wiped his mouth with a napkin and rose from the table. "Signor Prince! You must excuse us. Our dinner has taken more time than we had expected. But how delighted we are that you are able to join us for the ceremony of dedication. It would be a great sadness for us if you had returned to America and could not be present at this historic occasion, an occasion that you can appreciate as much as any living person."

Von Ribbentrop, also a diplomat, chimed in. "How fortunate we all are to be present at such a moment. A world-historical moment.

Would it not be a wonderful thing if we could travel backward in time to ancient Egypt, to the hour at which the cornerstone was laid at the Great Pyramid?"

"Or at which the last stone was centered at the apex." That was Speer, speaking in German. "Herr Prince, I congratulate you on your achievement. From every corner of Rome I see your building. To me, it is music in steel. It is an athlete suspended in the air. Who can read the future? It is no less difficult than the journey into the past. Perhaps at some time that we cannot know your golden dome will yet shine above the city and above the clouds."

Prince put a finger to his hat brim by way of acknowledging this compliment. But his words were directed to Ciano: "How come there ain't no chairs for us at this bank-quit?"

It was true; every place at the table, save for the Reichskanzler's unoccupied seat, was taken. The Foreign Minister ran his hand over his brillianteened hair. "I hope you will accept my apologies. We—"

Count Ciano was interrupted by his father-in-law. "Prince! Amos-a! I'mma happy to see you! I'mma delighted-ed you are no longer in Regina Coeli. Your *figlia*, *la bionda*, she make for her father the big *sacrificio*. It's like the opera by Verdi. No! A *tragedia*: Agamemnon, he make the *sacrificio* to the gods. So they gonna make the *brezza del mare*. The sea breeze. To fill up the sails of his ships! *Sì!* The gift of his daughter to the gods." The Dictator grinned. He sucked in the winds himself, swelling his chest, on which the medals and embroidery looked much like the tagliatelle still on his plate.

"YOU, WHO DINE AT THE DUCE'S TABLE! HE HAS A BIG IDEA! HE DECLARES THE SUPERIORITY OF ROMAN ART TO GREEK TRAGEDY! THIS IS VERY, VERY INTERESTING!"

Farinacci: "Tell us, Duce. In what way is Roman art superior to the Greek?"

The World's Greatest Thinker leaned back in his chair and stared, as if for inspiration, at the Lion of Saint Mark that was painted on the ceiling. "IN THE WORK OF SOPHOCLES, OF—OF—"

Goebbels: "Aeschylus, Duce?"

"AESCHYLUS. IN THOSE PLAYS THERE IS A BIG ERROR. THE GREAT MAN IS ALWAYS HUMBLED. HE MUST SUFFER BECAUSE OF THE SIN OF PRIDE. *HUBRIS*, RIGHT, FARINACCI?"

The maimed man nodded.

"BUT WE FASCISTS HAVE PROVED THAT THE HERO CAN BE LOVED IF HE IS FEARED. THE GREEKS DID NOT KNOW OUR SECRET: YOU MUST TREAT THE CROWD LIKE A WOMAN."

The little King, with both hands, twisted the tips of his moustache. "Was not Caesar loved, Duce? Yet even he could not avoid his fate."

There was, from round the table, an astonished gasp. Mussolini waved his hand. "No, no. It is nothing. This is not a problem. We are having a discussion. FATE? FATE? HEAR THE WORDS OF THE DUCE: A STATESMAN SPEAKS OF FATE ONLY WHEN HE HAS MADE A BLUNDER. Ha, ha, ha! Look at Pacelli. He grows pale at our words. He does not like to hear that we Fascists are without fear, that we care nothing for the sacredness of human life, and that we do not, like Christ, preach forgiveness. No, we are true Italians. We feel closer to Dante than to the Greeks or the Child of Palestine. *Dante*, who did not forgive his enemies even when their skin was bursting like a pig's in the fires of hell. YOU, PACELLI: THE DUCE GRANTS PERMISSION. DO YOU WISH TO DISCUSS THESE PROFOUND IDEAS?"

All eyes turned to the Pope, who had indeed turned pale. With both hands he gripped the edge of the table. Only those seated closest to him could hear what he muttered: "But before God you must tremble."

Mussolini, it seemed, could read those thin lips: "Ha! Ha! We are having a real *conversazione*. Goebbels! Did you hear? He said the Duce should tremble. And why? Does *he* tremble? Our honored guest who learned courage at the knee of us Fascists?"

Goebbels: "The Reichskanzler fears nothing, Excellency."

"YOU, WHO SIT AT THE DUCE'S TABLE: KNOW THAT WE TWO CONQUERORS HAVE MORE POWER THAN THE GODS OF OLYMPUS OR THAT OTHER GOD WHOM PACELLI WORSHIPS IN HEAVEN. HE MADE THE MOSQUITOES. WE DRAIN THE SWAMPS—WHICH EVEN THE ANCIENT ROMANS COULD NOT DO."

Here Mussolini reached for what appeared to be a glass of milk, took three gulps, and then, with a linen handkerchief, wiped his lips. "Not only that, the Duce has secret knowledge that the master of the Thousand-Year Reich has plans to get rid of his mosquitoes too."

Like an arrested pendulum, Maximilian's heart stuck to his ribs. He looked toward Pacelli, awaiting what must be his certain answer: *Human beings are not insects.* But the Pope sat mute, continuing to cling with white-knuckled hands to the table, as if he feared the torrent of words might blow him away.

"This God, the God of Pacelli, he is not as strong as those who made the Pact of Steel. We are ridding Europe of evil. But he? The old man in heaven? The one with the beard? What does he do?"

Not a soul at the table dared say a word.

Into the silence Mussolini thrust forward the barbell of his chin. "YOU, WHO HAVE STUFFED YOURSELVES WITH MEAT, WITH PASTA, WILL NOW HEAR THE DUCE USE LOGIC. HE PRESENTS YOU WITH A *SILLOGISMO*: THIS GOD ALMIGHTY, EITHER HE WISHES TO DO AWAY WITH EVIL AND HAS NOT

POWER; OR HE HAS POWER AND DOES NOT WISH TO; OR HE WISHES TO AND HE HAS POWER; OR HE DOES NOT WISH IT AND DOES NOT HAVE POWER; OR HE DOES NOT HAVE POWER BUT HE WISHES TO—Wait, did I already say that? OR HE WISHES TO AND, AND—*tutto è confuso nella mia testa* OR, OR—"

Farinacci: "He wishes to but he—"

"*SILENZIO!* THESE ARE WORDS. WORDS ARE TO DEEDS AS FLESH IS TO A SWORD. ON THIS NIGHT, THE NIGHT HE BECOMES IMMORTAL, THE NIGHT HE IS TO BE COMMEMO-RATED IN STEEL, THE DUCE WILL ACT!"

So saying, the Dictator seized either side of his tunic and ripped it asunder. Then he tore his black silk shirt into two pieces, reveal-ing the hair-covered chest, with its many scars, underneath. He got to his feet. Instantly everyone else stood up as well—save only for Aria and Pope Pius XII. Mussolini glared at the Pontiff. "ONLY ONE MAN IN ITALY IS INFALLIBLE. IT IS NOT HE WHO RE-FUSES TO RISE."

He Who Is A Genius Of The Violin pulled a stopwatch from a lower pocket and then, as certain animals are capable of doing, puffed up his chest even further, to what seemed twice its normal size. "HERE IS THE BREAST OF IL DUCE. YOU SEE IT AND ITS WAR WOUNDS, WITH THE SHRAPNEL STILL INSIDE. IF THERE IS A GOD, IF HE HAS POWER, LET HIM STRIKE THIS BREAST WITH HIS BOLTS OF LIGHTNING. THE DUCE IS GENEROUS. HE ALLOWS A FULL MOMENT."

There was a murmur from the crowd, each member of which took an involuntary step backward, as if toward a zone of safety. All heard the tick-tick-tick of the swaying clock; all watched as the chest, improbably, impossibly, grew still further, while the famous scars—created without anesthesia by the battlefield surgeons—elongated, like the uncoiling of shining snakes.

"AHA! AHA-HA! HA! THE MOMENT HAS PASSED! HERE STANDS THE DUCE! YOU SEE? THERE IS NO—"

There was a crack, like a rifle shot, or a knife embedding itself into a board. The Duce reeled, grasping his throat. Everyone turned toward the spot at the table where a seated boy—so small, so insignificant, that Max had taken no notice of him—had knocked his glass of orange-flavored water onto the floor. Who was he? It was not Helmut, Herr Goebbels's only son. It wasn't Romano, either. Was this an even younger scion of Mussolini? A love child with Claretta or Paola Borboni or some other singer or actress? Whoever he was, he—with his mouth turned down and his thumbs screwed into his eyes—was about to burst into tears.

"*No, no, Piero. Non piangere.* Do not cry. Look, I too can play the game." With the back of his hand Mussolini swept his own glass, still half-full of milk, to the floor. "Who can eat? A man with my stomach, he might as well be a monk!" Off sailed his plate. Off sailed his silverware. "The meal is *finito!* Take it away!"

Like cuckoos from a clock, a set of waiters appeared and bore off all the dishes.

"Look. Our friend, Signor Prince, he and his *famiglia* cannot sit. So we will continue to stand. Bring the demitasse! Bring the coffee!"

Through the same doors came a second set of waiters carrying little cups and saucers, steaming pots, and sugar and cream.

Maximilian, through this commotion, had not taken his eyes from the Pope. One question burned in his mind. While the others were standing, chatting, drinking their cups of espresso, he now had his chance to ask it. He took a step toward the end of the table. He took another. The Swiss Guard turned to block his way.

"Excellency, it's Maximilian. Maximilian Shabilian. You remember? The American?"

Pius lifted a single finger, the one with the golden ring. That was enough to cause the Switzer to withdraw. Max still refused to kneel before the Pontiff, but he did lean down. "Excellency, forgive me, but what happened? The plan. *Your* plan. What went wrong? The Jews are still disappearing."

"The plan has not been forgotten. It has always been in our thoughts." The Pope drew his legs beneath his chair. "Every detail was brought to the attention of the civil government. We have done what we could. We shall see if Caesar chooses to act."

Ciano, standing nearby, had overheard them. "*Scusatemi*, but I believe you refer to the Duce. Also to the plan for the Jews to work on his monument. Yes, the Palazzo Chigi, which is responsible for all foreign Jews, has received this idea. We have approved it. Farinacci!" The diplomat called out to his fellow Fascist. "Farinacci! The Office of Demography and Race, has it not also approved the plan? The one to put the Jews to work instead of subjecting them to deportations?"

Farinacci was with great skill balancing a saucer on his stump. "*Sì*, everything is in place. Permission has been granted by the Grand Council itself."

Then Vittorio Emanuele spoke up. "We made no objections on our part. Far from it! We thought it a stroke of genius. It solves so many problems all at once. It remained only for the Duce—"

He Who Forgets Nothing, hearing the mention of his name, looked up from the barely adolescent boy. "I will speak to this American in *Inglese*. This is not the plan of *Il Papa*. It is the plan of Il Duce. To think is to act! Therefore, this plan, she is already putta into, what-you-call-him? Into *operation*. Yes! The *Ebrei* will build the monument to Il Duce, just as they build the Arco di Tito and the *Piramidi dell'Egitto*. Of course, we hadda first get the *approvazione* of our allies. Our *fratelli in armi*."

Von Ribbentrop: "There was no difficulty. In fact, we welcomed the suggestion. People suspect us. They accuse us of terrible things. But this is an example of our humanitarianism. The Ministry of Foreign Affairs approved the plan. And so did that of Propaganda and Public Enlightenment. Is that not so, Herr Goebbels?"

The limping minister smiled. "That is correct. We thought it just. The Jews are eager to capitalize on the labor of others. Now we will let them labor themselves."

"You understand," Von Ribbentrop added, "that the final decision is not ours to make. It must be approved at the highest level. Yes—" And here he lowered his voice: "by the ultimate authority."

A hush fell over the room. Some people glanced upward, some down. Then Amos Prince cleared his throat. "You mean by the Furor himself? A-dolt Shitter?"

There was, at the mention of this name, a gasp.

Oblivious, Amos went on: "Let me get this straight. The Fearer, he's going to approve this idea? When? How soon will we see the plan in action?"

Farinacci: "Immediately!"

Von Ribbentrop: "Tonight!"

Ciano: "In only minutes. At the dedication of the Monument to Il Duce."

"I am honored," said Prince. Then, as if he could not resist, he added, "I've been waiting a mighty long time."

The architect, Butocci, spoke up for the first time. "Yes, that is why we have hurried to have the dedication tonight. So that you could be there as an honored guest."

Nina said, "What do you mean? Did you think we would ever miss such a moment?"

Farinacci: "Our fear has been that soon you might leave the country."

"But we're *not* leaving," said Franklin. "We weren't ever going to leave."

Magda Goebbels gave a lighthearted laugh. "I am certain you will not want to be here when your country goes to war."

The little King stood with his arm linked in hers. "That's right. It would be a mistake to wait even one more day. Tomorrow might be too late for you."

Goebbels hissed in German: "He's drunk too much. Will someone close that little fool's mouth?"

But it was his own wife who said, "Yes, tonight is your last chance. It is already too late to stop the Japanese."

"Japanese!" Max cried, and at once heard a garbled echo: "Jab-the-knees? What do they got to do with it?"

"*SILENZIO!* THE DUCE DEMANDS IT!"

But it was too late to prevent Max from recalling what Delle Donne had said in their interview. How the *Giapponese* would be rounded up, even though they were American citizens. What did that mean? Why was it too late to stop them? Stop them from what? Could it be that—"

The tipsy King broke into his thoughts: "*È una sorpresa.* A surprise! Boom! Boom! *Una sorpresa!*"

Ciano rushed to the monarch. "Please, your majesty! Not another word, I beg you!"

"It's so far away. Here, on the *Mare Tirreno*, it is already night. There, *sull'Oceano Pacifico*, it is only dawn. Surprise! Surprise! The attack might have started already!"

Farinacci: "Yes, the night is coming. We must hurry. Everything is timed. The *Cerimonia di Dedica* must begin precisely on the hour."

At that moment a motorcyclist—the same one who had conducted Shabilian to the Palazzo Colonna—stepped through the doorway. He wore the identical black uniform with the white holster on his hip. "Duce! I have the honor to inform you that the motorized escort awaits you."

"Yay-y-y-y!" That was the boy, Piero. He ran toward the door. Everyone else started to follow. Max stood rooted, his head in a whirl. "Where had he seen that boy? Where had he heard his name? And was there to be an attack? By the Japanese? On America? Shouldn't he do something? Raise the alarm? Call the embassy?

Now that the head of the church had at last risen, only one person remained at the table. Aria. Nina ran to her. Her father said, "Aria. Come. Tonight we are being honored."

His daughter rose. With one hand she swept her hair to the side. She smiled, quaveringly, at her sister. Then she nodded toward her father. And Max? Yes, she smiled at him as well. She even took a quick step in his direction.

The Duce had stopped in his tracks. He pulled the stopwatch from the pocket beneath his belt. He held it up by its chain, the way hypnotists are reputed to do. As it swayed back and forth he addressed the girl. "Let the others go. We have time. *È stato di otto ore.* My sun! My moon! Come to me!"

"No!" Franklin, of all people, cried. But as he moved forward, as if to seize her, he was caught up in the crush of bodies as everyone—Germans, Americans, Italians—swept in their excitement out of the Mappamondo and down the stairs of this ancient palace of the Popes.

The winter sun was well down by the time the guests reached the line of limousines that was waiting by the curb. Max thought they would surely drive south, past the Teatro di Marcello, directly to the Circus Maximus. He was surprised, then, to find their Lancia start off in the opposite direction, and then swing west along the broad Corso Vittorio Emanuele. Pulling aside the window curtain, he saw armed guards at every intersection and, silhouetted against the nighttime sky, atop the countless rooftops. In mere minutes they reached, then crossed, the river.

"Where are we going?" asked Nina. "This isn't the way to the monument."

"Don't worry. Look, there's the Vatican." Franklin was pointing through the window at the looming dome of St. Peter's. "We're going to drop off Il Papa. He goes to bed early."

But their caravan swerved around the southern border of Vatican City and was soon climbing the heights of Montespaccato. More soldiers stood along both sides of the switchback road. No one inside the car said a word; each knew precisely where the motorcycles were leading them—to the Mussolini Works, the steel factories embedded at the top of the heights. They could see the reflection of flames on the underside of the billowing smoke clouds. Ash began to drop onto the windshield, smearing in semicircles when the driver turned on the wipers. The constant low growl of the smelters overcame the whine of their own laboring engine. Max was filled with unease. Nor was he reassured by the glimpse of A.P.'s face, pale and twitching, that he caught in the rearview mirror.

The caravan arrived at *Il Vulcano*. The drivers hopped from their seats and opened the passenger doors. Impossible, with the noise from the factory, to speak. The window glass in the long, single-story buildings glowed orange. Heat seemed to rise from under the ground, right through their shoes. Now and then the chimneys belched out a cloud of sparks that flew stinging about them. Three men came forward, holding piles of coveralls. Speer motioned for everyone to put them on. Max thought he could hear

Magda's high laugh as she wiggled into the garment's stiff cloth. Another man held a box of goggles. In a moment they were all staring at each other like Martians through the tinted glass—all, that is, save for Pope Pius and Max, both of whom would be blind without their glasses.

"Over here! This way! I found it!" That was Franklin, screaming at the top of his lungs. He was leaning over a raised lip of soil that stood at the edge of what seemed a flat crater between the hilltops. He waved to the others. Prince went first, with Max and Nina at his heels. Max was amazed to see how with each step the earth eddied around his feet, as if the iron in it were attracted and repelled by the nails that studded his shoes. He raised himself on tiptoes and stared over the embankment.

Behind his spectacles, his eyes opened wide: perhaps they *had* all arrived from Mars. For there, settled on the plateau below them, was the spaceship, an enormous metal craft with hollow windows and two pointed ends. He knew at once that it was the next section—the ninety-fourth, ninety-fifth, and ninety-sixth floors—of the monument, precast and ready to be dropped over the core. Prince, seeing it too, raised his hands over his head, like a prizefighter who has just knocked out his opponent. Nina ran to her father, hugging him with both arms. All of Maximilian's doubts disappeared. Here was the section that on this very night would make *La Vittoria* the tallest structure that had ever existed on earth. Perhaps Speer had been right, and that one day, after the war was over, their tower would rise even higher, far above the clouds.

Now Prince looked up, away from the three stories of the precast segment, away from the mill, whose smoke and flame were proof that it was still smelting steel for the hundreds of stories to come. Instead he searched the skies, peering through the layers of smoke. Max knew precisely what he was thinking. Where were the motorized blimps? If Mussolini had released enough helium for this final flight, the armada of *dirigibili* must already be on their way.

But nothing appeared in the sky. On the ground, however, Farinacci called out from where the others had gathered by a tin-topped shack: *Ooover here. You mooost come here.* The architect and his little family trudged back through the magnetized dust.

At the side of the metal cabin the others were shouting to make themselves heard. "I don't like it here," Edda cried to her husband.

"I don't either," said Magda Goebbels. "My feet are hot; the rest of me is freezing."

"What are we waiting for?" asked Romano. "I was going to go to the cinema. To see Laura Nucci."

"Quiet! All of you! Don't you hear?" Prince held up the palm of his hand. He was still staring upward, though there was nothing in the sky that any of them could see. But they could hear: a clacking sound, a whir, which grew steadily louder.

"Listen!" cried Prince. A huge smile split his face. "It's the hail-the-captors! Those are the machines that will lift it; they will take it up to the heavens."

No such autogyros appeared overhead. In truth, the sounds they heard seemed to be coming from below. Even the architect lowered his gaze to the rusted shack, beneath which the whirring noise now clearly emanated. They all stood back as the side of the tin hut slid open, revealing the cage of the elevator that was waiting within. Vittorio, the Duce's son, strode to it. Romano was on his heels. The rest pushed their way inside. Nothing was going to roar into the heavens, Max thought. Far from it. They were about to descend into the bowels of the earth.

The journey went slowly. Their cage was suspended by ropes, frayed ones at that. It rocked as it fell, tipping ominously when any of its passengers took a step toward this or that edge. The result was that they huddled together in the middle of the platform, their bodies touching. The rate of descent was not much more than that of a languorous walk. Max calculated that after the first thirty seconds they'd sunk roughly a hundred feet. At that level the air grew stifling, thick, and somehow palpable, like the wool of a warm-blooded animal.

"Listen," said Nina. "Do you hear?" Her shoulders, under her coverall straps, were shining with perspiration.

"*Che cos'è quello?*" asked the beribboned King.

They all heard it now: thuds, and clanks, and scraping, accompanied by a cacophony of what could only be human voices. The next instant, almost as if they had crashed through the roof of a vast apartment complex, the earth around them opened up and they saw fifty, a hundred, two hundred men. Each was shirtless and wore a pair of striped cotton pants. All were at work, swinging a pick, wielding a hammer, digging a hole with a shovel. Some carried bags of soil on their backs or, like dray horses, hauled them by the straps on their foreheads. Others pushed wheelbarrows this way and that. Still others rolled boulders up an incline, like so many figures of Sisyphus at his hopeless task.

Oh, the noise they made! Not just from their labor, but from their speech. All of them, it seemed, were shouting orders or asking questions or simply jabbering away at each other in what must have been a score of different languages. Impossible, in this inchoate roar, to make out a single human word. Max ran to the side of the cage, tilting it precariously. But no sooner had he put his ear to the mesh than everything disappeared—the strings of electrical lights, the incessant noises, the workmen themselves. It was as if a blind had fallen over an open window. Yet in another few seconds that shade snapped upward and the same scene appeared—the glaring illumination, the underground cavern, the agitated workers, and the sound of their varied voices:

"Podaj lichtarku!"

"Vono za tyazhke dly mene!"

"Ils seront fâchés avec nous!"

"Der ridl kert tse mir!"

"Oogst het omhoog! Oogst het omhoog!"

Then everything went black again; to Max, it seemed that a great cloth shutter had fallen over the lens of a camera that had been shooting the scene. This time he counted. One-two-three-four: on cue the next image was revealed, men at work on the recalcitrant earth, together with the jagged boulders, the backbreaking burdens. Each scene had an identical script and was played by interchangeable actors. It was as if they, in their cage, were a spool of film running at four feet instead of sixteen frames a second, allowing shot after shot of the performers in their striped pants, their pale, glistening chests, with a soundtrack of constantly wagging tongues.

What was the subject of the drama? What else but Hell, Hades, the Underground, the Abyss: a warren of underground tunnels and caverns filled with laboring men. Was this the *Inferno* of Dante? Were they to pass all nine circles? Each filled with the images of sinful men? Were their skins to be gnawed by rats or, as the Duce had suggested, roasted over unbearable flames? Here was another such circle, and here, four seconds later, yet another. But where, in this underground mine, was the brimstone and sulfur? Where the fire? The rending of tortured flesh? Why were there no groans, no moans, no sounds of wailing? Instead, what Maximilian heard was an excited chatter in a dozen different accents. There was even laughter. Amazing: some were even singing songs.

Suddenly, Max felt that he could hardly stop himself from breaking into a ditty himself. He understood! This babel, this mixture of tongues: It was French. It was Ukrainian. It was Polish. It was Dutch. Above all, it was Yiddish. No wonder they were laughing. No wonder they whistled at their work. These were the Jews! *His* Jews! From all over the continent! He, Maximilian, had gathered them here. He had given them work! He had given them life!

The descent continued for what Shabilian estimated to be a total of four minutes—which meant, by odd coincidence, that they had gone below the surface of the earth as far as the monument to the victory over Ethiopia soared above it. Then they came to a jarring stop. If this was the bottom circle, the very pit, of Hell, it was not a place of human suffering. The fact was, there were no people here at all. What they saw, stretching out below them, was a huge underground cave, almost as vast as those that Max had seen at Carlsbad when he was a boy. Was it man-made? Hewn from earth and stone by the labor brigades? Or was it a natural formation, like those in New Mexico? He could not tell. Certainly men had been at work here. Unshaded light bulbs were strung through the darkness. Terraces had been cut into the rock face, rather like those that Chinese farmers dug into the sides of their misty mountains.

Now Speer pulled open the door of their lift and motioned for everyone to climb out onto one of those narrow ledges. "*Raus, raus! Geh raus!*" he commanded, his voice echoing off into what was otherwise absolute silence. They filed out and, as if their combined weight alone had been the anchor, the cage flew off, vanishing rapidly up its shaft. The little band of adventurers stood with their backs to the earthen wall, staring into the shadowy reaches of the excavation below. The heat from behind them was almost enough to sear their skins. What now? Max thought. Prince, his face obscured by the wilted brim of his Panama, had the same question:

"What's happening? This sure ain't a dread-i-cation."

Romano pointed overhead, to the ceiling of the cavern. They all looked up. Something, some object, was picking up the stray light.

Max remembered the stalactites that had hung for centuries at the top of the underground caves. This was no mineral, no shining spike of ice. It seemed to be the terminus of a large metal pipe that was embedded in the rocky roof of the cavern. What was it for? Air? But there was no lack of oxygen, which spilled freely from the shaft they had just descended. It was much too large for water or any of the other utilities the workmen might have employed. The sight of this opening, black and gaping, filled Max with anxiety. Dread-i-cation? *Dead-i-cation*, he could not stop himself from thinking, in a kind of gallows guffaw.

"*Eccolo!*" exclaimed Farinacci. He was pointing with his mangled arm toward the bottom of the lift that was speeding toward them on its return journey. It did not reach their terrace, coming instead to a halt well above them. The door opened. Foreshortened figures got out. Max struggled to see through the condensation that had gathered on his spectacle lenses: yes, it was Pius the 12th and his Swiss Guard. Piero, the child, was with them. Was he, then, some kind of altar boy?

Now the cage rose again, far from sight; but it soon returned from the surface. This time it stopped at a still higher level: impossible for Max to see who, if anyone, stepped onto the carved ledge. This cycle occurred yet again: the elevator rose to the tin shack, took on its passengers, and descended—on this occasion to a terrace far above Maximilian and the others who were marooned below.

Butocci, the Italian architect, thrust his wristwatch into the weak, electrified light. "*E ora,*" he said. "It is time."

Speer looked at his watch too. "Remember this always. *Viertel vor Acht, siebter Dezember, 1941.*"

"Why?" asked Nina. "Why should we remember? We aren't even at the Circus—"

"Max-imus!" It wasn't Prince who played with the word. It was
Frankie, who simultaneously slapped Shabilian so hard on the back
that his glasses flew from his nose. "Here it comes!"

Max dropped to his knees. He was groping at his feet for his
spectacle frames when he heard the thunderous roar. The sound was
far off, high above them; but it approached rapidly, like a falling
meteor or a charging lion. Everyone remained paralyzed, Max on
all fours, Nina clutching her father, and Franklin stiff at attention.
The others pressed back in various attitudes against the scalding
rock, like figures in a frieze.

"*Il tubo!*" Ciano shouted.

Max's eyes were riveted on the pipe, out of whose open mouth
came the ungodly clamor. What else was to emerge from it? A gas?
A liquid? Or a flow of concrete in which all of them were to be immured? Then, he, like all the others, clapped his hands to his ears.
"Ah-h-h!"

The cry came from one and all. The aperture began to vibrate
and then to glow. Suddenly it disgorged a thick stream of crimson
liquid. A nightmare! Max thought. This must be a nightmare! He
felt the earth trembling under his knees.

Magda, Goebbels's wife, uttered a scream. A wave of heat, like
the hot breath of an animal, swept over the huddled spectators. Still
the stream kept pouring, covering the bottom of the cavern and beginning to lap up its flinty walls.

Shabilian, without spectacles, stared at this blood-red sea. They
would be inundated! Incinerated! Where was the elevator? Gone!
He could see the fiery torrent reflected in the smoked glass of all
the goggles. Why hadn't he worn them? The heat, the glare, were
so intense he felt that, even through his shut eyelids, he was about
to be blinded.

"*Hier ist das geschmolzene Metall.*" That was Goebbels.

Von Ribbentrop shouted out a single word: "*Stahl!*" Steel!

To Max's amazement, the others did not share his nightmare. Far from it: they were grinning. Ciano and Edda were clinging together, but not in fear—in delight, in celebration. "*Bravo!*" cried the King, Emperor of Addis Ababa, Maharaja of Tobruk. "*Bravo! Bravo!*"

"Yes! Yes! It's perfect!" These words were in English. Max looked up to see Frankie's fuzzy face. His features were distorted by what could only be ferocious glee. He was pounding his fist into the palm of his hand. Now he cried out in Italian, "*Congratulazioni* to Signor Butocci! *Congratulazioni* to Herr Speer!"

Max, still on his hands and knees, called out to him. "What do you mean? Why are you cheering?"

Nina shouted too. "You knew! Frankie! You knew this was going to happen!"

It was true. He knew. They all knew. Only Max and Nina had been in the dark—and Prince, who stood doubled over, as if struck in the solar plexus.

There was, of a sudden, a new sound, a tremendous gulp. The pipe had emptied. The hissing lake of steel had reached its full height, at something like twenty-five feet. As it cooled it grew darker. The ripples of liquid metal grew smooth. Steam rose from the surface, which was already forming a crust.

Franklin turned to his sister. "I could not tell you. You would not understand."

"But what? Understand what?"

"There will be war. There will be bombs. *La Vittoria* is going to be destroyed."

"What has that to do with this? Why are we here? You're not making sense."

"Allow me," said Von Ribbentrop. "No bomb can penetrate into this earth, even if the British, the Americans, were to target the steel factories above. When the bombs cease, when the war is over, the soil will be removed—with machines, with dynamite. The entire mountain will disappear. The monument will remain."

Prince, still bent double, said, "The steel. Where will you get the steel?"

Von Ribbentrop: "That will be the task of Minister Speer."

Speer: "I am sorry, Herr Prince. Truly sorry. Yours was a noble vision. Full of daring. Someday it will be achieved. But in wartime, you understand, we had no choice."

"*La Vittoria?*" asked Prince.

Speer nodded.

Then a voice rang out, high and piping. "Yay-y-y! Yay-y-y!" It was Piero, the boy, who stood on the terrace above them. In a flash, Max knew his full name. The Duce had pronounced it on the *Hindenburg*. *Piero Cipriani*. From Calabria. The lad who had had the idea. Build a statue of a god. But with the face of Mussolini. Next to him stood Pacelli. He raised his hand in what must have been a gesture of benediction. Yes! He was blessing this idol, just as he had once blessed the tanks as they passed by the Arch of Constantine.

It was all clear now. This *was* a dedication—but not of *La Vittoria*. *La Vittoria* would provide the steel to build this monument, not a thousand feet up, but a thousand feet into the ground.

Now another voice, deeper, more familiar, thundered out loud. "YOU, WHO WITNESS THIS MIRACLE OF FASCIST TECHNOL-OGY, HEAR THE WORDS OF THE DUCE."

Maximilian, still without his glasses, peered still farther up-ward. He could see Mussolini, a blur of gray and green. Beside him, another blur: a purple robe, golden hair. Aria! At the side of her lover! The Dictator raised one of his legs over the edge of the preci-pice. For an instant it seemed he was going to jump onto what was already becoming a solid ingot of steel. Then he pointed to his shod foot.

"YOU SEE THE BOOT OF IL DUCE. THE BOOT, WHICH IN THE EYES OF THE WHOLE WORLD IS THE SYMBOL OF ITALY. THE BOOT WHICH KNOWS HOW TO CRUSH THE LIFE FROM ITS ENEMIES, TO REST WITHOUT MERCY UPON THEIR THROATS. AND HERE—"

The dictator gestured downward, toward the frozen foot of the sculpture. "HERE IS THE BOOT OF MY MONUMENT. THE NAKED FOOT OF A GOD."

A cheer went up. Then another cheer, louder than before. Max felt something at his hand. His spectacles! He wiped them; he put them on. It was as if the steam, still rising from the foot of the colossal statue, had lifted. He raised his head. He saw, on a ridge above them, the figure of the Pope and the young boy. He looked still higher. Yes, there was Mussolini and his mistress.

Then, straining, bending back as far as he dared, Maximilian focused his gaze on the topmost tier. There, enclosed in the last wisps of mist, and looking down on the entire scene, was the Master of the Thousand Year Reich. He did not move. He did not speak. His hands were clasped behind his back. Maximilian, with his sight restored, could see the flap of black hair that fell across his forehead, and the dark smear, like filth, above his lip—a lip that seemed to stretch in the slightest of smiles as his partner in the Pact of Steel concluded his peroration:

"NOW THE DUCE DEDICATES HIS MONUMENT. THE STATUE OF HERCULES. THE EIGHTH WONDER OF THE WORLD."

ALITALIA 607

Aborto Spontaneo

[2005: 1941]

1

We are the only ones left on the plane—Leda, Il Dottore, and I. Plus two of the green-capped stewardesses and a tall, stooped man in uniform who has turned out to be the pilot. The storm, I see, is still raging. I can feel it. The 767 trembles on the tarmac, just as it had in the air. "*Un tifone*," says the pilot, who hasn't once stopped wringing his hands. "*Un tifone terribile.*" The words disorient me, because we'd been over the Atlantic, not the other big ocean, the one where typhoons occur. The Pacific! Jesus, for a second I could not remember the name of the largest body of water on earth. Greetings, Uncle Al!

I don't know why we're in Gander. Did the—let's call it a nor'easter: did that storm force us down? Or did we land to get my granddaughter medical assistance? Good God: she's still unconscious, lying in the aisle, blank eyes open, her mouth open too. The bleeding has stopped. Mamiglioni's handkerchief has long since been discarded. They've had to use our linen napkins from first class. She's breathing, all right. I see her blood-spotted blouse moving up, moving down. The wind is whining and howling around the fuselage, as if the jet's engines were warming up. "W-W-W—" *When can we get off?* I want to ask. Are we going to stay on the plane all night?

Apparently not. Glancing out the oval window, I see that two or three vehicles have pulled up beside us. A cargo lifter, if that's what you call it, is maneuvering under the wing toward our door. Ergo, they're going to raise the platform and take the stricken passenger directly down to the E-C-N-A-L-U-B-M-A, a word that I fail to unscramble before she starts to groan.

"Oh-h-h-h."

We all turn toward Leda. She's blinking, the way they say sleepers do in a dream.

Mamiglioni: "Is good. Is very good. No coma. We take to hospital. We make the stitches. All is healthy. Only a little blood. Perhaps a small *trauma cerebrale*. Is nothing."

Is it possible I have more tears in me? No bottom to this well? I feel them on my right cheekbone, my right cheek. They pour down my face like the lines of rainwater on the window pane. *Amnon. Bram. Ozni. Nestore. Iris.* Oh, it's not that endless list of names. And it's not the words of the doctor. What moves me, this time, is the sight of the Signet Shakespeare, still clutched in my scholarly granddaughter's hand.

It was nearly dawn when we emerged from deep under ground. By the time our driver took us through the deserted streets, newsboys were already putting up posters that announced the beginning of World War II. Were we, this little band of Americans, the only ones in all of Italy, in all of Europe, who had not known that Japan intended to attack Pearl Harbor? We bought *La Stampa*, we bought *Il Messaggero*, and read them through. When we got out of the car we stood shocked and speechless on the Via degli Specchi. Except, that is, for Franklin:

"At last!" he exclaimed. "This is what we've been waiting for. Now everything will be decided."

Nina ignored him. "We still have the tickets, don't we? For the *Rex*? Our bags are still packed. We have to be on it. Papa, you see that now, don't you? There's nothing to stay for. They're going to use your steel for the other monument. Isn't that right, Maxie?"

"Yes. And soon. Before the Americans can bomb it to smithereens."

"The Americans!" Franklin exclaimed. "They don't even have a navy now. *That's* what's in smithereens."

Prince seemed to hear none of this. "My daughter," he said. "Where is she? We can't leave without her."

Frankie: "You can't leave with her, either. Where do you think you'll be going? America isn't our country anymore. We're at war with her now."

Nina's face, which always looked scrubbed, had been scorched a deeper red by the heat of the molten steel. "Don't you understand? That's why we *have* to leave. Before war is declared. Our country isn't fighting anyone yet—except Japan."

"You won't have to wait long," her brother responded. "It doesn't matter what America does. Germany and Italy will stand by their ally. That's what honorable nations do."

Again Nina ignored him. "Let's get Papa inside. Let's find the tickets. Maxie, you call the Linea Italia. Tell them we want to go."

I did as instructed, half-expecting the phone line to be cut. To my surprise, it worked. The ship would be sailing to New York on the afternoon of the 11th. All five of our berths were confirmed. Then

I rang up the Stazione Centrale and reserved a first-class compartment on the Rome-Naples express for that day. But I knew A.P. was right; we weren't going to leave Aria behind.

There was nothing to do but wait. That we did, huddled about the radio, the same instrument whose six glowing tubes might yet serve as the grounds for my banishment, imprisonment, or being strung to a wall by the thumbs. Mostly, no matter the bandwidth, there was music. Every hour or so I ran out to see if the papers had put out a special edition. Finally, late at night, the melodies stopped and we heard the text of Roosevelt's request for a declaration of war against Japan. *Un giorno che vivrà nell' infamia*, said the announcer, without a hint of mockery, without derision, though with a slight quickening of his breath. Then he went on to say that Congress had granted what the president had asked. There was no mention of Germany, however; nor was there a word about Mussolini or the Fascist state.

December 9th came and went. So did the 10th. No news. No Aria. Each morning I had Renato drive me to the station, where I could buy outdated copies of the *New York Times* and the *Tribune*, along with papers from Germany and occupied France. Nowhere, not in *Le Figaro* or any of the others, was there a sign that America was going to war with the Axis powers. There was nothing to prevent the departure of the *Rex*.

Early on the morning of the 11th the doorbell made its characteristic grinding rasp. We all jumped up. But it wasn't Aria. Four men climbed to the second floor. They pulled at the bills of their caps. "Signor Prince?" one of them, the sturdiest, with hair spilling from the V of his collar, demanded. Deep in his armchair, the architect nodded. It turned out these were the stevedores from the Linea Italia. They hauled our luggage down to the van that sat, its motor running, in the street below. Our train was scheduled to depart in three hours, at noon. The great steamship would leave from its new port of Naples just four hours later.

"We shouldn't have let them take the luggage," said Nina. "We can't sail. Not without Aria."

Without raising his head, staring at his bony kneecaps, Prince said, "She will come."

And, at the last moment, at 11:30 that morning, she did. She wore what looked like a man's overcoat, cinched by a cloth belt at the waist. Underneath it was the same formal dress she had worn at the banquet, though the hem was soiled and brown. She moved from spot to spot in the room, without once sitting down. What struck us all, and what made my heart leap up, was that her voice had returned. But an instant later I realized that she seemed to say far more when she could not sound her words. The first name she mentioned was mine, Maximilian:

"Hello, darling Max," she said. "Good morning, Franklin. Nina, how wonderful to see you. Oh, how I've missed you all. Papa, are you feeling well? Let me give you a kiss. What? Is it almost twelve? Goodness! It is so hard to keep track of the time."

Nina: "Yes, it's almost noon. Renato's waiting downstairs. We're going to have to rush to get to the station on time."

"Oh, give me a moment! I have to catch my breath. It's so *good* to see all of you. Gianna! There you are! Let me give you a kiss. A kiss and a hug."

She took two steps toward the servant, who turned quickly away, burying her face in the apron that perpetually hung down the front of her black uniform.

For a moment Aria stood, turning her head left and right, and making quick repetitive motions with her hands, thrusting them toward each other, as if she were knitting an invisible quilt. Then she brightened, talking away through the fixed smile on her lips:

"I must look a fright! It's so windy today. Yes, there, I knew it—" Here she walked up to the mirror, one of the few fixtures the stevedores had not taken away. "Why those swallows could make a nest in my hair! Look: you'd hardly know it was me. I'll never comb it out. Oh, I'm just a dishwater blonde! I used to pride myself on my hair. Bruno ran his fingers through it. *La Bionda. La Bionda.* Why is it so windy? I hate to go out in it again. Did you say you were late for something? I remember! The station! Are we going on a journey? Out into the terrible wind? Do you remember when we took the train together? How Bruno flirted! Vittorio too! I didn't know which one was more handsome. I didn't say a word while they chatted away. About poetry. About flowers. I didn't want to talk. The children! The fire! Papa's beautiful house! The Tree House! Those flames!"

Franklin moved toward her. "Aria—"

The girl jumped away, her hands still jabbing at the air. "Well, my goodness! If we're late we'd better leave, don't you think? *Get a horse!* That's what they used to say in America. America. Is that where we're going? Papa! Tell me! Are we going home? Papa? Where are you?"

Tears stung my eyes. I blinked them away. I saw that the armchair was empty. Amos Prince was gone. Franklin saw the same thing I did. He ran to the window and leaned out. "The Fiat!" he cried. "It's leaving!"

I ran to the window too. I just managed to catch the back of the Berline as it turned the corner and sped away. "Quick," I shouted. "Downstairs. We have to catch him."

As luck had it, we stopped a taxi on the Via Arenula and made our way eastward across the city. Aria did not stop chatting—no wonder the cab driver raced through the streets!—not even when we pulled up in front of the Stazione Centrale and ran inside. Our train was about to depart. Would Prince be on the platform? He was not. Would he be in our reserved compartment? No, not there either. It was no surprise. All too clearly the crazed man had fled the sight of, the sound of, the terrible price that had been paid for Pharaoh's limestone block.

With a hoarse hoot the express left without us. The next train, the last that would get us to Naples in time, left ninety minutes later. We exchanged our tickets. The others—save Aria, who paced, moving her arms in what might have been an imitation of the connecting rods of a locomotive—sat down to wait. I ran off to find Amos Prince.

My best guess was that the architect meant to seek a final audience with Mussolini. I told the taxi driver to head for the Palazzo Venezia, but the center of town was clogged with traffic. I got out and ran toward the piazza. Everyone else in Rome seemed to be running there too. A vast crowd had gathered in the square. It spilled into all the adjoining streets. Masses of people thronged the monument to Vittorio Emanuele II, like so many black keys on an enormous white typewriter. Everywhere, in the square, on the monument, in the choked streets, the men seemed to be saluting. I looked again: no, in the blasts of the wind they were only holding onto their hats. The same wind was ripping apart the words that began on the balcony of the Palazzo Venezia and issued in tatters from the hundreds of electronic megaphones:

DAY OF SOLEMN DECISION . . .

HEROIC JAPAN . . .

THAT TYRANNICAL DEMOCRAT . . .

THAT SUPREME FRAUD.

Those last words, I knew, were meant to describe Franklin Delano Roosevelt. The gale, as if in shock, briefly relented. I made out an entire sentence:

ITALIANS! ONCE MORE ARISE AND BE WORTHY OF THIS
HISTORICAL HOUR. *NOI VINCEREMO!* WE SHALL WIN!"
The strange thing was, at this Declaration of War there were
no cheers, no exclamations. The crowd, instead of throwing their
hats in the air, kept them clamped on their heads. Then the loudspeakers, which had fallen silent, crackled to life again:

Comrades! *Amici!* Old Amos speakin'. He's gonna do his
darndest to talk straight like a man of the pee-pull, not some
fancy flylosin'fur readin' big words out of the *New York Crimes*
or some other nose-wiper.

Old Amos! It was Prince! It was A.P.! His words were not coming from the megaphones. They poured from radios. Thousands of
radios. Echoing from every open window. How could this be? It
couldn't be. But there was no voice like his in all the world:

Now we got ourselves into a war. A Warburg, I otta call it. This
was cooked up by the Chews. That's right. By the kikes and the
hyperkikes against the Not-sees. They want to put a dent in Mister Hot-leer's prestige.

As I had once before, I found myself running toward the Circus Maximus: behind the monument to the King's father; past the
Forum; the Via dell' Impero; the Colosseum; the Via dei Trionfi.
And all the while the little radios of Rome kept transmitting my
mentor's terrible words:

Don't trust the Damn-mericans. Or their president. He wants the
Jew-hated States to fight against our Fast-shits. Bet you dolors to
donutz this was all done at the ordures of the international

bonkers—the Spittons, the Broth-chilleds, and those other fine-ass-ears. With the blessings of old Rabbi Wheeze.

I paused. The voice paused too. All of Rome seemed to be taking its breath. The high humming noise in the air came not from the transmitters but from the vibrating wires of the monument. And there it was, *La Vittoria*, thrust up into the sky, taller than the *Rex* if it had been stood on its end. I followed the twang of the voice to the Circus Maximus.

> *Amici!* Who speaks to you? A f-Amos architect? Heck, no. I am your *paisan*, a farm boy from Alley-noise. Used to sheer the wool off the backs of sheep. Used to milk the udders of whole-stain cows. That milk! That cream! Oh, let me tell you, my dear Romans, you ain't lived until you tasted Granny Tropp's ice cream 'n pee-chose. My mouth is waterin' at the thought. All cream, all peaches, nothing from a can. No fancy French chef gonna top that with his frogs and snails and airy sue-flays. Now where was I? Sometimes, you know, I lose the thread. The thread of my thoughts.

I knew where I wanted to go. The radio shed. I slid under a bulge in the wire fence and made for it. This was where Marconi had once sent his beams to the blimps overhead. I could just make out Renato, with the leather band of his headphones snug against his hairless scalp. But where was the broadcaster? His voice still rang out from thousands of invisible cardboard cones:

> People of Italy! Old Amos is your ill-eye. Hear my voice! I am going to eggs-pain why you and the Daisy, and not the Chooze, will live in freedumb and win this war.

I looked up to where the tower, in the wind, was swaying inches left and inches right. High above, it might have been on top of the forty-second story, I saw the tiny figure of Amos Prince. He was in his white linen suit and his white Panama hat. His legs didn't dangle over the edge of the ellipse. They were pulled to his chest. I had to imagine the microphone into which, from this gigantic antenna, he was lecturing to Italy and, in spite of the curvature of the earth, the nations that lay overseas.

> Why must we listen to what Moo-sez? Because of his Ten Cormorants? Hell, he wasn't even a Chew. Didn't speak a word of High-brow. That's why Hair-on had to do all his talkin' for him. Moo-sez there's only one God. Adenoid. Jay-hover. But he got that from the Egyptian King who married Nether-tittie. The Yids never invented a thing.

From where I stood I shouted the architect's name. I jumped and waved my arms. He chose not to see me. What was I to do? Yes, if one of the lifts still worked, or if I could race up the inner stairway, I might be able to confront A.P., calm him, persuade him to return to ground level. If I could do all these things, would there be time to make the train to Naples, to board the *Rex*, to make our escape? Escape? To where? How could a ship sail from one country to another against which it had just declared war? It seemed, from Prince's concluding remarks, that he had thought of that too:

> This minute I should be on a ship. I was going to sail to the Unheated Estates. But I changed my mind. I am going to fight for the Doozy and the Furor, our modern Honey-ball, our modern Joan of Irk. The Yanks are coming. We got to throw 'em back in the sea. We got to defend our land. We got to protect our

monuments. Old Amos, he gives you his word. I am stayin' right
here to fight by your side.

I sank down to the ground, pulling my knees to my chest, in
imitation of my master. Every muscle in my body trembled and
twitched. Even if by some miracle I could board the *Rex*, which at
that moment was preparing to move out of the Bay of Naples, I knew
I would refuse to do it. Worse, far worse: What if that great ship
were allowed to leave, and what if Aria were now actually aboard
it? Still I would choose to remain in Rome. A pain, the tip of a knife
blade, seemed to penetrate my heart at the thought of her: the hollows inside her collarbones, the green flecks in her gray eyes, and,
oh, the flaring, the quivering of her nostrils, always a little reddened,
as if she were perpetually recovering from a cold.

"Aria! Aria!" In my misery I called her name aloud. Years before, attempting to offer her a ring, hoping to make her my bride, I
had told myself that she was the reason I would not return to
America. Now I knew otherwise: it was this ranting madman, the
architect who was her father, to whom I was forever wed.

2

The cabin door opens at last. The wind and the rain come roaring
in. So does a medical crew, bearing a stretcher. They roll Leda onto
it. The stewardesses try to open umbrellas over her, but they blow
inside out. Covered with blankets, she is carried onto the portable
platform. I start after her. The stooping captain and the doctor hold
me back. I twist out of their grip.

"L-l-let me! L-l-let me go!"

They relent. One of them retrieves my wheelchair, which has
been collapsed in a forward compartment. The other one props me

up at his side. We all go into the whipping wind, the stinging rain. In an instant I am soaked through. My hair, white now, without any curls, is plastered to my forehead and my neck. The young men from the A-M-B-U-L-A-N-C-E lean over the stretcher, shielding the patient as best they can. A good thing Doctor Mamiglioni has taken hold of my arm; I'd blow off the platform like a sodden rag, a sodden leaf. We descend. The red lights on the ambulance are flashing below us. So are the blue ones atop a police car. Our escort, I realize. Count to a hundred. Goddamn it, that's how long it is taking us to reach the ground.

Here comes the emergency vehicle, backing up to us. We squeeze inside and speed off down the runway as fast as a plane taking off. Our sirens wail and wail; but those on the police car bray, in the European manner. The medics seem to be paying more attention to me than to Leda. They remove my jacket. They strip off my pants. They wrap me in towels. Two of them clasp hands across my chest, forming a harness. I manage to remove my glasses; I wipe off the fog. When I put them on again I see, to my horror, that the blanket above Leda's legs, Leda's thighs, is stained with blood.

Mamiglioni sees it too.

"Ah," he says, bending over her, "*è incinta.*"

"W-what? W-what is it?" I ask. "Is it a mis-mis-mis—"

"*Sì.* I fear it. *Un aborto spontaneo.*"

We continue to careen through the streets. The hospital is ahead. I smile at my granddaughter. She is wide awake. She manages to smile back.

"Don't let me lose it," she says.

SPIRAL NOTEBOOK

Betrayed

[1982: 1945]

I was a marked man. Taller than the wops. Billy-goat beard. Linen suit. By the grace of God my Panama hat. No point in camouflage. The Yanks, the Brits, the *partigiani*: somebody was going to get the prize. Figured it might as well be my own people. One day at noon, maybe a week after I left Salò, I walked over a hill and practically into the laps of four niggers. Sprawled on the side of the road, smoking something that wasn't Indian tobacco. They didn't see me. Far too busy with their live chicken. One big buck wanted to wring its neck on the spot. Another, the sentimentalist, said wait for dinner. The third, disciple of old Ben Franklin, I guess, said not to do anything because now they would have eggs for breakfast. The fourth, smiling, a gold tooth, I swear, just looked from one to another, swayed by whoever spoke last. Had the chicken in his arms. Smoothing the feathers with his thumb. Oh, Italy! Land of Augustus, Caesar, Virgil, Dante, as Mushroomy used to say. The Conqueror of Africa had Africa in his own backyard. What the hell? Reckoned I could settle the debate by letting them cook *me* in their pot.

Here I am. Yep, the one you been looking for. They didn't even get up off the ground.

Amos Prince. Talked on the radio. I surrender.

One of the quartet, the fiercest, the one who wanted to commit the murder: he held up his smoke for me to take a puff. The fella with the gold tooth offered a bar of Hershey chocolate. In a century of putting up with life, this might have been the greatest humiliation. A chicken! It meant more to them than the man who had built the tallest building in the world. I felt the debasement, but the opposite too: I was puffed with pride. My number wasn't up. It was not my time to die. The gods had more in store for Amos Prince.

I ended up haggling over a bicycle. For two hundred lire I bought their Bianchi racer. Painted in Bianchi grass green. Off I pedaled. Happy as the old lark. Whistled like one too. Nobody was going to turn me in. And nobody did. Mile after mile, hundreds of kilometers: my God, they stood up in the spring wheat and took off their hats. It was as if they knew I had been saved for some special fate.

The sun, watery as it was, is going down. Or else I'm going blind. The former. No more tap-tapping. The stone mason has knocked off for the day. Probably finished all eight sides of his stone. Genius of medieval Italy. One man. One day. One piece of rock. Nobody goes to the poorhouse. He'll be back, my woodpecker, in the morning. For a month, hell, six months, a lifetime's occupation. In the United States of America, they'd pave the whole street in an hour with a steamroller and a bucket of tar.

Feels like it's going to be a cold night. Winter coming on. Can't move my legs. Couple of frozen logs. Fingers ditto: can barely hold this stub of a pencil. Can't read my own writing. Just loops. Just swirls. I need a blanket! I need a cup of tea! Where the hell is Enrico?

I ring. I ring. I ring. No answer. Has he abandoned me? After two decades together? *Enjoy your soup, Maestro.* Traitor! Can't wait for me to kick the bucket. Probably picking the lock on the bicycle shack. Throwing open the doors to the newspapers. To the girls from Carnegie Tech. Is he going to say he invented the floating planet? But that is why the gods kept me alive. Enrico! It is cold. Cold in my chest. Goddamned hotel won't put up any heat. Where is the *minestra?* Gianna! Aria! Junior! Old Shabby-lion.

Rode the bike all the way to Milano. Every soul knew who I was. Fed me anyway. Fixed my flats. Bedded me down for the night. Good-natured people remember what suits them best. The ones loyal to Mausoleumy, they thought of the builder of his monument. The ones who hated him, and to tell the truth that was just about every wop in the world, they recognized the voice that had brought him down: *The reign of the imposter is over.*

I got to the city at the end of April. The streets were in turmoil. Everybody was shooting at everybody else. Old scores being settled. Bodies falling from the rooftops. Jumping. Being pushed. Americans zipping in jeeps from one end of an alley, Germans hightailing it out the other. Saw one big building, ministry of something-or-other, with the Stars and Stripes on one floor, swastika still hanging from the floor above. Didn't hide. Didn't run from shadow to shadow. Rode right through the crowds up to the Duomo. Didn't duck from the bullets, either. Watched them chipping the stones. Under divine protection, no doubt about it. Had a job to do. Promise to keep. Bring the corpse of the Dotty back to his tomb.

But where was old Ben? Alive even? In Switzerland, maybe? Making his last stand in the Valtellina? What did he call it? *Another Thermopylae.* Or was he coming back to Milan? To turn it into—I still remember: a *second Stalingrad.* What about that secret weapon? The electric bomb? The death ray of Marconi? For all I knew he had escaped to Japan in a submarine. No torpedoes, only sacks of gold. Or been captured already and on his way to, yep, Madison Square Garden. People would pay money to see him like the Ethiopian Emperor inside his cage. There were more rumors than bullets whizzing in the air.

Spent the night in a playground. Huddled up against the trunk of a tree. The bark had been shredded, maybe from an ice storm, maybe from where somebody had been stood up for an execution. Didn't care. Too tired to check for the poor man's blood. I woke at dawn. No bike. Pockets inside out. Last lira gone. Yet even that thief knew better than to put a knife to the throat of Amos Prince.

"*Americano! Americano!*"

Up against the railing of the fence, a crowd. They were grinning. They were waving their arms. Bells were ringing. For me? Or for the Americans who had run the Germans out of town. Or was it Sunday? I looked at my wrist, as if my watch could tell me the days of the week. It was gone too. Now more people appeared. There were shouts. There were cries. The streets filled up with the Milanese. They were running, trotting. Old folk hobbled as best they could. Fathers carried children on their shoulders. I got to my feet.

Old Amos: "*Dove è il Duce?*"

They all pointed in the same direction the masses of people were moving. I joined the mob. We pushed ahead. Shoulder to shoulder. Elbow to elbow. Impossible to move. Impossible to breathe. Suddenly the steet opened up into a square. Everyone surged ahead. Thousands were already there. Tens of thousands, it seemed. Had the Doughy indeed returned? Was he going to address his people as he had at the Arch of Titus?

BLACKSHIRTS OF THE ITALIAN REVOLUTION. ITALIAN MEN AND ITALIAN WOMEN—COUNTRYMEN AT HOME

AND THROUGHOUT THE WORLD: LIFT YOUR BANNERS, YOUR SWORDS, YOUR HEARTS—

Or at the Palazzo Venezia?

ITALIANS! ONCE MORE ARISE AND BE WORTHY OF THIS HISTORICAL HOUR. *NOI VINCEREMO!* WE SHALL WIN!

Far off, at the front of the crowd, large, dark objects were hanging in the air. We were not at the site of a public oration, but at a public market. I could see the carcasses of the slaughtered cows. Heaven forgive me: I laughed out loud. Is this why I had come all the way from Salò? From the *Lago di Garda*? To watch the citizens of Milano fight over meat?

Must have dozed off. Funny. No more pain in the head. Can't feel a thing inside it. Like old Paul Bunyan chopped it off with a blow of the ax. Read somewhere that victims of the guillotine go on smiling, or weeping, or speaking in French after the blade has descended. For a second. Or half a second. Is that what I'm doing now? Sure seems like it: looking at my toes a mile away. Take a gander at those fingers, still twitching and twitching, doing an imitation of writing. Like my old friend, *il pollo*. Niggers ended up slitting its neck with a bayonet. Kept running just the same.

I swear in my dotage I can hear the I-ties making a hullabaloo in the streets. Is it in the streets? On the radio? Or in my head? Never stopped yelling ever since they won the World Cup. Italy 3. Spain 1. Glad these wops can win something. Read in the *Herald Tribune*, maybe three months ago, that the Cardinals beat the Brewers. World Series. Four games to three. Also in the *Tribune*: Speer kicked the bucket. No, no, that was a year ago. Can't keep track anymore.

Who's alive. Who's dead. Maybe old Albert, he's still running around too, like that chicken without a head. Never knew they had a team in Milwaukee. When did that happen? For all I know people are singing "White Christmas" on Mars.

Looked twice. Not cows. Not lambs. It was Muscle-teeny! And his crew. Hanging in the air by the heels. I pushed forward. I fought my way through. Hadn't I taken an oath? Wasn't this my purpose in life? Like I said, to take the Dopey to his tomb. I stopped. I stared. They were raising someone else next to the others. A woman! Her belly, her breasts, her head were lost in the folds of the dress that hung down from her hips. Shameful sight. The madman called out his daughter's name. No one on earth answered. The fool cried again. The crowd was drawing away from the stricken father. Respect for his grief? Fear of what the crazed man would do next? Then the poor girl's hat fell to the ground and I raised my arms to the heavens. *Hooray!* The crowd fell back even more, so that I stood in a magic circle of my own. The next thing I knew an American jeep pulled up beside me. Two policemen seized my arms. They turned to the multitude. They demanded to know if this was the traitor. No one said a word. I was under the protection of the Italian people. Then one man stepped forward. He was not from Milan. He was not from Italy. Dumbstruck, I mouthed his name. And then Junior, that Judas, betrayed me.

———◆———

FLYING FORTRESS

[1943]

1

On the bright, hot, cloudless morning of July 19, 1943, the *Lucky Lady* opened her bomb bay doors and released, instead of the leaflets the Romans no longer bothered to read, a stick of sixteen five-hundred-pound bombs. There were more to come. The shells of anti-aircraft fire burst ineffectually a full mile below. The Flying Fortresses were aiming at the railway yards adjacent to the Tiburtino district. At twenty thousand feet it was not possible to be precise, which meant that the explosives also struck the medical school of the university, the densely packed apartment houses adjacent to the yards, and, with a direct hit, the Church of San Lorenzo Outside the Walls. As many as two thousand people were killed and an equal number injured, not counting the corpses awakened from their everlasting sleep when the explosives fell among the graves at the cemetery of Campo Verano.

The casualties that day might have been fewer if the population of Rome had not been swollen with new arrivals. Foreigners, refugees, Italians from everywhere in the country, German soldiers on leave, and Jews from occupied Europe—all had flocked to the holy city out of the shared belief that this was the one capital on the continent that would never be bombed. *"What is the best anti-aircraft battery in Italy?"* ran the popular saying. *"The Vatican!"*

It is reported that the Pope, standing at his windows in the Apostolic Palace, watched the attack through ivory opera glasses. He must have shuddered. All of his diplomatic efforts had been directed toward sparing Rome just such a bombardment. He could not have known then that the great basilica had been damaged or that the tomb of his own ancestors, the Pacellis, had been unearthed; but he surely sensed that the barrier that had separated the profane world from all that is sacred had been knocked down and would never be erected again.

Amos Prince, viewing the same events, seemed overjoyed. On the rooftop of his flat on the Via degli Specchi, he clapped his hands, as if the waves of B-17's and B-24's were props in a vast stage spectacle. On the other side of the low brick wall that separated number 8 from the adjoining building, a flock of doves were moving from perch to perch in agitation. Was this because of the sound of the architect's applause? Or the distant boom and thud of the exploding bombs? Or did they, with their heightened senses—the homing instinct, the skill to navigate by polarized light—feel the disturbance in the air created by the far-off concussions? Maximilian, staring from the parapet, watched the smoke rising above the heights of the Esquirial. He thought he could see, through the depths of his eyeglass lenses, the flyspecks of the falling bombs.

"What are you celebrating?" Franklin asked his father. "You look like you want to dance."

"I do! Yep, I do! What do they call this? Ain't this a tarantula?" Prince, in his flapping white linens, broke into a knee-slapping jig.

Frankie turned away in disgust. "Don't you know what this means? The Allies have taken Sicily. They'll land next on the coastline. Do you think our soldiers will fight? They'll throw rose petals at their feet! It's the end of the Fascist idea. The Italians were not worthy of it. Or of the Duce."

A.P. stopped his gyrations. "You wait and see. This is what I been waiting for. It ain't defeat. It's victory."

Nina had her hands to her ears, as if to block out the sounds of the continuing bombardment. "What are you saying? Are you saying this gives you pleasure? People are dying. Don't you see the smoke? My God! I can smell it!"

Aria stood with her arms wrapped around her body, as if she had felt a cold breeze. "It's the Americans," she declared. "They're coming for us. Isn't that right, Frankie? They're coming. Isn't that right?"

"Yes, they're coming," the boy said. "The army can't stop them. The government will fall. It's filled with cowards and traitors. Poor Duce. He was like a god. But not even a god can fight such hordes with his bare hands. These cowboys! These Negroes! With their white teeth! Only one person can save us. *His* Wehrmacht won't run. *His* soldiers will fight. You know who I mean. Only *He* can throw the Yankees back into the sea."

The little color that remained in Aria's face drained away. "Look. There they are. The Americans. Do you see?" Everyone followed her gaze to where the bombers in formation resembled a thousand Christian crosses in the sky. "And there will be soldiers. I know it. I feel it. Soldiers and sailors. Sailors and soldiers. Americans. Americans. Oh, Papa! They are coming for you!"

Nina: "Don't be silly. There are millions of people at war. What did A.P. do? Talk on the radio. Everything he said, all his words— nothing he did took a single life. They are not thinking of him."

Aria shook her head. "What will they do to him? Papa, you tell me. Will they put you in a cage? Oh, a bird cage! Like the poor doves!"

Frankie turned to his sister. "They'd like that: to put all of us in a cage, the Duce too. Don't worry. I told you. The German army is not going to let the Americans get to Rome."

Prince gave a laugh. He started toward the open doorway that led down to the interior of the building. "You think all I do is talk? That it was all hot air? That nobody heard a word? You wait. Just hang on. You'll see what happens when they hear my brayed-cast."

He started down the staircase. Max made to follow, but the architect, descending, held up his hand. "No, no, Jew-near. I'm going soul-attire."

Shabilian watched his mentor disappear down the stairwell. He resisted the urge to follow. After all, over the past year Prince had left the house for only one of two destinations. The first was the Mussolini Works, where he made sure the last three-story section of *La Vittoria* was still on the plateau and not fed into the forges for the statue of Il Duce. Max, who often tagged along behind him on these excursions—his "shad-roe" Amos would call him—never failed to be surprised by the deference the Carabinieri showed the older man. Off came their cloth caps as he trudged upward; some even put their hands to their foreheads. "*Salve, Maestro!*" they called, from both sides of the steep, winding road.

The other place Prince would visit was the tower. It may be that he feared it too would be demolished to make the Herculean knee caps, the Herculean thighs. Indeed, Max had been present in May when Herr Speer had driven to the site in a command car, from which he could be seen taking measurements with an instrument that looked like a seafarer's sextant. Next to him was a uniformed German, with a puckered dueling scar from cheekbone to chin. When the American architect demanded to know what the German one was doing at the site, Speer leaned over the side of the open Mercedes and said, "*Entschuldige mich.* I am sorry, Herr Prince. I admire this building as I do no other. It is, for me, the Parthenon of our age." In other words, thought Maximilian, *We need bayonets, airplanes, tanks.*

Yet the tower remained, if not any taller than the ninety-three stories it had stood on the day of Puerile Arbor, as A.P. called the catastrophe of December 7, then at least not any lower either. Its architect was convinced that it had been spared because of the broadcasts he had continued to make from high on the mast. It was as if the flow of his words had created a force field, a magic web, that nothing could penetrate—not Mussolini's hunger for steel, the requirements of the German war machine, or, now, the American bombs that were being deflected northward onto the Città Università, the chugging locomotives, and the graves of those already dead.

"That's the one thing that Rosenfelt and old Moo-so-loudly got in common," he'd declare, on coming down from *La Vittoria.* "Both of them are hanging on my every turd."

Which might well have been the case, though Max suspected the survival of the tower had more to do with the fact that EIAR, the Italian network, had been using the monument to transmit its broadcasts to Fascist forces overseas. The trouble was, those troops had suffered one defeat after another—first in Ethiopia, then in Libya, and finally, at about the time that Speer had made his springtime appearance, in Tunisia too. The only soldiers left were struggling to make their way homeward, some from as far away as the Russian steppes; there was no one to hear the patriotic songs, the exhortations, the accounts of victory.

On that July morning, Shabilian left the roof with the others. At 11 a.m., when the last of the bombs were falling, they turned the black needle across the lit arc of the dial to Radio Rome: "Amos Prince Speaking."

Wal, it looks like we're going to have some visitors to our Italian Penis-healer. They been dropping their calling cards all morning. Got one foot in the door on the island of Sicily. They come a long way, across the sea from Baruchistan and the far-off shores of Yidonia. I guess this is a curt-see call to return the visit of old Crusty-fur Column-bugs. Old Ferdinand. Old Isabella. They was smart enough to kick out the kikes!

In 1492, Columbus sailed the ocean blue
When he got back there weren't a Jew.

Now Frankie Finkelstein Roosenfelt is sending them back across the ocean. Watch out, watch out, my peep-pul! These Chewish butchers will treat our Stallions like they done to the meat in the U.S. of Hay. Each man is going to lose his foreskin! Old Amos knows what he's talkin' about. Back in Alley-noise, we used to make geldings. But you'll be gelt-ings.

My old great uncle had a wooden leg
And a goose that laid a golden egg
And a dog that wouldn't bark
Sold that farm to the barkers of New York—
Ohhhhh! New Pork!

I repeat: how is the Fascist man going to fight this infection? Is he going to let the sheenies beat his swords into pawnshops? Today the bombs are fallin' on our churches and our trains. Ha! Ha! Our church-choo trains! But tomorrow fighter planes will

305

be shooting our women and children. Shooting them in the
streets! We got to demand protection from our Dizzy. He's got
to listen to his Prince! Keep these airplanes away.

There was a crunching sound, like a giant cough, though
whether the clamor came from the radio's speaker or through the
open window none of those who had been listening to the broadcast could tell.

"A bomb!" Nina exclaimed.

"The old man is right," Frankie cried "They *are* bombing
people!"

But there was no second explosion; Max knew that meant this
was not an attack but a single weapon gone astray. He started to
say as much when A.P.'s voice, at a higher pitch, came back over
the airwaves:

I wunner if you heard that? You hear that? They just threw Old
Amos a fastball! I guess they got their rodeos tuned to his message. Guess they'd like to stop up his words. Dropped a sheenie
new blockblister on top of his head. *Amici!* Romans! They can't
hurt me! They can't hurt my tower! Just made a big hole in the
ground. Do what I said. If you get the right protection, they
won't be able to harm a Herr on your Hades. Demand it. Insist
on it. Now! This has been Amos Prince Speaking.

The broadcaster returned home in time for lunch, and ate
heartily. He held up a roll and joked about his "brioche with death."
He didn't take his usual nap. Instead, he went back to the roof. The
bombing had long since ceased. Even the smoke that had hung over
the Tiburtino district had blown away. Nonetheless, Prince would
not budge. The only concession he made to the heat of the day was

the umbrella he opened over his hatted head. He remained in that patch of shade, peering left, peering right, for all the world—or so it seemed to Maximilian—like a white-clad referee at a tennis match.

The July sun did not go down until well after nine. A.P. did not stir. His daughters brought him a pillow, a blanket. He insisted on spending the night.

At dawn, even a little before it, Prince began barking like a dog, crowing like a rooster. "I knew it! I told you! I said it would be a victory! Get up! Get up, everybody! Come up and see!"

Everyone inside the flat heard him, and began to race upstairs. The neighbors heard him too. Shutters were slamming. Heads poked out of windows.

"*Tacete!*"

"*Un pazzo!*"

"*Dormiamo!*"

Frankie was the first one to reach the roof, with Maximilian on his heels. "Look!" his father exclaimed. "They done just what I told them. Now we're in business! Yes sir! Look at 'em! Like marshy—! Like mishy—! Like mushy—!"

Both girls had arrived as well. They all looked out over the city. Rather, they looked skyward, over the rooftops, the domes, the spires. There, moored by a thousand cables, the barrage balloons stately swayed in the breeze. They had sprung up just as Prince, in his excitement, had tried to say: like *mushrooms* after a rain.

2

The Duce had not been in Rome during the bombing. He returned to the capital under cover of darkness—not so much because during his city's hour of crisis he had been conversing with the Reichskanzler in the safe town of Feltre, but because for some time he had no longer dared to expose himself to its citizens. Toward midnight, half-disguised, he did stop at the site of the bombing, where people were still digging through the rubble. He wept. He handed out one-hundred-lira notes. Then he sped off in his Aprilia 1500; no one in the small, sullen crowd had said a word.

The moment Amos Prince heard of the Duce's return, he did everything he could to get in touch with him. A day, two days, went by but no one answered the telephone at the Villa Torlonia. At the Palazzo Venezia they said the Duce was immersed in plans to defend the city and would surely call his friend, *l'architetto*, in just a few hours. The call never came. Prince wrote letters. He sent Max with a message. He went himself, only to be escorted away by plainclothesmen.

What was it that A.P. wanted from Mussolini? Max knew. At night, when there was no threat of either low-level bombing or strafing from the fighter planes based in Sicily, the cables of the barrage balloons—fifty would be more than enough, Prince had calculated—would be released from their concrete blocks and reattached to the enormous steel ellipse that was waiting on Montespaccato. Once in the air, the structure could be dragged to the Circo Massimo by a single motorized blimp. How, without escape valves, could the payload be lowered over the waiting core? A sharpshooter—in his letters A.P. had proposed "a marksman such as yourself, Duce"—could puncture three, four, at the most five of the balloons, which would allow gravity to pull the remainder with great delicacy over the target.

Still no answer came from the architect's private correspondence. That's why, on the morning of July 22, he broadcast his plan to the entire world:

Amos Prince speaking. I ain't going to bleat around the bush. People of Rome: the Yids and Zany-ists are trying to knock down your eternal city. You got to defy them by building it higher than ever. Higher than anything in Jew York. Old Amos forgives your Duce for not giving him the helium. It was an act of genius to keep the gas for just such an urge-to-pee. But what we got to do now is show them Yanks. We got to prove to old Mortgage-thou we ain't intimidated. How? By making something bigger, grander, better than what they got. Something taller than the Umpire Hate Building. Here's my idea. As soon as it's dark, at-tach the barrage balloons to the top section of *La Vittoria* and drop it onto our mound-of-mint. Overnight the more-ale of us Romans will soar! Will have the highest structure ever built by man! Do it tonight! Tonight! Until you do, I ain't budgin'. Old Amos is waiting.

Wait he did, through the whole of that day and into the night. When he did not return for dinner, Nina brought a hot meal to the tower. Max followed later with the same bedding he'd used the night before. Overhead, the barrage balloons hung as silent and unmov-ing as painted clouds. Below, in the deserted, blacked-out streets, chalked messages seemed to glow on the sides of every building:

MORTE A MUSSOLINI!

At dawn, *La Vittoria* was still the second highest building in the world. Prince's next transmission was directed neither to the people of the Eternal City nor to the citizens of America, but di-rectly to He Who Drained The Marshes:

Douche! Amos Prince speaking. I been up all night. Just me and the croquettes, chirpin' and a chirpin' away. Today I am giving you a warning. You could have been a great bewilder. Like a Knobby-cad-noisier, famed for the Hanging Gardens of

Babylon and the palaces that touched the sky. But he made the same mistake as you, oh Dunce! He made a image of himself sixty cubits high, just like your statue of old Heroic-lies that you would like us to bow down to and warship. Like Daniel, the Chew, Daniel in the liar's den, I prophecy: You, too, will be driven from men and live like a beast and have to eat grass. Like a ox! I'm givin' you one more night to act. Oh, Dizzy! The writin' is on the wail. MENE, MENE, TEKEL, HAIRRAISIN: *Morte a Duce!* Yes, the hand has writ and moved on: *E meglio avere gli americani sulla testa che Mussolini comprime i coglioni.* It don't take old Daniel to interpret the meaning of that. *Better the Americans on top of your head than Mussolini squeezing your balls.* I see! I see! Doozy is going to die like old Knobby and his son, Bel-cheesier. No Hanging Gardens: hanging by the heels instead. Upside down! Like a slut-tarred cow! Beware! The people are angry. They won't move to save you. You been warned. Amos Prince Speaking.

Did Mussolini hear those words? No one could say. But there was no doubt the Romans did. Cars halted in their tracks during the broadcast. As soon as it was over, people darted off to work or back to their apartments, so that the streets were as empty at noon as they had been at midnight. Through the rest of that day the tension only grew. Carabinieri took up positions at key intersections. Blackshirts, the *Squadristi*, stood guard in front of government buildings. Everybody sensed something was in the air, something thick, heavy, almost tangible, yet as unseen as the radio waves themselves.

What did not rise through the air, however, was the steel ellipse. Through the night it sat, silvery and silent, like a great ocean liner hauled into dry dock. The next day a hush fell over Rome: no shouts or curses, no voices raised in song, no honking horns. Pedestrians disappeared from the sidewalks. The very flags hung limp on their flagpoles. It was as if a cloud of ether had descended over the somnolent city, much as a current of smoke is employed to calm a swarm of agitated bees.

What everyone awaited was that day's broadcast. But the eleven o'clock hour arrived and nothing issued from the radio but the voice of the great tenor, Beniamino Gigli, as Pinkerton in *Madama Butterfly*, urging the soprano, Maria Caniglia, to come to his arms. What had happened? Had *l'Americano* been arrested? Had the Blackshirts seized the tower? Or had the opposite occurred: perhaps Mussolini had assured the *Maestro* that he would agree to all his demands. At twelve o'clock, the Lieutenant was in America and Cho-Cho-San was singing an aria about their handsome son. The opera was still on the air at one in the afternoon, though the abandoned bride had just stabbed herself through the cloth of her kimono and the voice that rang over the city was not that of the architect but of the naval officer, who—too late! Tragically late!—cried out, "*Butterfly! Butterfly! But-ter-fly-y-y-y!*"

At three o'clock there was nothing but dead air—sometimes static, sometimes a hum, as if the hive was about to emerge from under its anesthesia. Finally, at 4 p.m. on the 24th of July, the familiar voice began once more to speak:

> Citizens of Rome. Members of the Fascist Party. Those in the government. Those in the Army. King Victor Emmanuele III, of the House of Savoy. All who now hear my voice. The reign of the imposter is over. *Coragio!* Take courage. You must seize this moment. You must appoint a new leader. A man of vision. A man of daring. Amos Prince is speaking to you. It is he who demands it.

The moment the radios fell silent a tremendous clamor erupted. Thousands of shutters were clanging shut over shop windows. This was, after all, time to end work on a summer Saturday. But neither the shoppers nor shopkeepers appeared in the streets. Through the center of the city only a single procession of cars was moving. The vehicles traveled slowly, as if reluctant to arrive at their destination; some crept so sluggishly that it seemed the hot tar of the pavement was sucking at the treads of their tires. One by one the Lancias, Fiats, and Alfa Romeos drew up on the Via degli Astalli, at the back of the Palazzo Venezia. The passengers rushed quickly from their automobiles to the rear entrance. Nonetheless it was not possible for them to go unrecognized: Federzoni, Grandi, De' Stefani, Farinacci, Bottai. Why, it was the Grand Council! Scorza, the Party Secretary; Count Ciano, the son-in-law, the ex-Foreign Minister and now envoy to the Vatican; and here was Cianetti, Minister of Corporations. Everyone was there, all gathered together, for the first time in years.

If there had been a special bulletin on EIAR, or a transmission from the tower top, the news could not have traveled more swiftly. What was happening in the Sala del Pappagallo? Was it a revolution? A vote of no confidence? Had the King taken over? Or was Mussolini going to withdraw from the Pact of Steel and make peace with the Allies? Would the people of Rome wake the next morning to find that their city had been occupied by the Wehrmacht and the SS?

A thousand such rumors flew from house to house. It was almost as if the door of the little aviary on the Via degli Specchi had been thrown open and the doves had winged their way across the capital, each with a different message tied round its neck. What was the truth? All anyone could say for certain was that the limousines remained parked in a row behind the Palazzo Venezia, and that at midnight the chauffeurs had drawn black curtains over the windows and gone to sleep on the seats inside.

As more time went by, everyone put their faith in the most fantastic rumor of all: that Mussolini had passed out poison to all twenty-eight members of the council, and that like the Romans of old each had swallowed his portion to die at the feet of Caesar, Caesar, who, with a single shot to the skull—people swore they had heard it reverberating through the Piazza—expired with them. This tale was proved false when, at a little after three in the morning, Bottai, Farinacci, Ciano, and the rest appeared at the rear of the palace, got into their respective vehicles, and sped off into what was left of the night. The Duce himself walked out of the front entrance and was driven off in his limousine with the whitewall tires. For all anyone knew, the Grand Council might have been doing nothing more than holding a *festa*, a drinking party, or a lively *conversazione*.

The morning of the 25th dawned like any other: hot, dry, filled with sunshine. At 9 a.m. He Who Is Invincible appeared at his desk, just as he had for the last twenty years. Through the morning, ministers and generals came and went, carrying orders and dispatches and bearing the latest news, including that of the first bombing of Bologna. At midday the Japanese ambassador arrived at the Palazzo. When that visit was concluded the Dictator returned to the Villa Torlonia, making a detour through the Tiburtino district, where the crowds were as silent and brooding as they had been a week before.

Finally, at a little before five in the afternoon, the Aprilia 1500 set out once more, taking the passenger on its rear seat to an appointment with the King. That encounter took place not at the Quirinal but at the Villa Ada, the monarch's landscaped estate. Those few Romans who watched the slant-hooded limousine turn in at the gate on the Via Salaria could have no idea that they would be the last ones ever to see the Duce in the city of Rome.

Or almost the last. That privilege belonged to the family that resided at number 8, Via degli Specchi. At ten minutes to six the doorbell sounded through all four of its stories. It was followed by a thunderous knock. When Gianna opened the door two Carabinieri, bayonets fixed to their rifles, demanded to see Amos Prince. Max, looking down from an upstairs window, saw the white roof and red cross of an ambulance.

"Don't go!" he called to the architect. "They're going to arrest you." The appearance of the ambulance had an all too obvious explanation: word was going to go out that Prince had gone mad and been taken into custody for his own protection.

A.P., however, put on his hat and went down the stairs. The rest of the household trailed behind. The two policemen took the American by either arm and led him to the back of the vehicle, whose motor had not been shut off. The rear doors opened from within. Six soldiers sat on the metal benches, three to a side. Two of them held machine guns on their laps. Prince moved forward; he had placed one foot on the running board when a seventh soldier, seated in the shadows, held up his hand. He was dressed in a gray-green uniform, with, oddly enough, a cloth fedora pulled low over his head. Mussolini! The sleeve of his tunic hung loose on his upraised arm. His neck, a chicken's neck, poked thin and scrawny from the stiff loop of his collar. His face was a chiaroscuro of black and white: the pale, chalky skin, the dark stubble of a long day's beard.

"Dicey!" A.P. exclaimed. "Can that be you?"

"Amos-a! I'mma here to make the visit to my friend!"

"Wal, you're shore travelin' in style. An armed ass-carrot, even."

Franklin, from over his father's shoulder, cried out, "Duce! You honor us. Come in. Come upstairs. *Benvenuto!*"

"*Grazie*, I'mma thank you." So saying, Caesar stood, or half-stood, and took a step toward the open doors. Instantly, four rifles were thrust upward, crossing to form a barricade. Max could not help but gasp at the sight. It wasn't Prince who was the prisoner, it was Mussolini!

"Can it be true?" murmured Maximilian. "Are you under arrest? You? The Duce?"

The former dictator shrugged. "*Sì, tutto finito*. Alla is *finito*. I'mma the old man. The sick man. *Lo stomaco. La testa*. All is sick. *Ammalato*. Pain. I'mma tired."

"No, Duce!" Franklin exclaimed. "You must fight! Italy needs you! Give your orders! All will obey!"

"*Sì?* You think? *È vero?*" Before their eyes the Dictator flicked the switch that caused his body to expand. Once again his uniform shrank about his arms, his legs. His throat swelled over his collar. He snatched off his hat, revealing the shining dome of a skull that, like an artillery shell, seemed about to explode. "YOU! CARABINIERI! HEAR YOUR LEADER, WHO HAS BEEN SENT BY GOD: IF HE ADVANCES, FOLLOW HIM. IF HE RETREATS, KILL HIM. IF HE FALLS, AVENGE HIM. IT IS I, THE DUCE, WHO SALUTES YOU. YOU WILL ANSWER WITH THE SALUTE OF ROME."

The orator held out his right arm, which was once more writhing with powerful tendons. For an instant the soldiers, conditioned from childhood to obey that voice, sat in confusion. Then one of them raised, instead of his arm, his rifle. Mussolini staggered backward, rapidly shrinking, as if the point of the bayonet had punctured his skin. "You see? Is over. Is *finito*. Poor Benito. He's a *verme*. *Sì!* A worm. Step onna him. Cut him inna pieces. Put him inna what-you-call-him? The garbage can."

All this time Amos Prince had stood, staring down at his own shoes. Now, wonderingly, he raised his head. "Have I done this thing? I called for the barrage balloons: the balloons were there. I called on the people of Rome, the army, the party, the King: and they made the revolution. Is all this my work?"

Frankie pushed A.P. aside. "Don't listen to him! Listen to me! Where are they taking you? What will they do to you? Tell me! I shall notify the Führer. He'll send his troops. He'll put a stop to this outrage."

The look of wonderment on the face of the architect was suddenly replaced by a wide, almost boyish smile. The little beard waggled gaily at the end of his chin. "Haw! Haw! You mean A-golf Hitter? He can't help the Daisy now. He ain't nothin' but a has-Ben."

"*Sì*, no one can help the Duce. His fate-a, it's the same as the *leopardo*, the *tigre*, when brought to his knees by the race of the pygmies. *Sì*. Look at these men. Little tiny pygmy people. *Morte a Mussolini!* That's what they cry. And alla time he slaved for them. Day and night he worked to make them hard. Strong. Without mercy."

Here the erstwhile dictator performed his pneumatic trick again. From a barrel chest he cried, "THE DUCE GAVE THEM THE TEETH OF THE WOLF. THE ROMAN WOLF. HE TAUGHT THEM TO HATE. HE TAUGHT THEM TO LOVE THE SOUND OF THE MACHINE GUN. BUT THEY DO NOT REMEMBER. PYGMIES! ITALIAN PYGMIES! THEY WANT TO WATCH THE PASSING CLOUDS. TO EAT THE PASTA. TO SMELL THE PERFUME OF A WOMAN. THEY HATE THIS DUCE WHO WOKE THEM FROM THEIR DREAM. WHO TOLD THEM, *BETTER ONE DAY AS A LION THAN ONE HUNDRED YEARS AS A SHEEP*." Now the speaker so forgot himself that he stood erect, banging the bald pate of his head with such force that, on the metal roof of the ambulance, it left a visible dent.

"Is no good. Is *impossibile*. These people, they soft like the polenta. Even Michelangelo, he can no make the masterpiece outta the butter."

One of the soldiers looked at his watch. "*Sbrigati! Andiamo!*"

"You hear? You hear what he say? This pygmy, he wanna hurry up and kill Mussolini. *Perché?* Because the Duce, HE DESPISED OTHER MEN; NOW OTHER MEN TAKE THEIR REVENGE. HE GAVE THEM WAR: ETHIOPIA, ALBANIA, LA SPAGNA, WAR EVERYWHERE, AGAINST EVERYTHING— AGAINST FLIES, THE BATTLE FOR WHEAT, FOR STRAW, THE CAMPAIGN AGAINST STARCHED COLLARS. WAR! WAR! WAR! BUT THE DEGENERATE ROMANS WANT TO TAKE A WALK AFTER DINNER AND TIP THEIR HATS TO EACH OTHER. FOR THE DIGESTION! *TRADITORI!* THE DUCE KNEW HE WOULD BE BETRAYED. JUST AS CHRIST KNEW. CAESAR KNEW TOO. WAS HE NOT WARNED? DID HE NOT ACCEPT HIS FATE? *ET TU, BRUTUS?* THE DUCE IS SURROUNDED BY BRUTUSES! GRANDI, HIS JUSTICE MINISTER. THAT DINO GRANDI! BOTTAI. CIANETTI. SCORZE. CIANO! *O, DIO*, CIANO! HIS OWN SON! NINETEEN BRUTUSES. STABBING HIM, STABBING THEIR DUCE. NO CONFIDENCE. *UN VOTO DI SFIDUCIA!* ALL POWER TO THE KING, OF THE AUGUST DYNASTY OF SAVOY. HE IS THE WORST BRUTUS OF THEM ALL. 'MIO CARO DUCE. YOU ARE THE MOST HATED MAN IN ITALY. YOU HAVE NOT A SINGLE FRIEND EXCEPT FOR ME.' TRUE! IT IS TRUE! THE DUCE IS ALONE! ALWAYS ALONE. THIS IS HIS TRAGIC DESTINY. BODOGLIO: A BRUTUS. THE GENERALS: *TUTTI* BRUTUSES. COME, STAB YOUR DUCE. HERE IS HIS CHEST. COME, ITALIAN PEOPLE! YOUR DUCE AWAITS YOU. COME WITH YOUR FIFTY MILLION KNIVES!"

The onlookers, Prince, Nina, even Franklin, looked aside, as if the leader's bared chest, with its tightly coiled hair, its pink war wounds, was a sight they dared not see. Only Gianna faced the open ambulance. Breaking into tears, she rushed forward.

"Duce! Duce!" she wailed. "How could such a thing happen? We love you. Your people love you. We would die for you!"

Franklin: "Do you see her, Duce? Do you hear her? That is the true voice of Italy. Remember! Every Fascist has sworn an oath. To follow their Father to the death. We wait in our millions. We will pour into the streets this very night. You, soldiers. Carabinieri. Do not touch him. The *Squadristi* will devour all such traitors. They will feed them to the dogs. Come, Duce. Come now. These men will not stand in your way."

The soldiers sat unmoving, staring at each other across the narrow space of the cabin. They might as well have been drugged by the fumes that rose from the trembling tailpipe. Mussolini, when he spoke, was distant and small-voiced, as if he too had become stupefied by the odorless gas:

"Amos-a. Dear Prince. I'mma the fool. Always the fool. Why I no listen what you say? Now I'mma going to die. No, no! Is true. No be sad, my friends. Is only what-a-you-call-him? This body? *Uno straccio. Un vecchio straccio.* A rag. Is no importance. Ah, *ma la mia anima.* The soul. The thoughts. The words. The ideas. Prince: you make-a me *la promessa.* You search. You finda this body. You putta him like you say inna *la tomba. La tomba* inna sky. *Per l'Eternità!* The words of the Duce will fly up to the stars. He gonna live-a with the how-you-say-him? *Faraoni.* All the big Pharaoh. Inna *costellazioni.* He gonna be the energy, *la lunghezza d'onda,* the radio beam, the light. Isn't that right, *Architetto?* You putta Mussolini inna sky."

Prince: "That's right, Mister-loony. But we ain't yet built that Eighth Wonder of the World."

"No worry. Notta problem! You make *la promessa*; I make *la promessa.* You putta the *cadavere di Mussolini*—Ha! Ha! What-you-call-him? Mushy-linguini: is good joke. You putta inna *la tomba,* I already make the plan. I already give the secret order. You gonna getta the steel. You gonna getta alla Jewish *lavoratori.* Alla *schiavi.* The slaves, like *Arco di Tito.* You gonna make the *La Vittoria* the most biggest inna world."

"Douche, you have my word."

"Good. *Bravo.* I'mma *contento.* Happy. I'mma forgive my enemy like Gesù Cristo on account they notta know what they do. But IF THE DUCE SO WISHED, HE WOULD BITE THEM, THESE TRAITORS; HE IS SO FULL OF POISON THEY WOULD FALL DEAD ON THE SPOT. HA! HA! BITE THEM WITH THESE TEETH!"

On the instant, like a mad dog, his lips curled back and his wet fangs snapped together, clicking and clacking and grinding. "No, no, no. The Duce calms himself. *Calma. Calma.* He is *tranquillo.* He is at peace. You will look up. Inna sky. You see the star? The little star? Is that the Duce? That little a-winking, that little a-blinking light?"

There was, from the interior of the vehicle, a sob. One of the soldiers was weeping. At once the other Carabinieri, even the pair with the machine guns, were sobbing too. And not just the soldiers: tears streamed from Gianna's eyes. Franklin turned away, so no one could see that his own were falling onto the black cloth of his shirt. Max, to his own amazement, had to remove his glasses, which were inexplicably covered by a thin film of steam.

"*Piangi?* Why you cry? The Duce, he not sad. He happy. *Soldati!* Carabinieri! *Coraggio!* BE WORTHY OF THE UNIFORM YOU WEAR! Look. They cry like *bambini.* Why? For what? For the Duce? Ha, ha! *Bambini.* You gotta do the duty. You gotta kill your Duce. Always, this Mussolini, he gotta do every-a-thing himself. One day, inna *Anno Tredicesimo, era Fascista,* it's 1935, onna *giorno bello,* hot, a blue sky, the Duce, he goes inna the field. He take offa the hat. He take offa the coat. Inna hot sun he goes to show the people, his soft little pygmy people, how to make the Battle for Wheat. I'mma sweat. I'mma sore. I gotta big thirst. The wheat, she uppa to here. To the

Duce's waist. The Duce's head. And then: you look. The wheat, she no stand up. She bent alla down. It's the what-you-want-a-call-him? *Uccelli.* Birds! Black birds. Big black birds. They fly down. A hundred. A thousand. Ten thousand. YOU! SOLDIERS! *BERSAGLIERI!* ATTACK! FIGHT! FOR THE WHEAT! But they only stand. They only stare. *Stupefatto!* The Duce takes his stick. KILL THEM! KILL THEM! BEAT! BEAT! THE STICK! THE STICK! THE STICK!"

Mussolini had no stick. So with his bare fists he began to strike himself on the chest, on his shoulders, on his head.

"No! The cage! The cage for birds!"

That was Aria. The blond-haired girl moved forward, stopping in front of her father. She raised her hand, as if to touch the singed skin of his face or the brim of his battered hat; then before anyone could stop her she leaped into the back of the ambulance. No one spoke. No one moved.

Mussolini lowered his balled-up fists. A small trail of blood snaked down from where he had cut his own smiling lip. "You? You come? To the Duce?"

Aria, almost imperceptibly, nodded her head.

He Who Is Always Alone raised his bloodied hands. "SUN, IT IS I, THE DUCE, WHO SWEARS BEFORE YOU. YOU, SKY, THE DUCE DECLARES HIMSELF BENEATH YOU. CLOUDS, AIR, PEOPLE OF ROME: THIS IS THE WOMAN THE DUCE LOVES!"

Aria turned, as if after all she would leap from the platform. But instead of doing so, she seized both sides of the double doors and slammed them shut. Instantly, as if there had been some mechanical connection to the accelerator, the ambulance bolted ahead.

"Aria!" Prince and Maximilian called out the girl's name together. But when they started after the ambulance, the two remaining Carabinieri blocked their path. They could only watch as the vehicle turned the corner and drove out of sight.

3

That night the sun did not so much go down as fade out, as if it too were subject to air-raid regulations. A damp, heavy mist rolled in from the sea. People huddled at home behind black curtains. For some reason the telephones stopped working. The radios broadcast nothing but static. *Il Messaggero* did not appear in its Sunday evening edition, nor were any other papers delivered to the kiosks, which in any case soon shut down. Finally, at a little before 11 p.m., the transmitters of EIAR crackled back to life; an announcer declared that his majesty, Vittorio Emanuele III, had accepted the Duce's resignation and appointed a new government under Marshal Badoglio. Not everybody heard these words since the greater part of Rome—in their pajamas, in slippers, with the suspenders of their trousers slipped over their naked shoulders— was rushing into the streets:

"*Abbasso Mussolini!*"

"*Evviva Garibaldi!*"

"*Viva la libertà!*"

"*Viva la pace!*"

The entire nation was in a frenzy. The same crowds that had cheered Mussolini's speeches from the balcony of the Palazzo Venezia now gathered beneath it to call for his death. They smashed his plaster busts against the cobblestones; they threw the shreds of his portrait into the air. If a German dared to show himself in the street he was hooted back to his barracks. The presses of the Fascist papers were attacked with sledgehammers and the piles of newsprint burned, while the Romans danced in the light of the flames.

What of the Fascist Party members themselves, four million strong, each one of whom had sworn to fight to the death for Il Duce? One or two, with a handgun, with a terrible leap, ended their membership. Many more changed the pins on their lapels or sat down to write a letter of congratulation to Badoglio. Some, instead of taking to the streets to defend the life of their leader, fled through them to save their own. Farinacci, dressed as a woman, made his way to the German Embassy, crying out, "I didn't vote for the resolution! I am loyal to Mussolini! I am loyal to the Führer!"

The celebration lasted through the night. In the morning, people stumbled through the littered streets, like drunkards suffering a hangover. There were no more cheers. Everyone had the same thought: What would happen next? On the radio the marshal had said that the war would go on, with Italy on the Axis side. No one believed him. Surely the Americans would invade the mainland and drive toward Rome. The new government would find a way to withdraw from its entanglement with Germany and Japan. Perhaps it would sign a secret armistice with the Allies. Perhaps the Pope would persuade the Americans to make peace—or at least to cease the bombings. Was it not a good sign that in the week since that one terrible raid on the capital, there had not been another attack from the air?

The trouble was that if the people did not believe the assurances of Badoglio, the Furor, the Fearer, the Furrier—or the Phooey, as Chaplin had famously called him—did not believe them either. Every day Wehrmacht brigades poured through the Brenner Pass. Recruits from the Tyrol were pressed into special police units. Squads of SS openly patrolled the streets of Rome. Soon there would be more German soldiers in Italy than there were uniformed Italians.

"I told you," Franklin said, while gazing down from the rooftop at the armored columns. "They're here to rescue the Duce. His own people, his own party have abandoned him. But not his one true friend."

If that was in fact the mission of the foreign troops, they were taking their time about it. The last week of July came and went.

So did the first week of August. No one, least of all the Germans, knew what had happened to Mussolini. Of course there were rumors: that he was on this or that island, brooding like Napoleon on St. Helena; or, like that conqueror on Elba, plotting his return. Some said that he had already escaped and had been seen at Berchtesgaden, staring down from the Eagle's Nest at the Alps that, like Hannibal, he would soon attempt to cross. But there was more dire speculation: that Badoglio, eager to get his prisoner off his hands, had handed him over to the Americans on Sicily and that he was now in New York, about to be displayed in a cage—the same unbearable punishment that Aria had feared—at Madison Square Garden. Many were convinced he was already dead: that the Carabinieri, on orders from the King, had left a loaded pistol in a sequestered hotel room in Brindisi, and that the Duce had put the muzzle in his mouth, clamped his iron jaw around it, and pulled the trigger.

If Mussolini was a prisoner, of course, he could not keep his promise to make his tomb the tallest structure on earth. Moreover, as each day went by without another attack from the air, more and more of the barrage balloons were untied from their moorings and collapsed in their shelters. The steel ellipse, the crucial ninety-fourth, ninety-fifth, and ninety-sixth stories of *La Vittoria*, remained on the ground.

Nor could the defunct Caesar fulfill the second half of his commitment—the pledge to allow Jewish workers to complete his monument, as they once had those of Titus and the Egyptian Pharaohs. But had he not said that he had already given a secret order? Why had it not been obeyed? The Duce's subjects had already smashed every image of the former Dictator to pieces. Surely the new government would not allow them to continue work on a Colossus that would be ten times larger than the one at Rhodes. More days went by, but the Jews did not appear. What was their fate? As the streets began to fill with German soldiers, Maximilian returned obsessively to one terrible question: Had his great idea, his plan, brought the Jews to Rome only to lead them into a trap?

On a late afternoon in August he crossed the Tiber in order to determine the answer. He knew that, what with the rationing of petrol, it would be almost impossible to find a taxi. The few trams that were running were so overcrowded that people were trying to force their way inside through the windows. Even bicycles were hard to come by, though he had kept a flat-tired Montecane model in his basement bedroom for years. He pumped up the inner tubes and headed wobbily toward the river.

Dodging the thousands of home-bound pedestrians, he arrived at the outskirts of St. Peter's Square and began to circle behind it. A series of steep inclines lay before him. Pedaling in earnest, he entered the unlit tunnel that took him to the hills beyond the Vatican. Standing on the pedals, he started up the even steeper grades that led to Montespaccato. He broke into a cold, clammy sweat. His eyes stung. He snatched at the air for breath. It was too much for him. He swerved from one side of the road to the other, and then, abandoning his two-wheeler, he strode, neck down, like a broken nag, up the serpentine road.

"Halt! Achtung!"

He stopped at the command. He looked up, his magnified eyes bulging with astonishment. These were Germans! SS troopers! Where were the Carabinieri who had cried out, *Maestro! Maestro!*? These men had him by the collar. They were shouting:

"Wer bist du? Sprich! Papiere! Identifikation!"

Max tried to answer, but the sight of the skull on their caps, with crossed bones beneath it, had turned him into a dead man himself.

One of the officers clubbed him with the edge of his hand. "*Gib Antworte! Sprich!*"

Another said, "*Dies ist ein Jundenschwein.*"

They all burst into laughter.

"*Ein Kapitalistisher Hund!*"

"*Ein Parasit auf dem Volke!*"

These Stormtroopers were giants, six footers and more. One pushed Max to the left. Another caught him, shoving him back to the right, as if he were their ball in a game of soccer. The sport continued, minute after painful minute, until Max, sprawled headlong, saw a column of men, hundreds and hundreds of them, trudging down the same winding path that he had been determined to go up. He recognized them at once. The Jews! The Jewish workers! Of course! The Italians would not finish the statue of Mussolini, but the Germans would. Franklin was right: Hair Hatter was the Duce's one true friend.

Down and down came the weary men, their eyes peering from soot-covered faces as black as those of the Africans who had labored before them. Max, unmolested, ran to the first of the refugees. "Hello! Hello! I am happy to see you! I am glad you are alive!"

The column went silently by. Was it the gauntlet of German soldiers? Or were they simply too exhausted to speak? Maximilian fell into step. He pulled at the sleeve of the nearest worker. "Do you speak English? Do you understand me? Have you been building the statue? The statue of Hercules?"

The man, whose bare head, like a penitent's, was covered with ash, remained mute. The man behind him, tall and bony, spoke instead. "Hercules? Hercules *kaputt*. No more Hercules."

Max: "Then what are you doing? I thought you were working. You have to be working. That was our agreement. Our plan."

Another man, this one had blondish eyebrows, said, "We work. At the *Fabrik*. The factory."

"The Mussolini Works!" Max exclaimed.

At those words, those within earshot started to laugh. The ripple of merriment spread all along the column.

"I don't understand," Max stammered. "What's so funny? It must be terrible work, making steel."

"*Ja! Stahl!*" someone shouted. "Steel for tanks. Steel for bullets. Steel for bayonets!"

As if the man had been a comedian, the others started to howl. They slapped their knees. They hugged their sides. They wiped the tears that washed their darkened cheeks. "Do you not see?" asked the light-haired worker. "The Jews are making weapons to kill Jews! We are making war on ourselves! Ha! Ha! Ha! Is that not a good joke?"

Everyone seemed to think so; even the SS troops were laughing. To Max's astounded eyes, the skulls on their caps seemed to be grinning too.

"Listen. Listen, Jews. You don't have to do this. Tomorrow you must come to the Circo Massimo. That was our agreement. You were to work on the Duce's statue. Now you can work on his tomb. Do you hear what I'm saying? Do you understand? Don't work here! Don't work for your enemies. Come tomorrow. Come in the morning. Come at dawn." Max buttonholed his coreligionists, one after the other. But they pushed by him, not heeding a word.

What more could Shabilian do? He remained motionless as the last of the refugees plodded past him, toward the low, windowless shacks in which they would spend the night. He roused himself only when he saw a new group, also in their hundreds, depart the barracks and start marching toward where he stood. He would not speak to the new shift. Why bother? They were the Führer's Ethiopians now.

He brushed the dirt from his clothing. He stared through the gathering gloom for his *bicicletta*. There it was, its front wheel turned back toward its flanks, like a sleeping animal. He walked over, slung a leg over the saddle, and pedaled back the way he had come.

At dawn the next morning Maximilian arrived at *La Vittoria*. He took the motorized lift up the side of the monument. He rode past the broadcasting studio of EIAR on the twenty-first floor and A.P.'s on the forty-second, then stopped at the sixty-third, at which point the corrosion on the tracks made it impossible to rise any higher. He moved through a utility cable to the central ellipse and dragged himself up the interior steps another thirty flights. Then he climbed out of the trap of the ninety-third floor. On the ground it had been windless; a thousand feet in the air there was a perpetual breeze. A.P. himself stood nearby, staring off to the east. There the haze had begun to brighten; but to the west, over what he thought must be the *Mare Tirreno*, there was only darkness. For a dizzying moment he thought this is what morning must look like to Apollo in the heavens, or to a man in space: the rallying sun, the withdrawing forces of night.

"You know what a birdy told me," said Prince, turning toward his apprentice. "He told me you went up to that factory for steel. What did you find out? Are they still working on that statue of Hercuticles? Is the last segment of our tower still there?"

Before Max could reply he heard a noise floating up from below. An engine. A second engine. He looked down. A string of trucks was moving along the Via dei Cerchi. Some had already come to a halt; men were jumping from the covered beds at the rear. Soldiers? No, workers! Those were not guns on their shoulders but all manner of tools. The laborers scrambled though the line of parched, half-leafless trees and down to the floor of the site. More were arriving on foot, not in formation but in the straggling manner of men on their way to work. They looked for all the world as if they were free. But how could that be? Those trucks, their drivers, were German.

He turned toward his companion, but Prince had ducked down the trap to the interior of the top story. A half hour later he heard the distinctive chug of the elevator as it made its way down from section to section. At ground level, the architect emerged. He waved his arms. He took off his hat and used it to point this way and that. Straining, Max thought he could even hear the odd, distorted word, and then, more clearly, the familiar *Haw! Haw!*

People were running in every direction. A small crew of rivet men—Maximilian could see their blowtorches and how their metal helmets were pushed back on their heads—crowded into the elevator, which immediately began its ascent. Others made for the core or fanned out toward the machinery that lay, scattered and untended, about the site. Within minutes dust was curling upward, along with the sounds of shouting men and the screech and roar of their drills and pulleys and motorized saws.

There was no lack of work for the refugees to do. Over the last two years the monument had fallen into utter disrepair. The rails for the lifts had to be scraped of rust and realigned. The cables that stretched between the circumference of each ellipse to the hub at the core had to be tightened or restrung. Much of the glass that had been installed was now broken. The utility system—the pipes for gas, water, electricity, pneumatic mailing—was in a shambles. Many of the tasks would be backbreaking, and some, such as riveting a full quarter-mile off the ground, actually death-defying. Max watched as the Jews, *his* Jews—shopkeepers in a former life, leather cutters, accountants, theater critics—set about their tasks.

Then, just as Maximilian had decided to make his way down through the steps of the core, a new sound, a wasp-like buzzing, filled the air. Those on the ground, those in the building, heard it too. All activity stopped, aside from the echo of a hammer, metal on metal, metal on wood; then that sound ceased as well. Max looked down. The workers were running about in what looked like a random pattern; it was almost as if they were the insects whose wing beats were creating the growing reverberation. They were all looking up, heads back, fingers pointing. Max looked too. The southern sky was filled with airplanes! American bombers! They were heading directly for the monument, as if it were a compass point. Now the workers saw them. They ran for the paltry shelter of the trees. Already the buzz had deepened into a drone and then, as the first of the B-24's drew ever closer, an ear-splitting roar.

This, the raid of August 13, was not conducted from high over the city, as that on Tiburtino had been three weeks earlier. Indeed, the approaching Liberators were flying at such a low altitude that Max feared they would crash into the tower. Or was *La Vittoria* the target? Retribution for the broadcasts that Prince had made over the years? Would they bring down the symbol of Mussolini, now that Mussolini himself was hidden away?

On came the aircraft, their propellers flashing in the morning light. They did not strike the tower, but passed so closely over it that Max could see the blurred faces of the pilots and copilots and the cramped bodies of the belly gunners enclosed in glass. Poor Maximilian! He did not know whether to leap in the air and cry out *Hurrah* to his fellow Americans: *Do it! Kill them! Kill them all!* Or whether he ought to cower in shame at having lived at peace with the enemy of his own country. In the event, he did neither, standing silent as the young men in their airplanes flew over him in unending waves.

They did not continue north after passing the tower but banked westward, following the course of the river, before turning again, farther left. Max braced himself for the sound of anti-aircraft fire, for the sight of the Liberators breaking apart or spiraling down in flames. There was, however, no ack-ack at all. Rather, the salvos that went up were scattered and ineffectual, almost certainly coming from the few German batteries that had been implanted near their own barracks. Max had a sudden thought: the bombers were flying this low because they knew there would be no resistance. Perhaps the rumors were true: the Italians and the Americans were negotiating. They had reached a truce. Soon there would be an armistice.

Only a minute later Max learned the real reason for the low-altitude flight. Under the aircraft the familiar flyspecks appeared. The bombs were falling on Montespaccato! The target was not Mussolini but the Mussolini Works. A half mile, a quarter mile, above the Vatican. How daring the American pilots. How precise they had to be in their attack. This time any bombs that went astray would land not on the ancestors of Pacelli but the living Pope himself.

The explosives brightly burst; a second later Maximilian heard the sound of the concussion. The Jews, the steelworkers, came out from the protection of the trees. They stared off in wonderment. Only yesterday they had been at work in that factory. If it were not for a stroke of good fortune, they would be there now. They saw that the smoke rising over their workplace was thicker and blacker than that which had poured from the stacks of *Il Vulcano*, even when it had been turning out ingots at one hundred percent of capacity.

Above the tower the last waves of aircraft were banking off to the left, preparing their approach. Already a thick cloud of suspended ash hung over the city. Bomb blasts, like lightning flashes, lit it from below. Suddenly, there was a tremendous detonation, greater, it seemed, than all the others combined. Max blinked repeatedly, unable to believe what appeared before his eyes. Far off, where the bombs were falling, the landscape of Rome had altered. Half of

Montespaccato had disappeared. In a blur, an erasure, one part had folded into the other. It dawned on Max that the hollowed-out earth, the network of caverns and mines, had collapsed. The statue of Hercules was forever buried.

Now the ground began to tremble. The entire city seemed subtly to shift, like a fleet of boats on a wave. The ripple spread, as would a line of force in an earthquake. The tower swayed, then steadied. But the trees, already half denuded, lost the last of their fluttering leaves. Then the planes flew off, losing themselves in the man-made cloud.

A shout went up. The men on the ground were screaming. Their voices, in a dozen, in two dozen languages, rose higher and higher, until the mingled words reached Max's ears.

"*Pesach!*"

"*Passahfest!*"

"*Pâqueunshei!*"

"Passover." That is what, in their separate tongues, the Jews were crying. The miracle of Passover had saved their lives. In their midst stood the figure of the foreshortened architect, holding the brim of his hat in his hands. But those around him were not addressing him. Instead they were pointing upward, high in the air, to the idol of Maximilian Shabilian.

"*Moise, Maximiliano!*"

"*Moshiach, Max, Max, Max!*"

"*Le Messie! Max!*"

"*Megmento! Max!*"

He is our Moses, they were crying. Our Deliverer! Our Messiah!

ALITALIA 607

Grounded

[2005: 1943]

1

I've been spending the night rolling up and down the corridors of the hospital. No one tells me anything about Leda's condition, except that, as the *Dottore* declared, the blow to her head caused nothing more than a concussion. Have no fears for her, that's the last I heard from Mamiglioni. I think he went off to one of the hotels that Alitalia has provided the passengers. The rumor is, we won't take off until a crew from Italy, or maybe the Boeing people, check out the plane. That clacking sound. The dimming lights. You can't tell me that was caused by the weather. They better take a look at the rudder while they're at it. Those chunks of ice weren't beanbags. Just the thought makes me shudder, as if the frozen missiles were still flying by. No wonder half the passengers have rebelled. They swore they'd never return to that 767. They're going to wait for a turboprop to take them back to New York.

We're going to Rome, Slapsy Max, Leda, and the baby in her womb. Lots of women bleed when they're pregnant, that's what the medics said in the ambulance. So did the nurse, a real harridan, with her glasses dangling from a black cord. I am surprised by how much I want this great-grandchild—a great, great one for Amos Prince— to live. Though it appears to be fatherless. The result of some binge at the Dramat. Who knows the kind of lives these kids live. Even my serious-minded Leda, her thumb in the pages of her book. She could not be very far along—not with those slim arms, the fleshless throat, the bony shoulders. A month? Two? Or even earlier? This child, for all I know, is little more than a collection of cells. Nonetheless, I believe I can see it, as if the thick glass of my spectacles gathered enough light to penetrate hospital walls. I can't get the picture, like a smoky sonogram, out of my head: tough little fellow, lying on his back, like an orange peel. I cross my right-hand fingers: good luck, Buster!

The window at the far end of the corridor is starting to let in the northern light. Here comes the dawn. I wheel, one-handed, underneath it. A treeful of birds are making themselves heard through the glass. I turn, to prepare for the return journey to the other end. There, coming around the corner, are birds of a different color. Four nuns, in black, but with a stiff white bib, like magpies, are pushing a cart. I remember of a sudden we never did get our *risotto con funghi*, our *tonno*. My stomach churns. I feel a discharge of saliva at the side of my mouth. One-armed, I propel myself forward. What lovely ladies! What round, pink cheeks. And what have we here? Hot cross buns! With butter. With jam. I want to sing like a bird myself:

One 'a penny
Two 'a penny

I taste the spices. I roll the currants on my tongue. They laugh, these sweethearts; when I tear open the fourth one and butter it up, they break into applause. I guess they think they've made a convert. One of them, from inside that starched bib, takes out a handkerchief. She doesn't dab my mouth; she wipes the tears from my eyes. *Ota. Ondrej. Neda*— Damn! Damn it! Here they come again: *Saskia. Felicia. Ugo. Ketziah. Ermanno.* Oh, I'm not weeping for them this time either. Or for little Buster. Or for *L'uomo dei Miracoli* and the miracles he could not work. It's the kindness that moves me. Catholic charity. These darlings would not hurt a fly.

Moise, Massimiliano! Mosaich, Max, Max, Max!

Why did the men who shouted those words show up each morning to labor on *La Vittoria*? It was no more likely that they wanted to create a tomb for Mussolini than that the Jews in Egypt had wished to create a memorial for Ramses the Great. What did they care about creating the world's tallest building, or reaching what was for them the meaningless goal of an English or American mile? They certainly did not work the long, hot hours for Amos Prince. No, I was the one they followed—a greater figure than any of the other Maximilians: the ruler of the Holy Roman Empire; the King of Hungary and Bohemia; the tragic Emperor of Mexico. Whenever I appeared at the Circo Massimo they rushed after me, trying to touch the fabric of my coat, crying "Rabbi! Rabbi!"

The rule of Maximilian the IV, Emperor of Emigrés, lasted no longer than that of Marshal Badoglio. That is, we each lost our authority at 6:30 p.m. on September 8th, 1943, when an American voice went out over the airwaves. It wasn't Amos; it was Eisenhower, Supreme Commander in the Mediterranean. He announced that the government of the King and the marshal had surrendered. An hour later, on EIAR, Badoglio declared that Italian forces must cease all acts of hostility against the Allied armies and that they must oppose an attack from any other quarter. *Any other quarter!* That meant Germany! Italy and the Thousand-Year Reich were at war.

Before that same dawn, the Americans landed at Salerno, too far to the south to intimidate the German soldiers who now, under Field Marshal Kesselring, poured into the streets of Rome. Previously, those members of the Wehrmacht stationed in the city, even those belonging to the Waffen SS, behaved correctly, entering the shops in the old ghetto and, like any Roman, haggling over the price of a *torto di ricotta* or a striped cravat. That charade was over. Kesselring strode forward and, overnight, like an omnipotent god, caused his ten commandments to appear on every wall. But this was Mars, not Moses: any act of resistance was to be met by summary execution. No wonder that those Jews who could fled from the city or vanished inside it, like so many drops of water on bone-dry ground.

In just three more days the fallen Caesar had risen. Eight gliders landed on what was presumed to be an unapproachable mountaintop and whisked him off in an airplane to Pratica di Mare and then Munich for a reunion with the Furor. Listening to our *Superinduttanza Sei* was now a capital offense. Yet I sat well into the night trying to pick up Radio London, the Allied Armed Forces Radio, anything that might tell me whether, inside that tiny Storch aircraft, there had been room for both Mussolini and an American girl.

"I told you! I told you!" cried Franklin, who strode into our room wearing the uniform of a *Bombamano*, with two bands of grenades, like suckling mammals, crisscrossed on his chest. "This is loyalty. This is friendship. The leader of the Master Race keeps his word."

Before I could reply, there was an explosion, a bomb blast, and then a burst of gunfire. All of us—Franklin, Nina, Gianna, and I—

stood stock-still, listening to what sounded like the rattle of popcorn kernels against the lid of a kettle.

"It's the Americans!" I cried. "They have begun their attack. They will be in Rome tomorrow. They might be here tonight."

Franklin grinned, his teeth glistening. "Look out the window," he commanded.

I did so. I saw three or four men, dressed like Prince's son, step from the shadows. They waved. They shouted up to their comrade. At the same time, two motorcycles, each with a sidecar, raced down the Via degli Specchi toward the south. A half-track followed, with a machine gun mounted on its roof. Each vehicle had the Kreuzer of the Wehrmacht painted in gray and black on its side.

If possible, Frankie was grinning even more widely than before. "Those aren't the Americans you hear. They're partisans. A handful of Communists. We beat them down at the Pyramid of Cestius. We'll take care of this bunch in less than an hour. We are going to teach these dancing Italians. They'll pay for their celebrations. How they will pay! Rome is now as German as Berlin. Or, my Maximilian, as Warsaw."

The last word chilled me through. By then everyone knew what had happened in that doomed city. But I also knew there had been no Fifth Army in Poland.

"You can't frighten me," I declared. "The Americans *are* coming. No one can stop General Clark. Or General Montgomery. The Germans will have to retreat."

"The Wehrmacht never retreats. It is idiocy to think so. It is you, little Max, who must run away like the rest of the Jews. If the Gestapo does not capture you, the Americans will. Do you think they are coming to save you? That you will be liberated? General Clark knows who you are. Even Eisenhower has heard those broadcasts. You are a man without a friend in the world."

Just then the sky lit up to the south, on the other side of the river. Mortar shells hummed in the air. Down in the street, the little squad of *Bombamani* whistled again. Franklin shouted back through the window and, before racing down the staircase, addressed me one last time: "Run, Maxie! Run, Maximilian! Or you will spend the rest of your life in jail."

But where could I run? Into the arms of my countrymen? What could I tell them? That I had remained in Italy to assist a genius with his plans? That I had had a plan of my own to rescue the Jews? Or that I could never abandon the girl who was now the mistress of Mussolini? They would laugh in my face. Never, not in a million years, would they believe that I had cheered them from the top of the tower; that I had wanted to wave at the pilots and beg them to drop their bombs and *Kill them! Kill them all!* No. They would come for me, as surely as they would come for the man who had aided the enemy with his broadcasts.

As it turned out, however, it was the *Totenköpfe* of the SS who arrived for me in a black Daimler sedan. For a moment I stood lost in admiration of their physiques: the clear eyes and unblemished skin, the golden hair, the height of giants. Could the rumors be true? That these Death's Headers were not allowed so much as a cavity in their teeth? The next thing I knew I was thrown headlong into the backseat and we sped off across the heart of the city. Glancing through the swaying curtains, I saw that we were racing down the Via Labicana and then the Viale Manzoni. Could our destination be the Via Tasso? That was the location of the new Gestapo head-quarters, which was also—everyone knew it—a torture chamber, a jail. No sooner had that dread thought darted through my mind than we did indeed turn onto the street named for the poet who had composed the *Gerusalemme Liberata*; we pulled to a shuddering stop at number 155.

At once my head began to ache, as if the infamous electrical helmet had already been placed upon it. My guards held me by either arm as we walked up a curving staircase to the offices of the former Major Kappler, who, as a reward for discovering Mussolini's hiding place high in the Apennines, had just been appointed to the rank of Obersturmbannführer. As soon as I saw him behind his wide wooden desk, with a new iron cross pinned to his blouse, I recognized him. The protruding nose, the receding chin, the colorless gray eyes—above all, the snaking scar on the side of his face: this was the officer whom I had seen months before, surveying our site from the back of Speer's Mercedes.

"Please, won't you sit?" he asked, as if I were not a prisoner but a guest. But I stood, head cocked, listening for—well, what was I expecting to hear? Screams in the courtyard? The rattle of chains? The muffled sound of a pistol?

"Why have you brought me here?" I managed to ask.

"Surely you know. This is the place where we seek information."

"But why me? I know nothing. I can do nothing."

"You are too modest. You know a great deal. For instance, the location of the *Judenlisten*. With names. With addresses. Family members. Occupations. Even the dates of births. Book one: every Roman Jew. Book two: every Jew who has moved to the city."

At these words I accepted the invitation to drop into the waiting chair. "The *Judenlisten*? Why would I have such a thing? I am, you know, a free thinker. I do not go to the temple. I don't think you could even call me a Jew."

"We have no time for this nonsense, Herr Shabilian." So saying, the Gestapo chief pressed a button on his desk. He said three words in German. The door opened and two pairs of disembodied arms thrust a complete human being into the room. I stared at the man who stood on the carpet.

"Zolli!" I cried.

It was indeed the rabbi, hatless, half unbearded, with one lens missing from his glasses and the other one pushed high on his forehead.

"They've beaten you! How could such a thing happen? This is the Chief Rabbi of Rome."

Kappler ignored my cry. With his chin resting on his interlaced fingers, he addressed the rabbi. "If you would tell Herr Shabilian what you have told us—"

Zolli stood, with the lining coming out of his jacket. He began to tip to one side, further and further, until, as with the optical illusion of the tower at Pisa, it seemed he must fall.

"Rabbi," said Kappler. "Tell us who now has possession of the lists."

Now Zolli snapped upright. He raised an arm, from which the cloth cuff was missing. "*Lui le ha,*" he said, pointing at me. "He does."

It was a warm, mid-September day. Perhaps it was the breeze that blew through the window, occasionally lifting the corner of this or that paper on the officer's desk, that made me break into a stinging sweat. "Me?" I said. "Ha! Ha! There must be a misunderstanding."

Herr Kappler slammed his fist on his desk with such force that the cap flew off an inkwell and spun there like a silver coin. "Jews! Believe me! Your situation is desperate. I am going to speak frankly with you. More frankly than I should. I will say these things only once. You must pay attention to my words."

Either because his voice, which had begun with a shout, had dropped to a conspiratorial whisper, or because of the crimson-colored blur of exasperation that had appeared on his brow, I found myself leaning forward; and Zolli, who had begun once more to list, righted himself.

"Herr Shabilian. Herr Zolli. I am certain I do not have to tell you that Germany has declared war on the Jewish race. It is a war that will be won, even if—" and here he dropped his voice even lower, as if he feared he might—through the open window, the closed door, or any one of the three telephones on his desk—be overheard: "Even if the other one, against the Allied powers, is lost. In truth, this first war has already been won across the face of Europe. Need I point to Poland? Rumania? The Ukraine? Holland? All the Baltic states? France? Not to mention the Greater Reich itself. Soon there will not be Jews anywhere. Anywhere! Not just in those countries. Not just in Europe. The question is: Will there be a single Jew left in the world?"

Zolli, tipping again, jerked himself to attention. "I gave them to him. He told me he would take them to America. *He* has the lists." Once more he pointed toward where I was sitting, glued by perspiration to the cushion of my chair.

"It's not true! I don't know what—"

Kappler raised his fist. I closed my eyes, certain that this time the ink itself would fly from the well. When I peeked through my lashes I saw that the radish-red blotch on the officer's forehead had crept across his cheeks and brow. Only the scar, from ear to jaw, remained an ominous white. "*Meine Herren*: I am doing the impossible: I am putting myself in your position. You are asking: *Why does he want these documents? He is head of the Gestapo. He will drive us from our homes. He will gobble us up.* I do not deny that in this war Italy is now the battlefront. I live in fear that today, tomorrow, the day after, I will see on my desk a directive from Reichsführer Himmler. A white piece of paper. Or else one of these telephones will ring. I shall be ordered to settle the Jewish question in whatever territory our forces occupy."

There was a thud. Zolli had finally toppled—not to the floor, but against the wall, to which he now clung, like a drunkard to a lamppost.

Kappler barely paused. "When the order comes, the order that the Jews of Rome *sie zu liquidieren*, that they be liquidated, I will have to obey it. Yes, with a heavy heart. Yes, with pain. But I am a policeman and I must act. We will not need your lists. We will not need cooperation—either from the Roman population or the Jews themselves. In this we are expert. We seize people by their throats. We drag them by the hair. The children. The infants. Those, *Meine Herren*, still in the womb."

The Obersturmbannführer paused to take a breath; we two Jews held ours. I saw how, outside the window, in the courtyard, the wind was blowing the foliage from a tree. In this brief interval of silence I could hear the death rattle of each leaf as it was tugged—*by the hair!*—from its branch. Ah: there was a bird, a little Roman robin, going about its business.

"Now listen with care," Kappler continued. "In all of Poland only a single ghetto remains, that of Lodz. *Warum?* Because there the Jews have been put to work. They sit at their machines, sewing for the German army. In spring, we of the Gestapo say, it is time for the *Judenaktion*. The Wehrmacht replies, wait, we need the uniforms for the fall offensive; and in the fall, when we come for the round-up, the Wehrmacht says, wait, we need the uniforms for the winter campaign. So there they sit, the Jews, in their tens of thousands, clothing the backs of their oppressors."

"But Lodz is a textile center," I protested. "In Rome we make nothing."

"Think for a moment of Tunisia: when the SS arrested the Jewish leaders there, Field Marshal Kesselring mobilized the Jewish people to make fortifications. Not a single one was deported. You see? You are not without friends. And not without hope. This same Kesselring is now in Rome."

"I don't understand," I responded. "What do the sewing

machines in Poland, the fortifications in Africa have to do with the Jews of Rome?"

"You should know, Herr Shabilian, better than anyone. After all, the idea is yours. Yes, we are going to put them to work. On your mile-high tower. The first thing the Duce asked upon arriving in Munich was that his monument be completed; the Führer, who has never abandoned his friend, agreed. Not even Himmler can overrule such an order. The Mussolini Works must be rebuilt. The ore in the statue must be recovered. The two projects together will require ten thousand workers. You will now produce the lists, Herr Shabilian: not so the Jews can be deported, but so they can be saved."

What was I to say? What was I to do? Could I believe the words I had just heard? They sounded reasonable. I knew nothing about the ghetto in Lodz, but I thought I remembered that the Jews in Tunis had been spared. Kappler was smiling, nodding. In spite of myself, I smiled back. Then I looked toward Zolli, who was still clinging lizard-like to the wall. Then I looked again. Did I imagine it? Had not the rabbi, with an all-but-invisible tic—a message in code, from Jew to Jew—shaken his head: *No*. If only I could send a message back: *Don't worry, everything is safely hidden*.

"Why do you say this to me?" I finally asked. "I told you: I don't have the lists."

"Fool! Stubborn fool! Don't you understand that at this moment we are searching your building? We shall go through it centimeter by centimeter, from your room in the cellar to the very rooftop. Don't imagine you can hide the books from us."

"No! Wait! Don't search the house."

"And why should I not?"

"Because the *Judenlisten* aren't there. They're nowhere in the building. I swear it."

"Then where, Herr Shabilian, are they to be found?"

The officer leaned backward. In the slanting beams of sunlight that poured through the open window his body seemed to dematerialize, to evaporate, save for the slash of the pale scar and the black bars of the iron cross. What was that? The quick blur of color? Of course, the robin. Gathering twigs, was she, for some hidden nest? Pecking for grubs? Hip-hopping simply for joy?

"Naples."

"What?" It wasn't Kappler who said this; it was Zolli. "*Che? Come? Napoli?*"

The German, still awash in the light, said, "How could that be?"

How, indeed? I squinted into the sunshine. The redbreast turned its head, staring at me with an open, innocuous eye. "I sent them there. Two years ago. On December 11th. We were going home. All of us. Aboard the *Rex*. But the Duce, he declared war. That very day. The boat never sailed. The *Judenlisten*: they must still be on board."

"You expect me to believe such a story?"

"You believed the rabbi, didn't you? Didn't he just tell you? That he asked me to take the lists to America."

Herr Kappler swung back, out of the blinding light. "Well, Rabbi?"

"I asked him. It's true."

"Very well. Every road from Rome is in our possession. We have occupied Naples as well. We control the harbor and everything in it. If I sent you, both of you, to the steamship, would you be able to recover the book of names?"

Zolli: "No."

I took a deep breath. I glanced out the window one last time. The little songster had flown out of sight. What I said was, "Yes."

2

I have never been a fan of hospitals, even though I designed one in Marin County that finally won me the Pritzker Prize. Of course I stole the idea for the steel cables from *La Vittoria*. If I thought about it, I wouldn't be surprised if every idea I've ever had came either from that monument, or from one or another of Prince's buildings. If I had the guts, I should have turned down every one of my honors. Look twice: that hospital is nothing more than a suspension bridge turned on its side. Rosellen is the one who knows my secret: that underneath everything there's only little Max, the shad-roe of Big Amos. Maximilian Shabilian, the laureate, is a fraud. Or at best, like those angels of mercy, a thieving magpie.

I had my tonsils out in a hospital three hundred years ago, back in the days of the Harding administration. My mother told me we were going on vacation—to Baja California, I think. Good heavens, look what I have found in the brain cells of the attic: a sombrero. Jesus! Black with white trim and white tassels. That was part of the grand disguise. I wore it inside our Chevrolet, but instead of Caliente or Encinada, we ended up at—I guess downtown at St. Vincent's. Here's another trick of my short-circuited brain. At this very moment, even with my disabled sniffer—No-Nose, they should call me, like a Dick Tracy character—I believe I can smell the black mask they lowered over my face, a mixture of rubber and ether. They don't use that gas any more, but I can smell it all right, just as I do in any hospital. Ruined cells trumped by the power of association.

Here comes the harridan. I look up at her, I suppose like a beggar with a tin cup. *You should go to the hotel*, she tells me—commands, rather. *We'll call you the minute we have any word.* But I don't budge. If she doesn't sleep, why should I?

After her stroke, we took Nina to Columbia Presbyterian. She was, goddamn it, only in her sixties. When she came out she could not sit upright in a chair. All she did was spoon up vanilla ice cream and give out sticks of Doublemint gum. Her only pleasure, for years, was making a ball, as big as a basketball finally, from the silver wrapping. Was that what Amos was doing in his dotage? With this crazy tale of a floating metallic sphere? Was that just a ball of tinfoil too? You can guess what they brought me after my own brain exploded. Vanilla ice cream. They must have thought, the way I spat it out, or twisted my head away from the spoon, that I was nuts. How to explain, voiceless, tongueless, that that's what they gave me as a reward, everyone smiling, my own mother smiling, when I had my tonsils out. Oh, Nina, that lively girl! I should have warned her: don't waste your love on Slapsy Max.

This is my fear: that it was I who turned her hair gray. Sometimes, not copulating, but doing the dishes perhaps, I'd say, with my hands in the soapsuds, *Aria, would you hand me that cup?* Could it be? Did those three syllables, *Ar-i-a*, place the blood clot in her brain? Did they, I wonder, put the embolus in mine? Will all this crazy mooning send Rosellen to the hospital too? As I said, there are no secrets from that woman. What a look she gave me when I showed her the airline tickets. She did not have to say a word. She knew the real reason—the mission of a madman, Mister Loony—I was returning to Rome.

The rabbi and I rode to Naples in the cab of an empty truck. We took the Appian way as far as Lago Albano, at which point we pulled off the road.

"What's happening?" asked Zolli. "Why are we stopping?"

The driver, nothing but a lantern jaw and a helmet, only shrugged. "*Ich spreche kein English. Ich sprech kein Italienisch.*"

Suddenly a score of twenty soldiers, camouflaged and armed, trotted from a stand of nearby trees. Zolli and I stared at each other: Were we to be seized, dragged to the water's edge, drowned like cats? But the infantrymen swung themselves up into the bed of the truck, and at once we moved on. A half hour later, near Cisterna di Latina, we halted again, while a procession of trucks and half-tracks and mobile artillery units pulled onto Highway 7 from a staging area close to the railway tracks. Our own vehicle fell in behind a flat-bed transport that carried three Tiger tanks. With a sickening feeling I realized that we were part of a convoy that was going to join the counterattack at Salerno.

As if he had had the same thought, the rabbi groaned. But there was something else on his mind: "Are we really going to Napoli? Is that where the registers are? If only you *had* taken them to America! To the city of New York!"

I put a finger to my lips, indicating our silent driver.

"This *Dummkopf?* He does not understand a word."

At that moment, from just behind our heads, the squad of soldiers burst into song. The rabbi began to rock back and forth, as if to the martial rhythm. "Hopeless," he muttered. "Hopeless. We are doomed. What if the lists aren't on the boat? Luggage from 1941! Ah, but what if they *are?* What then? Mother of God! Shabilian! Tell me! What are we going to do?"

Even if I could have made my voice heard over the full-throated, high-spirited song, the only thing I could have told my coreligionist was that I had not the slightest idea.

The drive to Naples took hours and hours. The highway, pock-marked by bomb craters, was everywhere under repair. Even the un-damaged sections were clogged with traffic in both directions. Whatever gratification I took in seeing the ambulances moving north-ward with wounded Germans was more than spoiled by the terrible sight of captured Americans, crammed into trucks or dragging themselves on foot, being herded away from the battle in the south.

Twice we stopped because of aircraft above. The first time Zolli and I found ourselves alone in the cab—alone in the convoy, for that matter, since everyone else had abandoned his vehicle and was lying in the ditch alongside the road. False alarm. The planes, twin-engine bombers, were marked with the insignia of the Luftwaffe and were almost certainly returning to their base at Foggia.

The second attack was real. A single plane, a boxy P-38, appeared noiselessly out of nowhere and strafed us head-on. I saw the sparks coming from the nose of the craft, signs of the cannon fire that ripped though the canvas-topped convoy and clanged dully on the metal fenders and hoods. A hundred yards ahead some kind of truck exploded; even inside our cab, I could feel the heat of the flames. With an incomprehensible shout, our driver snatched up a rifle from behind our seat. Leaping to the ground, he just had time to squint, aim, and fire, as the plane, audible now, roared overhead. Had he hit his target? Or had the anti-aircraft guns on the half-tracks hit theirs? The only thing that was certain was that the next time I saw the airplane it had veered off, slithering seaward like a silverfish, leaving a smear of smoke.

The convoy split up north of Naples. The men in our truck moved onto one of the transport trailers, squatting among the tank treads or leaning against the turrets. Our empty van, joined now by a motorcycle escort, drove through the city proper. And what a changed city it was! The effects of bombardments—by American ships? American planes?—were everywhere. Buildings had cracked open or fallen into piles of rubble. Every block had its burned-out shell. High overhead, in an apartment missing three walls, I saw a woman combing her hair in a mirror. The remaining wall was painted the same blue as the sky.

A sky of Capri, perhaps, but not that of Naples. Here the heavens were covered by a perpetual cloud so dark, low, and ominous that for an instant I thought that mighty Vesuvius had erupted. Then I realized that this thick cumulonimbus, along with the accompanying rumble of thunder, came from the south, where the two armies were clashing on the beaches of Salerno.

We made our way circuitously to the waterfront. The instant we climbed down from the truck, we were surrounded by a throng of children.

"You must not look," said Zolli, who covered the single lens that remained in his glasses with the flat of his hand. I saw why: behind the children a group of women, some little more than children themselves, were standing in their petticoats. One of them, her eyes fixed on me, virginal Max, pulled a strap from her shoulder so that the cotton cloth fell from the white skin of her breast.

The motorcycle men waded through the crowd as they might through waist-high water. We trailed them into the terminal for the Linea Italia. It was, of course, empty, save for enormous rolls of newsprint, as big as haystacks, that had never reached their presses. The uniformed escort led the way through a sliding metal door. There, spread out before us, was the great harbor, filled with what must have been hundreds of unmoving vessels, like ships becalmed on the Sargasso Sea.

"Boom!" exclaimed one of the goggled cyclists. "*Sie sind alle gestrandet, alle kaputt.*"

"*Ja, Ja,*" answered his companion. He too was looking out at the steamships, the freighters, the occasional iron-gray destroyer. "*Wie haben sie alle vermint. Wir sprengen sie alle in die Luft.*"

"What are they saying?" I asked the rabbi.

Zolli, Austrian born, said. "They have mined the boats. To

blockade the harbor. They'll explode the minute the Americans try to come in."

Now our driver, still with his sharpshooter's rifle slung over his shoulder, drew us past a series of cement blocks and cement pillars, some upright, some upended. The *Rex* was floating at the end of a deep-water pier. I was surprised at how bright, how new she looked. I knew she had rotted in port ever since the declaration of war on the United States. Yet even now I could see a dozen men hanging by ropes from the top of the rear funnel; some were painting its red stripe, some its green. On a scaffold at midships, other men were starting a decoration in red. Only the rust mark, dripping like a tear from the eye of the anchor hole, suggested that for years now the ship had not once left port.

What I saw when I emerged from the gangway and looked down on the sun deck amazed me even more. The swimming pool, both swimming pools, were full of water. White sand was heaped up around them to make a beach; here and there on this lido were gay umbrellas, red and yellow and green, as if awaiting the men and women who were about to appear in their swimwear and order tall, frosted drinks.

For a dizzying instant I clutched the rail. Wasn't there a war on? Wasn't the harbor mined? I thought of the woman who, in her exposed apartment, high in the air, was combing her hair and about to put on her hat. Was she insane? Or was I? Why was the ship being refurbished? Were the Fouler and the Doozy, those old friends and allies, about to take a cruise? Was Aria, still Mussolini's companion, going to share the journey? Was she going to swim with her paramour in the blue water of these pools?

"What are you dreaming of?" asked Zolli. "The baggage is in the hold. That's where we must go." And that, with a great sense of foreboding, is where we went. Our helmeted driver—who was all too obviously also our guard—led the way to the promenade level, to the A, B, and C decks, down one staircase after another to the bottom of the ship. There, in what looked like a vast warehouse, we saw many of the goods that on December 11, 1941, had been destined for the port of New York: decaying foodstuffs, crates of porcelain and paintings and wine, racks of finished clothing, even a few automobiles. Whatever luggage that had not already been claimed by its owners had been placed in a roped-off section at the rear. At once the German stepped forward and began throwing the valises about. I kept shaking my head: *no, not that one; no, not that one either.* In the end he hurled down a large metal trunk and cried out, "*Verdammt! Die Juden haben uns ausgetrickst.*"

Zolli turned as white as the remaining half of his beard. "He says you tricked him." With his coat cuff he blotted the sweat that had beaded on his forehead. "Have you? And me as well?"

"But can't you see?" I stammered. "It's been lost. Or they sent my bag to the wrong address. There must be an explanation."

"*Folgen sie mir zum Schiffskapitän,*" commanded the German. We had to follow him to the ship's captain, which we did, retracing our steps past the quarterdeck, the upper deck, the boat deck, up and up to the chief officer's cabin.

We were met outside its doorway by a short man with black, slick hair. His eyes were large, and the liquid in them reflected the rays of the overhead light. The name stitched to the front of his uniform, which had a row of little stars on the shoulders and bands of silver on the sleeves, said, simply, DALIO. It might have been the uniform of a doorman or a bandleader; in fact, it belonged to the captain of the *Rex.*

"Welcome, Signor Shabilian and Rabbi Zolli," he declared, obviously forewarned of our arrival. "I am happy to see that a member of the Hebraic faith has kept his position, just as I, during the government of Badoglio, was restored to mine. He smiled, and I saw that, like a violinist settling his violin, he kept his head perpetually bent to his shoulder. Now he inclined it further toward Zolli. "Yes, we are both captains, eh? I of the ship and you the Rabbino Capo di Roma. Let us hope you do not go through my difficult experience and suffer a demotion. And lose your *capo*, eh?"

At this little joke, Zolli, as was his habit, leaned weakly against the door jamb. I looked toward our armed guard. But he did nothing more than push by *il Capitano* Dalio into the cabin and sink at once onto one of the leather couches that lined the walls.

"*Ma, scusatemi,*" said the officer, with yet another smile, displaying teeth that gleamed with the same quicksilvery brightness as the pomade in his hair. "I make apologies. Please. Gentlemen. You are welcome. Come inside."

We followed our host into the cabin, which was paneled in stained mahogany and seemed to stretch across the full width of the ship. The leather furniture glowed with brass studs. The walls on either side had been turned into bookcases, filled half with books and half with antique nautical clocks. A free-standing desk, the size of a pool table, and with a pool table's green felt, stood in the center of the room. Against the forward wall a sliding door had been thrown open, revealing a bright, glass-enclosed chamber that I at first took for a solarium until I realized it was in fact the bridge of the ship. There was a section of the spoked wheel, and there a bank of gauges and dials. Was that instrument, in brass, with a brass handle, the throttle that signaled the engine room? I thought I could hear the low hum of the diesels. Were they merely idling? Or were they about to propel the *Rex* to some unknown destination? Then I saw that the buzzing sound came from our driver; he was sprawled in sleep, his boots pointing in opposite directions, his helmet pulled down to his pink, prognathic jaw.

"Do you like the appoint-a-ments within the cabin?" the captain resumed, though I could not be sure he had ever stopped speaking. "Look here, please. This is the famous Blue Riband. Won by this ship, which is named for the head of the House of Savoy. On the average, 28.92 kilometers. It is possible that his majesty, when he was restor-ed to authority, also returned to me mine, because I was at the—*come si dice?*: at the *helm*, when in crossing the Atlantic Ocean we won for Italy this prize."

But I was looking not at the ribbon but at the painted face and torso of a man who, save for a black moustache and the many medals on his chest, might have been Signor Dalio himself.

"You think what everyone thinks: a painting of my father. *Ma, no.* Here is the brother of my father, *Zio* Alberto, who was an admiral in the naval forces of Italy during the last war. And here, you are looking at his father, my *nonno* Ernesto, who from his recognitions you can determine was also in the naval ministry, but who was most known in all the world for conducting the great Garibaldi and the Red Shirts to the Island of Sardinia. The family Dalio, it has always been connected to Genoa and to the sea."

Ernesto, the *nonno*, had the same family resemblance, the exophthalmic, glittering eyes and the same way of holding the head at an angle, as if it were propped on an invisible finger or fist. The difference was that these portraits were mute, whereas the living descendant chattered on, as if some elastic band had been wound in him the way a spring is in a music box.

"Ah, ah: might I offer you an American cigarette?" Dalio lurched in his disjointed manner toward a humidor on his desk. I waved my hand to decline, even as I wondered how such a little man—really no taller than I was—could command such a big ship. His arms seemed as unhinged as his legs; it was almost as if some

Geppetto were pulling strings from a hidden balcony above him, flapping open his mouth and throwing his own voice inside it:

"One, you see? I allow myself one. To celebrate each day my restoration by Vittorio Emanuele." There was an instant of silence, while the captain drew the flame of the match toward the tobacco.

Without thinking, I said, "I don't understand. How now—? I mean, at a time when—?"

Dalio's lips moved around the lit cigarette. "I grasp your meaning. This restoration, it is only just. It is in recognition not only of my family but the tradition of Italians of Israelite descent in our navies. Even under the Duce we had Ambrosino, Segre, Marfutti of distinguished service; perhaps even a non-Italian such as yourself knows that Angelo Modena became at one time president of the Supreme Army and Navy Tribunal. Of course every American has heard of Cristoforo Colombo. Do not smile! We Genoese have long known that secret. Let us go further back, gentlemen, to the Phoenicians in their boats. It was they who landed on our peninsula long before the days of Gesù Cristo. Imagine, this Mussolini, this schoolteacher, he would make in the family of the Dalios a demotion."

The rabbi, grim, unsmiling, spoke next: "But we are no longer dealing with the Duce. You are facing something worse than a change in rank."

"Ah! What you speak of: it requires of me to take a number two cigarette." At which this doll of a Dalio crushed out his first— Camel, was it? Lucky Strike?—and plucked up a second. "Because of the anxiety, yes? The fearfulness, that such an anticipation causes me." On this occasion the flaming match actually missed the tip of the cylinder and had to be applied again.

"Is it possible," I asked, "that you have simply been overlooked?"

At this Dalio shrugged, his shoulders rising almost to his ears. "Who can say? I do not think so. Forgetfulness is not in the nature of the *Tedeschi*. After all, it was not his majesty or the government of Badoglio who told their new captain to return to the *Rex*. No, it was the Germans. And it is they who have painted and made beautiful my poor and abandon-ed ship. In obeyance of their orders, I, *il Capitano* Dalio, am to make preparations to sail. To where? To Genoa. I am soon to leave Naples with a German crew. *Perché?* To pick up the *Tedeschi*. All those the Americans have wounded. Yes, gentlemen, the *Rex* is now a hospital ship."

At those words, our German guard stretched his arms and opened his eyes. Then, with an expulsion of air from his lips, he let his lids drop shut again.

Zolli clutched my arm. "The *Judenlisten*," he hissed. "The lists. *Capitano*—" he turned now to Dalio. "This boy. He was to sail to America. He sent his luggage. Two books. Big books. Covered in leather. Have you seen them? We must find them. We're under orders from—" and here the rabbi lowered his voice, even though the sleeping soldier could not hear him utter the German word. "From the Gestapo."

Dalio answered in a voice that was even lower: "*Orribile. Che orrore.* A terrible thing."

"Yes. If you do not possess them, the list of the Jews—it will be awful; if you do, it will be even worse."

"The *orrore*: not lists. Not books. *Il viaggio.* The voyage."

"The voyage?" I echoed. What voyage? You can't mean December 11th. You never sailed."

Instead of answering, Dalio crooked a finger, beckoning us out of the cabin and onto the bridge. There, the last light of the afternoon fought its way through the smoke, the clouds, filling the entire glass enclosure with a saffron tint. For a brief spell the three of us stood mute, like insects that had been fossilized in a crystal of amber. Then, still in low tones, Captain Dalio began once more to speak:

"But we did make that voyage, *signori.* Not to America, but to the *Inferno* of Dante. The famous Amos Prince was not on board. None of his family were on board. But *your* family was, Signor Shabilian. And yours too, Rabbi Zolli. I mean to say, the ship was filled with Israelites, those who hoped to cross the ocean of the Atlantic as their ancestors had once crossed the Red Sea.

"A day of great wind, that *Dicembre.* The heavy sea, which for this craft is nothing. Yes, like the baby that rocks in his mother's arms. From here, through this window, I see what for me is a joyful thing: the *attendenti* in their white jackets as they move below me with their trays of *il brodo.* Ah, bouillon. Yes, I am seeing the people in their deck chairs, wrapped in blankets; how they reach for the white bowls, the dark broth, the little clouds of steam."

A pause. A quick smile. The slanting sunlight caught in the wet irises of his eyes. "After two hours—no, two hours and one half, when the red sun was descending before us into the sea, we received the order of the Duce: *Ritornate a Napoli subito. Guerra dichiarata agli Stati Uniti.* I could not believe what was before my eyes. I did not believe what was entering my ears. *Ritornate!* You must understand me when I say I did not wish to obey. Oh, *signori!* If only we had one hour more! We might then have passed the Sardinia Island, where the signal is often flawed and where I could have made the pretense not to have heard. We might have made the Straits of Gibraltar. We might have made the open sea.

"But I had no choice. An order from the Duce. For my crew, for the Italian people, this was a commandment from God. Here, you see, into this speaking tube I uttered my instructions. With this wheel I began the one hundred and eighty degrees of our turn.

"Ah, what wailing then! What cries! Such was their desperation that the Israelites began to throw the same deck chairs in which only moments before they had been sipping the hot infusion over the rails and into the waters! Listen! You must listen. Now comes the worst."

Instinctively I drew away from the speaker. Zolli took a step back too. The captain's eyes were glittering. His smile was fixed. We might have been listening to the voice of the mariner in the famous Coleridge poem.

"The deck chairs. Why did they throw so many into the sea? I did not know how to assess this until the poor refugees began to treat themselves in the same manner. *O Dio!* They were leaping overboard! At first only two, three. Then five. And more! It was a contagion. I saw with horror a family go over, holding hands each with the other. I stopp-ed the boat. I signaled a movement in reverse. Then I ran with the speed of an athlete to the rail at the stern.

"I understood then the purpose of the deck chairs: these people hoped in their crazed mentality to bind them together, to make therefore a raft. They wished to float to Africa. To the Island of Majorca. Hopeless! *Disperati!* Already the canvas had grown wet and was pulling them down. Still this man insisted on making the leap, and so too this woman and child. It could only be the wish to self-destruction. It was not the ocean's water that weighted them. It was the heaviness of despair. The heads of the swimmers—one by one they were vanishing, as if a sea beast were pulling them down. Poor Jews! Poor people! They even fought against our sailors who arriv-ed in the boats. We saved only five. Five of fifty-five! Children! So many children! If only I could have made the rescue of all. Not of the fifty drown-ed souls. Of the hundreds! Hundreds and hundreds! The Jews I forced to make the return. On board this ship! *Una nave di fantasmi!* A ship of ghosts! Like—what is it you say? The Flying Dutchman!"

"You can! You will!"

Both men turned toward me, Max Shabilian. I almost turned myself, to see who had spoken.

"*Che cosa?*" said Dalio. "I can? What is it I can?"

"Save them! The Jews! Save them all! Every one!"

Zolli: "Have you gone mad? What are you saying? What can this little man do? He's as helpless as we are."

Dalio: "Please. I am not understanding. How could I save those who have already been doomed?"

I stood, my eyes blinking and batting in the near-horizontal beams of light. What had I been thinking? I had not been thinking at all. I grinned like the village idiot. I shuffled my feet like an idiot, too. My mind went over what I had just heard. What dread those people must have felt when they circled back across their own wake. They knew the ship was turning, going back to Muscle-loiny! Better to have jumped. Better to have been sucked down by the waves.

The captain, his head bent, as if on a chopping block, touched me on the shoulder. "Tell me, my dear Signor Shabilian. Tell me how I am able to live once more without these tortures."

I looked at the captain. I looked at Zolli. Suddenly it was dusk: the sun, like the wick of a candle, had been snuffed by the sea. A gull flew by, in search of herring. *Ow!* it cried, like a human being. *Ow! Ow! Ow!*

"You must follow your orders. When they tell you to sail, you must sail." I, Slapsy Maxie, heard these words with as much astonishment as the others. "You will turn north, as if to Genoa, but you will stop at Rome. Not Rome. The Tiber. Where it runs to the sea. Wait. Wait as long as you can. You do not have to come for the Jews; the Jews will come to you. Yes, down the river. In a procession of deck chairs."

Zolli: "I can't believe I am hearing this. It is insane. You will kill us all."

"If you arrive first, wait. If the Jews arrive first, they will wait for you."

"And Kappler?" said Zolli. "And Kesselring? Do you think they will allow us to go on this cruise?"

A good question. To which I had no answer. "Well?" I said to the grandson of the courageous Ernesto. "This is your ship. You command her. Will you bring her to Rome? First to Rome, and then—not to America. Not to Africa. And not Majorca. You must sail—quickly, quickly, with such speed that you will win a new Blue Riband—to Palestine! The only place Jews can be safe. Can you do it? Will you do it? Tell me!"

Dalio looked at the spread fingers of his hands, as if to inspect the polish on his nails. Then he raised his head almost to a vertical angle. But before he could speak, there was a loud thud from behind us. Then a curse, *Verdammt*, in German. I glanced through the sliding doors. The sleeping sharpshooter had slid from his couch. The three of us rushed into the cabin. Our guard was just getting to his feet. For a moment he stared at us, his eyes red and inflamed, like those of a bulldog. Then he pushed his helmet to the regulation position on his head and jerked his thumb over his shoulder.

"*Schnell oben! Wir gehen nach Rom. Zum Gestapo.*"

We started forward, to obey his command. As we reached the exit, I heard the captain of the *Rex* say, apparently to himself: "What choice do I have? I am not able to help myself. I must take cigarette number three."

3

Broad daylight. I must have slept the whole of the morning away. In my hand, the pages of A.P.'s notebook. On my lap, a tray of— what are they? Scrambled eggs. Untouched. I sense, with what is left of my hearing, with the eyes in back of my head, that someone is moving behind me. I turn my chair. It is the nurse, the harridan, with her arms folded across her bosom.

"W-w-w—" I don't have the breath, or the skills, or the courage, to say more. "W-w-w—"

I don't have to. She takes off her glasses; she lets them dangle by their black plastic straps. I am aghast to see that the eyes that had been hidden behind them have their share of tears. She does not seem able to speak any better than I can. Instead, she shakes her head, which, in Canada too, must mean *Failure. Affliction. Grief.*

SPIRAL NOTEBOOK

Villa Feltrinelli

[1982: 1943-1945]

Boots, that was the main thing. Boots and a stick and a knapsack filled with eggs. Had to be more careful than a fella carrying nitro-glycerin. One false step and, kerplooey, an omelet. Got out of Rome on the Via Flaminia. Ponte Milvio packed with rats jumping ship. Didn't stop walking for God knows how long. Year and a half, I guess. Boots didn't last half that long. Used rags instead. Plenty of blood if anyone wanted to follow with bloodhounds. Blisters turned hard as stones. Walked whole winters, though I took time out to sleep a week at a time. A bear hibernating in a haystack, in a tree stump, in a goddamned hole in the ground. I'd wake up amazed I wasn't dead. Wished I was plenty of times.

    Which reminds me. If I should kick the bucket tonight, or to-morrow, or the day after that, I don't want to be buried in Italy. Not in Gubbio, not on that island in Venice full of the big shots, not in the Campo Verano in Rome. I ain't an Italian, that's the long and short of it, even if I lived half my life in this country. It's not that the Italians failed me. Hell, the Americans failed me too. I belong in

Illinois. At the Tropp family site. Tombstones all washed out, all smooth, like whale bones stuck in the ground. No *La Vittoria* for me.

Did I drop off to sleep again? Must have. Somebody covered me with this fuzzy blanket. It wasn't here before, was it? Kind soul. Gianna? Came in on tiptoe. Tiptoed out. Feel much better. Not so cold. Maybe I am going to fool them. Did it once before. Doctors said I had a heart attack. I don't know when. Oh, twelve, thirteen years ago. In '69. When they landed on the moon. Dropped like a ton of bricks on the lawn behind the Montegranelli. Hit my head on a sprinkler. Woke up. Enrico weeping and wringing his hands. End of the old meal ticket, eh? Saw the bellboys and maids and a chef with a hat like what you'd pick up a lamb chop with: all of them running around and yelling, *Dottore! Dottore!* Young fellow, had on a swimsuit, pool attendant, I reckon: he was leaning over me with an ice pack and kept rubbing it over my heart. Had a white nose. Zinc oxide for the sun. "*Perché disturbarsi?*" I asked him. "Why put ice on something that's already frozen?"

No. Not possible. Gianna long gone. I won't see her again.

Got to Lake Garda at the start of April. More krauts than wops. Salò like a Bavarian village. Even had, on the bandstand, an oompah-pah band. Old story: sentimental songs, Strauss and Lehár, on the deck of the Titanic. *Wien, Wien, nur du allein.* Moustaches and a stripe on the pants. Came over the Alps with their tubas. Where was Missed-a-long-pee? At Gargnano, everyone said. At the Villa Feltrinelli, right on the shore of the lake. Couldn't get near, of course. Must have looked like a hobo. German guards on all the approaches. Got a glimpse of the dock. Saw red bathing caps in the water. Warm day for April, but lake must have been freezing. Maybe not swimmers. Buoys? Or German frogmen.

Hiked around to the humpbacked mountain in the rear. Climbed up. Climbed down. Took half the day. Guards in back too, but I slid through the evergreens into the park behind the villa. Birds not happy to see me. Outraged, really. Hopping up and down on the branches. *Architetto! Architetto!* they kept chirping. But only one guard: asleep in a lawn chair, his Mauser across his knees.

Heard 'em before I saw 'em: Dicey and his pals playing tennis. Red clay, the fences all covered with ivy. Crawled up to one end for a peek. Benzine in white shorts and a white shirt almost black with sweat. Recognized his opponent: Lucchese, the Italian National champ. Davis Cup, too. Famous for his serve. No sweat on him. White pants, cream sweater, a red and blue stripe at the neck. Not a curl out of place on his head. Ball goes back and forth. The Daisy panting plenty. Finally the champ slices a crosscourt backhand into the corner.

"*Fuori!*" cries the umpire up in his chair, raising a truncated arm. Farinacci! "Game to Il Duce!" Applause from the grandstand. Eight or nine people. Sipping lemonade. Eating biscuits. Can't help salivating at the sight. Vittorio there. Also Romano. Women in wide-brimmed hats.

Farinacci: "The Duce is leading. Five games to zero."

It's Lucchese's turn to serve. Real cannonball. Right on the line. A little tornado of chalk.

Up goes the arm, like a railway signal. "*Fuori!* Second serve."

Lucchese hits a looper, underhand. Benzine takes a tremendous swing. Ball hits the wood of the racquet, angles off top of the net, falls dead on the other side. Standing ovation.

"*Magnifico! Duce, quindici. Lucchese, zero.*"

They played on. It wasn't the biscuits I hungered for. Not the lemonade. I wanted to be on that court, yes, with my feet wrapped in rags and my nose sprouting whiskers. I clung to the fence. I pressed against it. The machinations of war, the worries, ambitions, all the shed blood: gone, vanished. Nothing left but the desire to hit a ball in the air, to chase it down, to feel the bliss—ain't a thing in the world like it—of lobbing it over the other fella's head: which is just what the champion did to the Doozy, a good three feet inside the line. On came Massive-loiny! Charging like a freight train right toward where I stood in the ivy.

"*Fuori!*" cried the ump.

But nothing could stop the momentum of Big Ben. Huffing and puffing, he crashed into the fence, staggered, and looked up. "Amos-a!" he cried, going as white as the ball that lay at his feet.

"First set to the Duce."

Lucchese hung his head. The grandstand stood and cheered. But the Deuce just stared, his mouth hanging open as if he'd seen the grim reaper.

"No, Prince. You come for the Duce. Like you made the *promessa*. Good! Good! But is too soon. The Duce, he's notta ready. He's reading the books of Plato!" He leaned forward, putting his face close to mine. His words came out in a whisper. "Listen, Prince. Everything, it's the fault of that Führer. I'mma like-a what-you-call-him? A *prigioniero* inna my own country. Inna my own house. You look. I gotta more Germans than a *leopardo*, he gotta the spots. But you no worry, eh? You go away. Go away, Prince. I'mma like the Lazaru, I'mma come back from the dead!"

Old Ben, he turned back to the court, the umpire, the gallery of family and friends. He sucked in his breath, and sucked it in again, so that his arms, the thick trunks of his legs, the shaft of his neck, seemed to burst from his shorts and shirt like the water boiling out of a spaghetti pot. "THE DUCE CONTINUES THE STRUGGLE. ITALY WILL THROW OFF ITS OPPRESSORS. THE GREAT MARCONI HAS LEFT US A SECRET WEAPON. WE HAVE AN ARMY READY TO SACRIFICE, TO DIE. WE SHALL MAKE OF THE VALTELLINE ANOTHER THERMOPYLAE. IF THE ENEMY

ATTACKS AT MILAN, MILAN SHALL BECOME A SECOND
STALINGRAD. NAPOLEON IS NOT YET AT WATERLOO!
SOCRATES IS NOT YET READY TO TAKE HIS POISON. ITALY
HAS NOT YET SEEN THE END OF HER GLORY."

He bent. He picked up the ball. "*Avanti*, Lucchese! I am an
old man. You are young. You eat meat. But you have not won a
point."

Peaches! Ripe peaches! Furry peaches! A man ain't lived until
he's tasted them mixed up in Granny Tropp's ice cream. Sweeter,
even, than tennis. Close my eyes. Can't remember what I had for
breakfast. Or whether I had breakfast at all. But the boy I once was
is intact inside me. The peaches. The eggs. The milk. The sugar
from our sugar beets. Rock salt, that's the only thing we had to pay
for. Even the bucket was from our own trees. The pines. I turned
the handle. A family responsibility. Meant more to me than any
building I ever made. Took two hands to do it. My tongue out, half
because of the difficulty of the task, as the milk cooled, as the custard thickened; half in anticipation of the treat to come.

"*Our* peaches," said Granny Tropp. Let's see: in a man's over-
alls on top of a ladies' blouse, with lilies printed on it and the stems
from lilies. "*Our* milk from our cows. *Our* eggs from our chickens.
Our sugar beets. Not going to let a Jew in a bank take that away."

I know. Don't have to tell me. Should have stopped my churning. Should have used that damned fool tongue that was hanging
out of my mouth. Used it to say something. Anything. A single word
would do. But the truth is of course I wasn't cranking the bucket.
The bucket, with the whole world turning the handle, was cranking me.

Before the Ducky could throw up his serve, something hard,
something cold, pressed the back of my neck. Barrel of the Mauser.
The guard had awakened. Two more with him. Took my arms. Led

me out of the park, round to the front of the villa. The beach. The dock. The water. Looked back over my shoulder. Swimmers close to land. One reached up, took off a red rubber cap. Gold hair spilling out. "Aria!" I cried. Guards tightened grip, hustling me down the road. Not seeing, not hearing, my daughter walked up the slope to the shore.

"Aria! The fire! The twins! There was an updraft! There was an electrical spark! I tried to save them! Those boys! You can speak to me! Your father! I loved them too!"

Wind, I guess, took the words away. Girl didn't hear. Walked steadily out of the water. That's when I saw she was pregnant. My God in heaven! Nine months pregnant if she was a day.

"Aria!"

Guard had his hand over my mouth. Marched me down to Gargnano. Sprung a surprise. Took off his boots, first one, then the other. Held them out to me. A perfect fit. Then he dug into his pocket. Took out a wad of bills. Peeled off five hundred lire. Gave me that too. German boy. But what he said next came out in Italian. "This is the gift of the Duce."

TIBER

[1943]

1

When Maximilian returned from Naples to Rome, nothing happened. To his amazement, there was no knock on the door of the Via degli Specchi and no summons to the Via Tasso. Ten days, each hot and heavy with humidity, went by. At Max's call, many of the refugees came out of hiding. He set them to work in two shifts, by day and night. The first completed the repairing and refurbishing of the tower. They fit glass to the windows. They managed to get the elevator to rise as high as the eighty-first floor. They tightened the guy wires between the circumference of each segment and its hub, as a piano tuner might tune a piano, or a violinist his violin.

The second shift addressed the discarded husks of the *maltagliati*. Each half of the core had had its own container, which meant that almost two hundred of the hollow shells lay scattered about the site. Groping about in the blackout, like a nocturnal species of ant, the men swarmed over the casks. They caulked up any cracks in the boards with steaming tar. They drilled a single hole high up in one of the triangular ends. Then, struggling with ladders, they piled the empty pods upside down in stacks of ten, like little apartment buildings with only their pitched roofs showing.

And where, while the Jews were at their tasks, was their Moses, their Messiah, Maximilian V? Not in their midst but high above them, on the ninety-third floor of the tower. All day long he stood at its westernmost axis, gazing out through a window that had not yet been glassed. The taut wires whined ceaselessly in his ears. The floor beneath his feet swayed, as designed, at the threshold of perception. Against his spectacles, as if fixed to them by the suction of their rubber cups, were a pair of binoculars. If one looked closely, and could remember back over seven long years, one might recognize them: the same heavy, black Zeiss Optikon model that Captain Eckener of the *Hindenburg* had bestowed on the victorious Amos Prince.

From his high perch, a quarter mile in the sky, Maximilian could peer over the city and the suburbs twenty miles to the sea. His arms ached, his elbows ached; but he never lowered his gaze. On the flat waters, alternately blue, green, or gray, the minuscule fishing boats danced like so many floaters in the irises of his eyes. At night he strained to distinguish the movement of shadows in the shifting blocks of fog. Nothing. Only the dark waters and the faint lines of the breaking waves, like chalk marks on a charcoal slate.

Then, at midday of September 26th, a disturbance broke out on the ground below. Work, Max saw, had stopped. The men were standing and staring upward. He refocused his powerful instrument until he could actually see the tongues moving in their mouths. But there was nothing to amplify their voices, which, what with the wind, the humming chords of the wires, reached him as little more than a moan. Now the lift started to ascend, and its chugging engine further masked the din. It arrived at the eighty-first floor. Then the doors swung back into the body of the capsule and Nina stepped into the aperture. Her breeze-blown hair, the whole mop of it, flapped from one side of her head to the other.

"Oh, Maxie!" she called. "The Germans! The Gestapo! They're stealing the gold from the Jews!"

Kappler, the Obersturmbannführer, had had no need to put posters on the walls. He simply told two or three prominent figures what he required and overnight every Jew in Rome had heard the news: fifty kilograms of gold must be raised in thirty-six hours, or two hundred—some said five hundred, and others two thousand—members of the community would be deported to Germany or further east. What were the Jews to do? Many had given their wedding bands to support the Ethiopian campaign. Were they now to hand over their rings of iron? Worse, the wealthiest Jews had fled from Rome or gone into hiding. The story was that so many had moved out of their own homes that when a German soldier asked where he might see the Moses of Michelangelo, he was told that he was staying at the house of a friend.

But this was no joke: when Max stepped out of the elevator the refugees crowded around him, begging him to save them from being sent back to the lands from which they had already escaped. Many still had their wedding rings, which they pressed on him, along with the occasional cigarette lighter or cigarette case in gold. Nina herself slipped a bracelet from her wrist and kissed it, instead of him. He was moved by the gesture, which perhaps accounted for the recklessness of what he now declared: "Listen. Listen, Jews! Stay alive! Keep working! It won't be long now. Only days. Your salvation is near!"

It took him almost an hour to arrive at the Main Synagogue; that was because, when he reached the Tiber, he was brought to a halt by the sight of men standing knee-deep and waist-deep in the water. Work gangs! Slave labor! These were not his refugees but the Jews of Rome, the poorest of the poor. Did they think that because they dredged sand from the river, their old foe, this Haman, would set them free?

He hurried on to the Tempio Maggiore, where a long line stretched down the Tiber to the Teatro di Marcello and beyond. Everyone had some trinket in his hand: a baby chain, a locket, the frames of a pair of glasses. Two tables had been set up on the sidewalk outside the bars of the synagogue's black-painted fence; at each stood a dentist busily wrenching out fillings or even a whole gold tooth with his pliers. Among the Jews, Max noted, were a number of Gentiles, ordinary Italians. One of these, in a homburg, tapped the American on the shoulder. "*Permesso*," he said. "You must not laugh. I have never before entered such a *tempio*. Tell me: do I or do I not remove my hat?"

Shabilian climbed the steps and pushed his way inside. The line stretched all the way to the Sala del Consiglio on the second floor. At its head, behind a long table, sat two men: one was the Rabbino Capo di Roma; the other was clearly a goldsmith. With his jeweler's eyepiece he was examining whatever was placed before him. Sometimes, like one of the dentists, he would scoop an emerald from a brooch or a diamond from a ring and hand it back to its owner; then he would weigh the gold on a springless scale and add the figure to his list. Seated beside him, Zolli wrote names in a registry, as if at some future date he meant to return the gift to the donor. Seeing Max, he said—what were his words? It was as noisy in the synagogue now as on a Saturday morning. The rabbi raised his voice:

"*Che follia*," he said. "What folly."

Max glanced at the cardboard boxes, in which the treasure was heaped; then he looked back at the sum on the jeweler's list: 4.35 kilograms. He groaned aloud: "Not even a tenth!"

Still, the lines kept moving forward. One man, with clouded blue eyes and white-blond hair, moved to the front. "I am a publisher of books," he declared, even as he began to stack a pile of coins, each stamped with the image of a pagan goddess, on the top of the table. "All of my life I have taken gold from the Jews. Now it is time for the Jews to take gold from me."

The first box filled up. Then the second. And half the third. That was more than enough to meet the quota. As the last ounce was weighed, all those waiting in line broke into a cheer. "We are saved!" they shouted. "We won't be deported!" Then everyone began to dance around the heaped-up treasure, just as, Max thought, their ancestors had danced around the golden calf.

Rabbi Zolli, standing next to the young American, had the same idea: "Look at these prancing Jews," he declared. "They never change. They have made a new idol. It will weigh fifty kilos. They think if they worship it, it will save them. Yes, they are fools, my young friend, but not one of them is such a great fool as you."

"*Io?*" said Max. "Why me?"

"You trusted the Gestapo. One look at that man Kappler should have told you he was a killer. But you believed him. Because of the ghetto at Lodz. Because of the Jews of Tunis. Better if you believe me: they are not done with Lodz, or Tunis either. They are not able to rest. Something in them grinds and grinds and makes them kill and kill. Only now they wish to rob us first. And why? It is because you tricked them about the lists."

Suddenly the shouting, the dancing, ceased. Everyone stood frozen. Kappler himself stood at the door to the Sala del Consiglio. He did not need to say a word. The Jews picked up the boxes and followed the Obersturmbannführer out the door and to the street below. The Mercedes, its top down, was waiting. Kappler got into the back. The Jews stacked up the treasure beside him and retreated behind the iron fence that marked the boundary of the synagogue. The driver of the Mercedes started the engine.

"Wait! Wait!" That was Maximilian Shabilian. He came running up to the side of the command car. "Was it my fault? Because of the lists? I went to the ship. I swear it. The books were gone. They lost them. They threw them overboard. Forgive me! Please forgive me! They no longer exist."

Kappler turned toward where the American stood wringing his hands. "You mean the *Judenlisten?* That does not matter now. Nothing matters. It is too late. Far too late."

Max took a step back, away from the automobile. "Too late?" he echoed.

"The worst has happened."

This time Max could not even repeat the words out loud. He simply mimed them: *The worst.*

"See for yourself." The lieutenant colonel reached inside his tunic and took out a white piece of paper, which he slowly unfolded.

Himmler. That was the word Max saw first. The rest of the message was nothing but a blur, as if it had been written in smudged ink and not in neat rows of type. *Transport nach Osten. Judenaktion.* And the most feared of all: *Liquidiert.*

Max gripped the side of the car, to stop himself from falling to the pavement. "The gold," he stammered. "The ransom. It is all a trick."

The officer lifted his cap, ran his hand through his thinning blond hair, and settled it on his head once more. "I would not call it ransom, Herr Shabilian. I would call it a bribe." He leaned closer, so that the driver in front could not hear his words over the hum of the engine. "*Ja, eine Bestechung.* The last chance to save your people."

At that, Maximilian found his voice. "Are you mad? Can you mean it? Do you think you can bribe Himmler? With gold? He doesn't want gold. If we gave him every filling in our mouths, if we emptied the vaults of the Rothschilds, he would not stop. Neither will—" Dare he risk it? *Der Fouler?* "His master. No, not until they have killed every Jew left on the earth."

"I do not wish to bribe Herr Himmler. And certainly not the Reichskanzler. This gold is not for them."

Max: "For who, then?"

Kappler leaned even closer, so that Max could, if he so wished, place his own cheek against the smooth skin of the officer's scar. "Why, for you—or rather, for the crew of your ship. All good German sailors. Do you think without this gold they would follow the commands of a Jew?"

Shabilian could not be sure he had not fainted. Had a second gone by? An hour? A season? He blinked his way to consciousness. "A ship? A steamship? Do you mean the *Rex?*"

"*Nein*, not the *Rex*. The House of Savoy has become a house of traitors. What we have now is the *Spitalschiff Hindenburg*. It will sail from Naples to—well, we know where, do we not, my friend? But we must hurry. Naples is under attack. Soon it will fall. The ship sails within two days, three days at the most. We must carry this gold to the crew if we have any hope of bringing her to—let us say, to her new destination."

With those words, the Obersturmbannführer made a sign to his driver, who immediately slipped the Mercedes into gear.

"Wait!" cried Max. "Can it be? How did—?" But his voice was lost in the roar of the engine as the car lurched from its spot in front of the Main Synagogue and sped away.

Two days. Three days. That's how long Kappler said they had to bring the ship from Naples. But those days came and went. Night after night Max sat with his ear to the brown box of the *Superinduttanza Sei*. All sorts of voices, from any number of countries, came through the speaker of the forbidden instrument:

Hello, Suckers! This is your favorite gal, your favorite pal, Sally, also known as Midge at the Mike. I'm broadcasting from the overseas service of the Reichsrundfunk on a beautiful fall day in Berlin. Where, by the way, I have just come from the hospital visiting Corporal Jim W. Thomson, dog tag number 51-52-9875, of the 5th Army. Poor Jimmy! Lost his leg even before he landed at Salerno. The way he tells it, the round that fell on his landing craft was from one of his own ships. What a terrible way to die. Of course a lot of you fellows are also being betrayed by your leaders. When I see the pale, bloodless face of Corporal Thomson, I am filled with Hate for Franklin Roosevelt and Winston Churchill. Damn them and all those rich Jews who are shooting you from the rear. Jimmy asked me to tell everyone in Cleveland, Ohio, that he loves America and wishes he were back there with his fiancée, Mary June. I didn't have the heart to tell him that she has been seen riding all over town with Ernie Glickman in his flashy red convertible. I sure didn't say that last week she moved in with that big-money Jew. I guess it's about time for me to play some of those tunes you've been waiting to hear. But before I do I just want to say how much I feel for you, Private First Class Dave James, under that terrible sniper fire from the Capodimonte district in Naples. I bet you're yearning for someone else too and hoping she is not running around with some fat, four-eyed, flat-footed 4-F like Ernie back home. Gee, I hope old Jimmy makes it. It doesn't look good. So pale! No blood in his lips. Well, boys, I've got a heavy date

tonight, if you know what I mean. A girl has got to get
herself together. So here, with a big kiss from Sally, is a
good old American tune, played by Berlin's own Three
Doves of Peace:

> *Kumm aun alongk*
> *Kumm aun alongk*
> *Alegkhazander's Riegkthem Bent*

Hearing this broadcast, Max was torn in two. Half of him
wanted to laugh. If only this woman knew that *Alegkhazander's
Riegkthem Bent* had been written by a Jew! The same one who had
composed "God Bless America," which Kate Smith sang every night
on Armed Forces Radio. But no laugh came from his lips. The other
half of him had been far too anguished by five simple words: *The
Capodimonte District in Naples.* Did that mean that the Allies had
already arrived in that city? And if they had, what had happened to
the harbor? What had happened to the *Rex?*

His worst fears were confirmed the next night—not by Axis
Sally but by "Colonnello Buonasera," the announcer on Radio London. Following the usual three dots and a dash, the V for Victory,
the familiar voice came all too clearly through the speaker:

Tonight we have a report from Naples, where the four days'
uprising has ended with the departure of all German forces
and the Allies in full control of the city and most of the
outlying districts. The scene that meets the eye is one of
chaos and devastation. The harbor is filled with the overturned hulls of at least one hundred and thirty ships, some
sunk by the Allied bombardment, the majority by enemy
mines. The approaches in and out are completely blocked.

The port itself is a shambles of overturned cranes and other heavy equipment. All along the great crescent, hotels, shops, apartment buildings, the warehouses of the sea trade: everything has been leveled to the ground to a depth of three hundred yards. The sewage and water systems, the means of delivering gas and electricity, have all been destroyed. Every stray perambulator, each anonymous corpse might well be a booby trap. The German policy of scorched earth—

It was Prince who snapped off the radio. He had just returned from a visit to the Via Tasso. But he wasn't trembling in fear of that torture chamber. He was beaming. He was exultant.

"You don't need to turn on that radio. Not for another two weeks. That's when you're going to hear something worth listening to. Yep, me and old Kappler, we made an ogre-meat."

"An agreement?" cried Nina. "What about? What for?"

"They want me to start up my talks on the radio. *Amos Prince Speaking.* Not to the Italians. Not to the world. Nope. To the American soldiers and sailors. On the beaches of Salerno."

"Salerno!" cried Maximilian "The Americans! You can't. A.P., you must know what that would mean."

"And why can't I? Those poor boys need some comfort. A friendly word from one of their own. They thought they would wade onto the beaches and stroll along to see the sights. Like a tourist with a Baedecker. Why, half of them have drowned in a sea of their own blood. Now they've arrived in Naples. Next they want to come to Rome. There'll be a massacre. I've got to warn them: *Go back to your ships, my lads! Go back to your darling wives!*"

Max wanted to seize the architect by his scrawny shoulders, to shake him. But before he could act, Nina cried out, "Why are you doing this? Did they force you? Have you lost your mind? Papa, it's treason."

"No, no, it won't be that kind of talk. People hear what I got to tell them, they're going to fall on their knees. They'll weep, but these will be tears of joy. Then no one will attack the city of Rome. I'll save her from destruction. Her monuments, her temples, her tower—all will be saved. And not just Rome. I have a message that will end the World Whore. Old Hot-leer, old Ass-in-shower, they'll throw down their arms. We need peace. We need to be friends. All men—the Two-tons, the Talons, the Anguish, our own dear Marrow-cans: I will teach them how to be *brothers!* Even the Moo-slums and Cretins and Chews!"

Franklin laughed out loud. "*Her tower!* That's what you want to save. The monument. They made you a deal, didn't they? What did they promise you? To make this speech?"

"Wal, we agreed that in two weeks I am going to make a talk. The night of October 15th. Why at night? Why that date? Because it's only safe to remove the barrage balloons after dark. And we'll need these two weeks to get the monument ready. You got to crack the whip, Shabby-lion. Get the cranes! Get the riveters! Get the polishers too! Because as soon as I start my breadcrust, the Not-sees are going to lift the last three stories and carry them to the site. By the time I finish speaking to my fellow citizens, *La Vittoria* will be the tallest structure ever built by man. Yup, we're going to break that world record. At last! At last!"

What ravings! Max paid them no further heed. It was the voice of Colonnello Buonasera that rang in his ears, as if the radio had never been turned off. *One hundred and thirty ships!* The harbor *completely blocked!* His last hopes faded away. The Americans had invaded the southern port. The explosives had surely been detonated.

Neither the royal *Rex* nor the hospital ship *Hindenburg* would ever sail from the great bay of Naples.

Though Amos Prince had two weeks to refurbish the tower, through sheer will he did it in one. But a difficult task remained. The refugees had to raise the two halves of the core, join them together, and polish the surface so that the hub of the final airborne segment could be lowered onto it with absolute precision. Ordinarily this could be done in twenty-four hours. But during the six days that remained before the architect was to make his broadcast, any number of things went wrong.

First, when the workers looked closely at the rim of the old core, they discovered it was as frayed as the edge of a discarded blanket. The halves of the new one, each protected in its pastry shell of excelsior and wood, were perfect. But the seated ellipse had been exposed to years of sleet, rain, and wind-borne particles of dust. Even the droppings of gulls, which had used it for a perch, had eaten away at the metal. The new hemispheres were not going to fit. A crew of daredevils had to file and grind away for forty hours until the rim had returned to its prescribed tolerance, a microscopic thousandth of an inch.

The two cranes had also been exposed to the elements. Would they buckle under the load of the great steel parentheses? To test their strength they hauled a broken-down city bus to the base of the tower and filled it with bricks. It got as high as the ninth story before it came crashing down with as much force as one of the bombs from the *Lucky Lady*. The crane had not buckled, but one of the links in its chain had given away. On inspection, it turned out that hundreds of segments had partially, or in some cases completely, rusted through. This was a greater problem than the corroded rim. It would not do simply to remove the weakest parts; the chain would be too short. Nor was there any scrap metal available in Rome. In the end they melted down the same red and green bus and forged the necessary links from its frame.

Then, when everything was set to make the lift on the morning of October 13th, the wind decided to blow—and keep blowing through the whole of that day, the next day too, and most of the day after. Impossible to raise the hemispheres; their curved edges would punch holes in the side of the tower the way a pair of bull's horns puncture a matador's flesh.

The gusts died down late on the afternoon of October 15th. They would have to hurry to get everything in place before, simultaneously, Prince addressed his audience and the final three stories, numbers ninety-four through ninety-six, were dropped into place. It was almost 4 p.m. before the chains were secured to the two halves of the core. All other work came to a halt. The refugees, both shifts, some two thousand men, gathered around. On either side of the building the iron links grew taut. Max, high in his watchtower, could see how both pieces of metal swayed, rocked, and then rose an inch from the ground. Five minutes went by before the hemispheres had ascended a full foot. *Too slow!* he thought. At this rate it would take days to travel the quarter mile to the top.

"Faster!" he shouted. "You have to go faster!" Then, as if the operators of the cranes had actually heard him, the two slices of steel began to accelerate, traveling the next foot in only a minute, and the foot after that in only a few seconds more.

Now Max wished the two pieces would move more slowly— or even come to a stop. He gazed down at the men through the twin lenses of his Optikon. Their faces, bearded and unbearded, darkened by the sun or strangely pale, were turned upward, following the passage of the core. Their spectacles flashed in the light of the sinking sun. Their teeth, exposed by their grinning lips, gleamed too. In awe, it seemed, they had removed their caps. *Fools!* Max thought. *Children!* Why were they smiling? Did they not understand that as soon as *La Vittoria* was completed, when they had topped off this building, their labor was done? Without that work their sole source of protection would have vanished. Poor Jews! Poor smiling people! They had completed a monument to their own destruction.

Just then, from a thousand feet below, a shout went up and a palpable shiver went through this topmost ring of the building. From opposite directions the two sides of the core had joined. A moment later the rim in which Max was sitting dipped and shuddered again. The pieces were in place. A second cry arose, louder than before. Why shouldn't they shout? It was a memorable moment. In a technical sense they had raised the tallest structure ever constructed by man. What did it matter that it would not be complete, a true world wonder, until the actual segment was dropped over it a few hours hence? He heard, closer by, excited voices, and then a series of pops, as if the men at the hub were opening bottles of champagne. It was, he knew, no celebration —only the jets of gas exploding at the tips of the welders' wands.

One last time he picked up his binoculars and, from nothing more than habit, looked out over the countryside to the sea. The sun was slipping into the waters of the *Mare Tirreno*, like the pate of a drowning man. All about it the mists of an autumn evening were starting to rise. A blur moved over the estuary of the Tiber. A fog bank? Maximilian, with the cups of his instrument attached to his eyeglasses like a pair of black leeches, looked again. This was no vapor but a solid shape. He squinted. He rotated the dial for focus. From out of the mists one funnel emerged, then another; they both disappeared in the swirls of effluvia, as a warship will hide itself in deliberate smoke.

In Max's eyes the whole scene began to dance, to wiggle, to dissolve; that's how much his hands were shaking. He propped his elbows on the window ledge and peered outward. This time the fog was not out at sea; his own quick exhalations had coated the binocular lenses. He put the instrument down. Through nothing more than his spectacles he saw that the sky was now an indigo blue; on its surface, like bubbles bursting in a glass, the stars came popping out. What was this? The size of a cocktail onion? Ah: the moon. He peered through the binoculars into the last light. For an instant the mists parted. Thus he was able to see, against a black metallic backdrop, the international symbol of man's mercy: a tiny, telltale red cross. It was the *Rex!* She had escaped from Naples! The gold! The gold! The gold had done it! Dalio had sailed his ship into the open sea.

2

That same round moon, exempt from both curfew and blackout, rose high over Rome in the course of the night. In its light the refugees had to move with great stealth. Those with families—wives, children, an elderly parent—gathered them together and moved through the shadows to the banks of the Tiber. The others went directly to the meeting point downstream from the Ponte Palatino. Before midnight, most of the *maltagliati* had made the portage from the Circus Maximus to the water's edge. Twenty men, ten to a side, hoisted each burden onto their shoulders—like so many pallbearers, Max thought, with a coffin; except that these caskets would carry their passengers to life. As each new craft arrived, it was lowered from the embankment to the surface of the river. A long wooden paddle, meant to act as a rudder, was inserted through the hole that had been cut into what had been arbitrarily chosen as the stern. The women and children collected at the narrow tips at either end. The strongest men, each with a pole in his hands, collected at the low point in the center. They would have to push each craft off any of the sandbars that the Jewish work gangs had not succeeded in dredging out of the way.

And what of those poor Jews, whom Max had seen at their labors just two weeks before? Were they not the descendants of re-publican and imperial Rome? Was he to leave them behind while his refugees fled to safety? But what could he do? Even if, with Zolli's help, he had been able to reach them, and supposing that at a moment's notice they would have been able to leave, there would simply not be enough room. The problem was not with the *Rex.* Max knew they could squeeze every Jew in Italy—and probably every survivor left in Europe—onto the luxury liner. The problem was the *maltagliati.* They had had only enough time to make eighty of the boxes watertight. Sixty of these were already in the Tiber, hiding under the camouflage of the leaves that still clung to the plane trees along the Aventino embankment. Each held thirty Jews. One by one the others were being filled by the refugees crowded at the shore. There would not be a seat to spare.

Amazing how silently the embarkation proceeded. The babes in arms, and even a three-legged dog that ran worriedly back and forth atop the embankment, sensed they must not utter a whimper. There was nothing to hear save for the slap of the wavelets against the hulls of the makeshift vessels. Now the last of these pointed polygons was lowered toward the water. One minute later and those who had carried it took their places inside. The last handful of Jews scrambled in too. There was a soft whistle. The white-whiskered mutt lurched down the moss-covered steps and into the arms of what looked like a ten-year-old boy.

There was no reason to delay. Max waved his hand. The first of the boats pushed out from under the protection of the foliage. Then the second, the third. Soon the bulk of the whole fleet, all four score, was drifting down the river toward the Ponte Sublico. But Max Shabilian still had his feet on the ground. Why? Per-haps because his mind had suddenly filled with thoughts of Amos

Prince and his tower. Just before he had himself moved down the side of the embankment, he had taken one last glimpse of the monument on which he had labored for so many years. The welders' torches, the red-hot rivets, had transformed the looming black shape into something resembling a gigantic, guttering candle. Was its architect high on the summit? Or had he moved to his studio on the forty-second floor? Was he about to broadcast to the sleeping city? But if he truly meant to speak on behalf of peace, of brotherhood, if he were even going to acknowledge the suffering of the Jews, would it not be wiser to wait until the final, record-shattering segment had been dropped into place? Max felt a pang. If only he could hear those words! And then embrace the man who had uttered them. How could he desert his master, his *maestro*, at the moment of his greatest triumph and most fearful danger?

"*Moishe! Moishe!*"

What was that? Max strained to see. The rudder man, standing upright at the stern of the eightieth boat, was calling to him. His passengers took up the cry. "Moishe! Moses! Our Messiah! Come with us! Take us across the Red Sea!"

Without further thought, Maximilian stepped into the vessel. At once it set off, taking its place in a flotilla as trembling and fragile as a line of newspapers that had been folded into paper hats.

The voyage continued in silence. All one could hear was the grunt of a steersman; the rattle of the hulls as they scraped over the pebbles in the shallows; or the occasional sharp crack of a pole as, caught in some buried obstruction, it snapped in two. Max, starting out last, floated beneath the Ponte Sublicio and then the Ponte di Ferrovia. By then he was no longer at the end of the line. Again and again a boat at the vanguard would become so lodged in a tangle of reeds or a hidden shelf of sand that its passengers would have to get out and help rock it free. These craft, which then trailed the others, were like minesweepers, clearing the way for the rest of the fleet.

Indeed, as if to reinforce the notion that their armada was sailing into enemy territory, the moon shone down with the full force of a searchlight. In its beams Max suddenly saw that each boat had a name painted on its hull, *Enrica. Shirli. Mojzesz.* A child was it? A parent? Some lost lover? *Bernhard. Orazio. Ellise.* Not a single craft was without its inscription. *Sandra. Ilena. Annette.* He leaned over to check the hull of his own little boat. *Bianca.*

Alas, that same moon made each of the vessels all too visible to the members of the Wehrmacht or the Fascist police, the only forces out at that hour. What would they think if, glancing down from the Artigiani or Papareschi embankments, they saw a fleet of boats lit up in the silvery stream? One such soldier, armed with an automatic weapon, could sink them all, like *anatre ferme*, sitting ducks, or so many *pesci in barile.*

Yet no guard appeared. No one sounded the alarm. On sailed the little flotilla, around the great right and then left bend of the river. How much time had gone by? Had it really been less than an hour? It felt like half the night. Old Rome, as well as the center of the modern metropolis, was far behind. Now wild grass and stands of woods stretched down to the water. High up, atop the bluffs on the port side, Max could make out the towers and turrets of what seemed to be a city, its arches of marble and alabaster glowing in the moonlight like the white pieces on an abandoned chessboard. This was the Duce's Olympic site, the Esposizione Universale di Roma, at which the swift runners, the high-leaping hurdlers, the hurlers of javelins had never had the chance to perform.

For a moment, with his elbows crooked over the gunwales and his head thrown back, Max allowed himself an easy breath. No one could see them from those distant heights. Was this a flotilla of frightened Jews? No, no, they might be tourists on a summer excursion or so many English swells, Cambridge and Oxford men, punting along the Cantab and the Tam.

Italians! Fast-shits and Not-sees! Wake up! Get out of your beds!
You been tricked!

Max stiffened. Was he having a dream? That voice, its puns, its inflections: it had to be that of Amos Prince. But where had it come from? He glanced at the other boats, which were sailing blithely on. The refugees in his craft, those without poles, had nodded off to sleep. Those in the trough of the boat were trailing their hands in the sluggish stream. Yes, he must have heard those words in a dream.

They fooled Old Amos, too. Said they were gonna make my
money-mint taller than the Emperor's Hate. But they didn't.
Because of those Chews! They escaped! They're running away!
I know where they are. I know their plan. They're sailin' down
the river!

It was no dream. Prince's voice came from the riverbank—at first from the left side only, where it was solitary and indistinct. But in no time it was magnified, echoing from one side of the Tiber to the other as more and more of the Italian people, roused from their sleep, turned on their radios.

They think they can get away! You got to pursue them the way
Old Furrow did the Juice. Go to the Tiber. Chase 'em! Shoot
'em! Kill every one!

All along the river the scattered dwellings—farmhouses, converted mills, even the eel-gatherers' shacks—were coming to life.

Max watched in horror as shutters were thrown open and human figures leaned from the back-lit windows. What was that? Headlights! A convoy of trucks, personnel carriers, was speeding down the Via del Mare. They were only a stone's throw away.

What could they do? The river was straight and narrow; there was no foliage on either side. Alas, there was hardly any strength to the current. How slowly the boats were moving! *Pascal. Dinah. Lotte. Zuzanne.* Slow as snails—and, worse, each left behind a snail's trail of moonlight, like a silver arrow showing the riflemen precisely where they should aim. A groan went up from the trapped Jews. It was answered by a shout from the riverbank and an answering cry from the other side. They had been seen! The chain of headlights slowed. The canvas-colored vehicles came to a stop.

At that near-hopeless instant, a cloud passed between the doomed figures on the Tiber and the moon. In the ensuing darkness, Max could not see the boat in front or the boat behind. All was lost in the gloom.

"*Un miracolo!*" came a voice from the gloom. "*Il nostro Mosé ha fatto un miracolo!*"

Poor Jews. They thought their new Moses had saved them. But Moses himself realized this was only a brief respite. The wind that had blown the cloud to its station above them would soon disperse it. Oddly, this did not occur. The little vessels floated on through the narrow straits and soon began to bend around the angle that swept them apart from the roadway where the motorized convoy remained at a stop. Amazingly, the cloud traveled with them, as the cloud in the Bible had followed the Israelites.

Max squinted upward. Only then did he hear the faint drone in the heavens. He peered more intently. The cloud, he saw, was composed of a number of cloudlets, all in formation. The moon itself was totally surrounded, much like the planet Saturn by its accompanying rings. The truth dawned on him: this was no cloud; it was the great steel segment, *La Vittoria's* last three stories, suspended beneath the city of Rome's barrage balloons!

"*Un miracolo!*"

"*Un miracolo!*"

Perhaps the Jews were right. That a ring of steel, weighing hundreds of thousands of tons, should hang in the sky, kept aloft by nothing more than the atoms of a gas that had been manufactured in the furnace of far-off stars—was that not as great a miracle as the parting of the Red Sea, or the turning of a rod into a serpent, or mere water into wine?

On went the fragile fleet. The classical *Pericles.* The classical *Erasmiròs.* The local *Paolo.* The balloons, pulled by their single blimp, kept pace, like so many sheep following their shepherd. To Max, the greatest miracle of all, more supernatural than the physics of the lifting capacity of helium or that of nuclear fusion in the cauldrons of stars, was the fact that the human beings above, almost certainly citizens of the Third Reich, should have chosen to provide them such protection instead of depositing their cargo over the hemispheres of steel that stood waiting one thousand feet in the air.

The Jews moved unmolested past Ostiense and then, after the *fiume* widened, along the great sickle-shaped curve that ended at Ostia. Here they paused to await the stragglers. In the black of night, they could not see the ocean; but they could hear it, and its repeated sighing; and smell, on the rising tide, its sharp, biting brine. The boats, like those in a shrimp fleet, gathered together. Max counted sixty-three, sixty-four, sixty-five. The *Annika.* The *Sylvie.* The *Eve.* Just then the same German convoy came sweeping down the Via del Mare. This time they did not slow down, much less stop, but roared off westward, toward the nearby sea.

The *maltagliati* remained an hour, and almost an hour more. By then their numbers had grown to seventy-seven, with the *Pietro* the last to pull in. They dared not wait for the three missing craft. Already a pink glow was spreading in the east; the menacing moon had begun to slide down the incline of the sky. Max glanced at his rudder man, who had stood at his station throughout the night. With his fringe of red beard he looked more like a Viking than a Jew. His eyes, meeting Max's, were as pale as a Viking's too. Max pointed down the river. Their boat started off; the others, with their high prows, their high sterns, followed just behind.

They sailed into the estuary of the *Fiume Tevere*. With their poles, the Jews pushed hard against the ocean current that seemed to want to thrust them back the way they had come. Each boat struggled to find a channel among the deposits of silt, thick with flattened sea grass. All about them the waves were breaking, sizzling like the whites of frying eggs.

Maximilian, peering ahead, saw that the mists were growing whiter, brighter, as if lit from within. Then he realized that the source of illumination was the light that blazed from every porthole of a great ocean liner. How could Max not feel he had lived this very moment before? Just as the enormous volume of the *Hindenburg* had loomed out of the mists on the Lake of Constance, so the black bulk of the *Rex*—or was it, too, named for the old German soldier?—rose up before him now.

The Jews saw the apparition. A great shout went up, a cry of joy. Now the boats could not move quickly enough. Over their sides leaped the men and women. They splashed from sandbar to sand dune. They slipped on the kelp-covered islands, the reefs sharp with shells. Knee deep they went, waist deep, with their children on their shoulders.

Then the mist, like the curtain on a tragedy, slowly rose. The Jews came to a halt, with the foaming sea swirling about them. Their cheers were replaced by a heart-rending moan. The *Rex*, plain to see, had beached herself on a submerged spit of land. Worse, even, than that, there was a gash in her side, with shards of metal, oddly like chrysanthemum petals, around the fringes of the gaping hole. Water gushed from it, like blood from an artery. Other pumps sent gushers down the black plates of her hull. Palestine? A voyage to Palestine? For all the frantic activity aboard the liner—the blaze of her lights, the jets of water, the smoke that poured from both funnels, and the waves that churned about her whirling propellers—the grounded ship could not escape from the grip of the mud.

What would happen now? The Jews were wallowing in the shallows. They cried and beat their breasts. Maximilian feared that in their despair they would drown themselves, like those who had leaped from those same listing decks two years before. Amidst the shouting, the splash of the waves, the thud of the ship's twin screws, it had not been possible to make out the drone of the hovering blimp. Indeed, no one would have heard it now if it had not been for a series of popping sounds high overhead. They all looked up. The great ellipse was descending! There was, in the air, another detonation. Max saw one of the balloons shrivel and its tether grow slack. Someone was shooting at the sacks of air. Even as he watched, two more shots rang out and two balloons collapsed, their skins wrinkling, like two gray elephants brought to their knees.

Down, down came the steel segment, toward the submerged spit of land from which the *Rex* still strained to free herself. Max could see the blimp, with its spinning propellers. A window in the gondola was open, and a man with a rifle leaned out. Maximilian recognized the silhouette of jaw and helmet. It was the sharpshooter.

The Obersturmbannführer must have sent him. All Max's doubts disappeared. Kappler was their ally. He had been their ally all along.

Now the SS man got off one last round, and another balloon doubled over, as if struck in the solar plexus. No need to shoot more. Gravity brought the steel oval down to the hidden reef. Slowly the segment landed, with as much caution as a cormorant settling onto the eggs in its nest. Nonetheless, a large wave spread in all directions, lifting the Jews, submerging the sandbars, until it broke up amid the reeds and dunes.

On board the *Rex*, the crew was rushing toward the stern. They leaned out, stretching forward with poles and hooks. Some leaped atop the stationary ellipse; they swarmed among the levitating globes. Together the sailors removed the taut tethers—there must have been forty balloons still inflated—from their moorings on the precast ring and affixed them to the rails of their wounded ship. How swiftly they went about their task—in fear of the lightening skies, perhaps; or the lurking Germans; or out of eagerness to catch the crest of the incoming tide.

Meanwhile the refugees were splashing, stumbling, swimming to the side of the vessel. They climbed up the ladders of hemp that dangled from the lower decks. Others made their way along the portable gangway that hung to the surface of the sea. Up they went, hundreds and hundreds of them, like troops storming a redoubt. Then, as the final balloon was fastened to a strut at the prow, the last of the Jews, an elderly woman in a soaked, nearly transparent garment, was drawn on board by an improvised net.

Not quite the last of the Jews. Old Shabby, Shabilian, stood rooted, with the surf swirling at his hips. He did not move as, in mere seconds, it rose to his diaphragm. Could the tears that poured from his eyes, as salty as that surge, be raising the level of the sea? No: the same moon that had threatened to undo them was now laboring to provide a means of escape. The infinitesimal gravitons that passed between the earth and its satellite, drawing the ocean up from its basin, were no more palpable than the prayers that the American was sending from his lips to a mute and unknowable God.

A full minute went by. The tide rose to Max's armpits. Seaward, the smoke belched dense and black from the ship's two funnels. The screws roiled the waters. The balloons, straining like huskies, pulled on their leashes. Then, with the ocean waters lapping at his throat, Max saw the ship heave itself upward and break free of the land. The last thing he heard, before the full force of the *Mare Tirreno* inundated his ears, was a cry of joy from two thousand Jews, and the answering call, a cheerful hoot and toot, from the whistle of the *Rex*.

Eagerly, clutching his spectacles to his nose, Maxie kicked for the shore. He pulled himself up on a heap of mollusks, barnacles, and mussels, which gasped almost as much as he. On this barbed bed, he looked outward. The vessel was steaming out to sea, though with a pronounced list. Even with the support of the balloons, the gash at midships was barely above the waterline. She could never make it across the Mediterranean to Palestine. But what did that matter? She had only to sail as far as Sicily or Salerno, or even back to the port of Naples—anywhere, anyplace, under the control of the Allies and out of the Germans' reach.

What Max, shivering on his precarious perch, saw next filled him with disbelief. The ship had started to turn—not merely southward to safety, but—he confirmed this both by her wake and the echoing figure described by her smoke—a full one hundred and eighty degrees. The *Rex* was making a circle!

How could this be? Once before, nearing Sardinia, she had been ordered to return to her starting point. Had another such message gone out? Over the radio waves? Oh, the poor Jews! Such suffering! Unimaginable the scene on those decks. Unhearable their bitter cries, their curses: *this savior, Shabilian; this Messiah, Max. He has doomed us all.* Then, before Moses's own eyes, the ship that was supposed to carry his people to the promised land steamed instead straight onto the Lido di Ostia.

"No, no, no!" cried Maximilian. But before he could take a single step toward the site of the catastrophe, a hand fell on his shoulder. It was the guard, the driver, the SS sharpshooter.

"Now we have caught him," he said, in perfect English. In his own tongue, he added, "*Dieses kleine schmutzige Judenschwein!*"

3

His captors threw Max into one of the trucks parked behind the hump of a sand dune. There, crouched in a puddle of seawater, he understood that the vehicles had been sent out not to deliver German soldiers to the beach but to transport the captured Jews back to Rome. Why, he wondered, this elaborate ruse? Could the Waffen SS not have surrounded the Circus Maximus any time they wished? But then they would not have been able to seize the families or complete their work out of sight of the city's population. But if the German navy, or the SS itself, had already commandeered the *Rex*, why the farce of trying to free her from the land only to beach her again? Either the enemy had lain hidden until the ship had made for the open sea or else—and Max thought this far more likely— they had acted solely to raise the hopes of their victims in order the more completely to dash them. At the heart of Fascism there was a certain playfulness, the same malignant merriment that ran through all of nature. Thus did the German cat toy with its Jewish mouse.

Max was alone with these thoughts for not more than a few brief moments. Then the blue-lipped refugees were led in from the nearby beach. No one spoke. There was no weeping. In Max's vehicle no one pointed an accusing finger or uttered a curse. He would have preferred either to the empty, dull-eyed gaze they cast upon him, as if he were no more than a flap of the surrounding canvas. It did not take long to fill their truck. Still, there was room for one more: Dalio, *il Capitano*, with his black hair matted to his head and without the stars of office on his shoulders or the braid on his cuff.

The skies never cleared. In fact, as the trucks started their engines, it began to rain. The entire convoy started forward, rolling over the damp dunes and lurching back onto the macadamized surface of the Via del Mare. The journey that had taken most of the night was retraced in less than an hour.

Through a crack in the pinned-down tarpaulin, Max saw that the city streets were shiny and slick. Scattered in the puddles, lying helter-skelter on the cobblestones, was all matter of debris: clothing, suitcases, broken chairbacks, kitchen pots, books and pages of books. It looked as if a hurricane and not just a rainstorm had swept up the right bank of the Tiber.

Max, eager to see, pulled the canvas aside. The side streets perpendicular to the Cenci embankment were blocked by barricades. Armed troops stood at the corners of every block. Here and there groups of people were dragging their belongings toward the ruins of the Teatro di Marcello, before which their own vehicle had stopped. One stooped man had a nonsensical chandelier balanced on his shoulders. Suddenly the rear flap of their truck was ripped open and a score of Jews were forced to squeeze inside. Their luggage came flying in behind them. For a moment no one spoke. In that short silence Max heard through all the Via del Portico d'Ottavia and the streets that adjoined it, a shrill, high-pitched noise. The Germans, like an army of salesmen, were ringing the doorbells of the Jews.

There was a new sound, that of grinding gears; their overloaded truck started forward. Across the river, in Trastevere, the scene was much the same. The streets were littered with footwear—galoshes, bluchers, summer sandals, ladies' pumps—as if the fleeing Jews had run out of their shoes. Max saw, on a church step, a white bird, a pigeon or dove, perched atop a single upright boot, as if it had mistaken the stiff leather for the black cylinder of a stovepipe.

On and on they drove, along the Farnesina and then the Gianicolense embankments. Nearing the Vatican, they swung off onto the Via della Lungara, ducked under an archway, and came to a stop in a courtyard where a crowd of more than a thousand milled under the outstretched arm of what Max recognized to be the inscribed statue of Julius Caesar: *Romana Virtus Romae Discitur*. This was the Collegio Militare. At once, trampling over the American as they went, the truckload of Jews swarmed over the tailgate and onto the pattern of interlocking tiles. More trucks came up and disgorged their own loads of passengers, who began to wander aimlessly in the packed square.

Between the four stone buildings of the college all was chaos. What a deafening din! Over and over the Jews called out the names of their missing family members. A German officer, standing on a table, barked orders that no one could understand. The transports, nosing through the crowds, sounded their horns. Everywhere babies were howling. Outside the archway, held back by a line of sentries, a new crowd—the friends and relations of those who had already been seized—were cursing and screaming. Amazing that in all this uproar Max Shabilian could close his eyes and fall asleep on the bed of his military van.

Amazing? Had he not been up the whole of the night, while his people had been dozing and drifting? It was not fatigue, however, that made him oblivious to the pandemonium around him.

Awake, he could not escape one recurring thought: it was he, and only he, who had driven the Jews into the net that had ensnared them. Rather than face that accusation, or see, always before him, the blank gaze of the refugees' eyes, he allowed his own to be stitched tightly closed.

When he woke for the first time, Dalio was shaking his shoulder. "You must to eat. You must to gather your strength." The *Capitano*, reaching over the tailgate, placed beside him a bowl whose contents were thick enough to hold upright a spoon. The rain, Max saw, had stopped. The clouds hung low and gray. Suddenly ravenous, he picked up the bowl with one hand and shoveled the polenta into his mouth with the other. He swiped two fingers over the concave surface, and licked them. He did the same thing again. Then the bowl slipped from his hand; before it had stopped rocking on its rim, Shabilian was once more in a dreamless sleep.

The next time he woke he was still in the transport, but the truck itself was no longer in the Collegio Militare. In fact, they were speeding over what must be—yes, there was the hospital of Santa Spirito just behind them, and behind that the dome of St. Peter's— the Victor Emmanuel Bridge. He checked the green-flecked hands of his watch: 4:52. But whether it was almost five in the morning or almost five at night he could not determine. Was this the same Saturday, the Jewish sabbath, on which he had returned to Rome— or had he, like some Rip van Winkle or a similar sleeper in Italian folklore, snored his way through a week, a year, or a whole generation, so that all the pain he had experienced could now be forgotten in the turmoil of another world war?

No such luck. There was the overturned bowl, as white as one of those clamshells on whose little island he had been captured. But his clothes, once wet from the sea, had entirely dried. Sunday, then. A day for the Gentiles. The van turned right onto the Banchi Vecchi and came to a stop. The driver and two Death's Headers got out of the cab and walked back two houses, comparing the addresses next to the doorways to those on a list the driver held in his hands. Then all three men kicked open a heavy *portone* and rushed up a flight of stairs. A moment went by. A moment more. Then the same high-pitched ringing that he had heard on the morning of the previous day filled the air. They were at the door of a Jew! A Jewish family! They had the name on a list!

Instantly Max clambered over the tailgate and dropped to the pavement. Where to go? His own house? It would not be searched because the only Jew in it—the *schmutzige Judenschwein*—was already in custody. But it was not southward, toward the Via degli Specchi, that he trotted now. Instead, he moved back to the Ponte Vittorio Emanuele and made his way across it. The skies were darkening: dusk, then, not dawn. He increased his pace, until by the time he turned onto the broad thoroughfare of the Via della Conciliazione he had broken into a run.

Ahead lay the great columns of Bernini and, beyond, the basilica of Michelangelo. Max slowed to catch his breath. How was he going to get by the German guards who patrolled the Roman side of the colonnade? Simply by walking, as it happened. They gave him no more than a glance. But the Swiss Guards closed in. They wore their usual blue and yellow uniforms, but now they carried rifles instead of ornamental pikes. Two of them seized his arms. A third was shouting at his ear, demanding to see his papers, while the last of the quartet was already thrusting a hand into his pocket. What could Max do? He threw back his head and began to shout:

"The Jews! Holy Father! Revered Bishop! They are killing the Jews!"

The Guards sought to throttle him, grabbing him by the neck. He wriggled free.

"You have to save them! Do it now! *Liquidiert!* Pacelli! Papa! Pius! There won't be a single Jew left!"

All through the vast square, the scurrying nuns, the seminarians, came to a halt. Plainclothed Germans, tourists and faithful—all stopped in their tracks. Max kicked at one of the Switzers. He bit the palm of the hand that attempted to cover his mouth.

"Excellency! Holiness! Only you can save them. *Liquidiert! Liquidiert! Liquidiert!*"

Overhead, a pair of shutters clanked open. A figure leaned from the papal apartments. "What is the meaning of this? It is a disgrace."

Max gasped. It was not Pacelli. It was the Rabbino Capo. Was this, of all the hiding places in Rome, where he had taken refuge?

"Rabbi!" he called. "Dear rabbi! It's happening! Everything we feared! Worse than we imagined!"

In the dimming light, little more than the white triangle of the clergyman's beard remained visible. "*Va bene,*" the elder man called. "*Fate salire l'Americano.*"

At once the Swiss Guard stepped back. Max knew precisely where to go. He stepped between the looming columns and pushed through the familiar door. It was as if, on his previous visit, he had left a trail of breadcrumbs or notched invisible trees: he dashed up the marble staircase, past the allegorical figures and what seemed to him the same group of cardinals sipping at what must now be cold cups of tea. On he went, up the Scala Mobile and into the room with the fresco of the martyr who was about to suffer what had almost been the fate of St. Maximilian: gasping beneath the weight of the sea. He went into the warren of cubicles, through the papal library, and by those still sewing on their tapestry. At last, in the shadowy anteroom, someone reached out and seized him by the shoulder. It was Zolli.

"Fool!" said the rabbi. "Little fool! What have you done?"

Shabilian slipped from his grasp and forced his way into the Pope's private study. There was, on this occasion, no blinding light. The sun may or may not have set behind the leaden clouds. Yet Pius the Twelfth, if not blazing, still seemed to collect every available beam of light. On his chest, as if designed for this purpose, was a large crucifix. Its diamonds managed to wink and sparkle, if not from the residue of the dusk, then from some reserve of previous illumination, the way the stones of a Roman fountain will reflect well into the evening the warmth they have gathered in the course of the day.

And, Max was certain, the lenses of his spectacles, and the spectacle frames, would also be aglitter, had the Pontiff, seated behind his desk, not hidden them by clutching his head in his hands. Max, not bothering with a bow, his calibrated curtsy, strode over the carpet, already starting to speak:

"Pius! Your Holiness! Excellency! I beg you! Listen! The Germans! They are sending the Jews to their death!"

Zolli, hurrying after, caught Max by the arm. "Hush. Hush, foolish boy. Do you think the august Pontiff is unaware? He knows all. He suffers all."

"But it's his fault too! Our plan has failed. We did their work for them. For the Death's Headers. We gathered them from all over Europe. We rounded them up. Now we have to save them."

The Pope did not move. He remained, his elbows on the table, his head in his hands. Once more the Rabbi of Rome spoke in his place. "What would you have his Excellency do? The city is ready to explode. The least spark will set it alight. Do you want to cause an insurrection? A war between the citizens of Rome and its occupiers? *Then* you will see death. Death in the tens of thousands. And these will be tens of thousands of his own people."

Max could hardly believe the words he had just heard. "*His own people?* And the Jews? Does he think they are a different species? Not human? Pacelli! Papa! Say this is not true!"

"You must understand. The Holy Father feels for all men. None are outside the sphere of his loving kindness. You must understand that the august Pontiff has done everything in his power to alleviate the suffering of all innocents, of whatever race. But this is a delicate moment. Thus far the occupying power has acted toward Rome with correctness and restraint. The Holy Father knows it was not the Luftwaffe that destroyed the sanctity of his family's tombs. But if there is an insurrection, if the Americans bomb, and the partisans bomb, the Germans will be forced to retaliate against the Eternal City and against the Vatican itself. In this conflagration, which was prophesied so exactly by Our Lady of Fatima, the devil in the form of international Bolshevism will attempt to seize power. The red terror! Not universal love. Universal ruin. Patience, my young friend. Patience and calm and prayer."

At these words Maximilian, contrary to his country's Constitution, fell on his knees before Pope Pius the Twelfth. He would have been glad to prostrate himself before him if only the Pontiff would hear his words:

"Holiness! Pacelli! Papa! Pius! Grant me one wish. One! Stand up. Come with me. I must show you the truth."

To the astonishment of both the American and the rabbi, Pacelli removed his hands from his head and placed them flat on the surface of his desk. Pushing with his palms, he rose. In his slippered feet he moved to where Max, leaping upward himself, stood waiting.

"This way, Papa. Here. Father, follow me."

He led the Bishop of Rome across the room to where the very last of the sun's rays were attempting to penetrate the two framed panes of glass. Maximilian threw them open. Then he pointed down toward the rooftops below. "There, Holy Father. Over there. Inside the Collegio Militare. Can you see them? The Jews in the courtyard? The Jews of Rome. The refugees from all of Europe. Will they be there in the morning? Excellency, they will not. Zolli: you know it. The Himmler order. It has arrived. Tell him. Tell Pacelli, the Pontiff. Tell him what will happen tomorrow. *Liquidiert!* Tell! Tell! Tell!"

The rabbi said, "If the Himmler order has arrived, all will be sent to their death."

"Holy Father, save them! You must speak! You must act! This crime is occurring beneath your very windows. Before your very eyes!"

The Bishop of Rome continued to gaze out over the rooftops. No one said a word. Nothing broke the silence. Then a white bird, it might have been a dove of peace, fluttered by and landed on the window ledge. The Pope, startled, turned round. His eyes, which had taken in the spectacle below, were filled with tears. "Such suffering is too painful for words," he said. "Therefore I shall speak none."

Max emerged from the twin claws of the colonnade. He walked, as everyone must, to the river. He turned southward, toward the Collegio Militare. The crowds there, the friends and families of those trapped within, were beginning to disperse; rather, the officers of the Gestapo were driving them away. When the entrance was deserted, and only Caesar remained to express the Roman virtues, Max started forward. He did not walk willfully; a hand, that's what it felt like, was tugging him by the collar. It was, of course, the pull of conscience: he had brought the Jews to this prison; he would share their fate.

Shame on Shabilian: at the last instant, he veered aside, moving south to the turrets of the Garibaldi Bridge. He crossed to the midpoint of that span and stared down to where the rapids were churning. In the deep, black water, something was shining, like one of those coins he used to dive for as a boy. He hauled himself onto the balustrade. Senselessly, he removed his shoes. Then he put his hands together like a man at prayer. Who knows? He might actually have jumped had he not realized at the last moment that this was no shiny dime, no quarter, but his old antagonist, the double-dealing moon.

He resumed his walk, aimlessly, and painfully too, since he had left his shoes behind. It was past the start of curfew. He was alone in the city streets. He limped in the shadows, along the sides of buildings. Soon he found himself doing nothing more than walking up one side of a block and down the other, over and over, hour after hour, until, inevitably, he was caught in the spotlight—not the moon, this time, but the headlamps of a sleek Fiat 509. A girl jumped from a front seat. Where had he seen her, with that Gypsy's tangle of ringlets and curls? Apparently, she had seen him too, since she pointed and said, "There's one. I know him. He's a Jew."

Immediately two men in green uniforms came forward. *I Repubblichini!* The Fascist police! He'd have been better off if this had been a Daimler manned by Death's Headers. They dragged him, limp and unresisting, to the car, on the front of which yet another white bird had alighted, like an ornament for the hood. His betrayer, getting in, passed through the headlight beams: this was no Gypsy, it was the girl he'd seen years before, directing her fellow Jews to walk beneath the forbidden Arch of Titus.

"Hotel Savoy," one of the Fascists told the driver, and when the Fiat pulled up before the palm trees that flanked the hotel's entrance, his confederate said, "*Camera 341.*"

This raid took only a minute. The two men reappeared with a short, fat, whimpering man. The girl, the informer, did little more than glance at the unshaven jowls, the belly that spilled over the waist of the silk pajamas. "*Sì, lo conosco. Lui è un Ebreo.*"

The 509 model rolled off, headlamps still burning, though the dawn was upon them. Max thought they must be driving to the Collegio Militare, but soon realized they were heading not west, but east. They drove by the Stazione Centrale, the Policlinico, and then the Campo Verano, where through these long months the tombs still gaped wide and the bones that had been in them lay scattered on the ground.

They drew up at last at the Stazione Tiburtina—not at the passenger terminal but, after maneuvering down the narrow Via dello Scalo Tiburtino, at the maze of tracks that crisscrossed the loading zone for cargo and cattle. Here in the early morning light were all of the transport vans from the convoy. Down the tracks, on a siding, stood a locomotive at the head of what seemed an endless train for freight. Each of the wooden, rust-colored boxcars had a large central door and a small, square window high up on the wall. The Jews from the first of the trucks were being loaded onto the last of these wagons. When the car was full, a guard slammed shut the door, secured it with a bolt and hasp, and the door of the next car was opened. By Max's old Bulova, it had taken nearly half an hour to make the transfer. At that rate they would be there for the better part of the day.

And that day was going to be hot. Already the sun was up, glittering on the switches and rails. Dark splotches of perspiration spread on the backs of the trudging Jews. What struck Max was how quiet everything was. The trucks had shut off their engines. The locomotive gave off, with a wisp of steam, a barely audible hiss. Now and then a face would appear at one of the tiny windows and a voice would ask, as politely as one would of a waiter, for a glass of water. There were no screams; there was no weeping. No one made a dash for freedom. To a man they were convinced they were heading to a labor camp in Germany, a life that could hardly be worse than continuing to starve in Rome. Max weighed his chances: Could he escape from the Fiat and, before he was brought down by a bullet or a club, shout out, as he had to poor Luisada on top of the ellipse, *Run! Run! Run!*? He finished his calculations; the course he took was no different than that of Pius the Mum.

He dozed, woke, and dozed again. His turn came in mid-afternoon. One of the *Repubblichini* opened the rear door. Shabilian's fellow prisoner stepped out first. In the light and heat of the sun, the fat on the man seemed to have melted away. Holding up the cord of his pajamas, he moved down the length of boxcars. Max followed, flinching as the gravel bit into the bare soles of his feet. At every window he passed, a single face looked down—almost always that of a child, a Roman boy, who must have been crouched on his father's shoulders. Well ahead, at the wagon that abutted the locomotive and tender, he saw a group of officers, some in black, some in brown. He limped ahead, keeping his eyes upward, as if the blue of the sky were a liquid he might gulp down.

"*Halt!*"

An officer, in a black cap, complete with crossed bones and skull, was pointing directly at him. "You! What do you think you are doing?"

Max stopped in front of the wagon's gaping door. The SS man took a step toward him, then stamped one of his shiny black boots on the ground. "You don't belong here," he said, folding his arms across the front of his tunic.

Max stared. The round face, wide-set eyes, the full, red-tinged cheeks: it was Frankie! He even recognized the white, wet flash of his teeth when he opened his mouth to speak again:

"This train is solely for Jews. *Die Juden*. It is not for you."

"But, I—"

"You!" The young man was now addressing the former guest of the Hotel Savoy's room 341. "Why are you standing there? On board!"

Two SS men came forward. They took the Jew by his elbows, lifting him in the air; then they deposited him on the wagon bed, which was already crowded with his coreligionists.

Without thinking, Maximilian started to follow. Franklin barred his way. Max could smell the peppermint on the boy's breath as it hissed by him:

"Are you mad? This train is going to Poland. Understand? Poland! Turn around, Slapsy Max. Or you too will go up in smoke."

Max hesitated, feeling the gaze of the SS men upon him. Then he saw yet another white bird. It flew by him in a whir of feathers, heading for the tender, where it settled on a black lump of coal. As if a spring had been released, Max turned on his heel. Behind his back he heard the rumble of the door, as big as a barn's, slamming shut; then the clank of the bolt; and finally the blast of steam from between the locomotive's iron wheels and the hoot, on two notes, of its whistle.

He did not have to look; he knew the train had started down the tracks. He looked, nonetheless: a second cloud of steam rose into the air above the moving boxcars. Not steam: birds, white birds, a whole flock, startled by the caterwaul.

Suddenly, with a pang of despair, Maximilian knew why, night and day, these birds had been wheeling over Rome. They were the doves from their neighbor's rooftop. No wonder Kappler had wanted Max out of the way—on the river, at Ostia, by the sea. Little wonder, too, that his men now knew the address of every Jew, whether it was that of a flat in the ghetto or a room in the city's fanciest hotel.

The Obersturmbannführer had searched not in Number 8, Via degli Specchi, but on the roof of Number 10.

There was another whistle, which, because of the effect of speed and distance, was lower in tone. The cloud of birds broke apart, vanishing randomly into the sky. It was as if the compass needle embedded in each of their brains was spinning, sending them off in haphazard directions, without regard for the magnetic lines of force that emanated from what had once been the fixed northern pole of this earth.

ALITALIA 607

Rome

[2005: 1943–1945]

1

The bravest of us are lined up under the wing of the same 767 that brought us to Newfoundland in the first place. The 'fraidy cats are still waiting for the turboprop that will take them back to New York. What's to fear? We've all heard the story of how a crack team from Boeing has checked out the aircraft screw by screw and wire by wire. Supposedly, they took her out over the Atlantic and performed all kinds of tricks. As we move toward the portable steps, everybody keeps telling everyone else how this, short of Air Force One, must be the safest plane in the air.

Leda and your narrator, Slap-happy Max, are at the end of the line. Dottor Mamiglioni is pushing her wheelchair, though she insisted, and is insisting now, that she is fine and wants to walk. I guess I could drag myself out of mine, but I rather enjoy sitting here with the stewardess's boobs hanging an inch over my head and the sound of the song she is humming floating along with us like an audible perfume. Now and then I get a whiff of the real fragrance too, which is encouraging for several reasons—the rebirth of a sense of smell, for one, and taking what I shall call a man's interest in such a nosegay for another—though the scent is mingled with the fumes of kerosene and pierced by the disinfectant in which my granddaughter's bandage has been soaked.

Our turn to board. No cargo lift this time: we're paying passengers, or more precisely guests of the Italian government, not damaged goods, not freight. Leda pushes herself from the chair; at once her face, always pale, turns the color of her cotton gauze, and she staggers against our own private *medico*. The little brown nut of a fellow is holding her in his arms.

"*Fa niente, cara.* This is only dizziness. From the descent of the blood."

Cara? Where does that come from? I feel, no mistake about it, a stab of jealousy. Same question: where does *that* come from? Don't I have my big-bosomed companion fussing around me? Listen: she's whispering her own endearments into my working ear:

"*Venite, caro signore. Coraggio, mio eroe.* I am giving to you every assistance." *Caro.* Why should I worry that good Doctor Mamiglioni has placed his sinewy arm around my granddaughter's waist?

"Mister! Hey, Mister!"

I twist my neck as best I can. There, running across the macadam, is Little Miss Marker. Her sandals slap through the puddles of water, sending up rainbows of spray. Arriving, she is too out of breath to speak. I give it a try:

"Hello, D-dimples! Coming on-on-on: *comingonboard?*"

She takes a deep breath in and blows it out with her words. "No! We're going on a *safe* airplane. We're going back to Kennedy Airport."

Another disappointment, surprisingly sharp. "I am sorry to hear that."

"What's the matter with *her*?" She points, of course, to the linen that crisscrosses Leda's brow.

"She has a s-s-s: a surly temple! Ha, ha."

She looks at me, the Littlest Rebel, as if I had lost my mind. "But that's not funny."

"No, it's n-n-not. I have picked up a very bad h-h-h: a very bad *habit*."

"Okay. Goodbye."

She says this first to Leda, hugging her, with her plump little arms, hip-high. Now it's my turn. Her face looms close and closer. Ringlets, that's all I can see, these springing curls. Then astonishingly she kisses me on what must be the tired blue lips of my mouth. An instant of this, and she is gone, this time hopping with both feet into the various puddles left by what had been a new fit of rain.

I was, in May of 1944, no longer Slapsy Max. I don't mean that, with my beard, and the bones sticking through my skin, and the green cap and scarf of the Monte San Martino Brigade, I was not recognizable. My spectacles, slipping down my fleshless nose; my duck walk; the fact that I still measured, head to toe, a Mini-Max's sixty-five inches—all of that would have given me away. The name on my forged papers was Oreste D'Avanzo. My nickname, and code name too, was Gesù. But to my own mind, in my own thoughts, I was Max the Murderer.

I knew that every Jew on every boxcar had long since been *liquidiert*. When the train pulled out of the Stazione Tiburtina, I set off to kill one person more. With a gun, if I could find one; with a knife, if I could not; with my bare hands and teeth, if it came to that. But Amos Prince was not on the Via degli Specchi when I got home. Nor had he returned on the night of the 15th, when his broadcast had betrayed the exodus of two thousand Jews. Nina, alone in the flat, said that he had headed north, to Lake Garda, where the Duce was going through the motions of administering the new Repubblica di Salò.

"You've got to stop him, Maxie. He's crazy. Crazy like you've never seen him. Can you believe it? He still thinks he can talk the Duce into letting him finish the tower."

I had no trouble believing that. But the next morning, when I headed north myself, it was no longer the architect I was after. The person I was determined to find was his other daughter.

Where could she be? Either with the Duce himself at the lake, or, more likely, with the foreign nationals, Jews, and prisoners of war who had been recaptured by the Fascists after the fall of the Badoglio government. What was more horrifying than the reopening of the camps was the way in which one by one they were being closed: not to liberate those inside but to send them to labor in Germany or, in the case of the Jews, to die at Auschwitz.

No help could be expected from the Allies. For months on end, seasons on end, they remained bogged down well south of Rome. The only resistance to the occupiers had to come from the Italians themselves. And that is what I became. Name: Oreste D'Avanzo. Age: 28. *Occupazione*: telephone repairman. Place of residence: that changed according to which province and which brigade I happened to be operating in, as did the length of the beard on the photograph that was regularly reinserted into my forged papers. I never did find that gun, that knife, or squeeze the breath from a man with my bare hands. No, Max the Murderer slaughtered the Germans, and the members of the *Brigate Nere*, the *Battaglione della Morte*, the *Repubblichini*, with nothing other than words.

I had a crystal set once, like every kid on the block. I could still tap out maybe twelve words a minute in the International Telegraph Code. That's why the first group of partisans I stumbled onto handed over their wireless, which was stuffed into a wicker suitcase, to me. The fact is this brigade, goatherders from Monte Terminillo, rock-cutters from the nearby quarry, had never listened to a radio, much less attempted to use one to send a message. When I ordered one of the youths, at ease with sixty-kilo boulders, down to Terminillo to recharge our six-volt battery, he hoisted the pack onto his shoulders and said, with real worry, "If it weighs so much now, how will I be able to carry it when it is full?" Impossible for them to encode their message or decode the groups of scrambled letters that came click-clacking back—especially when, if they took more than fifteen minutes, they risked being discovered by the directional finders mounted on the roving German trucks.

Though I managed to master the cipher books, it soon became apparent that my real talent was for getting our beam on signal. All too often, whether high in the mountains, where our antenna had been stretched from tree to tree; or in a city, where we camouflaged it behind chimneys, we received nothing but interference. But if I happened to touch the wires, the transmission immediately cleared; and the more of the antenna I came in contact with, the more precisely the keys clicked out the alphabet soup of our code.

Who could explain such a phenomenon? I was a Raffaello of the radio, the Michelangelo of the Marconi. The CLN, which coordinated all the different partisan units, began to send me from one crucial mission to another. There were no more heavy packs to recharge, no wicker suitcases to carry. The miniature wet cells of the batteries were distributed through my pockets. The radio itself was shaped to fit the contours of my body, and the antenna was wound round my waist, coil after coil of it, until the porcelain insulators at either end poked through my jacket like a pair of fancy buttons. In order to establish a signal I had only to stand erect and spread my arms, which is why over the course of that winter of 1943–1944

I became known not only to our own forces but also to the Wehrmacht and SS as Signor Gesù.

What miracles this Jesus performed! No sooner would he transmit a message that might just as well have been in Aramaic, than—over a forest clearing or mountain meadow or field of snow, each ringed by signal fires at night or, in the day, a pattern of colored clothes—the drone of a circling aircraft would make itself heard. Then—*There! Look! Out of the clouds!*—all would turn their eyes skyward to where, descending from heaven, the parachutes were swaying like the pale thoughts of a god.

And the Max who was not the Messiah? Plain Max? Silly Shabilian? He wept, he sighed: for in this delirium of dandelions he could make out neither the bell of Aria's silk dresses nor the golden filaments of the missing girl's hair.

Toward the end of that bitter cold winter Oreste D'Avanzo arrived in the mountains above the Tenna Valley—purportedly to repair telephones in the province of Ascoli Piceno. In our little twig shelters, unable to light anything but the smallest of fires, we almost froze. Because the Germans had either occupied or burned the farms on both sides of the river, we almost starved as well. Worse, the Monte San Martino Brigade had used up virtually all its ammunition in attacking the railway line that ran along the Adriatic. Two airdrops had missed their targets, another had to be aborted because the Germans had triangulated our transmission site; and now, through the whole month of April, no plane dared penetrate the rising mountain mists. All we could do was huddle together, hoping for a break in the weather.

My task, aside from transmitting meteorological reports, was to become the "whistler" for the brigade. The whistle itself was an oblong piece of wood with a notch cut in one end and a hole in the other to accommodate a length of twine. The partisans had erected a large, circular net from the threads of old parachutes. At the center, on the ground, they set up a number of carved birds, decoys that seemed to be pecking at a handful of genuine maize. In no time live birds, as hungry, perhaps, as we, came whirling down to begin the feast. Time for Comrade D'Avanzo to go into action. I picked up the *fischio* and whirled it around in a circle, creating a high-pitched shriek. "A hawk!" cried the wrens, in their own tongue. "A hawk!" cried the finches, in theirs—and all went peeping into the near-invisible cords of the net. We survived on these tiny roasted creatures, washed down with draughts of grappa. Gesù, crunching wings and brittle skulls between his teeth, felt a twinge of guilt—over his shoulder, so to speak, since Assisi, home of the protector of all winged things, lay westward, on the same line of latitude as our camp.

In May we learned from informers in the valley that the Germans were about to evacuate the concentration camp at Servigliano and deport all those inside—the great majority of them Jews—to Poland. I put out my arms, with the insulators in both palms in lieu of stigmata; the commander of our unit—he had the appropriate name of Volterra—tapped out the coded news. Confirmation, a coded "click," was to come over the BBC, which broadcast every two hours on the half hour. We waited through the day and into the afternoon: 4:30, 6:30, 8:30. *"Apricots are in season,"* declared Radio London at long last. That meant our drop, weather permitting, would be at midnight. The target zone was the flat, rocky ledge below the walled city of Monsammartino. We managed to line up six old Fiats and signal the circling aircraft with our incandescent headlamps. The mists, as if frightened by the sudden blaze of light, withdrew. Then the steel capsules floated downward beneath their air-filled domes.

We spent the rest of the night cleaning the Cosmoline from our haul of Sten guns and long-range Berettas. In the hours before dawn the brigade moved into position above the camp. The German transports, meant to bring the prisoners to the railway line at Porto San Giorgio, had already arrived. Before the evacuation could begin, however, the Royal Air Force struck from a rare blue sky. The shiny little Vickers each made three passes—the first to strafe the row of canvas-covered vans and the next two to dive bomb the walls that surrounded the camp. Volterra had deployed his forces so as to keep the Germans pinned down, while the Jews came running through the smoking breach. The Italian guards, mostly retired Carabinieri, did not stir from their quarters; in fifteen minutes the prisoners had made their way to our lines. I went up to them all, fixing each with my bespectacled eyes. Aria was not among them.

2

"Why are you laughing? What's so funny? Before you were crying. You've been crying for the whole of this trip. I never saw so many tears from a grown man. Are you laughing at me? Jesus Christ! Jesus H. Christ! I'm doing my best, you know. I've put on my brave face. Can you give me maybe just the littlest break?" My granddaughter, buckled into her leather seat, scratches at her wrists as she speaks.

Contrite, I try to wipe the smile from my face. What a grimace, lopsided, one-sided, it must be. I can feel the whole right side of my head stretch into a grinning mask. The sound of my laughter—ghastly to me, must be like that of a zombie to Leda, a cackle from the pit of the grave.

"Now I'm going to worry about you, Mister Max. These changes of mood. I thought I—"

"L-l-look it up," I interrupt. "It's the only time in history. We d-did it! *La Brigata di Monte San Martino*. Not Churchill! We begged him. But he said, n-n-n—"

"No—?"

"Yes. No. They could have b-b-b—"

"Built? Bombed?"

"*Bombed*. Smart girl. They c-could have bombed the railroad tracks. They could have bombed Ausch-Ausch-Ausch. You know. But no! Never! They r-r-refused. But *we* did it. Haim Vito Volterra! Slapsy Max! Not that goddamned F-Franklin F-fucking Rosenfelt!"

My special stewardess looks up from her Italian magazine. Her lipstick is smeared, as if she's been kissing somebody. She grins, in sympathy with my outburst. My eyes, I confess, go down her throat, past her open collar, to where her breasts are pushing upward against her uniform, as if she too had batteries placed about her body.

A thought: what if, when Leda is sleeping, I ply her with wine? Malevolent Max! What if, alone, helpless, I have to take a pee? I feel, between my legs, a little jump, on the order of an undersized trout breaking water. Could it be? A miracle: Gesù, cruelly crucified, rising again—or at any rate Lazarus no longer under wraps. I slide my eyes over, to take another peek at my Magdalene. She's on the jump seat, legs crossed, like any girl on a barstool. Little green skirt. Charcoal stockings. A black pump dangles from her toes. Another twitch from the trout, after the bait of the fly.

A tear, of bemusement, I think, as much as gratitude, makes its way down the right side of my nose—a nose that, quivering like a collie's, detects the molecules of rosewater that are floating off the nape of my *signorina's* neck, where her black hair is gathered in a bun; and from the hollow in her throat, in which I have to imagine a green vein is beating; and from armpits that I dare to hope this goddess of a land *born between the fires of Etna and the snows of the Alps*, to quote a well known historical figure, has not shaved. This fantasy, with its convolutions, leaves me breathless. Let's go back to the beginning. I'll attempt to get out of my seat. She'll get up from hers. May I help you, Signor Shabilian? *Sì, grazie.* To the *gabinetto, per favore.* Give me your hand.

Damn it! What's the matter with Leda? Why is she scratching her wrists? First one hand, then the other. To my shame I realize that all through my little lover's interlude, she has not once stopped the flow of her words:

"Tell me the truth, Mister Max. Are you shocked? Are you disappointed? Is it like a slap in the face. Ha! Ha-ha! Slapsy Max. Little Leda. Your snow-white swan. Am I, you know, *sullied*?"

"No. I am not dis-dis-dis—"

"That poor baby! Is that even the word for it? *Was* it a baby? I mean, with fingers and toes? I only found out three weeks ago. I wasn't absolutely sure. I am going to have another exam. As soon as I get back to New Haven. I mean, I *was* going to. Maybe it's for the best? Isn't that why these things happen? Something must have been wrong. Fucked-up genes. My own little two-headed monster. Oh, Max! If you knew how happy I was! I was *hugging* myself. Lucky Leda! Lucky girl! Listen, did you see it? Did they tell you? Was it a girl? A boy? When can they figure that out? I should have done research. I'm a Yale scholar. Well, here's one thing I know. He— or maybe she: this baby was black. How do you like that, Mister Max? The proud papa is from Senegal. Well, he *would* have been proud if he ever found out. I didn't tell him. I was afraid to. Because of this superstition. If I said a word I was going to lose it. Oh, Maximilian! He is a lovely boy! So tall! So thin! He has this wrinkle in his brow. His beautiful brow. It's a vein of Senegalese skepticism, I guess. I think maybe he is an angel. I mean, a real one, the kind on the head of a pin. I don't think he knows how to raise his voice. Once we were having breakfast and there was a picture in the paper, a picture of a little boy. He had been raped and he had been strangled and thrown into a well. And there was another picture, right next to it, and this was the rapist—you know, the man who had done it. So I get up to get the coffee and the cream—because that's how he likes it, the cup so full it will take just one teaspoon of cream; and from the corner of my eye I see he has picked up the *Register* and he kisses the photo of the murderer. I dropped the teaspoon on the kitchen tile. I said, 'Why did you do that?' And he said, in this *accent*, he said, 'Because he is so unhappy.' I wanted to give him a son! But I wasn't worthy. No, no, not worthy. He doesn't say anything; he just looks at me with these mournful eyes if I—I don't know, if I swat a fly. Do you think he actually felt it? The murderer, I mean. Do you think so, Mister Max? Through a disturbance in the ether? Did he feel that he, or his picture, all the little dots that made up his picture, was being kissed?"

It isn't this talk, this constantly babbling brook—I don't think she's paused once to take a breath—that disturbs me. Or not only this. But she is still scraping, scraping, scraping the skin of her wrists.

"D-don't," I say, and move my penny-arcade arm across my body and lower my hand on top of hers. Should I tell her? How much she, in her gestures, her chatterboxing, resembles her great aunt? The way she kept stabbing and stabbing invisible knitting needles. Fucked-up genes!

"You-you-you—"

"What?" she asks, her hands tense, twisting underneath mine.

"You remind me of someone."

She grows still. "Aria?" she asks.

"You k-know—?"

For some reason her whole body goes slack. She exhales. Then her eyes begin to spill tears, as if, it occurs to me, one teaspoon too much has been added to the coffee cup's reservoir. "It's no secret, dear man. Grandma told me. About her sister. About you. Such a sad story. Oh, sweet Max: she was the love of your life. But you always were, for Nana Nina, Nina Nana, the great love of hers."

In the spring of 1944, Max the Murderer had been shivering in the mountains that overlooked the Tenna Valley. In the spring of '45, I was no less cold, and in addition was soaked through by the intermittent drizzle and downpour that swept the hills above the surface of Lake Como. Another similarity: around my neck I wore a scarf; but the green one that had belonged to the partisans of the Monte San Martino was now exchanged for the red one of the 52nd Garibaldi Brigade.

It had taken the whole of that year for the Allies to capture Rome and occupy the remainder of Italy. Finally, with the melting snows, the prolonged battle became a rout. As the Germans retreated beyond the Po and as one city after another rose in insurrection, the services of Gesù, like those of any other radio operator, became superfluous. The leaders of the resistance could give their orders face to face or, when need be, over the telephone exchanges they now controlled. The last message I received was a general directive from the *Comitato di Liberazione Nazionale* to every partisan unit. Mussolini and his entourage at Lake Garda were under no circumstances to be allowed to fall into the hands of the British or Americans, under whom they might escape the dictates of revolutionary justice.

No one doubted how summarily that justice would be exercised or what form it would take. The word that struck me was *banda*, entourage. That didn't refer only to the ministers, retired soldiers, and die-hard fanatics who made up the Repubblica di Salò. It meant the friends of Mussolini, his aides, bodyguards, family— and perhaps even the mistress whom all of Italy knew to be ensconced only a few hundred meters from where he was living at the Villa Feltrinelli.

Gesù was going to do his best not to let that happen. Not *Gesù*: for within an hour of hearing that broadcast I had shaved my beard, removed my neckband, and thrust my telltale spectacles into my rear pocket. Max in masquerade was after Mussolini. I arrived at Lake Garda on the 22nd of April, only to learn that my prey, with his ministers, had departed for Milan a few days before.

I set off on foot for that city, and finally caught a ride in a family car that had been equipped to run on handfuls of charcoal. The moment I sat down on the rear seat, I felt my spectacles snap in two. Perhaps that is why I, waking from a doze, did not recognize the figure, a blur of white, who was pedaling a green bicycle at the side of the road. By the time I reached Milano, the city was in open revolt. The Wehrmacht command post had just been seized by the laborers at the Pirelli plant. Trucks with red flags raced through the streets. The same loudspeakers that had once transmitted the declarations of the Duce now broadcast the decrees of the CLN, including the one for the unconditional surrender of all Fascist forces.

At dusk I made my way to the Via Monforte, where the Prefectural Palace had been turned into a bunker for the remnants of the Salò regime. This time I learned that Mussolini and his German escort had fled only hours earlier. *Where to?* I asked the milling crowd. *A Como*, they shouted.

"Was there a woman with him? *Ha una donna con lui? Una signorina?*"

But that no one knew.

My luck was no different in Como, which was like Milan in miniature. American forces were closing in from the south, while those of the resistance were fighting the Fascists—desperate now, since they had at last run out of territory in which to withdraw—in the center of town. As for Mussolini, he had once again departed just before me. But where? In what direction? Was he already in

Switzerland? Had he withdrawn with the Brigate Nere to the Valtelline? At the waterfront a group of fishermen swore they had heard a seaplane land at three in the morning and take off again at three-thirty. The Duce, they claimed, was now safe in Spain. And Aria? Was she with him? In Basel? In Geneva? In sunny Seville?

I slept through that night beneath the hull of an overturned skiff. In the morning I rose to continue the search along the lake. Flip a coin: east bank or west? West. I began to trudge northward on the narrow, winding road. No one dared stop to pick me up. I walked from village to village: Moltrasio, Laglio, Brienno. Above my head the clouds began to release a fine, stinging rain. In Argegno, in Tremezzo, no one had seen any trace of the Duce.

I arrived at Menaggio in the late afternoon. The roofs of the buildings were lost in a swirling mist, much as the legs of the men standing about in the central square had disappeared in the fog that had rolled in from the lake. I looked down at my own feet; they were wrapped in the same gray-colored puttees. We all seemed to be floating, like the ghosts of the people who had once lived in the town.

By now I was asking my question by rote: "*Dov'è Mussolini?*"

This time a voice came out of the fog: "Who wants to know?" There were a series of clicks and three men, all holding rifles, materialized from the droplets of the cloud. One of them said, "*Parla.* Who are you? What are you doing here?"

"*Io,*" I stammered. "I am looking for Mussolini."

"So are we," said the man. In the thick fog I could just make out the narrow moustache over his lip and the star at the front of his peaked cap. "But not to join him. To kill him. Identify yourself, or we will kill you."

For a moment my tongue seemed to swell in my mouth, filling it like a clam fills its shell. "*Un Americano,*" I stammered.

"Signor Shabilian. No, no—I mean, *partigiano.* A member of—
A member of—"

"Colonnello," said one of the men. "This is a spy."

The man with the cap responded. "I know it. Take him to the wall."

To the wall? That could mean only one thing. I was to be shot!
Before I had even finished this thought, two of the partisans had
pushed me against the stones of a small hut at the side of the road.
I heard, in the gray coils of vapor, the sound of feet, dozens of feet,
running away. I opened my mouth to speak, but no words came out.
The Colonnello did not speak either. He raised his weapon. So did
his companions. Then I heard, from out of the mists, the death sentence:

"*Morte ai Fascisti.*"

A sheer reflex answered for me, "*Libertà ai popoli!*"

At that instant a fourth man came dashing from the bank of
fog. "Oreste! Oreste!" he cried.

He ran past his companions and threw himself on me. "No
beard. No glasses. I did not know you. Signor Gesù!"

Who was this man? With only two fingers on his hand and a
broom of black whiskers on his chin? Then I recognized him: the
boy who had once carried my six-volt battery down the mountain
on his back and who thought it would be so much heavier coming
up. "Urbano!" I cried. "Is it possible? Is it you?"

It was at that moment that Signor Gesù joined his last brigade.

I slept that night in a cottage that Urbano had found above the village of Giulino di Mezzegra. At dawn we walked down the footpath, where the Colonnello picked us up in a battered Fiat 1100. We
drove as far as Musso, where our men had set up a roadblock near
an enormous boulder, the Val'Orba. Around my neck I wore the

red handkerchief of the 52nd Garibaldi. The rain had not let up. I sat, chilled, soaked through, ready to feed Urbano the belt of bullets for his automatic weapon.

Behind me, wrapped in canvas, was an old wireless machine. Calls to Milan, ordinarily routed through the exchange in Como, could not get through because of the battle in that city. Gesù was reborn. From this instrument we learned that the Duce and his ministers were still on the shore of the lake and that—again I had missed him by no more than the proverbial whisker—he had spent that night in Menaggio. Where he had gone that morning, no one knew. Hoping against hope, we sat behind our guns at the Val'Orba.

It was not He Who Is Immortal that the barricade halted, but a retreating column of Luftwaffe vehicles. At the front was an armored car with a machine gun mounted in its turret. Behind came some three hundred German soldiers in a line of trucks, each with wooden sides and a canvas top. Urbano fired the first shots, hitting the tires of the armor-plated vehicle and forcing it to lurch to the side of the road. A few more shots rang out from both sides. Then the convoy came to a halt. A white flag went up from the open turret, and the Colonnello went down to talk to the major who commanded the Luftwaffe column.

The stalemate lasted for hours. If only those in the road had known they outnumbered us by a factor of ten to one, they surely would have overrun our position in the rocks and trees above them. But we moved from spot to spot, shouting as we went, set a series of small fires, and in general managed to create the impression that we were a formidable force. Shortly after noon I received uncoded instructions from CLN headquarters: the convoy would be allowed to proceed toward the Swiss border and then on to Austria, if the soldiers first submitted to a thorough search. It was Fascists we were after, not Nazis. After another hour of negotiations, the Germans agreed. The line of trucks started off to the waterfront town of Dongo, in whose piazza the inspection would take place.

Half of the Garibaldi Brigade rode on the running boards of the trucks. The rest of us followed on foot. I came last, carrying the radio in a sling on my hip. By the time I reached the stationary convoy, the town was in an uproar. The search had uncovered an unexpected prize. Poor Duce! He had worked too hard to make his face recognizable for him to be able to disguise it now under a German helmet and with a Luftwaffe greatcoat slung over his back. "*Cavalier* Benito Mussolini": that's how one of our men addressed the soldier in the back of the enemy truck.

"*Sì*," answered the huddled figure. "I am Mussolini. I make no trouble."

He was escorted at once across the square and into the town hall—the same stone building against which a large crowd was now excitedly pressing, heedless of the armed guards who stood under the arch of the entrance. Another crowd had gathered beneath the windows. They stood on each other's shoulders, hoping to get a glimpse of the tired old man inside the ground-floor room.

I moved in that direction myself, then halted. The hair on my head was erect and tingling, a sensation that I imagined must be like having been struck by lightning. Over the tailgate of the last truck a woman was climbing down. Without my glasses I could make out only the shape of a brown fur coat and a dark, broad-brimmed hat. *Aria!* I cried, only to discover that that same bolt of lightning had broiled my tongue to a crisp.

I tried to run toward the line of trucks, but the men, the women, the children who swarmed by me, frantic in their desire to reach the town hall, made it impossible to take a single step. Like a swimmer fighting a riptide, I moved sideways, parallel to the row of trucks, whose engines I could now hear roaring once more to life.

I burst through in time to see the Fiat 1100 pull up next to the fur-coated woman. A hand reached out from the open door in the rear and pulled her inside. Then, fishtailing in its eagerness to get away, the automobile and all those inside it vanished from the square.

Two shots rang out, followed by a third. The guards, my own brigade members, were firing into the air. The crowd had begun a rhythmic chant: *Dateci la bestia!* Give us the beast. The mayor of Dongo appeared under the stone arch. He held up his plump, white hands. The streaks of moisture on his face, like the dark patches under the armpits of his straining jacket, were composed of sweat, not raindrops. "*State calmi!*" he shouted. "We are civilized people. We must not behave like those we have defeated." His words were drowned out by catcalls and curses.

Someone was pulling on my arm. It was Urbano, pale above his curly beard. "You must contact Milan," he said. "These people, they are coming down from the hills. They are crossing the lake. We cannot protect him. The CLN must take responsibility."

We moved down from the square and onto a wave-washed jetty. But I could not get a signal there or anywhere else on the waterfront. "I need more height," I told my companion. He pointed to the top of the Municipio. To get there, Urbano had to lower the muzzle of his Beretta and force our passage through the mob. The guards, reinforced now by submachine guns of their own, let us through. On our way to the central staircase I caught a glimpse of Mussolini, staring at a glass of water on the table before him; his head was bent, as if the scrawny neck could no longer bear the density of that skull.

I hauled the wireless up three stories and into an attic with a single window and a skylight to the roof. As soon as I set up the apparatus I realized that not only did Urbano not know the international code, he could not read a single word in Italian. I posted him as a guard on the floor below while I stretched the antenna from one spot to another, crisscrossing the whole of the room. There was still too much interference from the storm clouds and the mountains that rose up so steeply on the far side of the lake. Would the old magic work? I wound the wires around my body and inserted the insulator buttons between forefinger and thumb. At once I established contact. Using alternate hands, I sent and received a message. Not without difficulty, sweating as much as the mayor, I put down our orders on paper:

> *According to Article 5 of the Decree of 25 April, jurisdiction of Fascist war criminals is to be exercised by the local brigade, which in emergency conditions will constitute a military tribunal. He whom you have named and all in his party must be taken at once to the public square of Dongo and executed before the citizens of that town. The bodies will then be transported to the Square of the Fifteen Martyrs in Milan.*

> *Signed for the Comitato di Liberazione Nazionale:*

> *Valiani*
> *With the approval of General Cadorna.*

At that moment a roar went up, as if this message had been read aloud to the masses of people. I ran to the window. The cheer was for the Colonnello, who lay across the fender of the Fiat as it slowly made its way through the crowd. For a moment my breath caught in my throat: at the end of his rifle some dark-colored thing was waving? Was it Aria's fashionable hat? Her fox-fur coat? With my unspectacled eyes I had to wait until the car had drawn up almost directly below us before I could determine that the garment was in fact the greatcoat in which the Duce had tried to disguise himself, with the German helmet on top.

"We must hurry," Urbano shouted upward. "Have you received instructions?"

"*Sì*," I replied, in a voice that was weak and trembling: the Colonnello, I knew, would be only too eager to carry those orders out.

"*Presto, presto*. If we do not act, the people will."

I climbed down from the attic, leaving the radio behind. I followed Urbano out to where the Colonnello was, with both hands on the butt of his rifle, waving the ghastly scarecrow in front of the crowd. His face was red with blood lust. Urbano moved close beside him. "Colonnello, we have orders from the CLN."

"*Bene*," he cried, his voice high with excitement. "Give them to me."

I stepped forward and held out the message, folded lengthwise. Then I watched as his face turned as white as the paper in his hands. I knew each word he was reading because I had made them up myself:

> *Mussolini and his mistress must be brought together. They are to spend the night in the cottage two kilometers above the town of Giulino di Mezzegra. At eleven in the morning they must be transported to Milano, where both will stand trial and receive the judgment of the Italian People.*
> *Signed:* etcetera, etcetera, and etcetera

I spent that night at the Municipio—not because I wanted to but because the throng of milling Italians gave me no choice. They had howled when the brigade brought Mussolini, bent over and bareheaded, through the stone arch. Almost instantaneously he was inside the Fiat, which was already moving across the square toward the low wall that separated Dongo from the waters of the lake.

"*Al cesso! Al cesso!*" shouted the gleeful crowd. What better place to end the life of the great Caesar than against the public urinal of this tiny town? For a moment I too thought this would be Mussolini's fate. Suddenly the car veered left, veered right, as if caught in a fit of indecision; then it swung ninety degrees away from the wall and disappeared up the same road it had taken before. The mob, cheated of its prize, turned on the building that had housed him, and began to pelt it with stones. I was imprisoned for the night.

In the morning both the crowd and the rain clouds had dispersed. Rays of sunlight pierced the attic window, waking me with as much force as a tugging hand. I sat bolt upright. It was already ten o'clock! I dashed outside. The square was deserted. I looked for a car. I looked for a bicycle. Nothing stirred. Was this the same piazza that had been teeming with people the night before? Had I been whisked to a different village, or had the citizens of the new republic taken to their beds, to catch up on the sleep they had lost?

I trotted back to the main road and turned south, in the direction of Como. Not a truck, not a jeep, not even an oxcart moved in either direction. I could not keep up that pace for long. My strength was evaporating faster than the rainwater that still filled the hollows and ditches of the road. A fresh breeze blew the clouds over my head. A sailboat tipped toward what were now the lake's blue waves. The scene looked like a picture postcard from before the war. I checked my Bulova: 11:15! If the Colonnello had obeyed his orders, he would already have picked up his prisoners and be on his way to Milan. The very thought made me break into a run, which all too soon reverted to a trot, and then a dragging walk.

Hours later I turned off the road at Azzano and climbed the paved path toward Giulino di Mezzegra. Why I did so I could not

say: the cottage would surely be empty. And what if, for some un-
likely reason—an accident or a breakdown or resistance from the
prisoners themselves —the mission had been delayed? What did
I, weaponless, mindless, intend to do? All I could hope for was
some relic of Prince's daughter—a dropped handkerchief, as in an
old-fashioned play; a cylinder of lipstick; or perhaps a single hair,
stretched over a bar of soap.

I continued to trudge up the road. For a moment the sun disappeared, the rain fell out of nowhere, and then the beams of light
shone once more through the freshly unfolded leaves of the trees.
Well above me I could glimpse the buildings of the little town. Much
closer by, I saw the stone walls of a garden and the iron gates that
opened onto a secluded villa. Then, from well up the road, came
the sound of a car: the low, humming engine, the hiss of the tires
on the wet asphalt. I dashed off the road, taking cover behind the
thick, ivy-covered trunk of an oak. A minute later the car came into
sight. It was the battered Fiat 1100. Six members of our brigade rode
on the running boards and on the fenders. They blocked any view
of who might be inside.

But I knew perfectly well who the passengers were. I also knew
I could not let the automobile pass by unchallenged. Time to gather
my courage. On the count of three, I told myself, I would step forward, into the center of the road. *One. Two.* Before I reached the
last digit, the car came to a halt. The partisans jumped from the
chassis. Two took up positions above the villa, two below, so that
no one could approach the spot from either direction. Another man
stood spread-legged directly opposite the stand of trees in which I
was hiding. I gasped: it was Urbano, his machine gun in his hands.

Before I could move, before I could speak, all four doors of
the vehicle flew open. The driver got out from one side, the
Colonnello from the other. He gave an order. Mussolini emerged

from the rear. Without a word he walked to the stone wall and stood next to the concrete pillar that supported one side of the garden gate. The Colonnello faced him, with his own submachine gun in the crook of his arm. He shouted out that in the name of the Italian people he would carry out the sentence of death.

The Duce took a deep breath, and then took another. His chest expanded. And expanded again. The great chin rose once more into the air. Simultaneously, from the back of the car a female figure, but without her fur coat, came flying forward.

"No," she screamed. "You cannot kill the Duce!"

She leaped at the Colonnello and grasped the muzzle of his gun. He pulled the trigger, but there was only a click; no bullets came out.

Myopic Max! Strain as I might, I could not make out this woman's features, which were still shaded by the brim of her hat. I stepped from behind the oak tree. I was about to call out, *Aria! Aria!*, when Urbano, who had saved my life, now threatened to take it. He had me squarely in the sights of his Beretta.

The Colonnello had thrown down his weapon and snatched up another. He aimed at the Duce's chest, across which his inamorata, like a true Roman, now threw her body. She took the first shot and fell to the ground; the rest, too many to count, struck her lover, so that, with his back to the wall, he slipped to the earth and toppled onto his side. The Colonnello walked to the tangled bodies and fired a last shot into the Duce's heart. His body stirred once and lay still.

The driver got into the Fiat, which rolled to the garden gate. The Colonnello got inside; the two men drove off together. The partisans did not move from their stations. I stood, blinking and blinking, swallowing and swallowing, while not ten feet before me Urbano raised one of the fingers that remained on his hand and put it to his lips.

3

Everyone, except the pilot I hope, is fast asleep. The computers, riding the radio beams, will be flying us to Rome. They could land us too, even if—carbon monoxide, perhaps?—we had become a planeload of corpses. Nice thought! Should I try, yet again, to get forty winks? Hopeless. Here's Leda, slightly snoring, with a thin strand of saliva attached to my jacket sleeve. Leda in love. Max a great-grandfather. Almost. Slapsy of Senegal. I feel a stab of pity, like the thrust of a knife blade, for that African boy, the perpetual wrinkle of worry on his brow. Oh, I remember: no one will have to tell him; he did not know. Imagine! Kissing the face of the murderer. *Because he is unhappy.* What has Leda gotten herself into?

Sixteen: that's how many come back from the Stazione Tiburtina. Out of the thousands sent away. Sixteen! Are any of them still alive? Living in Rome? What if I should come across such a person? In a restaurant? In the street? Would little Max be recognized? I'm even shorter now. My black curls white. Perhaps this was the reason, not the sight of the churches and monuments, for not wanting to return to Rome. What will I do? Drop to my knees? *Don't you see what time had done to me? Forgive me! I am one of the walking wounded, the living dead.*

This is no way to get to sleep. My heart, still plugging away, is pushing the blood around my body at breakneck speed. Let's raise the window shade. There's our right wing, silver in the moonlight. It's as steady, no, steadier, than the extended arm of an athlete in his youth. Or someone giving the Fascist salute. Above, the black night, the gleaming stars. A certain percentage with planets; a certain percentage of planets with something like life. Algae, maybe, but here or there, in a parallel universe, superior beings. Hell, a horse would do. Or cabbages. Anything that does not eat its own young. I see that

I am subject to a certain turn of mind. What keeps me from sleep, however, are not such waking nightmares, through which the serene wing of our 767 cuts, as if through so many wisps of clouds; on the contrary, I am restless with: let us call it hope. The undeniable evidence that I—one in a Maxi-million—am coming back to life.

I gave up on the physical therapy a long time ago. So did the therapist, who could not stand my shrieks and howls. He wanted to play Chinese gongs. And burn incense, even if I couldn't smell it. Sadist! Torturer! Even Rosellen said it didn't matter; I'd reached my plateau. Not so bad: left half dead, right still twitching. Down the middle? Compromises. The tongue tastes but twists itself into knots on consonants. *Lots of coconuts*, as A.P. might say. Down below, we piss but not play. As for *il naso*, well, things seem to be improving. Even now, if I set my mind to it, I can make out the medicament beneath Leda's bandages and, from some place not far off, the mix of rosewater and perspiration released by the pores of my paramour.

At that thought, my member gives another twitch. It's improving, too. Who would have thought it? Rosellen likes to cuff it around, but I suspect that's why, when I ask—very well, beg—her to marry me, she says not on your life. She is, after all, half my age. She says she had a husband once. Got a Mexican divorce. She'll sleep in my bed every few months, for no rhyme or reason. Mostly, she's in another wing of the house: sometimes, summertime, when the windows are open, and the wind currents right, I can hear her moan—I hope in her sleep.

It's not nurse R. who appears to me now. I don't mean in my mind's eye. No, in real life, peeking over the seat before me, in Curly Top's place: it's the sleek black hair of Signorina Rosewater, Rosa for short, and now her olive brow, the thin plucked eyebrows, and the wide-set, slightly bulging eyes. She's batting the lashes, which her mascara has clumped together, like insects' legs. There: the broad nose and finally the full, poorly painted lips, which are parted in a smile.

"*Professore, mio,* you not want to sleep?"

"Shhhh," I caution, inching my head toward Leda, who does. "N-no, I can't."

"*Architetto, mio,* then what are you doing?"

"Nothing. Looking at the stars." This, I note, comes out flawlessly. God in heaven! Has that, Slapsy's stutter, been cured too?

"*Ah, le stelle!* They are beautiful, no?"

"Yes," I reply, looking squarely at her, "very beautiful."

Is that, beneath the shade of olive, a blush? "Massimiliano, *mio,* what is it you need? What is it I can do for you?"

It is a moment from adolescence, when everything in one's experience had a double meaning. "Is your name Rosa?"

"*Io?* Rosa? No."

Here she draws herself higher, higher in fact than she has to, so that both of her breasts seem to spill over the seat back. Above the left one I see the name badge that must have been there all along: *Bianca.* My God! *Gott im Himmel!* The name of my floating triangle! My little boat! And wasn't it also a name from *Othello?* I resist the sudden urge to nudge my granddaughter awake. She knows her Shakespeare better than I.

"Ah," I say. "Bianca."

"*Sì, posso accomodarlo?*"

She remains in place, bat-bat-batting her lashes and smiling wide enough for me to see, within the cavern of her mouth, the slow movement of a sluggish tongue. On the instant I am as excited as the lusty Moor.

"Yes," I say, to create a distraction. "I must, you know, the g-g-g-g—"

"*Gabinetto?*"

Suddenly I *do* have to pee, achingly so, dangerously so, though at the moment it is a physical, or perhaps psychological, impossibility. *Rosellen.* I want her here. I have through the whole of this journey. I push on my armrests, which unsurprisingly makes me topple sideways, toward where my granddaughter, in her white bandages, is in her mummified sleep.

Bianca—wasn't it her handkerchief? The one that led to so much trouble? Bianca abandons her seat and approaches. I reach up, across my body, to take the hand she has extended toward me. Her bulging eyes—or so I imagine—skip across the disturbance in my trousers. I let her help me quaveringly to my feet. She crouches, as it happens belt high, and draws my left, lifeless leg over Leda's primly locked limbs. My right arm falls around her neck, with an inadvertent hand on her breast.

"S-s-s—" *Sorry,* of course, is what I want to say; but she does not react, makes no attempt to remove what must feel like the five fingers of an echinoderm clamped on the soft belly of its next meal. What the hell? I don't move my arm, either. I lean into her. Like a couple of drunkards we make our way down the aisle.

As we go, I see the lolling heads of this passenger and that. Everyone's on their sleeping pills. The smell of this woman! The perspiration that glues us together! Her hefty hip, green-skirted, grinds in its socket against mine. On we stagger, and on. *Show me the way to go home!*

My foot, the good one, kicks something that had half projected from under one of the seats. A little liquor bottle goes spinning along the carpet. Instantly I am not on Alitalia 607 but on LZ 129, watching Romano's red rubber ball roll mysteriously toward the rear of the airship. Is he alive or dead? Here's what I know: that he married the sister of Sophia Loren and that the little boy under the aluminum piano became a jazz pianist. Benefit of the doubt: alive. And what of that other boy, Harald, the stepson of Joseph Goebbels? Everyone knows what happened to his step-siblings, those poor little towheads. Poisoned. The pity of it!

We are at the door of the first-class toilet. Bianca turns, to fumble at the handle. As she does so, the middle of me, my epicenter— why these niceties? My penis—rubs against her flank. She turns back. No doubt about it: her cheeks are rosy red now. What did Freud say about the maidenly blush? That the blood that engorges the lips and cheeks below is displaced to those above, a gesture that both confirms and denies what one is actually feeling. I'm feeling plenty myself. My own lips can barely express my gratitude: "Th-th-thank y-y-y—"

"*Di niente*," she answers, panting a little, I think. "It is a service we are happy to perform."

She pushes open the door and steps to one side, allowing me to precede her into the little cabin. Suddenly, from the depths of the economy section, a voice rings out:

"Wait! *Aspetta!* One moment, please!"

It is *Dottor* Mamiglioni, charging forward with as much mass and at the same velocity as the unrestrained food cart. Bianca pulls backward. Without support, I teeter in the doorway. The squat man, brown-headed, bald-headed, catches me before I can fall.

"I see you need assistance. This is a thing between men, eh? I am accompanying you. Yes, yes: no need for remonstrance. I am *un medico*. So. Now, together, we go inside to make the business."

With one arm around my waist, he draws me after him. I cast, outfoxed Othello, one last look behind me. But Bianca, Desdemona's buddy, has already retreated well up the aisle. The door closes on the tragedy; the comedy is about to begin.

I returned to Milan the next day, a Sunday morning. The Duce had already arrived at what the CLN liked to call the Square of the Fifteen

Martyrs, but which everyone else continued to call the Piazzale Loreto. His body, along with those of a score of others who had been executed in the last few days, had been dumped in front of an abandoned filling station. By the time I reached the scene, a huge crowd had gathered. It must have numbered in the tens of thousands, much like the throng that used to gather under *Juliet*, the Duce's balcony in Rome. No one was cheering now. They were swearing, cursing, jeering. They surrounded the mound of corpses, pushing aside the handful of partisans who were trying to protect it.

I could not get near the front of the mob; I knew full well, however, what was occurring. The Milanese were rushing forward to attack the bodies. I could hear the crack of the breaking bones. The favorite target was the Duce's jaw, which was kicked repeatedly, the way, elsewhere in Italy, one might touch the bronze head of a statue for luck. Somebody fired five shots; as if through a telegraphed message, everybody knew that a crazed mother had put a bullet into the Dictator for each of her dead sons. Was it possible for such barbarism to grow worse? It was. The men opened their pants; the women, kneeling, lifted their skirts. They soaked the bodies in urine, as if they meant to douse them with kerosene.

How long was this carnival to last? Until everyone had had a chance to spit on the corpse? Or carry away a scrap of his clothing? A piece of his flesh? Two of the partisans turned a fire hose on the mob, but it only became wilder, more intoxicated, as if the hydrant were filled with champagne. I looked around for the American soldiers. Hadn't they occupied the city? Weren't they in charge? But all I could see, well off in the side streets, were a few idling jeeps.

A roar went up, louder than any that had come before. I turned back. The Duce was rising, floating above the crowd, ascending like one of the saints to heaven. No: someone had tied a rope around his ankles and thrown the other end over a girder. They pulled him up, feet first, like a slaughtered bull. The crowd rushed forward, leaping high, striking the corpse with sticks, with scraps of lumber, as if it were a piñata that, battered, the head cracked and misshapen, could yield no other prize than its blood. Messy-linguini!

Now a second corpse went up, and a third, and a fourth. I saw the stump of an arm dangling downward. Farinacci! Once so fierce. More and more of the Fascists rose into the air. Ah, there was Delle Donne, the poor vice minister, whose toupee tumbled earthward as he rose upside down in the air.

I gasped at the sight of the next body: it was that of a woman. She still had her hat on her head, but her dress fell about her hips, revealing the shame of her nakedness. Someone, a lady, the angel of modesty, came forward and raised the fallen skirt about the thighs and tied it with something—a cord, a string, a length of belt. Yet nothing could prevent the force of gravity from seizing the long-suffering article of millinery, which by inches slipped from the inverted head.

"Aria!" It was not I who shouted this word, and then cried out again: "Aria!"

But this was not Aria; even I, with my 20-200 eyes, could see that the hair that fell in a cascade was not blond but brown. I knew this woman. She had been the Duce's companion in the lift and on the *Hindenburg.*

"Petacci! Petacci! The Clarinetta! Hooray!"

There, a full head taller than all the Italians, stood the architect, fully erect beneath his Panama hat. For some reason the crowd around him was pulling aside. I soon saw why. A jeep had forced its way forward; two military policemen were jumping from either side. The masses of people melted away. A.P. did not move; he allowed the two soldiers to seize his arms. One of them turned to where I was standing. "Who is this? Tell us. Is this the traitor?"

My fellow American saw me. Ever so slightly he shook his head. In a dumb show he mouthed my name. I stared past him, as if he no longer existed.

"Yes," I replied. "That's the one you are after. That is Amos Prince."

4

Time for breakfast, American style, ham and eggs. I see that my meat has been precut into bite-sized pieces. Thoughtful Bianca, *posso accomidarlo?*, though now, serving others, she avoids my eyes. Leda, less pale this morning, sips black coffee from a porcelain cup. Then she takes out her compact and looks in its mirror. They've cut away a segment of her hair; what remains, plenty of it, she lets fall over the same side of her face, still in the style of—what's peek-a-booing is my age, I fear—Veronica Lake. "What do you think, Mister Max? Pretty rakish, huh?"

"I think," I say, "you'll be the rage of Italy."

She looks at me sideways, as if deciding whether to remark my perfect enunciation. She clicks her compact shut and lets the moment go. Bianca has started to move about, collecting the breakfast china. Even as she is at work the chimes go off, the engines relax, and we start our descent. I took the *Conte di Savoia* to Genoa on my first trip to the city. I have not been back for sixty years. As we drop lower, even my left hand seems to grip the armrest, fully as tense as my right.

Again I have to wonder why I insisted on the window seat. So I would not tumble into the aisle? Or trip someone with my dead left foot? I don't dare look out now. Neither do I pull down the shade. We're coming in from the north, so maybe all I will get is a glimpse of the Tiber exhausting itself into the sea. That's enough to set my heart racing. Determinedly I close my eyes. When I open them again, there is nothing to see but a layer of clouds. Nonetheless, I am in a sweat, my ears ring-ringing. What I fear isn't any of the seven fabled hills, which at any instant I expect to see break through the cloud bank like a pod of humpbacked whales. Not the Colosseum, either, the Capitoline, or even the Dome of St. Peter's, beneath which the services are going to be led by a new Pope.

No: what I half-wish, half-dread, to see is the top of *La Vittoria*, the tomb of Mussolini, soaring out of the overcast, a double ellipse at one thousand feet. In fact, according to the computerized map on the wall, we're already lower than that—a blip in the clouds at three hundred, two hundred, a hundred and fifty meters. Silly Shabby! Muddle headed Max! To think that we are going to crash into a building that I know perfectly well no longer exists. I transmit the information to my body, but it is wiser than I. Not exist? It is a monument that will remain standing forever; I will never be able to avoid the collision. Suddenly, with a jolt, I feel the impact: our wheels have touched down on a runway, the engines roar like caged tigers, and we gradually slow down at a fume-filled airport that I know must be miles from the center of Rome.

SPIRAL NOTEBOOK

The Blanket

[1982]

Dark. Cold. My head. The blanket. Junior.

FLOATING PLANET

An Epilogue

[2005]

What a builder, the Duce! Greater than Caesar, Constantine, and Hadrian; than all the Popes and Emperors combined. And what a destroyer, since in order to realize his dream of a metropolis that extended unbroken to the sea he decided to demolish everything constructed in the twenty centuries of decadence between the Emperor Augustus and the *Anno Primo* of the Fascist Era. Nothing would survive save for the Colosseum, the Pantheon, the Capitol, and the rebuilt Tomb of Augustus himself. Alongside those monuments there would now soar an immense Palace of Fascism and a *Foro Mussolini* so grand it would cover all of what had been Renaissance Rome. For *Anno Ventesimo*, 1942, the twentieth anniversary of his revolution, the Duce planned the Esposizione Universale di Roma, whose buildings and monuments would not only celebrate the city's imperial past and its present glory but serve as the permanent center of the Olympic games, at which all of civilization would periodically gather.

Let us, along with Maximilian and his granddaughter, who had at last arrived on flight 607, take a tour of twenty-first century Rome.

The *Foro Mussolini* has had a change of name; its heroic statues, marble-muscled, stare down at the Romans who jump rope and perform calisthenics under the auspices of Big Gym, the franchise that now controls the whole of the stadium. Our tourists cannot visit the *Palazzo del Fascismo* because it had never been built. The Tomb of Augustus? Unresurrected, though the acres around the weed-spotted mound have indeed been stripped of their medieval streets, their dark churches, and the tenements that had so affronted the Dictator's eye.

After all these years the city has not yet marched to the sea; the great *Esposizione* that the Duce designed to be at the center of the new metropolis remains isolated to the south, on the heights above the river. On the morning that Leda pushed her aged grandfather's wheelchair over the scallop-shaped tiles in front of the *Palazzo dei Congressi* and up to the steps that led to the Palace of Labor, the complex looked much like a De Chirico painting, windswept and uninhabited. As Max had once looked up from the Tiber to see these ivory chess pieces at night, he now looked down at the same river—no, not the same; as Heraclitus had pointed out, the molecules were a different mix—by day.

That afternoon they went to the Vatican but the Pope, made of new atoms himself, did not appear at the high, rectangular window. No one appeared on the balcony of the Palazzo Venezia either; the loudspeakers attached to its walls, and to the walls of so many other buildings, had been replaced by the cell phones that everyone held to his ear.

They stayed away from the Via Torquato Tasso. Nor did Max allow himself to be wheeled under the Arch of Titus; he kept to tradition, though his fellow tourists, Jews and Gentiles alike, did not. The Collegio Militare had a plaque on its walls, to commemorate those who had spent two days and two nights within them. The Regina Coeli had no such marker, but it was still full to bursting with its unwilling guests. The *Monumento a Vittorio Emanuele II* was as white and gleaming as ever. What had A.P. called it? A wedding cake? A typewriter? A urinal? Dentures! The Circo Massimo was overgrown with grass, the leaves of the poplars along the Via dei Cerchi dusty and dog-eared in the heat of the sun. You would never know that the crowds shouting at a chariot race, or the world's second tallest building, had ever been there.

After a few days the two Americans hired a car and drove to Gubbio. Max could not remember the street on which he'd first searched for the architect. He knew it was high up. He knew from Prince's notebook it was near San Ubaldo. The driver went back and forth along the narrow passageways, but nothing, for Shabilian, rang a bell. They went to the Montegranelli. They rolled over the eight-sided cobblestones in front of the hotel, but it wasn't easy to push the wheelchair on its gravel paths. Max, to show off a little, got up and walked. They tottered along between the cypresses to the back of the villa. There was nothing resembling a bicycle shack. Max looked across the lawns: oddly, there was no swimming pool either. Inside, at the desk, no one recalled Amos Prince. No one remembered a waiter named Enrico. Max and Leda had a drink at the bar, for old times' sake, and followed their headlights back to Rome the same night.

No reason to go back to the Via degli Specchi, the street of mirrors, because the ceremony that had brought them across the Atlantic was to take place in the large, second-floor room of number 8. Was Marconi's secret weapon a time machine? Because when, on a hot, steamy afternoon, the event was actually held, everything looked just as it had a full seventy years before: there the armchair, there the table that Prince had cracked with an upward thrust of a knife, there the Philips *Superinduttanza Sei*.

There was a crush of people inside, more of them from Burlesque-phony's—no, no; as Max said, this is a bad habit: from Berlusconi's television stations, and from newspapers, than from actual participants in the commemoration. Sophia Loren was not present, nor was Romano, her brother-in-law. Looking around, Max saw dignitaries of every stripe: the Prime Minister, his cabinet, right-wing politicians, and a delegation from the *Consiglio Nazionale degli Architetti*. These gentlemen were the ones who stood and applauded, and kept applauding, as someone hauled a microphone stand in front of the Pritzker Award winner, and someone else shone a bright light in his eyes. He got up on his own to his feet. He pulled the papers from his left breast pocket.

"S-s-s—S-s-s—Excuse me. Pardon me. I am sorry. Si-si-si—"

Leda, in this emergency, stood up and greeted the Prime Minister, the Minister of Culture, and the American Ambassador; then she began to speak of how a long time ago the swallows had built a nest on this very window sill and had even flown into the room.

Why had Max's tongue failed him? The glare of the lights? The heat? The airlessness? Or had this journey backward in time occurred so suddenly that his thoughts, and the words to express them, had not yet caught up with him? These gentlemen from *Forza Italia*, from the *Alleanza Nazionale*, with their bull necks and the little pins in their lapels and their ramrod posture: did they not, each one of them, long to live dangerously? And what of this Berlusconi, with the hard plates of his skull and the chin that jutted over his stiff, starched collar? He stood now before the cluster of microphones and put his hands on his hips. "ITALIANS! AMERICANS! IT IS A TRAGEDY, *UNA TRAGEDIA*, THAT OUR COUNTRIES WERE TRICKED INTO BECOMING ENEMIES. NOW THEY ARE REUNITED IN THE RESPECT THEY BOTH HOLD FOR THE MEMORY OF AMOS PRINCE." Maximilian had to turn his eyes away from the gleam, the crazed light that ran over the speaker; it was as if the gaze of millions of Italians—far more than had ever seen Mussolini—had left on his skin a permanent shellac.

Up came his own country's ambassador, a shopping-mall king. Famous for placing addicted young men in concentration camps. Boot camps, they called them. Uniforms. Drills. Indoctrination. Discipline. What was he saying? That the time had come to look not just at the architect's buildings but at his ideas, which had been misunderstood because they were ahead of their time. Max lost track of the words. The time machine was whirling him around. He fought back a wave of nausea. He clung, with his good arm, his good hand, to the metal wheel of his chair.

We celebrate today the life of the greatest man of the twentieth century, a man whom a new generation of Italians have come to remember with respect, gratitude, and love in their hearts.

Who was speaking? Who said these words? A woman. And what could she possibly mean? That Amos Prince was greater than— an Einstein, a Churchill, a Gandhi, even a Marconi? At that instant Maximilian realized he had been wrong. The fear that had so gripped him aboard flight 607 had not been caused either by the anticipation of seeing the Eternal City and its monuments or the chance of coming across one of those who had survived the journey from the Tiburtina Station. Nor had he feared the kind of people who surrounded him now, each of them dreaming of the past glory of Rome. No, what he had dreaded most was a woman, some aged crone, as old, almost, as himself; in that bent and gray figure he was bound to recognize the daughter of Amos Prince.

No such witch stood before him now. This was a full-busted blonde, thick-lipped and clear-eyed and smooth-skinned. Nor was she speaking of Amos Prince. The man she wished to honor was Benito Mussolini. And why not? This was Romano's daughter, granddaughter of Il Duce. She was only repeating what she had said on many occasions: that Italy must never apologize to anyone, to any person or nation or race, for its actions during the Fascist era—and that to do so would dishonor the memory of her family and the history of her country.

As she spoke, Maximilian clutched his chest. He could feel the blood circulating through his veins faster than the charioteers with their whips had driven their chariots around the Circo Massimo. He stared at this member of Parliament, the blonde: those hands that gripped the stalk of the microphone; in his eyes they seemed aged and spotted. The breasts, the lips: had they both been pumped with silicone? Had the hair been dyed? The skin around that jaw, that chin: clearly it had been lifted and tucked. And why was the neck covered with a gray and green scarf? *A hoax! It was a hoax!* He wanted to stand and shout those words aloud. This Alessandra was not in her forties. She was sixty! Sixty! Nor was she the daughter of Romano and the sister of Sophia Loren. No! No! No! She was the love child of the Duce! The Duce and his mistress! Aria!

Leda, seeing Max topple sideways, ran to his wheelchair. She feared he had suffered another stroke. In truth, he was only exhausted, his head spinning from the whirligig of being spun about in time. Here's another truth: a voyage to the past requires no invention of Marconi. It returns on its own. Josephus, describing the downfall of Jerusalem, spoke of history as a wheel, ceaselessly revolving. Let us briefly leave Maximilian Shabilian, so that he might catch his breath and clear his head. Perhaps we need to recover from our own dizzying journey. It will take no more than a moment to discover how the great wheel, in turning, reduced those caught beneath it to dust.

A-daft Hatter, to begin at the top, killed himself just two days after Mussolini was lined up and shot against the garden gate. At the same time Magda and Joseph Goebbels committed suicide, though they had first taken care to drug their six towheaded children and force poison down their throats. Harald, whom we met as an adolescent on the *Hindenburg*, though presumed lost on the Eastern front, in fact survived the war; similarly Hugo Eckener, whom Maximilian feared had perished in the crash of his airship, was not on board and survived the conflict as well. Von Ribbentrop and Obersturmbann-führer Kappler were both tried as war criminals; the former was hanged but the latter escaped from prison—some say in his wife's large suitcase—and died not long afterward from natural causes. Albert Speer served his full term at Spandau and spent his last years of free-dom writing books about the Third Reich and his role in it.

What of Pius the Mum? In spite of his reticence and the recent revelation that he ordered the bishops of France not to return bap-tized Jewish children to their surviving parents, it seems certain that one or another of his successors, perhaps the Pontiff who was him-self a member of the Hot-air Youth, shall succeed in making him a saint. Israel Zolli, Chief Rabbi of Rome, converted to Catholicism, taking the name Eugenio to honor that same Pius XII, his friend, his protector. In the eyes of the Jewish community he was disgraced, but much honored by his new coreligionists, who noted that in his spiri-tuality he would weep for a flower picked before its time.

As we already know, Haile Selassie, Lion of Judah, was not in the cage that the Romans had pelted with their coins, but safely in exile at Bath. He reclaimed his throne when the Italian armies were defeated and, after many years of productive rule, was overthrown by his own army and died in captivity. Vittorio Emanuele III, an-other Emperor of Ethiopia, as well as King of Albania, was also sent into exile, where he expired; the male members of his line have at last been allowed to return to Italy, though his grandson, the would-be Vittorio Emanuele IV, has said the racial laws of 1938 were not all that bad—a remark quite similar to that of Silvio Berlusconi, who claimed that Mussolini never killed anyone, but merely sent them away to holiday camps.

Another Vittorio, the Duce's son, who admired the bombs bursting beneath his plane *come fiori*, died in 1997, two years after his sister, Edda. Her husband, Ciano, was executed by his father-in-law in 1944, to punish him for his vote in the Grand Council meeting that followed Prince's broadcast. Butocci, the architect, faded into obscurity and must surely have long since passed away. Paola Borboni, who sang "The Continental," and whom Max thought he saw running naked up the staircase of the *Hindenburg*, lived to the age of ninety-five—enough time to appear in both Fellini's *I Vitelloni* and *Roman Holiday*. Putzi Hanfstaengle, her piano player, lived almost as long, expiring in the course of things at Munich. Margherita Sarfatti, *So-fatty*, Prince had called her, fled to Argentina to escape the laws restricting the rights of the Jews; she returned to Italy after the war and died there in 1961. The girl whom Max mistook for a Gypsy, and whose real name was Celeste di Porto, also converted to Roman Catholicism and served seven years of her twelve-year sentence for turning in her fellow Jews.

Il Capitano Dalio was not one of the sixteen who returned from Poland to Rome, though there is a possibility, however negligible, that he made his way back to Genoa, where his family had lived for so many years. As for his ship, the *Rex*: after the liberation of Rome she was pulled off the reefs of the Lido di Ostia and repaired. For her own safety she was sent into the Adriatic. The Germans sought to sink her in order to block the harbor at Trieste; before they could act, however, the British sent a group of Bristol Beaufighters to hit her with rockets. The *Rex* rolled over in the shallows of Capodistra Bay, one year to the day after General Eisenhower had gone on the radio to announce the surrender of the Italian government to the Allied armies.

A small turn of the wheel—less perceptible than the movement of an hour hand on the face of a clock: this time forward instead of back, to the months following Maximilian's and his granddaughter's return to New York on another Alitalia flight. Leda is back at Yale. Everyone raved about her performance as Portia, the self-mutilator. Max, in the audience, kept his eyes out for anyone resembling a tall, willowy Senegalese, but there was not a single black man in the cast. As for Max himself, the first thing he did upon reaching home was ask Rosellen to marry him; as was her habit, she said no. But she did not fail to note that his middle organs—a true Gesù, our Shabby-lion, capable of resurrection—had been restored to working order; which might explain why she now spends more nights than she had in the past in his bed, and why Max no longer hears the sound of moaning when she sleeps in her own.

Amos Prince was buried in Gubbio, after all, in a corner of the *Cimitero Della Pace* at the Church of San Francesco. Leda, upon reading the spiral notebook, decided that the last wishes of her great-grandfather should be respected and began the process of removing his remains to America. As she soon discovered, that kind of thing is, even in the best of circumstances, a long, tedious business. At the moment, however, it does seem likely that A.P. will soon be interred, without fanfare, and with the simplest of markers, in the Tropp family plot in the state of Illinois.

Oh, yes, the Little Chickadee: well, Bright Eyes made it safely back to JFK, but her family, thoroughly shaken by the experience aboard Alitalia 607, canceled their vacation to Rome. On the smaller turboprop, she had to raise her voice to make herself heard over the whine of the engines. *Why does a golfer have two pair of pants?* A pause. A giggle. *Because he might get a hole-in-one.*

What happened to *La Vittoria?* Everyone Maximilian encountered had a different story. Some said that over the winter of '43–'44,

Speer had pulled down the tower and shipped off the steel ellipses to various armament works in the Ruhr. Others claimed they had seen a squadron of Flying Fortresses make run after run over the target, until they had reduced it to rubble. In any case, the bones of Mussolini rest with those of Bruno in the family vault at Predappio, and not, as in the wild fancy, a mile high in the air. The statue of Hercules, or at least its lower extremities, is still at Montespaccato, a thousand feet below the surface of the ground. Or so the Romans will tell you.

What is not in the realm of myth is that the Obelisk of Axum, which had long stood near the eastern end of the Circo Massimo, was hit by lightning in May 2002. The government of Berlusconi, taking this to be a sign from Jupiter, hurler of thunderbolts, decided to return it to those whose ancestors, the descendants of Solomon and Sheba, had made it untold centuries in the past. To get it into the Antonov aircraft, they had to chop it into three pieces and lengthen the runway at Axum. The middle segment alone constituted the heaviest object ever transported by air. In April 2005 the last piece reached the capital of Ethiopia, from which it had been plundered by the victorious armies of Mussolini almost seventy years before.

When the ceremony was over Maximilian told Leda he did not feel well enough to attend the gala dinner and asked that she represent him instead. He remained behind until the last person had left the building, and continued to linger after that. Outside the light gradually faded from the sky. An hour, perhaps a second hour, went by. It was now too dark inside the room for him to read the dial of his watch. He turned his chair and pushed his way to the staircase. With his right hand he grasped the banister rail and hauled himself upright. That was nothing; the real task was to climb the stairs. He found the strength to do so, a step at a time, a flight at a time, until he passed his old attic workshop and reached the door that led to the roof. For a moment he rested, then thrust his shoulder against the bolt that secured the portal. It flew open. Dragging his bad leg behind him, Max stepped outside.

The first thing he heard was the cooing of the doves. He moved to the low brick wall that separated 8 Via degli Specchi from Number 10. There they were, order Columbiformes, owing to the consistency of genes identical to those of all the intervening generations: white-muffed, pink-toed, short-billed, orange-eyed. Another feat of strength: he hauled himself over the bricks and approached. Inside the dovecote the birds were wide awake, in spite of the black cloth of the night. They preened and hopped. They unfolded their wings, as if in a beauty pageant, and folded them again. Max, breathless and trembling, kneeled down.

From the shadows, a voice said, "You won't find them."

Max turned, twisting his neck to see the speaker. A figure came forward. The shock of hair on his head was as white as the feathers of the doves. There was just enough light, from the moon, the stars, the electrical fixtures of Rome, to make out something boyish—the little balls of the cheeks, the flash of white teeth—in the aged and wrinkled face.

"Franklin!" he cried.

The old man ignored him. "The *Judenlisten*. The lists. Where you hid them. They aren't there."

"I know. Kappler found them, didn't he? Underneath the dovecote."

"His men did."

"Did you help them? Did you show them?"

"I tried to keep them away from the roof. I didn't succeed. I hope you'll believe me."

For an instant Max's mind spun backward. All those wheeling birds—the ones at the Pope's window, on top of the black boot, clinging to the locomotive: he knew where they'd come from. He turned to the aged figure beside him. "At the station, you saved my life. I believe you."

There was a pause. Then Franklin said, "Did you get the notebook?"

"The spiral notebook? You sent it?"

"To Leda. But I knew you would read it first."

"Did you go to Gubbio?"

"On the day he died. He had the pencil in his hand. I went to the shack. I got the models. I got the plans. For the floating planet. Took us thirty years. To build it. But we did. In time for the celebration. In time for you."

Max had to grip the side of the dovecoat for support. What was this—he almost thought *boy*: what was this old man saying? That the sphere, the aluminum planet, had been constructed? "What do you mean? Frankie, tell me. This was his masterpiece. Greater than all the rest. Who built it? Where? Is it ready to rise?"

Franklin stepped closer. Yes, he was old—gray, withered, stooped. But with a start of dismay Max was forced into the realization that he was nonetheless a good deal younger than himself. Without a word, he stepped closer still. He took Max's dead arm and put it over his own thin shoulders; for a moment they stood there, as if in an embrace. Then A.P.'s son helped him over the brick barrier and all the way down the stairs.

It was now the deep of night. The streetlamps were on and the monuments lit, but the avenues were largely deserted. Franklin, in what turned out to be an old brown suit with a faint blue stripe, stood behind Maximilian's wheelchair. He pushed it first to the Teatro di Pompeo and then onto the Via delle Botteghe Oscure. The few passersby stopped to stare: two old men, one pushing the other, like characters in a morality play. The blind lead the blind. The halt, the lame. They skirted the monument to Vittorio Emanuele II and trudged along the wide Via dei Fori Imperiali. Franklin began to slow down. Behind Max's head the puffs of breath grew coarse and labored. On they went, nonetheless. Were they to take all night? Max allowed his chin to fall toward his breastbone, jerked it upright, but was powerless to prevent it from descending again. He dozed—and was still sleeping when they came to a stop.

"*Ecco!*" cried the former Fascist. "There it is!"

Max lifted his head. He looked. He looked again. But he saw nothing, only the floodlit Colosseum.

"See! See! Do you see?"

Maximilian twisted about in his chair and saw, glittering above him, the eyes of a madman. Then he turned back. A number of things combined, perhaps, to create the illusion that now appeared before him: the low angle of his chair; the moon, tumbling about behind the tatters of the clouds; his own excitement, his own exhaustion; the play of shadows around the bright fluorescent lights. The great ruined bowl rose into the air. It hung there, carrying with it the shades of Emperors and slaves and the citizens of Rome. Roaring lions. Gladiators. The young man who had clung to the topmost fragment to watch the spectacle of the victorious armies passing below. Max blinked, but the monument, with its ghosts, remained in the air. It was the only planet in the heavens not made by the gods but by the hand of man.

A GLOSSARY OF THE PLAYERS

Amos Prince [1882–1982], famed American architect who wins a competition to build a monument, *La Vittoria,* for Benito Mussolini. Arrested by United States Army and tried for treason.

–*Aria* [1918–?], his first daughter. Betrothed to Mussolini's second son, she then becomes the Duce's mistress and perhaps the mother of his child.

–*Nina* [1920–1991], his second daughter, eventually the wife of Max Shabilian.

–*Franklin* [1922–], his son, who rises under Fascism.

–*Leda* [1982–], his great-granddaughter and granddaughter of Max Shabilian and Nina. During her flight with Max to Italy in 2005, she suffers a wrenching loss.

–*Odaline,* his first wife and mother of Aria, Nina, and Franklin.

–*Granny Tropp* [1801–1893], his grandmother, full of worldly wisdom and recipes for ice cream.

–*Gianna,* his devoted servant from 1936 to 1974.

Maximilian Shabilian [1914–], as a young man, Amos Prince's protégé, then his son-in-law. He adores Aria but marries her sister after the war. Attempts to save the Jews of Rome. As an old man, he flies to Italy with Leda, his granddaughter; on this flight he recalls his youth and for the first time reads the journal of Amos Prince.

Benito Mussolini [1883–1945], He Who Is Never Wrong. Ruler of Italy, Conqueror of Ethiopia, Leader of the Battle for Wheat and the War against Flies. Lover of Margherita Sarfatti, Claretta Petacci, and Aria. He both desires and fears the monument meant to celebrate his victory and become his tomb. In death, hung by his heels in Milan.

MEMBERS OF HIS FAMILY:

–*Vittorio Mussolini* [1916–1997], his eldest son and a pilot in the Ethiopian campaign.

–*Bruno Mussolini* [1918–1941], his second son, also a pilot. While engaged to Aria, he is killed in an air crash.

–*Romano Mussolini* [1927–2006], his last son. After the war, married the sister of Sophia Loren and became a celebrated jazz pianist.

–*Donna Rachele Mussolini* [1890–1979], his wife.

–*Alessandra Mussolini* [1962–], his granddaughter and daughter of Romano (though Max thinks she may be the love child of Aria and the Duce). A member of parliament devoted to the memory of Fascism and its leader, she will attempt to become Mayor of Rome.

–*Edda Mussolini* [1910–1995], first daughter of Il Duce, married to Count Galeazzo Ciano.

–*Galeazzo Ciano* [1903–1944], married to Edda Mussolini, Minister of Foreign Affairs and later Ambassador to the Holy See. Shot on orders of his father-in-law.

THE ITALIANS:

Guglielmo Marconi [1874–1937], Nobel Laureate, inventor of radio. Assists Amos Prince in winning the architectural competition and in building *La Vittoria*. Some believe he was working on a death ray at the time of his death.

Roberto Farinacci [1892–1945], Secretary of the Fascist Party, later the Duce's right-hand man, though lacking a hand of his own. Killed by partisans.

Eugenio Pacelli, Pope Pius XII [1896–1958], also known as *Pius the Mum*. Before 1939, Cardinal Secretary of State. A devotee of the Lady of Fatima and an anti-Bolshevik, he watches the roundup of Roman Jews from his windows at the Vatican.

Vittorio Emanuele III [1869–1947], King of Italy, Emperor of Ethiopia, King of Albania. Small in stature, with a white moustache, he does the Duce's bidding until he has him arrested in July of 1943.

Michele Delle Donne [1901–1945], Vice Minister, Office of Demography and Race. Killed by partisans.

Silvio Berlusconi [1936–], ex-cruise ship crooner and balding Prime Minister, now twenty-fifth richest man in the world. Like He Who Was Even Balder, he compared himself to Churchill, Napoleon, and Jesus Christ, but was nonetheless defeated in the campaign of 2006. Like MacArthur, he vowed to return.

Il Capitano Dalio [1899–1943? 1944?], captain of the steamship *Rex*. Assists in the flight of the Jews from Rome, but is captured himself and sent to Auschwitz.

Claretta Petacci [1912–1945], mistress of Mussolini and with him hanged by the heels in Milan.

Paola Borboni [1900–1995], bared her breasts in a stage show in 1925 and for the Duce in 1936. Went on to act more modestly in many distinguished films.

Margherita Sarfatti [1880–1961], the Jewish mistress of Mussolini, she pretends to leap from the *Hindenburg* and then flees Italy after her former lover's anti-Semitic decrees.

Israel (later *Eugenio*) *Zolli* [1881–1956], Chief Rabbi of Rome and confidant of Pius XII. After the war converts to Catholicism and attempts to give his side of things.

Celeste di Porto [1926–?], also known as *La Pantera Nera*. Mistaken by Max for a Gypsy, she is in fact a Jewess who betrays her own people to the German occupiers–including, in the end, Max himself.

Pietro Badoglio [1871–1956], Duke of Addis Ababa and briefly head of the Italian government after the fall of Mussolini.

Renato Giavagnoli, a chauffeur and a good deal more. After the war he appears at the trial of Amos Prince.

Georgio Butocci [1896–?], a leading Italian architect, he competes for the monument to Mussolini.

Luisada [?–1941], a citizen of Rome who leaps from *La Vittoria* so that his children, Lorenzo and Antonia, will no longer be burdened with a Jewish parent.

Ambrogdio Ratti, Pope Pius XI [1859–1939], blessed Il Duce's adventure in Ethiopia, but would have condemned the spread of anti-Semitism had he not died a month, or two months, too soon.

Dottor Mamiglioni [1950–], a physician aboard Alitalia flight 607, he ministers to the stricken Leda.

Wanda, owner of an eponymous pensione in Rome.

Enrico, a waiter at the Villa Montegranelli. Serves Amos Prince a memorable bowl of soup.

Piero Cipriani, a small boy who has a big idea.

ITALIAN PARTISANS:

Haim Vito Volterra, Il Colonnello, Urbano, the last two of whom assist in the capture and death of Mussolini; and the first of whom conducts a raid on the Servigliano concentration camp, which frees many Jews, though not Aria.

VISITORS FROM GERMANY:

Joachim von Ribbentrop [1893–1946], an ambassador and then Foreign Minister of the Third Reich. A supporter of the Axis with Italy and the Pact of Steel, he quotes Juvenal on the subject of the Jews. Hanged after the Nuremberg trials.

Herbert Kappler [1907–1978], SS Obersturmbannführer and head of Gestapo in Rome. Apparently a lover of both gold and a good German joke.

Albert Speer [1905–1981], an architect and Minister of Armaments in the Third Reich. He competes for the monument to Mussolini and then thinks of various ways in which it might be torn down. Writes his memoirs after a long term in Spandau prison.

Joseph Goebbels [1897–1945], Minister of Englightenment and Propaganda in the Third Reich. Dances with his shortened leg aboard the *Hindenburg* and finds other paths to pleasure before killing himself as Russian troops close in on Berlin.

Magda Goebbels [1901–1945], wife of Joseph and mother of many children, six of whom she poisons at the end of the war.

Harald Quant [1921–1967], her son and stepson of Joseph Goebbels. As a young man he challenges Max aboard the *Hindenburg* and goes on to become a German flying ace.

Albert Kesselring [1881–1960], Generalfeldmarschall, also known as Smiling Albert. Occupier of Rome and defender of occupied Italy.

Heinrich Himmler [1900–1945], Reichsführer SS. In 1943 authorizes the liquidation of the Jews of Rome, and, for that matter, everywhere else. Eagerly takes capsule of potassium cyanide as war comes to a close.

Hugo Eckener [1868–1954], chief of operations, *Deutsche Luftschiffahrtss-AG.* As captain of the *Hindenburg,* he aids Amos Prince in making his demonstration and rewards him with a pair of binoculars. A portrait of the Führer is aboard his airship, but not in its captain's heart.

Ernst "Putzi" Hanfstaengel [1887–1975], Harvard graduate who was an early and loyal supporter of Adolf Hitler, for whom he played the piano–though not the same songs he played in the lounge of the *Hindenburg.*

The SS sharpshooter, lantern-jawed, steel-helmeted, he knows more languages than Max and Rabbi Zolli imagine.

Adolf Hitler [1889–1945], Reichsführer, who beneath his nose sported a *Rotzbremse,* a snot-stopper, and possibly possessed only a single testicle. He appears at the dedication of the Hercules monument. Also known, at least by Amos Prince, as *A-daft Hatter.*

Mildred Gillars [1900–1988], also known as *Axis Sally* or *Midge at the Mike* [1900–1988]. An American citizen, but because of her radio broadcasts on behalf of the Third Reich, let us make her here an honorary German. Tried and convicted of treason against the country of her birth.

AMERICANS:

Curly Top, also *Little Miss Marker, Dimples*, etc., a witty young passenger aboard Alitalia flight 607.

Rosellen. Though she does not appear in the novel, this nurse and companion is never far from the older Max's thoughts.

Franklin Delano Roosevelt [1882–1945], American president; like Rosellen, without a speaking part, but Amos Prince's great antagonist, always in his mind and in his words.

Breckinridge Long [1881–1958], Ambassador to Italy during the procession to celebrate the Duce's victory over Ethiopia. Afterward, indifferent to the plight of Europe's Jews.

Melvin Sembler [1930–], American Ambassador at the time Maximilian and Leda return to Rome. A shopping-mall king and contributor to the campaign of George W. Bush, he is thought by some to have run camps for addicted youths that in their methods rival those established by the Duce.

James W. Thomson, a wounded American GI.

Ernie Glickman, owner of a red sports car; overweight and 4F, he is said by Midge at the Mike to be in pursuit of Thomson's girl.

Judge Bernard Andrew Katz, presided at the trial of Amos Prince in Washington, DC. Noted for irascible nature and hawk-like nose.

Richard "Dick" Mosk, also known as The Penguin. Prince's natty attorney.

Dr. Weinstein, at St. Elizabeth's Hospital and before, the psychiatrist to Amos Prince, who calls him *Wine-Stain*, etc.

A Girl from Carnegie Tech. Interested in Prince's last great project, the Floating Planet.

ASSORTED PLAYERS OF VARIOUS NATIONS:

Colonnello Buonasera, also known as *Colonnello Stevens*, Broadcaster to Rome on Radio London.

Soldiers and Sailors and Death's Headers.

Carabinieri, Architects, Psychiatrists ("Squirmy," "Sleazy," and "Slime"), and Patients (notably Chief Wahoo), Nuns, Stewards and Stewardesses, Lighter-than-Air Crew and Mechanics, the Jews of Rome as well as Jewish Refugees, Grand Council Members and other Politicians, Prosecutors, Members of the Jury, Prisoners at Pisa, large crowds of Italians, etc.

IN HISTORY:

Ezra Pound [1885–1972], American poet whom Mussolini once called diverting. He made broadcasts of his philosophy on Italian Radio and almost certainly would have been found guilty of treason, and perhaps executed, had a jury not declared him "of unsound mind." After a long stay in St. Elizabeth's Hospital, he returned to, and died in, Italy.

Frank Lloyd Wright [1867–1959], American architect who designed a mile-high tower.

R. Buckminster Fuller [1895–1983], American designer, inventor, and architect. Dreamed of delivering prefabricated buildings by dirigible and drawing up their inner parts by pulley. Some of his designs may be found on the endpapers of this book.

Haile Selassie [1891–1975], the Lion of Judah, Emperor of Ethiopia, descendant of Solomon and Sheba. Defeated by Mussolini's forces in 1936, he returned victorious to his homeland in 1941.

Solomon [?–971, BC], King of the Jews, lover of Sheba and father to her son, Menelik I.

Sheba, Queen of the land of Sheba, now Ethiopia. Bore the son of Solomon, who became the first Emperor of that kingdom.

Titus [39–81], Titus Flavius Sabinus Vaspasianus, Conqueror of Jerusalem, whose victory is celebrated by the Arch of Titus in Rome.

Obelisk of Axum, built some 2500 years ago and looted from Axum by Mussolini's occupying forces and carried to Rome. It appears in the Duce's triumphant parade as well as in the search for the perfect spot to erect *La Vittoria*. After being struck by lightning, it was returned to Ethiopia in 2005.

The *Hindenburg*, the great Zeppelin airship on which the final round of the competition to build the monument to Mussolini is held. It was destroyed by fire while landing in Lakehurst, New Jersey, in 1937.

The *Rex*, the steamship of the Italian Line on which Max, with the assistance of *il Capitano* Dalio, hopes to rescue the Jews of Rome. Sunk by the British in Capodistra Bay in September, 1944.

La Vittoria, the monument to Mussolini's victory over Ethiopia and designed to be his tomb. Originally planned to reach one mile in height, it eventually did surpass St. Peter's, the Mole Antonelliana, and the Eiffel Tower to become the highest structure in Europe. Whether it exceeded the Empire State Building to become the tallest in the world depends on whether the observer counts the core, which indeed topped its rival in New York, or the final three stories, which were lowered into the sea instead of onto the monument. It no longer exists in the Circus Maximus, but persists in the mind of anyone who ever saw it, and in that of Maximilian Shabilian, who gave much of himself in the attempt to build it.

FIC
EPS

Epstein, Eighth WOnder of the